ASHES OF THE RAHN'KA

Book Four in the Pantracia Chronicles

ASHES OF THE RAHN'KA

Amanda Muratoff & Kayla Hansen

www.Pantracia.com

Cover design by Andrei Bat.

ISBN: 978-1-7337011-6-7

Third Edition: February 2024

To new beginnings.

The Pantracia Chronicles:

Prequel:
Dawn of the Thieves

Part 1: The Berylian Key
Book 1: *Embrace of the Shade*
Book 2: *Blood of the Key*
Book 3: *Unraveling of the Soul*

Part 2: A Rebel's Crucible
Book 4: *Ashes of the Rahn'ka*
Book 5: *Pursuit of the Hawk*
Book 6: *Heart of the Wolf*
Book 7: *Rise of the Renegades*

Part 3: Shadowed Kings
Book 8: *Sisters of the Frozen Veil*
Book 9: *Wings of the Eternal War*
Book 10: *Axiom of the Queen's Arrow*

Part 4: The Vanguard Legacy
Book 11: *Daughter of the Stolen Prince*
Book 12: *Fate of the Dae'Fuirei*
Book 13: *Oath of the Six*

Visit www.Pantracia.com for our pronunciation guide
and to discover more.

Prologue

Spring, 2609 R.T. (recorded time)

WOLVES SNAPPED AT JARROD'S HEELS.

Blood pounded in his ears, sweat dripping down his temples as he ran.

With a hand braced against a wooden crate, he leapt over it, rolling under wooden beams. Dust from the ground clung to his palms, aiding his grip on a horizontal pipe protruding from wooden scaffolding.

His breath heaved, howls reverberating through his bones with each heft of his body to the next bar. Pulling himself up, he perched for only a moment before launching to the next. Glancing down at the arena floor, no flashes of fur chased, but his past manifested in a snarling maw gnashing at his ankles.

He dropped, swinging clear of the final obstacle, and a cloud of dust wafted up around his boots.

Turning to face his pursuers, Jarrod found himself alone.

No wolves.

Only the one tattooed on his back.

After rubbing his dirty hands on his breeches, he wiped his brow with his forearm. Casting another quick glance behind him, he eyed the doorway.

Already midday, the desert heat discouraged anyone else from joining him in the training arena.

Jarrod sucked in another deep breath as a distant, familiar screech drew his eyes up. He couldn't see the sky beyond the raftered roof.

Liala.

Finding reserved energy, he ran for the aviary.

His eyes shot skyward as he skidded to a halt, searching for his hawk.

She screeched again, and he whistled his response, squinting in the daylight.

Without truly needing to see, Jarrod caught Liala on his outstretched arm, and the hawk flapped her umber wings with a screech. "Easy, girl." He reached towards the parchment secured beneath the hawk's metal cuff at her foot, still trying to catch his breath. His hand stilled when he saw the smudged drawing of an arrow on the outside of the rolled paper. "Shit."

"What is it, boss?" Braka meandered through the guild's aviary door with a sandwich in his burly hand. The big man could terrify the bravest of men, yet couldn't resist their chef's roasted duck between slices of homemade bread.

"She didn't reply. Again," Jarrod grumbled, unrolling his unread note.

"You look like you just ran 'cross Xaxos." Food muddled Braka's words.

Jarrod frowned at the freshly recruited thief. "Was working the arena. You were supposed to be, too."

Braka grunted and took a large bite of his meal. He spoke around bits of bread. "I was hungry."

The Helgath spring had already turned into summer in the desert. A hot wind tore through the dark fabric hanging overhead, protecting the sandstone courtyard from the blistering sun.

Jarrod shoved Liala into the air to join the others, all belonging to senior members of the Ashen Hawks. The criminal guild used them as messengers, but the last three notes he'd sent Rae had been returned unopened. Only her drawn arrow confirmed she even lived.

I suppose I should be grateful she hasn't thrown Liala's charm away, then I wouldn't be able to reach her at all.

He sighed and spun, boots grinding against the thin layer of sand coating the city of Mirage after a recent windstorm.

"Sika will come around." Braka spoke out the side of his half-full mouth, using Rae's guild-given name.

"Aye." Jarrod looked at the crystal-blue sky through the fabric. "But when?"

"When she's ready. I know you miss her, but seeing Theo die shook her. Give her time, she'll come back. She seemed pretty fond of you."

Clenching his jaw, Jarrod hoped Braka was right. As his closest friend and ally, he wouldn't know what to do with himself without Rae in the Ashen Hawks. "But what if..." His voice trailed off as the door clicked shut, and he turned to see Braka had retreated inside.

He scuffed his boot over the ground and followed, finding his way through the guild's extensive hallways to his room. Rifling through the drawers of his desk, he found a fresh paper and withdrew it. With it, came a gold chain necklace that fell to the floor. Scowling, he picked it up and tossed it onto his desk before sitting with a quill to write Rae another note.

If I don't hear from you soon, I'm coming to find you.

He scattered pounce on the ink and folded the letter before returning through the maze of hallways to the aviary.

A new screech echoed from above, and he looked up to see Rae's grey hawk circling. His heart soared, and he pulled his whistle charm from his pocket and blew it twice.

Din swooped down and landed on his bracer.

Jarrod pulled the paper out, sending Din to join the rest of the hawks before unrolling it. Reading her message took time. They used a cypher code between the two of them, and her uncharacteristically sloppy hand slowed the translation process.

Jarrod. I found a possible deserter in Olsa. Is Helgath looking for one right now? Could be a big bounty if the Hawks want to get involved outside our usual area of expertise. Sorry I haven't written. Needed time, but I'm fine. Let me know.

She signed the note with an arrow with an X through it, and he read it again.

The Ashen Hawks avoided bounty jobs, often aligning with other criminals, rather than aiding in their capture. Most deserters never made it as far as Olsa, so if Rae was right, the bounty would be substantial.

Chapter 1

Two days earlier...

COOL COINS STACKED WITHIN RAE'S fingertips, varying in thickness and diameter. A hand in her satchel, she sauntered over the Jacoby rooftops. The money pouch weighed more than she'd expected, and she silently chastised the merchant for leaving it so readily available in her back room. Lifting her hand, she withdrew the largest coin. One side displayed the face of the god Shen Tallas, a swirling maelstrom on the back. A silver florin.

Not bad. Worth more than the pair of dice I left behind.

The unfortunate shopkeeper's incessant flirting with the baker made Rae's escape simple. However, as an extra precaution, she kept above the streets.

No one ever looked up.

The shallow incline of the roof posed no threat to her soft-soled black boots. They'd been a gift, crafted for her. The squeak of unbroken leather could ruin her graceful steps.

A warm breeze kicked up her chestnut-brown hair, the long, straight strands tickling her elbows. Braids wove through the length on the top of her head, keeping it out of her face. Having left her cloak behind due to the beginning of spring and the new year, she donned worn black leather pants and a sleeveless brown tunic. All tight against her frame to limit the risk of getting caught during her escapades.

"This is Helgathian garbage!" A gruff voice carried over the wind.

Rae's steps faltered as she looked at the source.

"Are you blind?" A young man faced a weathered cart vendor on the edge of the city's main square. "This is genuine military-issued armor. Made with the finest Helgathian steel. It's worth a fortune."

Rae crouched on the rooftop, narrowing her eyes at the exchange occurring. The mention of her home country alone would have gained her attention.

"How do *ye* know it's genuine, boy? The bush ye *found* it in tell ye?" The mocking bellow rang through the air, bringing a chuckle from Rae's lungs.

Pink flushed the young man's cheeks, his lips pursing together. He dropped the collection of metal pieces onto the makeshift countertop in front of him.

The wood groaned at the onslaught of heavy armor, and the shelf's hinges snapped, sending everything clattering to the ground.

"Ye clumsy fool!" The vendor stomped around his cart and shoved a finger in the younger man's face. "Pick yer trash up! And while yer at it, ye can reimburse me for the damage ye done!"

A boyish smile crossed the young man's face, a golden-blond beard dusting his chin. He leaned back from the vendor's accusatory poke. "Apologies, Mister." His baritone voice dripped with insincerity. "I merely wanted to display the authenticity of the armor. The weight is one way to identify Helgathian craftsmanship."

The vendor scoffed and shook his head. With a heavy boot, he kicked the fallen helmet clear across the street and laughed. "I hear how far it flies is also an indicator. The price is the price. Don't like it? Take yer trash elsewhere."

Rae traced the helmet's path and watched a rotund male patrol guard stoop to lift it from the dirt street with a huff.

The guard lumbered over to the arguing men and wheezed. "Is there a problem here, Rowley?"

Rae sat on the roof, crossing her legs.

"I'll say." The younger man glowered at the vendor. "This *thief* is unwilling to barter fairly. And he's damaging my property." He snatched the helmet out of the patrolman's hands and tucked it under his arm.

Rae rolled her eyes.

If that man is a thief, what does that make me?

Anyone could earn the title, it seemed.

"Damaging *your* property?" Rowley howled. "This idiot broke my cart, Lloyd!"

Lloyd tutted his tongue, nudging the crumbled ledge of the cart with the toe of his boot. "Well, you're going to have to pay for that, son."

"What?" The man's voice rose. "You can't be serious? All I ask is a fair price for my wares. It's basic trade law."

Lloyd looked down at the armor and grumbled. "I trust Rowley knows his armor. If he says this ain't worth more..." His voice trailed off as he bent to lift the chest plate from the ground. His face turned purple at the effort, and his breathing became ragged. Giving up, he dropped it and stumbled backward.

"You'd best clear this out." Lloyd wiped his hands on his uniform. "Take the offer, or I'll write you up for property damage."

Rowley smiled smugly and crossed his arms over his chest.

The young man's face contorted into a look of astonishment, his mouth gaping.

Rae laughed, and it echoed into the street before she slapped a hand over her mouth.

All three of the men stared at her.

Well, shit.

"You!" Lloyd shuffled forward as he pointed up at her. "What in Nymaera's name are you doing up there? Those rooftops are strictly a non-walking area."

The young man seized the opportunity to gather up his armor, but Rowley snatched the helmet from his hands.

Rae smiled. "Watching a comedy. Titled *the soldier, the cheapskate, and the incompetent guard*." Leaning forward, she propped her elbows on her knees. "Besides, I'm not walking. I'm sitting."

This time, the soldier laughed, and it came with a charming grin.

Lloyd's face flushed. "Young woman, I demand you come down immediately. Then I'll be taking the both of you..." He wildly pointed back and forth between the young soldier and her. "To contemplate proper manners."

Rae feigned consideration before answering. "Mmm... No."

The guard grumbled at her. "You can't say no. What do you mean, no? Get down here. Don't you understand the law?"

"I'm afraid I must decline. Unless you'd like to come up here and arrest me?" She held her wrists together out in front of her. "But that would require walking, and these rooftops are strictly a non-walking area."

Lloyd's face darkened to burgundy.

The soldier laughed. “She’s got you there.” Amusement glimmered in his eyes. “I’ll give you a boost if you want.”

The guard spun on the young man and jabbed a fat finger at his chest. “You go get ‘er, smartass. Or I’ll arrest you right now for disturbing the peace.”

Rae frowned.

You’ve got to be kidding me.

“Seriously?” The man eyed Rae. “I can’t catch her.”

“It’s true, he can’t.” She received a pair of glares from them.

“Not my problem. You’ll be sitting in jail if you fail. We take peace seriously here in Jacoby.” Lloyd crossed his arms over his round belly.

The soldier gave no clear response, his jaw tightening before his fingers closed at the latch of his belt. He tossed it, and the sword hanging from it, onto the pile of armor with a clank. His short cloak came next, falling as a loose drape over the entire pile. Beneath, he wore a simple stained white shirt with sleeves rolled up to his elbows. He tucked the bottom of his shirt into his worn tan breeches.

Tilting her head, Rae watched the man being sent after her and rose to her feet. She gave an exaggerated frown. “That’s all?” She could see the definition of his muscles beneath the thin material. “What about the shirt? It’ll get in your way.”

“You’ve enjoyed enough of a show already.” The soldier walked towards the building she stood on.

"Aww. But watching the fat man bend over was hardly a show. I'd rather watch you."

As he neared the wall, she lost sight of him but heard him laugh.

Is he actually going to chase me?

Taking a step away from where he climbed, she glanced behind her. The buildings were close enough together to facilitate an escape, but her horse was halfway across town.

The soldier's hands closed on the edge of the rooftop, his body following with an exhale of breath. His shoulders flexed as he wrestled his arm beneath him. "You know." He huffed as he threw his leg over the roof edge. "I'd appreciate it if you didn't run."

Rae stepped back again, poised to sprint once she deemed it necessary. "But where would be the fun in that? I thought all men loved the chase."

"COMMON MISCONCEPTION. I'M RATHER FOND of mutual agreement and shared interests." Bastian groaned as he pulled himself over the edge of the roof.

His muscles ached from lugging his old armor all over Jacoby, trying to find a vendor willing to purchase Helgathian armaments. No one wanted unlawfully sold armor, the property of the Helgathian military, and now he was being forced to climb onto a roof.

Perhaps my choices of late haven't been the best.

Lloyd reminded him too much of the entitled Sergeant Rynalds, a man he'd served under before becoming his superior. He certainly ordered Bastian around in a similar fashion.

And here I am... obeying.

The woman's vibrant green eyes pierced him now that he was closer, nearly inhuman in hue.

Auer, perhaps?

Her rich, tanned skin suggested the possibility. But with her shorter stature and warm brown hair, her blood couldn't be pure. He hoped, for his own sake, that conclusion was incorrect. He suspected she'd be difficult to catch, but auer grace and balance would make it impossible.

"How boring." She sighed and feigned a yawn. Other than her initial steps, she'd made no move to get away from him.

Finding his balance, he slowly advanced, trying to gauge when she'd run. Her apparent hesitation, or perhaps confidence, made his gut rumble with anticipation.

He held his hands out to help steady his gait up the slight incline. His worn boots were too slick on the surface. Maybe he'd fall and break his neck. That'd be one way to deal with his problems, though not ideal.

"Boring is good sometimes." He watched her hips for a shift in weight. He spied a bulging satchel at her side, his soldier's mind jumping to conclusions about her purpose for roof walking. "Right now, for example... I'd love boring. What do you say we climb down together?" He held a hand towards her.

The woman touched her chin, before crouching and reaching for his hand. Her fingertips grazed his before she recoiled. "Mm, I don't think so." She swiftly spun on her heels.

Ready for the shift, he lurched forward, just missing her hand.

Running along the peak, she jumped down to the lower neighboring rooftop. Halfway across that one, she stopped and looked back at him as he paused at the edge. "Too high? Do you need a hand down, Corporal?"

He grumbled to himself.

This is not what I wanted to deal with today.

Jacoby had never been part of his original plan. He'd intended to disappear into the Aidensar wilds, but something drew him southwest. Justifying the change would grant him milder weather, he accepted the foolish draw to open meadows and known Reaper brigades. The threat required him to quickly exchange the identifiable armor for coin so he could continue further from Helgath.

He'd pried off the nameplates from his armor that read *Lt. Damien Lanoret*. It'd been weeks since he'd left his battalion, and they'd come for him soon.

I'm Bastian now.

He'd hoped a new name would hinder their ability to find him. The woman's blatant guess at a rank, however, threatened his confidence for blending in.

"Not a corporal," Bastian muttered. "Cautious, is all." He eyed the alleyway between the buildings. He could make the jump but wanted to throw the woman off with feigned reluctance.

She stopped to sass him. It'd be easy to lull her into false confidence.

Glancing up, he tried to estimate how quickly he could jump and advance on her. He wanted this whole situation to be over so he could get his money and leave town.

This is unduly complicated.

Before he could come to a conclusion, she took off again. With no more time for debate, Bastian darted forward and launched himself across the alley. He landed roughly on a knee, but it helped prevent him from sliding backwards. Momentum propelled him up to the crest of the roof, where he regained sight of her.

The following gap was smaller, but the next home's roof stood a full body length higher than the previous.

She leapt with reckless abandon, her hands catching the edge of the shingles.

He almost wished she'd lose her grip and fall, saving him the trouble.

She wiggled her hips to shift her weight as she started to pull herself up. The sensuous movement made his heart beat a little harder, and he nearly forgot his purpose.

The slick soles of his boots allowed Bastian to slide down the slope. He jumped, reaching with one hand to grasp the shingled edge, while the other grabbed hold of her waist, yanking her into him.

In a move he didn't expect, her legs thrust forward, boots contacting the side of the building. She shoved him, and his fingers burned as they lost their grip.

They tumbled backward together.

He prepared himself for a long fall, but a jolt rocked through him as they landed on the incline of the lower roof. All the air expelled from his lungs as she landed hard on top of him, both his arms locking instinctively around her waist.

She struggled, twisting in his grip, forcing him to readjust and grab for a new handhold at her wrist. He bent his knee, pushing it against her hip. Rolling to accommodate her movement, he kept his hold of her. He locked his knees tight around her hips, putting the entirety of his weight on her thighs, and leaned over her.

To his amazement, she crossed her arms over her chest with a smirk, breathing hard. "You think you've won."

Bastian smiled and shrugged. "Looks like winning to me." He flexed his legs and sat up, scanning her up and down. No weapons that he could see. Her broken-in leather clothes were simple but well fitted. He couldn't help the moment his eyes lingered longer than they should have on her heaving chest. He returned his gaze to her face in time to see the playful scowl.

"You Helgathian men are all the same."

"Now, how would you know that? Besides, who said I'm Helgathian?" Her accusation, while it seemed frivolous, meant more if she somehow knew.

Her right hand reached up and grasped his jaw, turning his face so she could see his profile. Bright eyes bored into him. "Are you telling me you're not?" She tilted her head, her hair splayed out on the roof behind her. It cascaded around her pierced ears, one with a single silver hoop and the other with five.

He twisted his chin from her hand, seizing her wrist. "Are we going to do this the hard way? Or are you willing to admit I caught you, so we can get this whole thing over with?"

A grin spread over her face, and his stomach tightened. "You haven't caught me. You've merely delayed me. Could be worse, though. Better you than *Lloyd* sitting on me after all." Her other hand touched his hip and tugged at the hem of his shirt.

A flutter of sudden heat passed through him at the shock of her fingertips against his skin. "Whoa." He dropped her wrist and seized the other, pulling her touch from beneath his shirt. "Hey now. Getting a little handsy, aren't we?"

The woman rolled her eyes. "I'll show you handsy." Using her newly freed hand, she shoved his shoulder, catching him off guard.

He lost the precarious balance he'd obtained, but took her with him as he toppled sideways. He tightened his thighs against hers, shifting his grip on her wrist back to her waist. For a single, gloriously awkward moment, she was between his legs, but then they rolled again, his hand on her shoulder.

One over the other, they tumbled down the slope and off the side of the roof. The fall was brief, and he landed on his back with another huff.

She landed sharply on top of him.

His grip on her loosened, distracted by the dizzying pain in his back as he tried to regain his bearings. The high, dark walls harbored the hulking shadows of storage boxes and barrels all around.

She lay across him, her chest pressed to his as she shook her head. "This has been fun. But it's time for me to go."

As she rose from him, boots thundered, and Lloyd's silhouette appeared at one side of the alley's mouth.

A distraught, older blond woman followed him.

Lloyd wheezed, leaning over his belly to catch his breath.

"That's her!" The woman pointed a finger. "Thief! She robbed us!"

Bastian twisted his neck as he attempted to sit, looking from the accuser to the thief who'd been his objective. He reached for her, but she leapt away and hopped onto a crate, crouching within the shadows.

Cold hands clamped around his wrists as the guard seized him. "You're under arrest, son. For disturbing the peace, damaging property, and aiding the escape of a criminal." Lloyd clicked metal cuffs around his wrists in front of him.

"I did no such thing." Bastian growled, his head throbbing. "You're the one who sent me after her." In desperation, he considered bribing the guard. Not being put in jail was more important than how he would afford to travel to the next city.

Bastian awkwardly slid his cuffed hands towards his pocket, his fingers closing on an unfamiliar object. Confusion turned to panic as he withdrew a pair of white bone dice rather than the little coin he'd possessed. "Son of a bitch." He spun towards where the thief had been, catching only a glimpse of black as she disappeared onto the roof. "You've got to be kidding me."

"I do have some good news for you." The guard tugged on the chain between the manacles. "You'll have the jail all to yourself tonight."

Chapter 3

LYING FLAT ON HER BACK, Rae listened from the roof as the guard hauled her would-be captor off to the city jail. She stared at the sky and sighed, closing her eyes.

He was Helgathian. Most likely a military deserter, judging by the attempted sale of armor he claimed to have found. His story farfetched, she was willing to bet on her suspicions. The incompetent patrol guard would earn a hefty reward for turning the soldier in.

Helgath was infamous in Pantracia for its punishment of deserters, the crime equal to treason in the eyes of their courts. No one left the service of the military and lived to tell about it.

I need a drink.

Rae sat up. Peering down into the empty alley, she slid off the shingles, landed on her feet, and dusted off her pants before sauntering into the street. Picking the closest of the town's two dining halls, she pushed open the door to Telli's Tavern.

After doing a quick survey of the room to ensure Lloyd wasn't present, Rae found a seat near the hearth. A group of people gambled in the corner, drawing her attention, but she resisted the inclination to join them.

When the barmaid brought her an ale she reached into her pocket to find her coin. Her fingers maneuvered past several dice to retrieve an iron mark, giving it to the woman.

Rae withdrew one of the dice, turning it over in her hand. The enamel had been dyed green, and her gaze flitted back to the action at the far table.

Above the heads of the gamblers, a bulletin board hung on the wall. Posters plastered its surface, but one stood out more than the rest.

A wanted poster for a woman accused of deserting the Helgathian military.

Standing, Rae carried her mug over to the poster hanging from one corner. She tugged it from its place and eyed the reward amount.

No wonder Reapers pursue deserters.

Her lip curled at the thought of the ruthless soldiers sent to acquire practitioners of the Art for Helgath's academies.

A triumphant shout erupted from the table of gamblers, several rising to their feet.

A dark-haired man lifted his mug and stepped back from

the table. He bumped into Rae before she could step out of the way, her drink sloshing onto the front of her tunic.

She gasped, lifting her hands and looking down at her soaked shirt.

"Shit, sorry." The man's words slurred. "Let me get you a new one."

Rae huffed with a smile and shrugged, lowering her arms. "Not the first time I've been covered in ale."

The man blinked at the dampened wanted poster. He gave a charming smile, eyes flashing with interest. "Bounty hunter? That one's been caught already. Last month."

Rae smirked and crumpled the paper in her fist. "Too bad, quite the reward. Did *you* catch her?"

He sighed and shook his head. "Reapers did, I think. They pass through here all the time to check the postings. Bounties always get higher if the deserter makes it this far."

"Interesting..." Rae diverted her gaze to the clatter of dice being rolled at the man's table.

He caught the glance, briefly following it. "How about I get you another drink, and you join us for a bit? Seth, by the way." He held out his hand to her.

Accepting his grip, she nodded. "Rae. I'll join you, but just for one game."

"That's what Olrac said five games ago." Seth grinned, gesturing with his head to a pudgy, balding man who cheered.

Sure enough, one game turned into two, which quickly

turned into four. Each game came with several rounds of ale, blurring Rae's mind.

Seth put another pint in Rae's hand. The night's games over, they leisurely sat next to each other on a bench seat in front of the hearth.

"Why do I get the impression you needed a night off?" He smiled, leaning back and tucking a strand of fallen hair behind her ear.

Rae quirked a brow. "Probably because I did. Thank you for the games, took my mind off things." She smirked, admiring his blue eyes.

"Anytime." He propped a leg beneath him as he turned to look at her. "Even though you cleaned me and the other boys out of all our coin. Going to have to offer to do dishes or something to pay for the drinks."

Sipping her ale, she laughed. "Be careful who you spill on next time." She lifted her feet over his lap.

He rested a hand on her calf, above her ankle boot. "How long are you staying in Jacoby?"

"Not long."

"That's too bad. What brought you here then?"

Mistakes.

"I needed a break from Helgath."

"Helgath?" He frowned. "Didn't take you as someone who'd live in a country ruled by a tyrant. Perhaps you should stay here in Olsa."

Rae smiled. "Perhaps I should."

The thought of never returning to the Ashen Hawks caused a lump to form in her stomach. She never intended to leave permanently, just long enough to gain some perspective.

Since joining the Hawks at twelve years old, she'd earned an impressive rank, and she considered them her family. Weeks prior, she'd failed to save one of her comrades before he landed on the executioner's block.

She'd been unable to watch Theo's death.

"What are you thinking about?" Seth prompted, bringing her gaze back to him. He idly played with the laces of her right boot.

Shaking her head, she smiled. "Sorry." She took a gulp of ale. "I lost a friend recently, and it haunts me sometimes."

Seth's gaze sobered, but he loosened her boot enough to tug it from her foot and place it on the ground. His hands returned to her calf, working the muscle. "First time losing someone?"

Rae shook her head. "No. Not even close. But he took the blame for something he shouldn't have. It was my responsibility to protect him. He was just a kid." She rambled, forgetting herself momentarily in the drunken haze. Leaning her head back, she focused on the feeling of him massaging her foot. "If I'd done my job better, he'd still have his head."

Seth pursed his lips, running his hands up and down her calf. "Hazards of the job, sometimes."

"Firsthand knowledge?" Rae's chest tightened.

Talk about sleeping with the enemy.

He chuckled, returning to the pads of her foot. "Perhaps. Posters don't always give the best information on who you're after. Run into my fair share of more trouble than I should have bitten off." He shrugged. "But I'm still here."

Rae pulled her legs from him, leaning forward to study his face. "And are you chasing someone now?"

His shoulders tightened, a breath caught in his chest as she leaned close. He looked remarkably calm, but his eyes flickered down towards her chest. "Maybe. Why do you ask?"

Touching his chin, she lifted his eyes back to hers. "Professional courtesy," she murmured, trying not to slur. "Wouldn't want to step on any toes."

"Could partner." His hand slipped to caress her waist. "Plenty of money for two of us."

A tempting offer, if I wanted to switch careers.

"Depends who you're hunting." She eyed his mouth.

His lips parted, tongue licking his lower lip. "Just heard there's another deserter. Posters haven't made it this far yet, but word is he's headed this direction."

Rae's gaze returned to his, the man from the rooftop flashing in her mind. "What's the reward?"

Seth's eyes brightened. "Nine hundred silver florins. Plenty to share." His head inched closer, his breath tickling her lower lip.

Rae watched his advance, but her mind flitted elsewhere. As he kissed her, she wondered if the man in the city jail could be the deserter. Pulling away, she smiled at him and tugged her boot back on. "Do you live here?"

Seth still leaned forward at an awkward angle, reaching to touch her again as she tied her laces. "Sure, just down the road. Short walk." His fingers tangled briefly with the braids of her hair, trying to encourage her mouth back to his.

Turning her face in his touch, she kissed his wrist. "Maybe I'll see you again." She stood. "I'm sure I'll visit this place plenty while I'm in town."

Seth frowned. "You're leaving?"

"I have some business to take care of tonight." Touching his jaw, she angled his face up towards hers. "Poor timing is all. Next time." She dragged her thumb over his lower lip, smiling, before letting go.

Seth offered more protests, but she was too distracted to pay them any attention. The cool night air lightened her lungs once she stepped outside, conflict stirring within her.

The Hawks avoided getting involved in bounties, but nine hundred florins would go a long way. Betraying a fellow Helgathian criminal left a sour taste in her mouth.

He helped me get away.

Grinding her jaw, she walked towards the tree line, her steps uneven.

I can't just turn him over. Maybe Jarrod will know what to do.

Rae whistled with two fingers in her mouth to call Din. The grey hawk landed with ease on her outstretched forearm, chittering near her ear as he nestled in her hair. He did it for extra treats, and she could rarely tell him no. She ran her finger along the white speckles on his chest.

After sloppily scrawling on a bit of parchment, she wrapped the coded text around Din's leg with a modicum of trouble amid her fumbling fingers. "Jarrod." She narrowed her eyes at Din, trying to evaluate his understanding of her instruction. "Jarrod," she repeated, then launched the bird back into the sky.

Standing in the little clearing, she swayed as her mind ran itself in circles.

Turn him in, enjoy the payday.

Help him. He's a renegade like you.

"Guess it's time to go free the poor bastard," Rae muttered, sighing. "No point in figuring it out if he dies before I make up my mind. Can always turn him in later if he's a pain in the ass."

Using her cloak for the hood rather than the warmth, Rae led her red bay gelding to another tavern, conveniently close to the jail. Several horses lined the post, and hers wouldn't look out of place among them. She gave him the name Syga after stealing him from a trade caravan on her way out of Mirage two months prior.

Jacoby's streets ran in convoluted turns that suggested little forethought when new structures were erected.

Worn gravel and dirt roadways made for a multitude of imperfections, and Rae stumbled more than once in her tipsy state as she navigated her path.

The city jail, located at a three-way crossroads, looked to be built with more skill than the buildings around it. The stone walls rose into unmanned watchtowers with narrow windows, hinting at a possible former life as an armory. Only one unobstructed entrance existed off the main street since the back alley was blocked by a collection of boxes from the nearby tanners. It smelled rank enough to deter Rae from considering it an option.

Pausing to ensure no witnesses, Rae slunk along the side of the building to the door. She tried the handle, a gentle thunk of the lock catching confirming her suspicion. She fished her picking tools from a leather cuff around her upper arm.

This would be easier sober. But I don't have time to wait if Seth is already looking for him.

Her muscle memory aided her ability to insert the bent pieces into the lock, feeling and listening for the satisfying click of the mechanism releasing. It took a few breaths longer than it should have.

With a tentative push, she tested the hinges. They were quiet, and she remained crouched as she entered, delicately closing the door behind her. Impressed at her own success, she grinned beneath her hood.

Two boots crossed on top of the warden's desk to her immediate right, and raspy snores carried through the air.

She kept low, hidden from the slumbering guard by the bulky furniture. Taking her time, Rae examined the rest of the room. Large, with no interior walls. Instead, pillars supported the ceiling and at the far-right side, two holding cells stood in shadow. The space was hazy, sparse light seeping from hooded lamps hanging on the walls.

The jail's lone prisoner sat nearly invisible in the darkness.

Eyeing the holding cells, she made her way across the cold stone floor without standing. Within the right one, a head of blond hair was bent over, the man's hands laced together behind his neck, elbows against his knees. Defeat radiated from his slumped shoulders. It was unbecoming of the man she'd tussled with on the rooftops.

Glancing back at the sleeping guard, Rae approached the occupied cell with silent steps, albeit rather unsteady. The faint shadow she cast passed over the floor in front of the Helgathian's feet.

He started, his head lifting as his hands released his neck. Straightening his back, he looked at her, confusion and exhaustion on his face. Widening hazel eyes gave away his fear as he stood, his mouth opening to shout.

Rae yanked the hood from her head, realizing he may make assumptions that would get them in deeper trouble. She lifted a finger to her lips.

His mouth stilled, and his brows knitted. He stepped towards the bars, eyeing the warden's desk behind her. Crouching, his face leveled with hers, and he kept his voice low. "What are you doing here?"

Rae smirked. "What does it look like?" She pulled the lock-picking tools from her arm cuff. One slipped out of her hand, her reflexes too dulled by ale to catch it before it hit the floor with a clink.

"Shit." She clapped a hand over her mouth before glancing back at the still sleeping guard.

The soldier's eyes widened, head tilting as he sniffed. "Are you drunk?"

Rae scowled at him. "Are you complaining?" Pausing, she made a face and then smiled. "Maybe a little."

He lifted his palms to her in defeat. "Not complaining. I'll shut up." He stood, looking beyond her to the rest of the jail.

Keeping a third tool between her lips, Rae used the first two in the lock. "Ungrateful," she mumbled, the word hardly coherent as she worked. "Break me out." She mimicked a petulant tone. "But no drinking first. Be boring, be mundane. No one likes a drunk thief."

Twisting one of her picks, she pinned it against the other

and then held it with one hand while her other retrieved the third tool from her mouth. Inserting that one, she pushed and lifted the tip, and the cell door's lock lifted. She let out a soft cheer and grabbed the bars.

The soldier's hands closed on top of hers, holding the cell shut. "Wait."

She gave a slight tug again, to test him, and he glowered, holding it still. Her eyes followed his to the hinges.

He didn't need to say more for her to understand.

She frowned. "So complicated," she muttered under her breath. Replacing her tools in her cuff, she looked back at the warden's desk. She spotted her salvation flickering a sleepy yellow.

Leaving the cell door unlocked, Rae pulled her hood back up and retraced her steps across the room. Her boots made no noise, and she plucked the lamp from the tabletop. She returned to the cell and blew out the flame. Ignoring the soldier's impressed huff, she opened the spout used to refill the oil and poured the contents over the problematic hinges.

Satisfied, she abandoned the lantern and swung the cell door open. The hinges glided as if new, and she smiled.

"Not bad for a drunk thief." The soldier gave her a teasing grin.

"You should see me sober." She lifted her eyebrows. With a jerk of her head towards the door, she led the way back, and he followed silently behind.

Her heart leapt into her throat when the front door handle twisted and unexpectedly swung open.

"Gods damn you, Velch, you left the door unlocked again." Lloyd's voice echoed as Rae dove beside the doorway.

The soldier did the same in the opposite direction, pressing his back against the stone wall.

A snort sounded from Velch as his boots fell to the ground. "What—huh?" He rubbed his eyes.

Lloyd sidestepped, yanking his keys from the lock.

Rae saw her opportunity to slip through the half-closed door. Doubt whether the soldier would have time to follow rippled through her, and she hesitated. Sure enough, the door slammed shut a second later, confirming her suspicions. Turning, she met the gaze of the soldier she came to free.

Lloyd's eyes roamed to the side, landing on the empty and open cell. A dirty curse erupted from his wheezy lungs. "Nymaera's tits, you idiot! Where's the prisoner?" He stomped towards the cell, kicking the abandoned lantern.

Rae silently skirted the wall, Lloyd's attention turned away from her. Creeping around behind the sitting warden, she exhaled a steady breath. Scanning for a weapon, since she carried none, she located the hilt of a dagger at the warden's belt and frowned.

Men and their blades.

Velch's back straightened, looking in the soldier's direction. "Lloy—"

Stepping forward, Rae jerked the dagger free in a smooth movement, lifting the cold blade to his throat from behind.

The soldier hurried out of her vision, towards Lloyd, who let out a grunt shortly after.

The dagger felt foreign in her grasp, but she held it steady as she rocked her head back to look behind her.

Lloyd's back arched in an awkward position, forced to bend by the brawny arm wrapped around his throat.

Locking Lloyd against him, the soldier placed one hand expertly behind the city guard's neck.

The guard turned purple.

In front of her, the warden sat rigid, and she looked at the open, empty cell.

"Rise. Slowly." She stood as he did.

"You." Lloyd gasped through the soldier's chokehold, his beady eyes on Rae. "The thief who—"

The soldier cut off any further speech with a squeeze and Lloyd gurgled to silence.

The warden sniffed. "Are you drunk?"

Rae rolled her eyes. "Everyone's so interested in the state of my sobriety."

"You do smell like a keg." The soldier flashed her a grin from behind Lloyd's struggling body.

Sighing, Rae swayed. "I had a drink spilled on me. And *then* I got drunk." She poked the warden with the blade. "Move your feet."

"Easy there, I'm goin'. I'm goin'." He stepped into the darkened cell.

Lloyd, in a futile effort, struggled against the soldier as he dragged him to follow. The man's large body strained the soldier, but he tightened his hold and kneed Lloyd from behind. The guard squeaked, unable to right himself when roughly thrown forward.

Velch tried to catch him, but they tumbled in a pile on the ground as Rae slammed the door shut.

The soldier clicked the lock into place.

The warden gaped at them while Lloyd found his voice.

"You can add assaulting an officer, wrongful imprisonment, resisting arrest, and attempted murder to *your* list of charges, Son!" He rolled about, struggling to get to his feet.

The soldier laughed, the sound rich as he turned from the cell and crossed to the warden's desk. "I'd enjoy seeing you enforce those charges from that cell." He plucked up a dark emerald cloak draped over the back of the chair and wrapped it around his shoulders. He started opening drawers and rifling through them. He paused after opening one and snorted before he lifted the pair of dice between his thumb and forefinger as he turned to Rae. "Can't be leaving these behind, seeing as I need you to trade me back the coin you stole."

Rae looked at the dice, a grin breaking over her face. "You stole my dice?" She stalked towards the door. "Not very gentlemanly."

"I stole your..." The soldier rolled his eyes and moved to the next drawer. He withdrew a small coin purse and let it jangle as he turned towards the cell. "I'll take this as my reimbursement for your appropriation of my armor. Thank you for your generosity in providing a fair price." He moved from the desk to the weapon rack on the wall, tucking the dice back into his pocket.

Lloyd huffed.

"Taking that dagger with you, Dice?" The soldier retrieved his old sword from the rack.

Dice? Did he just nickname me?

"Not my style." Rae tossed the liberated dagger to the floor, its purpose served. Walking to the front door, she touched the handle and waited. "Shall we?"

The soldier nodded as he buckled the sword belt, tying the strings of the coin purse next to it. He glanced up at Rae before he turned back and secured extra knots.

She grinned at his silent implication.

On reaching the horses outside the rowdy tavern, Rae nodded at the brown and white paint mare with bulging saddlebags next to Syga. "That one is yours."

He hesitated, raising a brow to the apparent gift.

"Hurry up." Mounting, she steered Syga away and nudged him off towards the tree line. As the silence behind her drew out, she wondered if he'd follow. It'd been a risk to assume, but she hoped. Even with her plan uncertain, keeping him close reigned crucial.

The clamor of hooves caught up behind her, a steady gallop slowing to match Syga's canter as they neared the outskirts of the city.

"So, what's with the dice?" he yelled over the thundering hooves. "You leave them every time you steal someone's money?"

Rae laughed and eyed him. "That's what you have to say to me?" She scoffed as they entered the trees. "Not a *thank you for breaking me out of jail*? I see the manners of the Helgathian military haven't improved."

He scowled and looked ahead. The half-moon broke through the canopy in places, creating glimmering pools for them to see by.

Forced to slow, they wove through the trees.

"Why do you keep calling me Helgathian?" They passed close to each other, and he lowered his tone. "I'm not. And I suppose I could muster a thank you if you returned my property. Or is it payment for your services?"

Shaking her head, Rae withdrew his black coin purse from her satchel. She threw it in his direction and, surprisingly, he caught it. "You can't afford me, Helgathian." A thought sparked on how to keep him with her. "But it's your lucky day. *I* can afford *you*."

"Excuse me?"

Rae smirked. "You need money. I need a sellsword." She motioned to the blade at his side. "Assuming you know how to use that thing."

He frowned. "I do. And seeing as you apparently like to break into places while drunk, I could see why you'd—"

"Nope. While sober too."

He groaned. "Either way, I'm not sure we'd make very good partners in—"

"Nope. I'm not asking, just being polite. If you decline, I'll take that pouch back while you sleep and find someone else." Looking at him, she cocked one eyebrow as he eyed the coin purse in his lap. "Don't bother hiding it, there's nowhere I won't look."

The soldier's cheeks flushed in the pale moonlight, his spine straightening. "Insistent, aren't you? Why me?"

Hmm, I've never met a bashful soldier.

"I can't trust a bounty hunter." She waved her hand as she absently thought of Seth.

"Bounty hunter? You met a—"

"Yep." Rae cut him off again, grinning. "Seth. He spilled my drink on me. He's in Jacoby looking for some deserter, so I don't need him catching wind that I'm less than lawful myself. Does that mean you'll accept my offer?"

"I think I need you to explain the offer again," he grumbled.

"You don't understand the concept of a sellsword?"

"Well, of course I do. I don't understand why a *thief* needs one."

Rae sighed. "Because I do."

He pursed his lips, but then laughed, shaking his head. "Whatever you say, Dice."

"My name is Rae." She narrowed her eyes.

"Too bad, I was getting fond of Dice. You can call me Bastian. It might feel like less of an insult than Helgathian."

"*You can call me* makes it sound fake, you realize that?"

He laughed again and shrugged. "I do want to say thank you. You had a chance to slip out back there, and you didn't. You didn't even have to come free me in the first place."

"We'll see if you were worth it."

Too bad I can't give Jarrod Bastian's name until Din gets back.

"Now I find myself in debt for my new friend." He reached forward, rubbing the mare's neck. "What's her name?"

Rae, distracted by thoughts of what might happen to Bastian, nearly missed the question. Raising an eyebrow, she looked at the horse and shrugged. "You'd have to ask her owner."

Bastian heaved a sigh, ending in a regretful groan. "I stole a horse?" He leaned back in the saddle. "Great..."

"Too late to take her back now." Rae smiled. "Lloyd's probably found a way out of that cell and everyone will be looking for you. Sounds like he's got a few charges to hold to your name. Not to mention you being so far from your post, Sergeant—"

"I'm not a sergeant," Bastian interrupted in an exhausted tone.

"Was I correct with corporal?"

"No, I'm not in the military."

"Not this far from Helgath, you're not."

"Gods, how many times do I need to say I'm not—"

"You're cute when you're frustrated." She looked sideways at him.

His chest rumbled with a growl as he rubbed the back of his neck.

"That." Rae pointed at him. "You should keep that look in check, it could prove difficult to resist. I'm not sober yet."

"I wouldn't take advantage while you're drunk. And wouldn't you want to keep this relationship professional if you were to hire me to protect you?"

Rae looked him up and down, then shrugged again. "Not when you look like that. Professional boundaries be damned."

"I don't even know how to respond to you right now. Are you serious?"

Rae's shoulders slumped. "Has no one ever flirted with you? If you're not interested, you can say so. And please, if you're married, tell me now."

Bastian's eyes widened. "I, umm..." He scratched the back of his head in his cute nervous habit.

Rae sighed, assuming one of her inquiries was correct. "You still haven't accepted my offer."

"You'll need to be a little more specific. Are we back to talking about me being a sellsword?"

"Yep. This poor, defenseless girl is requesting your help."

"Oh?" Bastian laughed. "Believe me, I've encountered enough women like you to know you are not defenseless. But I do need the money, and I'd be a fool to pass up the opportunity."

"Good. Then we have a deal. But for the record, you've never met a woman like me."

"That, I'm beginning to believe. You have a way of keeping me on my toes, and it's hardly been a day."

Rae smiled, looking at him as they wove closer to each other again, the horses walking side by side. "If you enjoy being kept on your toes, just wait until you aren't wearing boots."

"You did suggest I take my shirt off before." Bastian grinned. "Sounds like you're already making more plans?"

"Is that a problem?" She tilted her head.

"What if I don't meet those lofty expectations?" A hint of pink colored his cheeks again.

Rae hummed as she looked him in the eye. "I think I've spent enough time in your arms as it is to know my *expectations* certainly aren't lofty."

"While we rolled around on the rooftop? How could you get a sense of anything?"

"I'm good at multitasking." Rae shrugged. "When I'm sober." She let her eyes linger on him to make him uncomfortable.

It worked, and he shifted his position on the saddle, averting his gaze.

"Shy?" She gentled her tone with a hint of sincerity.

"Unaccustomed. I'm not often in the company of a beautiful thief."

"Ah." She smiled. "You're right. There are far too many ugly thieves out there."

Chapter 4

As Rae pulled her ale-saturated tunic over her head, intent on replacing it with a fresh shirt, Bastian's entire body caught fire with a glimpse of her bare skin. The natural warmth of her tanned skin showed through the thin cropped chemise still covering her chest, and he averted his gaze from the sensuous curve of her breasts under the fabric.

Guess she's not shy.

He tried to remember how to swallow, kneeling beside the fire he'd just encouraged to life.

They'd established a camp within an outcropping of rock near the base of the Belgast Mountains. She'd identified Drych as her destination, but they were still somewhere east of Dyfor's Pass. It would likely be a few days before they reached Drych.

Traveling together was still a strange concept.

Bastian had no intention of finding a partner, yet Rae had thrust herself rather effectively into his life.

As Rae circled in front of him, Bastian caught another glimpse of the curve of her waist. A tattoo covered her side, but before he could make out the details in the dim light, she yanked a black shirt over her head. Tight sleeves clung to the middle of her forearms, with cutouts at the shoulder exposing her skin.

"Is it too cliché for a thief to wear black?" Walking towards him, she looped her arms through a black vest.

"I'm a little partial to the previous look," Bastian blurted before he could stop his mouth.

Rae quirked an eyebrow. "When I stunk of ale?" She sniffed her shoulder and frowned. "I think I still do."

"I was talking about the moment after that, but before the black shirt." He'd been too silent before, unappreciative of the attention she seemed intent to give him.

Her gaze flitted back to him, reflecting flames. "Bravo," she praised quietly. "Now you need to work up the nerve to relieve me of it." Leaning back against a tree trunk, she took her time in lacing her vest.

Bastian chewed on his lower lip, encouraging himself to only watch from the corner of his vision. He'd be a fool to be blind to how attractive Rae was. Her vibrant eyes always felt like they were undressing him, and it left him flustered in every conversation. But as a soldier, he knew how to act under pressure. He didn't want to let her attempts to disarm him succeed, even if they already had.

Fiddling with the fire, he rolled a small log into place, watching it catch. "Are you always like this with men? Or am I special?"

Rae opened her mouth with a glint in her eyes but paused and closed it, taking a breath. "No." Her tone turned serious. "I'm not, but I need a break from reality. The ale and the company of handsome men have provided ample distraction."

The campfire pulsed warm waves across him as he sat cross-legged. "This Seth you mentioned earlier? The bounty hunter. One of your distractions?" The mention of the knowledgeable hunter in Jacoby was enough reason for Bastian to leave town with Rae. He didn't know the region and even if he couldn't trust her, the company would make travel through the wilds safer.

"Seth." She rummaged through one of the stolen saddlebags sitting next to her. "Not as handsome as you, but something tells me he'd make up for it in other areas." Eyeing him, she smiled. "He thinks he'll see me again."

"Will he?"

"Nope." She pulled a whetstone from the stolen bag. Frowning, she motioned with it. "Want this?"

Bastian nodded and held up a hand as she tossed it, catching the sharpening stone. He considered asking more about the bounty hunter, but ultimately talking about another man sounded counterintuitive. He changed the subject instead. "Blades aren't your style?"

"Nope." She returned her gaze to the bag. "Does that surprise you?" The tone of her voice held less of her usual teasing air.

"A little. Those in your profession are usually rather fond of small, concealable weapons."

"True." She looked up. "I prefer my bow. Blades always felt rather... crude. Messy. I have a hunting knife in case I need it, but I could probably get three arrows in your skull before I managed to unsheathe it."

"A lovely image." Bastian laughed. "I'll take your word for it. I was never much good with a bow."

"Really? The Helgathian military has an impressive archery range." Rae narrowed her eyes at him. When he took a deep breath, she waved a hand in the air, dismissing whatever he was about to say. "If not Helgath, as you so insist, where *are* you from?"

He hid the wince at the question he'd been preparing for. He wasn't particularly keen on lying, but it was necessary for no one to know. Even one person was too much risk. He knew enough about the methods the military used to track down deserters and wished to avoid all of them. Lies needed to be his new reality, along with the persona of Bastian.

"Is there a physical trait specific to Helgathians I'm unaware of? Last I checked, they aren't identifiable on looks alone, so why do you think I'm from Helgath? I could be from Feyor and take great offense to your misidentification."

Rae gave him an unimpressed look and pulled her long hair up behind her head, playing with gathering it into a ponytail. "Aside from the Helgathian armor you were trying to sell? A hunch." She let go of her hair, and it cascaded around her face, the top still held in place by braids. "Nothing but a hunch. Where are you from?"

"Aidensar." He named the one country he felt confident he knew enough about. "Just outside Fort Tryssla. Close to Helgath, but still not in it. What about you?"

Her green eyes blinked as if she debated answering him. "Ashdale." Her tone softened. "In Delkest." The abrupt vulnerability in her voice struck him, and she averted her gaze. Pulling a dark orange tunic from the saddlebag, she held it up. "Want a new shirt?"

And now stolen clothing. Perhaps a life of criminal activity would suit me.

He'd already put a price on his head with the choice to disobey orders and subsequently walk away. He'd become a traitor in the eyes of his country, even as he sought to protect her people. How could stealing a horse and clothing be worse?

"I could give you some privacy if you wanted to try it on." Rae grinned.

He glowered.

She must have seen me turn away.

He could imagine his mother's berating tone as she lectured him on how to properly behave around women. It wasn't like he'd never stripped in front of others before. It was frequently required during his service in the military. But his compatriots were primarily men, and Rae's womanly curves made it impossible to pretend she was another soldier.

If she kept teasing him, he doubted he'd hold his resolve forever.

Bastian eyed the tunic she held up. "Little small, I think." His ratty white shirt neared the end of its life and needed to be replaced. Intended as an undershirt for the armor he'd been 'relieved' of, it was already heavily stained. Bastian couldn't remember the last time he'd worn a traditional tunic instead of a uniform.

She shrugged and tossed the tunic at him, anyway.

After filling their bellies with a simple meal of crusty bread and dried venison, Rae positioned herself with her back against a tree trunk, her hood pulled over her eyes.

Bastian settled with his back to the fire, balling the orange tunic under his head as a pillow. The hard ground didn't bother him anymore, having grown accustomed in the weeks since abandoning his duty. His money pouch formed a lump under his hip, and he shifted to untie it.

"Peaceful sleep, Bast," Rae whispered after he'd thought she'd fallen asleep.

Reminded of her presence, he reconsidered his sleeping arrangement.

She'll rob me blind if I give her the chance.

He unfastened the pouch as he sat up, unraveling the shirt and tucking the coin purse in the middle of it, then reformed his pillow. He eyed where his sword lay between him and the fire.

Rae lifted the edge of her hood, watching him.

"So, you don't like blades. Does that mean you won't steal them?"

A smile spread over her face. "It's cute you think your coin purse is safe there. But stealing from my sellsword is counterproductive. Just because I can, doesn't mean I will."

"Doesn't mean you won't, either."

Rae laughed. "I'd give you my word, but I suspect it would mean little to you." She let go of her hood, leaning her head back again and crossing her ankles.

"I'm not in a position to be picky, I suppose." Bastian sighed, laying back down. He didn't bother with the sword but wrapped the shirt as tight as he could and nestled it between his bent arm and head. "Good night, Dice."

"Good night, Captain."

Wrong again.

Glad she couldn't see his smile, he closed his eyes.

Slumber fell quicker than he expected, and he descended into dreams.

Voices whispered through the trees, which glowed with a faint, pale blue light, their bark emanating with a pulsating energy he'd never seen before. The wind blowing through the leaves left trails of flickering motes.

Looking up, Bastian studied the growing glow, flowing like a wave on the beach. The whispers echoed the movement, encouraging him forward.

He took a cautious step, his bare feet touching the cold forest floor. His step sent a pulse of light through the shivering grass, like dropping a pebble in a puddle. The next placement of his foot felt awkward, avoiding a little mushroom and an oak seed still pushing through the soil.

You came, a voice reverberated above the rest.

Bastian's gaze darted up, and a figure that hadn't been among the trees before settled in his vision. At first, he thought it was a woman, but the broad shoulders and height suggested otherwise. The person faded and in their place stood a massive stag.

Dark navy eyes bored into him, flecks of blue-white light drifting from the beast's ruff as it shook its expansive antlers.

I have an offer for you.

"What?" Bastian's voice sounded far away.

I brought you here to accompany me to the sanctum where greatness awaits you.

Bastian hesitated. An odd sense of calm filled his stomach. "I brought me here. Not you."

You wanted to go to Aidensar. But I brought you here, instead. This is important. With the power I'm offering you, you'll have no need to fear the petty thief you travel with, nor the grand threat of Helgath finding you.

"Power?" His forehead tensed as he frowned. "What power?"

An ancient and sacred one that needs a guardian like you. One who defends innocence.

"How do you—"

We know more than you could imagine, human child.

"I don't want it." Bastian backed up.

The stag didn't follow.

"I don't need your power." His foot caught on a root, and he fell, jerking awake. His eyes shot open, every muscle tensing as he sat up. Glancing toward the tree Rae had slept against, she wasn't there.

The confusion of the dream turned into panic as he slipped his hand into the still bundled orange shirt. Instead of finding his coin pouch, his fingers touched two small cubic shapes. "Son of a bitch."

Rae's laughter echoed behind him, stunted by a huff of her breath.

Twisting awkwardly, he turned to see her dangling from a horizontal branch before she hauled herself back up. Sweat glistened on her bare stomach, having stripped to her plain half-chemise.

"Daughter would be more accurate." Rae's ankles locked as she lifted herself again.

Bastian tore his eyes away from her, examining the familiar dice in his palm. Tapping his pocket where'd he'd kept the pair she'd previously left him, he found a different bulge. He tugged the coin pouch free, the money inside jangling together. He sighed with relief but followed it with a groan for her benefit. "Now you're just showing off."

Rae dropped to the ground, shaking her hands and brushing them off on her pants. "Just showing you that your efforts are futile. You're better off trusting me, it's less offensive." She cringed, closing her eyes.

"Well, I'd hate to offend a thief," he grumbled, reaching for his boots after pocketing his coin. His feet felt cold, and he anxiously covered them back up. "I'm surprised you're not with a guild somewhere with skills like that."

"Who says I'm not?" Walking over to him. Rae sat near the dead fire pit and leaned back. Hands at her head, she lifted in a sit-up.

Bastian shifted to support her ankles, holding them in place, and her speed increased. He leaned to get a better look at the ink on her side, making out a fox and a bird.

"That you're in the Olsan wilderness alone. Hiring sellswords." The vision of her muscled abdomen made his throat tighten, and he forced himself to stare at her knees instead. A subtle scent of mint touched his nose.

"How are you not hungover?" He dared to gaze at her face.

Rae looked from the sky to him. "I am." She lowered herself again. "Exercise helps."

Watching her, his body ached to join her. His usual morning routine of Helgathian training forms, however, would need to be modified. She was suspicious enough already. Shifting to put his knees on her boots, Bastian lifted an arm behind his head to stretch. "Hope you don't mind company, then."

Quirking an eyebrow, Rae paused at the high point, but didn't sit up all the way. "I don't mind." Her gaze trailed down to his chest. "Still insisting on keeping your shirt on, huh?"

He'd prefer not to, but his left arm carried a tattoo she might recognize as his military brand. "Still just as bashful as yesterday. I'll keep it on."

Rae sat up all the way, catching her breath. Lifting her hand, she offered him the coin pouch that had been in his pocket moments before. "You're easy to steal from. You should work on that."

Glowering, Bastian snatched the coin purse and tossed it behind him towards his sword. "You just can't keep your hands to yourself." He rocked back from her feet before she could go into another set.

She stuck out her bottom lip. "Is keeping my hands to myself a rule?" A coy smile overtook the pout. "If it is, tell me now. I'll take some time to adjust to such strict conditions."

"How about you hold my feet?" Bastian sat back.

Shifting onto her knees, Rae knelt on his feet and leaned with her forearms on his knees. "This is technically touching."

He allowed himself a moment to feel the stretch of his back before he lifted himself in the first sit up. His heart jumped into his throat as he realized the perfect position Rae had put herself in. With her arms beneath, he had a generous view of her cleavage. And he couldn't tear his eyes away for a mind-numbing breath before he remembered he needed to lay back and continue with the exercise.

Gods help me.

"Problem?"

Absolutely not.

Bastian imagined dunking himself in an icy river. "Nope." He lifted himself again. This time, with the forethought to close his eyes.

"Where did we land on that rule of yours?" Her tone sounded serious, arms leaving his knees, but her weight on his feet remained. "Believe it or not, I can respect your wishes if you prefer I stop... the extra attention."

"No." Bastian's mouth spoke before his mind could second guess. He opened his eyes and saw her sitting back, rubbing her temples. He continued his sit-ups. "I like the way you are. No reason to stop, Dice."

Rae lowered her hands from her head, and her smile touched her eyes before turning into another smirk. "Dice. I'm not shaking that one, am I?"

Bastian huffed a chuckle. "Would you rather I stop? I find it fitting."

Leaning on his knees again, she tilted her head. "I suppose it is." She winced and sat back on her feet. "Though right now it merely serves a painful reminder of just how many dice I threw last night." Looking at the treetops, she shrugged. "But I *did* get a foot rub too. That was nice, even if it was only one foot."

Bastian's brow furrowed as he came up and stayed, resting his arms on his knees. "Foot rub? How does that work into a dice game?"

Rae met his eyes. "The dice game, and the ale, came first. Then the foot rub. Something appealing about a man who's good with his hands. Maybe I'd have returned if I hadn't had other things on my mind."

Bastian silently cursed his mind and the places it ventured without his permission.

Rae, still sitting in front of him with barely anything covering her torso, didn't help.

He swallowed and cleared his throat. "Other things?"

Rae leaned back when he stood up. "Yep. I had to go rescue a certain soldier from dire circumstances."

"Ah, yes." Bastian turned towards the tree she'd used for her pull-ups. He felt a sudden need to keep his back to her. "You aren't regretting the possible losses by making that sacrifice, are you?"

"Not even a little." She shuffled around somewhere behind him. "Seth will find a lovely girl, I'm sure. Better than being caught up with someone like me."

Jumping to grab hold of the branch, Bastian took a moment to find a comfortable position for his hands before he fluidly pulled himself up. The tension in his muscles helped distract him from other discomforts.

Get yourself together, Lieutenant.

He focused on what she'd said instead. "Because you're a thief? Or because he's a bounty hunter?"

Rae fell silent as he waited for her answer, but he could hear her moving about their camp. Several pull-ups later, she answered. "Professions aside, I don't offer what respectable men want, and he seemed like a decent man. Didn't need me corrupting his life."

Bastian slowed his next pull-up with her words, frowning. Despite the yearning of his body for more, he released the branch and dropped to the ground.

Rae had put her shirt and cloak on and stood at her horse's side, checking her bow.

He shook out the bottom of his shirt, peeling the fabric from his skin. "You know that's a load of horseshit, right?"

Rae's gaze darted to him. "What?"

"Horse shit. Your past doesn't matter in that kind of situation. If there's something between you, that's all that matters. Love doesn't care about our perceptions of ourselves. And it sure as hells doesn't corrupt."

Staring at him, she turned from her horse. "Love?" The hint of a smile touched her lips, her shoulders relaxing. "You're a romantic, aren't you?"

Bastian shrugged. He'd never considered the notion before. "If believing that makes me one, I guess so."

"Then I hope you get your romance one day." She cringed and pulled her hood up. "We should get going before Seth begins his deserter hunt and finds me."

"No more foot rubs?"

She mounted. "Not from him. But if you'd like to fill the role…"

Bastian turned to pick up his sword and money pouch before she could see him blush. He secured his sword to his belt. "We in a hurry? No breakfast?"

Rae paused, pulling a vial from her cloak and dabbing the contents onto her fingers before rubbing her temples. "Breakfast? Is that something you do? I have fruit if you'd like, but if you're thinking I'll cook for you, you'll be sorely disappointed."

"Breakfast is a necessary part of the day." He sauntered towards his horse.

My stolen horse.

"But I would never dare assume you'd make it."

Rae huffed. "That's better for both of us. I'm about as good at cooking as I am with a sword."

"Well, now I want to see both."

Laughing, she shook her head. "Stick around long enough and you might, but it's not pretty. Maybe we can find a stream first, then eat? All I can smell is ale on my skin, and it's making me nauseous."

Bastian chuckled. "Fair enough. Stream first, then I can make us something to eat." He pulled himself up onto his saddle, settling into place.

"You cook? That might be better than foot rubs."

"Ma made sure of it" He gestured towards the narrow game trail along the mountainside. "After you, Dice."

Rae rode ahead of him, letting her hood down again as her horse maneuvered over the uneven terrain. Their speed limited, he watched her keep fidgeting in her seat. After a quick stop at a stream, they continued, looking for an appropriate location to build a firepit.

She leaned back, and he realized she'd tied her reins to her saddle, leaving both her hands free to retrieve something small from within a pack. Sitting straight again, she started braiding the hair at the sides of her head before pulling it into a high ponytail.

He didn't talk, his mind wandering back to the dream he'd had. Looking up at the trees, their branches rustling in the wind, he recalled the pulsing blue lights. Thinking about them brought a strange sense of peace to his mind.

"Bastian." Rae used the full name he'd given himself for the first time.

It jarred him from his reverie, realizing they'd stopped.

The thief slid from her horse, boots silently connecting with the ground. "Look." A childlike tone of curiosity filled her voice.

"What?" Bastian squinted in the direction Rae faced. They'd remained against the mountainside, the slopes turning into jagged cliffs in this part of the forest. Before them, two of the cliffs dropped together, suggesting a shallow gorge. A tall thorny bush grew in front of it, the leaves still sparse and re-growing from the recent winter.

Rae pointed at the bush, looking at him. "Use your sword to create a path."

Bastian narrowed his eyes. "To what end? That's a great way to dull down a blade."

"I gave you a whetstone, didn't I?" Rae approached him, reaching for his hilt. "Come on."

Bastian smacked her hand. "Again with being handsy." He

indulged her by dismounting. "What'd the poor bush do to you?"

Rae frowned, standing her ground directly in front of him, tilting her chin up. "It's in my way. I want to see what's in there."

Bastian rolled his eyes, staring down at her with his hands on his hips. "There's probably nothing more than rock and dirt... You're serious?"

The weight of his sword shifted, and he looked down, finding her hand on the hilt.

Rae tilted her head, a coy smile on her lips. "Aren't you curious?" She tugged on the weapon, not to remove it, but to guide him closer.

A strange flutter passed through his chest. He looked down, trying not to stare at the gap in her tunic. "What exactly am I supposed to be curious about?"

Rae's hand retracted from his sword, sliding over his belt. "Your sense of adventure."

Bastian's heart leapt into his throat, and he shivered with how she eyed him up and down. He caught himself imagining moving closer to her and feeling her fingers against his skin. "I think you mean my ability to act foolishly."

"Then we have something in common, after all. Be foolish with me." Rae's dark eyelashes flitted as she looked from one of his eyes to the other.

Without his conscious permission, his hand lifted and caressed up her arm, fingertips brushing the exposed skin at her shoulder. He watched, fascinated by the look of his pale hand against her deeply tanned shoulder.

"Something on your mind, Lieutenant?" Rae's fingertips walked up his abdomen.

A wave of heat mixed with shock rocked through him, hearing her appropriately name his rank. It sounded utterly seductive from her lips, rather than how he was so accustomed to hearing it.

It took everything in him not to react, and he smiled instead. "I thought you wanted me to cut through the bush, but here you are distracting me instead?"

Rae smirked. "It's nice to know I can distract you." Stepping backwards, she unsheathed his sword. She lifted it, aiming the point at his chest, her arm surprisingly steady. Her face beamed with play.

Bastian's heart pounded, the sudden lust for her mounting with the threat of the blade. He wanted nothing more than to step back into her and inhale the sweet scent of her hair and skin, fresh from the bath at the stream.

Disciplined, he stood still, watching her vibrant green eyes. "You're quite effective, but I know better than to show too much weakness." He held out his open hand to her. "But I'll take that sword back, if you please."

Lowering her arm, she turned the blade and pushed the hilt into his hand, wrapping her fingers around his. "Can we *please* go look?"

Bastian sighed. "Fine." He took a step towards the bush, and she let go of his hand. Examining the branches for the best entry, he rolled his shoulders.

Can't sword train in the morning, so I guess this will have to do.

He lifted the sword and swung it at the bush, severing branches with a satisfying snap. Stepping into it, he maneuvered deeper.

The area behind the bush proved empty, despite what he believed. The canyon continued beyond, opening into a walkway wide enough for a pair of horses.

Rae appeared beside him, wriggling past him and the last chunk of thorns. His shirt snagged, and he turned to free it without ripping the material, but it was too late.

He looked behind, seeing the horses tied to trees, and when he looked forward, Rae ran ahead.

She jogged towards a pair of tall pillars, their white facades worn with time to a mottled cream. Vines curled up them, still brown and barren. "Ruins." Her voice barely reached him as she walked deeper. "These look ancient."

The word resonated in the memories of his dream. *Ancient power.*

He furrowed his brow, contemplating what they had said to him. The stag spoke of a sanctum, and the bottom of his stomach dropped out.

Impossible.

He'd never shown an ounce of ability in the Art, which would've explained prophetic dreams. He couldn't manipulate the fabric of reality like those the Reapers hunted. If he had, Helgath would have snatched him up for their academies the moment he showed any talent.

"Hold up, Rae," Bastian called after her. "You don't know what's in there."

She turned to look at him, walking backwards. "I see your sense of adventure has disappeared again. I'm paying you to keep me safe, so you and that sword of yours should probably follow."

Bastian grumbled, cursing under his breath. He stepped forward despite every muscle in his body wanting to refuse the action. Knuckles tightening on his hilt, he readied the weapon at his side and jogged to catch up to Rae. "What about a bunch of old rocks could possibly interest a thief?"

Rae rolled her eyes. "Maybe there's treasure." Her tone mocked him. "I'm a person, too, you know, not just a girl with sticky fingers."

He frowned. "Never said you weren't."

As Rae explored deeper, the gorge widened into a canyon with rocky cliffs on either side. Monoliths of stone stood sentinel over the smooth surface of the ground, arranged in a wide circle. Vines danced over them, weaving a tapestry that draped between them like banners at a festival.

Bastian would expect to see such structures in Eralas, home of the auer. He'd seen pictures drawn in books when he studied the culture during tactical training. It was beautiful on paper, but in person, his heart stopped.

Rae kept walking ahead, but he hesitated at the entryway to the circular area, eyeing an eroded stone at the center.

At the sound of their footsteps, a flock of birds chattered and erupted from the low-hanging branches of an oak tree.

"I wonder what—" Her words cut short, and she stilled.

Life around him paused. Birds froze in mid-flight and leaves hovered in an absent breeze.

Bastian stepped forward. "Dice?"

Her eyes didn't even move, fixated on the stone altar in the center of the area. He studied her chest, but no air filled her lungs.

Advancing closer to her, his heart thundered in his chest. "Rae?"

She's not welcome here. You shouldn't have brought her. The voice from his dreams echoed from within his head again.

He spun, searching for the source, louder than it had been before and without the cacophony of other whispers in his dream.

The stag stood behind him, anger in its dark eyes. The white flames at its hooves licked up as it stepped forward. As the tip of the hoof touched the stone ground, it morphed into toes. A human foot emerged, and the vision rippled upwards, twisting the wisps of white and blue into the sway of a skirt over androgynous hips. Long trails of light pulsed behind them, curves akin to fabric blustering in the wind.

Their body tall and skin a rich navy blue, small, wizened wrinkles creased the skin around their doe-like eyes. Their nose maintained the structure like the stag, flat and long, and a set of antlers curled in a crown around their head.

They reached a hand towards Bastian.

"I'm still dreaming."

No, you're not. This is my sanctum, and she is not welcome.

"Who are you?"

I am Sindré, the guardian spirit of this sacred place.

Bastian looked back at Rae, a rock forming in his stomach at the stillness of her heart. "Is she..."

She lives, but not for long.

Bastian stepped towards the figure considerably taller than him. Tightening his grip on his sword, he lifted it towards the spirit's flat chest. "Let her go. She's done nothing wrong."

I can't do that. She is our enemy, even if her blood isn't wholly infected. She holds the potential for great power.

"Potential means nothing. And what you're saying doesn't make sense. Infected? With what?"

"Auer heritage." Their mouth moved with physical speech. "She must pay the price for her ancestors' crimes." They stepped forward, ignoring Bastian's blade.

His eyes widened as the spirit's body passed directly through the steel, a subtle pulse of the bluish haze dancing like he cut through smoke.

In a rush, he jumped between Sindré and Rae again, dropping the sword to his side. "You claimed you offered me power because I protect the innocent. Rae is innocent of whatever crimes you speak of. Spare her. There must be another way."

A thoughtful expression crossed the spirit's face. "There is." With a slow blink, they produced a thin glass vial from the folds of their robes. Approaching the altar, they outstretched a hand, and droplets of light blue energy fell from the vines above to fill the vial.

Sindré offered it to Bastian. "She can drink this."

Stowing his useless blade, Bastian took the offered vial, his stomach writhing with nerves. As his fingers closed around the glowing object, the energy shifted into water sloshing against the plain glass. The blue light faded from it. "What is it?"

"A compromise. One that will let her keep her life while prohibiting her bloodline from continuing."

Bastian gaped at the thing in his hands, resisting throwing it back at the spirit. "You mean it'll make her unable to have children? Who are you to make that decision for her?"

Sindré's head tilted, the antler crown coming near Bastian's face. "I chose death for her. You asked for another way. It is your choice. If you need more time, I can give you until sunset, but if the vial is not consumed by then..." They reached a long-fingered hand towards Rae's chin. "I will return for her life. But you may not divulge our arrangement to her."

"This can't be real," Bastian mumbled, glaring at the glass in his palm. Closing his eyes, he tried to will himself to wake from the dream. Squeezing his hand tight over the vial, his nails bit into his palm, eliciting a sharp pain.

"This might not have happened, had you accepted the power I offered."

His eyes snapped open to see Sindré standing patiently, the dark blue pools of their eyes watching.

It sent a shiver down Bastian's spine, and he pursed his lips in thought. "If the contents of the bottle are emptied, you'll let Rae leave here unharmed?"

"If they are *consumed*, yes. I will allow the auer to leave in peace."

"You swear it, upon the power you claim to protect?"

"Yes, human child. It is promised."

Bastian stepped towards Rae, studying the open vial in his hands. Her life relied on his decision, and it felt horribly wrong. He considered it was possible she didn't want children, but making that choice for her, even if she might never know it was him, made him sick.

He slipped between Rae and the altar, staring into her unmoving eyes.

"Would you prefer time to make this choice?"

Bastian shook his head. "It won't change my decision."

Before he could think about it any longer, he lifted the vial to his lips and drank. The cold hit the back of his throat, causing him to gasp. It slid down into him, the icy touch turning into a burning sensation that passed through every limb of his body.

Sindré approached beside him, reaching for his shoulder. Their dark blue fingers closed on him, a jolt of lightning passing into his body. "You've chosen well, Rahn'ka."

The gentle tone grew into a wave of sound as the things he'd heard in his dreams assaulted Bastian's mind. Forcing his feet to move, he stepped around Rae towards Sindré. "What are those sounds?"

"It is the power I offered you. It's yours to protect now."

Voices, speaking languages he'd never heard, roared through his head. Pain flared from his temples, driving him to his knees as Sindré vanished, and life resumed.

Chapter 5

"—THIS IS FOR." RAE'S EYES narrowed at a stone altar. Something thudded behind her, and she whirled around, gaping at Bastian on his knees. "Bastian," she breathed, hurrying to kneel in front of him. "What is it?"

His face contorted in pain, hands grasping his temples. "Headache." Despite the obvious discomfort it caused, he blinked up at her. "Rae, are you all right?" A hand fumbled for her shoulder.

Her brow furrowed, and she placed one hand over his. "Of course. I'm fine. Why wouldn't I be?"

Bastian winced and minutely shook his head.

"Come on." Sliding her arm under his, she helped him to his feet. "Let's get back to the horses."

After giving Bastian time to rest, they rode west.

Rae constantly checked on him behind her, confused by the sudden, unrelenting pain he suffered.

Something about the ruins? But it makes no sense.

They stopped when the sun dipped too low on the horizon, and she took care of untacking the horses while Bastian curled up on the only bedroll and fell asleep.

Taking her spot at the base of a tree, she pulled her hood over her head and watched him.

He tossed and turned, mumbling incoherently in his sleep.

A knot grew in her stomach, touched with fear by what she didn't understand.

He's not my responsibility. His pain is irrelevant.

But even as the thoughts rattled within her skull, empathy blossomed and threatened her stoicism.

They rose with the early morning sun, both bleary-eyed.

Bastian resorted to nestling his head against his knees, back curled beneath his dark green cloak. His body twitched, some invisible irritant berating him. He didn't speak, and she wondered if he'd even noticed her get up.

"How's your head?" She kept her voice low.

Bastian didn't jerk this time, but tilted his chin up towards her. His bloodshot eyes, rimmed with dark circles, made her frown. "Not good. I've never had one this bad before." The words themselves sounded pained, more than she expected. Like he suffered from a stab wound rather than a headache.

She hesitated, wondering if herbal remedies would have any effect. Debating for a moment, she sighed and glanced at her saddlebags. "I have something that might help, if you want."

"I would try anything right now." Lifting his head, he relaxed his knees.

Rae rose and rummaged through one of her packs. A small pouch of vials clinked as she withdrew it. It contained several herbal extracts, and she found the one marked for headaches she had used the day before.

Crossing the camp, she knelt in front of him. "I'm going to put this on your temples, all right?" She opened the vial. The scent of peppermint and eucalyptus, with underlying tones of citrus and fennel, filled the air.

Bastian nodded with his eyes closed.

"Try to relax. Tension will make it worse." Dabbing the aromatic oil onto her fingertips, she reached for him. The touch radiated differently through her than their previous playful banter. She hardly thought anything of flirtatious affection, but her empathy surprised her.

With her contact, his shoulders relaxed. A soft sigh escaping his lips tickled the collar of her shirt.

She swallowed, rubbing the oil in circular motions on his temples. "Keep breathing deep. Slowly." Her fingers continued their work, gently massaging as he obeyed.

What the hell am I doing?

As much as she tried to sequester her feelings, they kept surfacing.

Drawing in another long breath, he let it out slowly, and it teased her skin. His eyes remained lightly closed. "That feels good."

Rae smirked. "Probably better than rolling off a rooftop."

Bastian chuckled, but a wince followed. He opened one hazel eye a sliver. "At least you had a cushion. I recall being between you and the ground." His shoulders sagged as he closed his eyes again.

Rae indulged in remembering how solid his body had felt beneath hers, glancing toward where the collar of his worn shirt had opened. It revealed a small section of his defined chest. His skin looked soft, fanning her desire to touch him again, something she seemed compelled to keep doing.

Pulling her hands from his temples, she busied them by dabbing more of the oil onto her fingertips. "A lovely cushion, indeed. It'll help if I put some of this on your chest." Somehow, she kept her tone steady, and she watched his face for any sign of protest.

Bastian's back straightened as she touched his collarbone, but he didn't pull away. Instead, his eyes opened, and he pulled the collar of his shirt open for her. He watched her, but his expression was impossible to interpret.

The oil glided over his sun-kissed skin, lighter than hers. She traced the definition of his collarbone with the tips of her fingers, seeing goosebumps spread across him.

She slid her hands up and around his neck, rubbing the oil into the base of his skull with her fingers while her thumbs massaged his tight jaw muscles.

When his eyes met hers, only inches away, she stiffened.

"Rae..." he whispered, a hand rising to touch her bicep.

Rae smiled, swimming in the depths of his hazel eyes. "Can't a girl admire?"

His cheeks flushed a charming shade of pink, and he blinked. "Not much to admire." He slid his hand up her arm, taking her hand to lower it from his neck. "And you're teasing me again."

Rae frowned, wondering if his attitude arose from modesty or naivety. Pulling her hands back to herself before she did something stupid, she stood. "Any better?" She replaced the lid on the vial and stepped away.

He paused as she stored the medicine. "Better." Standing, he ran his hands through his hair.

She walked to him and took his hand, placing eight iron marks in his palm. "For yesterday and today."

Bastian frowned down at the coins in his hand. "Won't you just steal it right back? Maybe give me the dice now and we can save all the trouble. I bet I'm an easy mark right now."

Rae smiled. "And hardly worth your pay in your state. But I won't steal from you. You know, *again*." Pausing, she tilted her head. "For now."

He chuckled, but it was short-lived. "Let's get going before my head starts pounding more." He stowed the sleeping gear among his saddlebags, and they continued their way towards Drych.

Bastian failed at trying to hide his constant headaches over the course of the next two days. She used the peppermint concoction several times each day on his temples, but it seemed to only take the edge off.

Riding west, the trees thinned, but they kept to rural hunting trails.

She studied the ground around Syga out of habit. Around mid-afternoon, she spotted a familiar pattern. Suspicious, she brought her gelding to a stop. Lifting her hand, she silently instructed Bastian to do the same. Glancing around, she saw no one, but dismounted.

Bastian shifted uncomfortably in his saddle with a creak of leather, focusing his gaze on the trees in front of them. His dense body stiffened. Zaili, the name he'd given his stolen mare, pawed the dirt, and he patted her neck.

Studying the tracks in the dirt, Rae noted several sets of hooves and judging by a snapped spring bud, they were fresh. No wheel marks and no footprints. But the hoof prints ran deep enough to suggest riders. And they didn't follow the hunting trail.

"We're not alone," she muttered under her breath.

He nodded without question.

They had time, and she wanted to see if the riders were Helgathian.

They could have information about recent deserters.

"Let's get off the trail." Rae looked at Bastian, mounting Syga. Steering the horses into the slightly denser woods, she veered around the path, following the hoofprints without letting Bastian in on her plan.

After half an hour of tracking, campfire smoke tainted the air.

Bastian brought Zaili to a stop as soon as the smell thickened, and Rae turned at the cease of her hoofbeats. Stubbornly dismounting, Bastian frowned. "Are you crazy? We should avoid whoever is out here, not seek them out. I thought you were leading us away."

Rae scowled. "They might have something useful."

"Sure, and they also might be dangerous. Who do you think uses these back roads along the mountains? Fine, upstanding merchants waiting for you to rob them?" Bastian stepped beside her saddle.

Rae scoffed. "*We* are using these roads, aren't we?"

"My point exactly." Bastian gestured at her.

She rolled her eyes. "Look, I can't pay you if I don't have money."

Bastian sighed, touching the horn of Syga's saddle. "We should steer clear. No profit is worth the risk if you ask me."

Rae hardly heard him, watching the faint pillar of smoke

rising to the clear sky beyond the canopy. "I'm not asking. But I'll wait until dark to do anything. For now, I'll just get a look." She slid off her horse on the side where Bastian stood, her back to him before she turned around. Lifting her chin, she tilted her head.

His brow knitted. "You can't be serious." They almost touched. "Don't be stupid. They could be Helgathian."

Rae narrowed her eyes. "So what if they are?"

With any luck, they will be.

"It could... complicate things." Bastian winced and dropped his head with a quick hiss.

"Complicate what things?" She dipped her head to maintain eye contact. "Is there something I'm missing?"

He growled and shook his head. Flinching, he turned away from her.

"That's what I thought." Rae grabbed Syga's reins. "Stay here and out of my way. Mind Syga. When I get back, I'll give you more of the oil." She forced the reins into his hand, and he took them as she stepped away.

"I'll leave you, you know. If you get caught."

Her feet stilled.

He's bluffing.

Rae met his gaze. "Earning your wage, aren't you? I'll remember that the next time you're behind bars."

"Promise it's just a quick look?"

Rae nodded. "That's all. I'll be back before you know it."

Creeping within the outskirts of the strangers' camp, Rae examined the riders. Two men and a woman, with their horses on the far side of the small clearing. Low, gravelly voices barely carried to her ears, the pitch of the woman's setting her apart from the men.

Rae crouched behind a boulder and some brush, eyeing the formation of their camp while noting the location of their packs.

The woman lounged against a fallen log, cleaning her nails with the tip of a knife while two male twins sorted through a stash of weapons. The woman wore an armored pauldron on her left shoulder, the rest of her armor sloppily discarded to the side.

A collection of papers lay scattered over a cot beside them, covered in scrawled notes and a map of the region drawn with a grid.

Bounty hunters aren't this prepared, but Reapers are.

Rae scanned the horses and their saddlebags, preparing to back away and return to Bastian. Her eyes widened as a horse she hadn't noticed before emerged from behind another.

Four horses. Three Reapers?

She stepped back, realizing one of them must have wandered off.

A hand closed on her, yanking her by the hair from behind. Yelping a startled cry, she reached back to grasp her attacker by the wrist.

"Well, well, well, look what we have here, fellas." A deep voice echoed behind her.

The rest of the party looked up, eyes lighting with interest. One of the men sorting the weapons lifted a serrated blade as he stood.

The man holding her expertly avoided each stomp she attempted on his feet as he wrestled her towards their camp. He grabbed one of her hands and twisted it behind her back before throwing her into the clearing.

Hands free, her palms braced her fall. Small shards of rock cut her skin, and she gritted her teeth.

"Caught us a sneak, Jebth?" The woman rose from her relaxed position. She spun the knife she'd been using for her manicure. She'd tied her pale blond hair back in a tight bun, and her body appeared densely athletic.

"Don't you know it's rude to spy?" A wicked grin spread across the dark features of the man with the serrated knife. "Need some teaching, girl?" With his dark complexion and rich amber eyes, Rae should have recognized his homeland earlier. His black hair, cropped against his skull, complimented his strong angled features reminiscent of the people of the Gilgas Desert. He eyed his twin across from him, who sat calmly as if nothing unusual had happened.

Rising to sit on her heels, Rae wiped her hands on her pants. "Judging by my welcome. You must be well versed in manners." Her voice thick with sarcasm, she glared at the man with the knife.

"Smartass too." Jebth kicked her from behind.

Rae crumpled forward, pain howling through her. She used the momentum to roll, pushing her shoulder to the ground and coming to the balls of her feet, facing Jebth for the first time.

He was a giant of a man and monstrously muscled. Leather stretched tight across his chest, a spattering of red chest hair protruding from his collar. Blemishes and freckles covered his fair skin. It somehow made him more intimidating.

Rae considered if Bastian had been speaking the truth when he said he'd leave her behind.

I'm on my own.

She glanced around for an escape. Popping up to her feet, she lunged towards an opening between the Reapers. Her body tensed, ready to fight whatever hands grappled her. For an elated moment, she ran towards the tree line.

A high-pitched whistling sound whizzed through the air, and her feet ripped out from beneath her.

Chapter 6

BASTIAN'S HEAD THROBBED, AND IT only got worse in the densest sections of the wood. Since he drank from the vial Sindré created, there'd been no respite from the abundance of voices.

Rae's oil helped, but the effects never lasted long enough. It also provided an opportunity to relish in the feeling of her hands on his temples. Her intention might have been to relieve his tension, but her being so near stirred a different discomfort. Her delicate features and toned body made his heart thunder with little more than a glance from her.

Regardless of the feelings she evoked, her foolishness astounded him. He debated his threat and how much he meant it.

I can't leave her. She's already paid me for today.

The justification gave him at least a little comfort that he wasn't staying just to feel her hands on him again.

When his stomach rumbled, he remembered her mentioning she had dried venison in her saddlebags. Busying himself with a search for food seemed a reasonable course, and he crossed to Syga.

Rummaging through to find it, he pulled out the parchment wrap and unfolded it. When his fingers touched the dried meat, he hesitated. Something about it resonated in his gut, his aversion unexpected. He folded it back up, replacing it in the pack, his stomach churning.

Guess I don't eat meat anymore.

He paced, rubbing the tight knot at the back of his neck while trying to bury the rumble of voices in his mind. Agitation ran rampant among them, but he couldn't tell who they belonged to. They weren't his.

But who else would be in my head?

A startled voice asked an urgent question, one of the few constant timbres within his senses.

Zaili's ears twisted forward, and she stomped a hoof.

Bastian turned his head in the direction his horse focused.

With Rae gone, Bastian lost more than her physical presence. Another part of her felt far away, but not unattainable. He'd resisted the urge to play with the new tingle within his senses, the awareness of another plane of being. He didn't understand it, which encouraged his usual caution.

Alone, he considered the validity of his new senses. He wanted the blue-skinned spirit's compromise to be a feverish dream, his mind snapping in the stress of his situation. If it had been, surely nothing would happen if he attempted to focus the power he never had before.

It must be related to the Art. And Sindré forced it on me, after making me sterile.

He'd never seriously considered children, and the insistent voices left him little time to debate it now. Yet, something about the choice felt hollow.

Learn to use it then, you idiot. If other Art users can start a fire from nothing, you can figure this out.

Bastian stilled, planting his feet. Nothing but a bird song and a spring breeze touched his ears. But his surroundings sung differently in his mind, an elaborate orchestration with hundreds of instruments. The pain surged, and he closed his eyes. He plowed through to the voices that sounded out of place in the symphony.

Bastian tilted his head subconsciously at the strange impression he gained from a masculine voice. Somehow the emotions and feelings felt more understandable, more human. It was the intention behind them, the hungry lust for an attractive female body he felt he deserved. It made Bastian's stomach flip.

Panic rose in his chest, his throat clenching as he found another source of human thoughts. A desire to share in the fun.

His body reacted before his mind processed. The same startled voice from before sounded as Zaili sidestepped from Bastian's sharp movements. He snatched his sword from the saddle and ran a hand down his horse's neck to calm her.

Bastian never once considered himself graceful, but he raced through the underbrush without a sound. The voices, while not mentioning Rae specifically, felt targeted and made his chest tighten.

Reaching the camp, he crouched beside an oak tree, his fingers ready at the hilt of his sword. His head pounded, blurring his vision, but he blinked through it.

Rae, being dragged feet first by a tall Gilgas man, kicked furiously at her captor despite the bolas wrapped at her ankles. Her hand found a fist-sized stone, and she hurled it at the man.

It impacted squarely with his jaw, but before she could make any move to free herself, a blond woman kicked her in the back of the head.

Rolling away from the strike, Rae curled in on herself, eyes closed and body still.

Bastian recognized the maps and the ledgers of records. The weapons were all part of the standard package granted to any special duty battalion, which is what the Helgath military considered Reapers. Sanctioned by the king, they operated outside the country borders for the 'good' of Helgath.

Everyone well knew the unethical behavior of Reapers. Common foot soldiers had more morals, which seemed absurd when Bastian considered the atrocities he'd witnessed during service.

Everything within him numbed, his mind working faster than the pain to evaluate what he could do. He was no match for four of them. It would do little good for Rae if he got himself killed trying to play the hero.

"Where's the rest of your gang?" The woman narrowed her eyes at Rae. "No way you're out here all alone."

Breathing hard, blood ran from Rae's hairline down her face. "Waiting to kill you all, most likely." She looked at the red-haired man. "You first."

The woman laughed as she buried her fist into Rae's hair, yanking her head back.

The sky darkened, sunlight fading as clouds rolled in.

Rae's eyes flashed with defiance as the Reaper woman studied her. Whatever conclusion she came to was unclear as she threw Rae towards the ground.

"Go take a look, Les." The woman motioned at another Gilgas man, who stood twisting a knife between his hands.

He frowned, a flurry of protestations dancing in Bastian's mind.

"I'm alone." Rae frowned. "Though even by myself, I'm more of a threat than—"

Her smart mouth earned her a boot to the jaw from Les's twin, who she'd struck with the rock. The way her head jolted, it had to be spinning.

Bastian cringed, grateful for her attempt to protect him, regardless of how futile.

The unnamed twin rubbed his jaw. His hand came away from his beard-stubbled chin with blood from the abrasion left by the stone.

"Alone, then." Les grinned. "Means I can stay and me and Jebth can entertain our little sneak."

The woman gave a disgusted grunt.

"I'll double check." The twin yanked his bolas free of Rae's ankles, gesturing to the big red-haired Jebth, who obeyed and moved forward. His bear-like hand closed over the back of Rae's neck and tugged her closer to the firepit like a two-year-old and his toy.

Bastian could feel the tension growing within Jebth, an excitement mirrored by Les, who eyed Rae. His pulse beat fervently in his ears, the voices ringing together in a cacophony.

"Be careful, Fife." The woman squeezed the bolas wielding man's arm.

Fife stalked away from the camp, searching in the wrong direction for Rae's accomplice.

Damien's veins blazed as he watched the men handle Rae.

Jebth threw Rae into Les, who eagerly caught her, drawing his blade to her neck between them. The glint of steel played against her skin as he wrapped his arm around her hips, forcing her closer to him.

Rae spat her mouthful of blood at his face. "Helgathian scum." She heaved a knee upward to strike him between his legs.

Les released her and doubled over with a yelp, clutching his crotch, the knife thunking to the ground.

Jebth acted quickly, encircling his thick forearm over Rae's throat and preventing the flow of air before she could reach for the blade.

Rae struggled and gasped, kicking at the dirt as Jebth held her up.

The sky above cracked with thunder, and the storm clouds burst with rain. It soaked the ground, turning the dirt clearing into messy pools of mud.

Les rose and advanced, sidestepping to avoid Rae's feet. He twisted his knife's tip near her sternum, the sharp tip playing at the wet fabric of her shirt.

Lecherous voices whirled in Bastian's head, incomprehensible. They caused something in his restraint to rupture. A tangle of pressure swelled against his skin, the muscles in his torso tensing as if he lifted a great weight. His vision sharpened on Les's frame, feeling for the energies around and within him, guided by the man's dark thoughts.

A dim haze grew around Les's hand, unaffected by the rain. It pulsed into vibrant white, and shock echoed from him as he dropped the blade and withdrew his hand. The wisps, like smoke from the incense of the temples, wove up his arm like a serpent. He opened his mouth to shout, but his voice stopped when the power encircled his throat.

Bastian squeezed his fist, and the Art obeyed.

Les choked, gargled sounds of astonishment erupting from his mouth as his hands fought against the untouchable attacker. His fingers passed through the smoke, but that didn't stop it from strangling him like a hangman's noose.

Jebth shouted and tossed Rae to the ground. He hurried to his comrade as Les's face puffed, and he collapsed to his knees.

Rae wheezed for air, clutching her throat as lightning flashed in the sky.

"The bitch has the Art." Jebth hurried towards the weapon cache.

"Knock her out, you buffoon!" The woman growled as she slid across the mud and grabbed a baton.

Bastian turned his attention to the woman, who encroached on Rae, her knuckles white from gripping the metal rod. He sought to harness whatever he'd done to Les. He felt for the voices around her, entreating them silently.

The ground at her feet fogged, the grass and stone shedding white motes that struck her ankles. The weight drew her down with a huff of breath, and she kicked to free herself. It was unsuccessful, and the power consumed her as she screamed.

Jebth took up a double-bladed axe and swung the base of its handle down on Rae's head without another moment of hesitation.

Rae fell limp.

Les coughed, freed of the power as it changed focus to the woman. He scurried across the ground towards her, expecting the power to dissipate. It didn't, and her body contorted in pain as the haze spread up her chest. Les hesitated in touching her, holding his hands above the visible cloud.

"Lue!" Fife darted back into camp, sliding through the mud towards the female Reaper.

Les spun to Jebth. "What's taking so—"

"She's out!" Jebth's eyes darted to the tree line as water trailed down his face. The big bruiser was smarter than he looked.

Bastian only had so much time to manipulate the power he still didn't understand. He tried to breathe deeper, to access his Art, but it only caused the power around Lue to shimmer before fading.

Well, that's not good.

He closed his hand on the hilt of his sword.

Rae laid still, and he couldn't even tell if she breathed.

The rain stopped, but the mud would make everything more interesting.

As the power subsided, Lue coughed.

Bastian's advantage waned with each movement of Jebth's searching gaze.

The voices whispered assurances, and Bastian welcomed them.

He surged from the bushes, targeting Jebth. As the biggest, it was in Bastian's best interest to down him first.

Jebth let out a warning shout and lifted his axe in hasty defense as Bastian's blade arced down while he slid to a stop in the mud. Bastian threw his entire weight into the blow, and it forced the large Reaper back, their blades locked together.

Adrenaline raged through Bastian's veins, pulsing against the weaves of power twisting within his soul. The voices nurtured the rush as he reached for the strength of the same voices who aided in attacking Lue.

The motes around Lue leapt upward into the air. She struggled to her hands and knees, rushing to get away.

Fife pulled out a throwing knife, rising into a kneeling position.

Bastian urged the power to gather into a wave, ripping over the Reaper's head before engulfing him. It knocked him to the ground with a flash of light, faltering his throw into a bush.

The distraction of manifesting the power granted Jebth the opportunity to twist the axe and wrench the sword from

Bastian's hands. He followed by catching Bastian's ankle with his boot.

Bastian tumbled backward, hunching his shoulders to protect his head as he rolled away from the swing of Jebth's axe. His feet tangled with Jebth's and with a shift of his core, Bastian yanked the burly man to the ground with a resounding huff and muddy squish. He dodged the wild swing of the axe at his head and slammed his elbow into Jebth's gut as he slipped to his feet.

Fife came from behind, wielding another knife aimed for Bastian's right side.

Somehow sensing the attack, Bastian twisted. He brought his arm down and caught the Reaper's arm in the crook of his elbow before twisting and yanking.

A satisfying pop came from Fife's shoulder, accompanied by a howl of pain.

Bastian focused on the voice of Fife's agony inside his head and used it to grasp its energy. His hands scalded as he recalled the burning cold sensation of drinking the water from the vial. He found the source of life within Fife and yanked it to the surface.

The voice in Bastian's mind screamed as Fife's skin turned ashen. A film of glimmering white evaporated from him, twisting back on itself to flow down the arm Bastian held captive.

Fife convulsed, his eyes rolling back as the haze increased around Bastian's chest. His body sagged, dropping to the ground.

Bastian held fast to the harvested power, his chest tight and breath shallow.

A weakened Lue bellowed with rage as she drew up a crossbow from beside where she lay and fired.

The bolt flew before Bastian registered the danger. He lifted his arms instinctively over his chest, as he would when covered in armor on the battlefield.

A flash erupted, followed by a snap of wood. Heat seared across his arms as the energy balled in front of him and shattered the projectile. He thrust his arms forward, and the cloud coalesced into rods of light. A wall of bolts shot at Lue. They blanketed her body, and she had little time to react beyond a startled scream.

Fatigue struck Bastian before Jebth landed on top of him. His back struck the ground for what felt like the hundredth time in the last two days, cushioned only slightly by the mud. Jebth crushed him, a huge hand closing on his throat. Bastian bucked against him but couldn't find traction in the slippery mess.

The big Reaper's fist collided with his jaw, making the world flash white and the storm clouds above spin. The return of the pressure on his throat made it impossible to suck in a breath, and his body ceased its fight.

Jebth's grip vanished as he reared back. The length of the bolas wrapped around his neck, and he gurgled as it tightened.

Rae grunted, her legs around the big man's chest as she prevented air from reaching his lungs. Blood coated her face, tainting the whites of her eyes.

Bastian, too tired to fight, clawed at the ground. His nails bit into the muck and pain splintered into his palm. He found something sharp, and he gripped the broken wooden shaft of the crossbow bolt, slamming it into Jebth's side, wedging it between layers of leather armor.

The big man fell sideways, taking Rae with him. She held strong to the bolas, muddy hair clinging to her face as the rain fell again.

Blood mixed with the mud, oozing from the protruding weapon above Jebth's belt.

Bastian crawled through the muck, hurrying to find the hilt of his sword.

A whoosh of air left Rae's lungs when Jebth threw an elbow back, and she tumbled to the side.

Bastian abandoned the search, spinning back to Jebth. He grappled the man's ankle, twisting it and pulling him sharply towards him. Lunging onto Jebth, Bastian forced aside the knee the Reaper lifted to guard himself. He yanked the bolt from Jebth's side, tightening his grip on the slick shaft. With a thrust, he drove it into the Reaper's throat.

All noise ceased except Rae's gasping as she lay on her back in the mud.

Bastian rocked back, rising on unsteady legs from the blood flowing from Jebth's throat. Everything hurt. He scanned the camp, counting bodies.

Three.

"Fuck!" Bastian spun to look for Les, but he was nowhere in sight.

The coward probably ran.

The voices temporarily subdued, Bastian sought the fleeing Reaper with his Art-laden senses, but he wasn't nearby. Like a crashing tidal wave, the torment of the voices renewed, splitting his skull.

Groaning, he clenched his fists, fingernails biting into the gash on his palm. He fell to his knees beside Rae, unable to take the time to lower himself.

She stared at the sky, face cleaner after the latest downpour.

Bastian couldn't tell if rainwater or tears muddled her cheeks. He huffed, trying to catch his breath. Sighing, he put his hands on his thighs. "You look like shit."

Rae tried to roll away from him, but her hands shot to her head, and she dropped back down. Whining, she gripped her shoulder, injured from her fall from the bolas. "Have you seen yourself?" Her whisper came out gravelly.

He couldn't help but smile. "Sound like shit too." He glanced up at the sky, squinting at the clouds now failing to provide the rain that would've helped to clean them both.

Her brows pinched in the center, and wetness trailed from the corners of her eyes as she rolled away from him.

Wincing, Bastian tried to ignore the new rising pain in his head along with the aches of his body. And he hadn't been hit in the head and strangled as badly as Rae had. As strong as she was, he could see the extensive damage she'd suffered in every slight movement.

She crawled away from him before sitting back on her heels, running her hands over her face and hair.

He stared at the profile of her face, a small streak of clean skin where the tears she fought had fallen down her cheeks. If he'd been watching her back, perhaps she wouldn't have been caught.

Some protector I am.

The voices surged, and he took it to be them heartily agreeing.

With a grunt, he forced himself to his feet and leaned down to touch her uninjured shoulder. "Can you stand?"

Rae looked at his hand and then lifted her deadpan gaze to meet his.

He offered his other hand. "Let me help."

Chapter 7

LOOKING UP, A WAVE OF dizziness struck her, so Rae shut her eyes. Nodding, she clenched her jaw and reached blindly for Bastian.

His arms closed around her, and he groaned as he pulled her to her feet. Once there, neither seemed to have the strength to pull away, and Bastian's head rested against the top of hers, arms still encircling her.

Catching her breath, she leaned on him, touching his sides. Weakness trembled her chin, but she swallowed, remounting the soreness in her neck where Jebth's arm had cut off her air. "You're going to ask for a raise, aren't you?" She listened to the steady beat of his heart.

He snorted a small laugh, his chest shaking beneath her temple. "I was half-expecting a demotion."

A smile twitched her lips. "Nah… But now I know your threats mean nothing. What took you so long?"

"Sorry." His hand brushed through her hair, parting it. He hissed sympathetically. "This looks bad."

Rae flinched when he touched the edge of a wound she'd forgotten was there. Finding her resolve strengthening, she reluctantly pulled her head away from his inspection. Not leaving his arms, she looked at his face. Lifting her hand, she touched his cheek while she glanced at the redness at his throat where Jebth had tried to strangle him. "Thank you." Recoiling her hand, she swallowed, trying to ease the rawness in her throat, but her voice still came out hoarse. "I'd be dead if you'd left me."

"We'd be dead together if you hadn't jumped on the big guy." Bastian touched her jaw, then caressed her neck. He tilted his head, a frown forming as he grazed over the tender flesh.

Her hand closed on his, moving it away from her throat. Stepping back, she narrowed her eyes at him. "What did you do to them?" Visions of Les being choked by a glimmer of light flitted into her mind. Fear surfaced, banishing the cold feeling of leaving his embrace.

"What?" Bastian's brow furrowed, and he stepped back. "I defended you." His face hardened as he looked at the bodies.

"I didn't know you had the Art." The thought added a level of uncertainty in her thoughts of him. An Art user, while more valuable, was not someone she could restrain for collection.

I'll need to give Jarrod a heads up if he thinks we should try this.

She followed his gaze, eyeing the downed Reapers, and her heart sank. "Where's the fourth?"

His eyes widened, but he didn't answer at first. Stepping around her, he bent to retrieve his sword from the mud near one of the bodies. "Coward probably ran." He slid the weapon into his belt. Blood stains ran down his arms and chest, turning his shirt a muddy crimson.

Rae studied him, blinking away her dizziness.

Bastian winced as he stepped towards her, his hand lifting to his forehead. Inhaling sharply, he squinted at her. "I'll look at those injuries when we get back to the horses. And after I get some more of that headache medicine. But you probably need it too."

You can say that again.

Bastian turned back towards the camp and gestured with an open hand. "Did you want to take anything before we go?"

A coy grin spread across her face. "That's the most romantic thing you've ever said to me."

Subtle color rose to his cheeks beneath the grime.

She steered around the cache of weapons with a wobbly gait. Walking to the horses, she unfastened their saddles. They each fell to the ground before she removed their bridles.

"What are you doing?"

She jumped, not hearing Bastian stalk up behind her. "I can't leave them tied up. They'll die." She released the fourth horse. "I'm a thief. I'm not heartless." She waved a hand to the bags in the mud. "Want to look through these with me? If there's something you'd find useful..." Stumbling, she quickly crouched next to a saddlebag to hide it from Bastian.

The Reapers traveled light, so locating their coin purses should be easy.

"I didn't expect this to be quite so involved." Bastian plucked up one pack. He roughly tore it open and started rifling through it. "We shouldn't take too long. The one who ran..." He withdrew a cloth from the bag and cleaned the remaining mud from his face and hands.

"Yes, I know." The one who'd held his knife to her clothing. "That needs to be *fixed*."

"It will be, but I need some of that oil first." Bastian tugged a small pouch free and threw it towards Rae.

She lifted her hand, but the pouch sailed past her palm, landing in the mud as she swayed. Staring at it, then at her hand, she tried to make her eyes focus.

"They must have hit you pretty hard." Bastian slung a small pack over his shoulder and stepped towards her. He picked the pouch back up and put it directly in her hand.

She closed her fingers around it, furrowing her brow. Swallowing back the burning in her throat, she nodded and pocketed the pouch. "I can still feel blood running through my hair."

"You probably need stitches. We should get back to the horses." Bastian slid an arm under hers.

Rae stood with his help, her head spinning. She wavered, her surroundings blurring. Her stomach clenched, a wave of nausea coursing through her body.

She turned from him, clutching her middle as she doubled over and heaved, adding the contents of her stomach to the mess of mud. Pulling her hair back from her face, she spat, stumbling backward.

Bastian caught her, steadying her with a tight hold on her upper arm. "No more thievery. Sooner I get you cleaned up, the sooner I can track down Les."

"*We.*" She let him lead her towards the tree line. "The sooner *we* can track down Les. A few stitches and I'll be fine." Doubt invaded her confidence, increasing with each throb of her head inside her tightening skull.

"*We'll* see." Bastian's tone reminded her of a patronizing older brother.

After one too many stumbles on the way back, Bastian hooked an arm under her knees and lifted her from the ground.

She swatted his chest, but leaned her head on it, regardless of his filthy shirt. "I don't need to be carried." Her words were half-hearted, and she closed her eyes in resignation.

"Don't be so stubborn and accept the help. And stay awake."

How does he function if his head feels like this all the time?

"I'm not stubborn."

Arriving in the familiar clearing, Bastian deposited her on a stump and tossed his stolen goods aside. A low whistle pulsed from his lips, summoning the horses.

Zaili obeyed, approaching with a shake of her mane.

Syga trotted in a moment later.

"You whistle like a Helgathian." Rae prodded his chest with an accusatory finger.

Stop talking. If he thinks I'm a threat, who knows what he'll do.

"Still going on about that Helgathian nonsense." Bastian sighed. "Fort Tryssla, remember? *Near* Helgath."

Disregarding her own silent advice, she opened her mouth again. "Right, right. You're the non-Helgathian, non-Art user, who didn't serve in the military. I'm terrible at reading people. I'll get it right, eventually." Her eyes locked on the warm hazel of his.

Rolling his eyes, he gave an exaggerated sigh and turned to withdraw her supply pack from Syga's saddle, fishing out the headache remedy.

Kneeling before her, he settled the pack onto the ground before applying the medicine to his temples. He tilted the bottle again, dabbing more on his fingertips before reaching for her head.

His gentle touch created whispers of butterflies in her gut, the sweet scent of the medicine bringing instant relief.

"Maybe you're meant for skills other than reading me." Bastian poured water onto a cloth, lifting the cold compress to the cut on Rae's forehead. He sat up on his knees, a hand cradling the back of her head as he applied pressure.

Rae winced, reaching for the skin of water he held and lifting it to her lips. Filling her mouth, she swished it around to cleanse the acrid taste before spitting it to the side. She took a drink before setting it down. "Don't we have anything stronger?"

He chuckled. "You don't need alcohol right now."

Exploring with her tongue, she found where she'd bitten her cheek after the female Reaper kicked her in the jaw.

His grip returned, another gentle pressure to the injury near the back of her head. "This isn't so bad. I don't think it needs stitches."

"*Not so bad*. At least I won't be able to see the scar."

"Your hair should hide it. And scars aren't so bad. Something to help you remember the adventures you insist on."

Studying his face, she touched a scar interrupting the edge of his right eyebrow. "What's this from?"

As if taken by surprise, his breath caught, chest pausing in front of her. "No exciting adventure. I fell off a horse when I was seven." He refreshed the cloth then dabbed her jaw, his eyes following its path. "Nearly killed my ma with worry."

Rae smiled, appreciating his openness. "You're lucky. To have a mother who worries over you."

His expression softened, the caresses along her skin slowing. "All mothers worry for their children, but perhaps don't show it very well." He paused. "My ma... became almost too protective after my sister died. But I suppose that happens when a mother loses a child."

His words struck like a punch to the gut, and she swallowed hard. "That, or the opposite." She shook her head. "What happened?"

"An accident. My family owns a horse ranch, and Brynn fell off one day. She landed wrong and didn't wake up. At least that's what I was told. I was too young to remember."

"I'm sorry about your sister." Her heart wrenched at the familiarity of the pain.

Bastian discarded the cloth and drew out a clean one with a shrug. "It was a long time ago." He wet the linen. "I wasn't old enough to remember. But it sounds like you might know a little about loss yourself."

"My mother hates me." She sought solace in his steady gaze. "For killing my brother and sister when I was eleven." She kept her tone even, having built a wall around the emotions connected to her past.

Bastian frowned and bit the edge of his lip. Drawing his hand up, he gripped her bicep. "It couldn't have been your fault. It must have been an accident? You were only a child."

Rae absently toyed with the hem of her vest. "Some boys were picking on me. I knocked over a lantern, and the fire spread too fast." Shame riddled her memories.

Why am I telling him this?

Squeezing her, he placed the cloth beneath her jaw and encouraged her gaze up. "See, an accident. Your mother will realize her mistake someday."

She heaved a deep breath as she shook her head. "The fire destroyed much more than our home. Half the town burned that night. A lot of people died because of me."

Something flickered in Bastian's eyes, and she held her breath, prepared for him to pull away in disgust.

Instead, his grip tightened as he shifted closer. "That wasn't you." He cradled her face in his hands. "You didn't choose to start the fire. An accident killed those people. You couldn't have stopped it." His voice sounded rough.

Her eyes burned, and she clenched her jaw, forbidding her emotions from surfacing further.

She didn't want to speak about the horrors of her past or her mother. The woman blamed her and had taken every opportunity to remind Rae of the suffering she'd caused. As a lesson, she took her daughter to the charred area of town weekly, forcing her to watch her neighbors mourn. Months later, Rae ran away.

Breathing a fresh inhale to center herself, Rae sheepishly touched a scar along the left side of Bastian's jaw. His stubble didn't grow through the fine white line, which seemed fresher than his brow scar.

"Dare I ask?"

"One of your favorite things to do... A sword did that one." He seemed to accept the distraction from the somber subject, resuming his cleaning of her face and neck. He slid the cloth up over her chin, cleaning around her mouth. He slowed once there, his gaze intent on where he worked.

Her pulse sped. "I told you swords are sloppy."

"Sloppy can be good." Bastian traced the outside of her lower lip with the cloth.

Rae tilted her head with an inquisitive hum and smirked. "Name one situation where sloppy is better." She watched his eyes linger on her mouth. Even in her disoriented haze, she couldn't miss his distraction.

"Sloppy kisses are better," he murmured and then quickly clarified. "From a dog. We had dogs on the farm." He grew more intent on his work, going over areas he'd already cleaned.

"Dogs." Rae chuckled and pulled his wrist away from her face. "What about women? Are kisses from women better... sloppy?"

He makes teasing him so easy.

Color flushed his cheeks and his shoulders tensed. He stopped breathing at the question, fingers twitching on the cloth. "Women?"

"Or men?"

"Gods no, not me anyway. Maybe my..." Shaking his head, he paused. "Women.... What about women?"

"I don't know about you..." Rae ignored his flustering. "But I prefer my kisses from men... and women... less *sloppy*." She brought her face closer to his as she spoke, welcoming the dizzy world around her as she did.

"*Kisses*," Bastian repeated in the strange considering tone, his breath shallow as she moved closer. His jaw flexed, body stiff in front of her. He leaned ever so slightly back from her, a hair's width of movement she grinned mischievously at.

Rae traced a fingertip down his jaw to his neck and slowly brushed her mouth against his to temptingly kiss his upper lip. His lips felt as rigid as his body looked, but he didn't pull away.

Slowly, his lower lip rose to savor hers, a brief heat passing between them before it abruptly ended.

Bastian put his hands on Rae's arms, encouraging her back from him. His face looked warm, a playful gleam in his eyes. "That bump on your head is affecting your judgment." He locked his elbows straight to solidify the distance between them.

Rae smirked. "Are you questioning the soundness of my mind?"

"Yes." He cocked his head. "Your clear lack of self-control proves you aren't coming with me after the last Reaper."

"My clear lack of..." Rae frowned and shook her head too fast. She briefly shut her eyes. "If you'll use my *lack of self-control* against me, then I'll keep it better in check next time you stare at my mouth."

"I was cleaning it." Bastian stood. "You need to stay here and stay awake while I go track him down. Shouldn't take long."

Rae rolled her eyes and straightened. "I'm not allowed to come with you because I'm hurt, but I'm also not allowed to rest. You have some strange rules, non-Helgathian."

Bastian lifted his stolen pack from the ground and strode to Zaili. Settling the pack among her saddlebags, he sorted through it. "Besides my sister, I've known men struck in the head who never woke hours after the injury. I don't want that to happen to you." He flipped open a leather pouch. Sunlight flickered off an array of throwing knives. He quickly buttoned the container again and tied it to his belt, opposite his sword, before mounting his horse.

Did he dislike the kiss that much?

She wasn't sure what made her head whirl worse, the injury or his rapid departure. "And I've known men to be quick to leave at sunrise, but you're setting a new precedent for early exits."

Bastian's brow furrowed. "I'm serious. Don't fall asleep. I'll be back soon."

"You're cute when you're serious, too." She laughed. "I won't sleep, all right? I'll stay up and pine for your return." She paused. "Be careful."

"I will." With a tap of his boots against Zaili's flank, Bastian urged her into a fast canter and disappeared between the trees.

Rae sighed and settled herself on the ground against the stump, facing the direction he'd gone. Standing felt too daunting. Resigning herself to stay awake, she wondered why he agreed so hastily that Les needed to be dispatched. She hadn't expected it of a man so squeamish about robbery, but murder...

Probably because he saw your face, Bastian. The Helgathian deserter with the Art.

If he was everything he claimed not to be, an army would surely be after him. Helgath would never let such a powerful treasure live after shirking their control. The possible size of his bounty kept growing in her mind.

She bit her lip, remembering how soft his were.

Don't get attached.

Could she be pragmatic anymore? After what he did for her, the idea of betraying him left a pit in her stomach.

He saved you from those Reapers and your own foolishness. You owe him.

Her eyelids weighed heavy, and her surroundings spun. Closing her eyes, her breath came faster. She gripped a handful of grass, trying to open her eyes.

Stay awake, stay awake.

Chapter 8

BASTIAN TRACKED LES WITH UNPRECEDENTED ease. Running the Reaper down on horseback sped up the process. He followed the path Les took through the trees without needing to find tracks. One benefit of whatever strange power he'd acquired from the stag-spirit. The constant voices helped distract the rampage of his own thoughts.

He absently touched his lip as he rode. Rae's unexpected affection spiraled him into a descent of foreign emotions.

Maybe she hadn't only been teasing me.

The military allowed little opportunity for heterosexual males to explore intimacy. The enlistment of women was rare in Helgath and his entirely male battalion forbade fraternizing. Bastian had witnessed enough affection shared between comrades to know he preferred the company of women, even if he didn't get to experience it.

But Rae...

He couldn't help kissing her back, his lips moving of their own volition to meet hers in the soft exchange.

How can I possibly fall for a thief?

The way she'd opened up to him and revealed such tragic memories caught him off guard. More surprisingly, he related deeply to the events of her past.

It wasn't my fault.

Following orders, Lieutenant Damien Lanoret had ordered his battalion to search a village for a fugitive, finding it full of mostly women, children, and those unable to serve. Most accepted his soldiers into their homes, allowing the routine search. A small section of the city refused, leaving the lieutenant in an awkward situation when a colonel arrived to assess the situation.

The colonel's order came as a shock. "Seal them in. Burn the buildings to the ground. They're all traitors to House Iedrus."

"With all due respect, Colonel. There are children in those homes." Damien frowned. "They're hardly guilty of their parents' choices."

"Their blood is traitorous. The country will be better without them." Colonel Fenner tapped the hilt of his sword. "It's an order, Lieutenant."

Damien hesitated, his corporal looking at him.

Fenner growled. "You heard me, Corporal, burn them."

"Belay that order," Damien snapped. "I will not condone the murder of innocents."

"You dare—"

"I'll go down to the village and search those homes for the fugitive myself, invited or not. But I will not order my men to murder women and children for something they may or may not have done. The fugitive might not even be in the village—"

"You aren't here to make that kind of judgment." The colonel scowled. "Are you disobeying my order?"

Damien's chest tightened, his head spinning with the repercussions. "I will not—"

"Then you are relieved of your duty, Lieutenant." The colonel turned to the corporal, whose back straightened. "Due to Lieutenant Lanoret's delay, the fugitive may have relocated within the village. I suggest you obey my orders. Burn it all."

Staring down the rolling Helgathian hills, screams echoed, tearing at Damien's eardrums. He'd watched his own battalion herd people into their homes, boarding their windows and doors shut. The stench of smoke burned his nostrils.

The village blazed. Orange flames licked into the black smoke filling the twilight sky.

"This is what happens when you refuse to carry out an order." Colonel Fenner crossed his arms over his chest. "This is your fault."

How could I have been blind to the cruelty for so long? Helgath is corrupt, and I'll never return.

Zaili crashed through the underbrush, a low branch striking him across the cheek, returning him to the Olsa forest. He'd sacrificed stealth for speed.

Damien Lanoret is dead. Bastian is who I am.

The abundance of murmuring voices in his head grew, urging haste. It felt like an extra blanket buzzing alongside his conscious thought. The increase suggested a village, or some other collection of people nearby. An audience would complicate what Bastian intended for Les.

The Reaper had seen his face in their brawl and depending on the speed of Helgathian bounties, either knew already, or would soon, the potential prize Bastian posed.

Leaving Rae in her precarious situation was not ideal. He hadn't wanted to but feared if he hadn't pulled away from the kiss when he did, he never would have.

The woods thinned as Bastian caught up to Les, stumbling slowly through the forest like a drunk boar. Striking him down from behind didn't sit well.

The Reaper looked back and reached for the knife at his side.

Bastian reached for the throwing knives, not slowing his horse.

Les spun and picked up his pace, weaving behind a giant oak.

Yanking on Zaili's reins, Bastian followed the redirection despite the low-hanging branches and dense foliage. Outstretched twigs raked at his arms as he maneuvered, a rumble of the trees' discomfort echoing against his soul.

Les's bobbing head disappeared behind obstacles every time Bastian caught a glimpse.

The foreign voices in Bastian's mind grew louder and his temples throbbed. He narrowed his eyes, forcing them to focus through the pain as he ducked another branch.

The forest abruptly ended, granting the opening Bastian needed. He tensed, ready to push Zaili into a gallop to cut off Les, but an unexpected sight in the meadow ahead spurred a skidding halt.

Zaili let out a shrill whinny as Bastian took in the pair of maroon tents.

Pillars of smoke rose from campfires, silhouetting the soldiers against the amber sunset. Even without flags, Bastian recognized the two-post tent configuration. He'd set up enough of them.

Les raced towards the Helgathian encampment.

Bastian didn't have time to consider why they were so deep in their neighboring country of Olsa, or his desire to maintain his honor.

The balanced Helgathian throwing blade flew from his hand in a silent, deadly spin. Bastian hadn't intended the little pulse of power which followed it, but it hummed in his mind as the knife struck Les perfectly at the base of his neck.

The Reaper toppled forward, momentum crumpling his body as he struck the ground, already dead.

A distant shout from the encampment encouraged Bastian to reel Zaili back into the shadows of the tree line. He didn't wait to see how many there were. Two tall tents suggested a troop of up to forty men between here and Drych.

Time to convince Rae of a change of plans.

He guided Zaili through the more well-worn paths back towards Rae, his heart pounding. The voices returned to the humdrum he'd grown accustomed to in the forest, his headache fading.

Never the best at navigation, Bastian still found his way back with stunning ease. Syga's energies stuck out from the rest of the forest. He should have been able to sense Rae, but hers was oddly quiet.

"We need to change direction." Bastian dismounted, starting to secure the bags he'd removed. He didn't look at Rae, able to see her shape in his peripheral vision. "Rae, come on." His nerves insisted he keep rushing to get the horses ready. There was no telling how many scouts might be in the trees.

Silence.

His throat tightened, and he looked at her. "Rae?"

She hadn't budged, her eyes closed.

Bastian dropped the bag he'd been fiddling with, throwing himself to his knees beside her.

Her face looked so peaceful.

He'd told her not to sleep, hadn't he? Panic rose in the pit of his stomach as he reached for her hand. It was chilled, but he could feel her heartbeat in her wrist.

He shook her arm. "Wake up."

Her arm wobbled like a rag doll, her body slumping towards him. He pulled her to his chest, seeking to use his body heat to warm her limbs. He patted the side of her face, but when her eyes didn't flutter, he tried a little harder.

Nothing.

He couldn't delay in leaving. The battalion would look for whoever murdered Les and would likely find the other bodies at the Reapers' camp before dark. The danger grew the longer he delayed.

Rae slowed him down, especially if he couldn't wake her.

The thought of leaving her came, then abruptly passed as he looked on her unconscious face. He pressed his fingers to the pulse at her neck, feeling its distant rhythm.

It would be wrong to leave her like this. She was in as much danger as he if found. She carried stolen goods, some that the battalion could trace directly to the dead Reapers.

The whispers around him rose in his mind, creating a wave of nauseating pain that coalesced at the front of his skull.

He cringed, gritting his teeth to subdue the sudden nausea. He pressed his forehead against Rae's cool brow, shutting his eyes to the pallidness of her skin. The feel of her eased the agony, but the voices whirled in a mad frenzy.

Bastian added his to the din.

Wake up, Rae.

Something shifted in the energy surrounding her, and her breathing came faster. The pulse in her neck strengthened.

His heart thundered. He matched her breath and concentrated as hard as he could, blocking out the voices in his head. Finding the buried, soft tone of her soul, he coaxed it to stir by adding his own.

Damn it, Rae, wake up!

Her gasp made him jump, and he nearly dropped her. He drew his face away as her eyes focused on him.

She anxiously looked around, startled as she caught her breath. "What happened?" She grasped his shirt and then narrowed her eyes. "What are you doing?"

"You were unconscious." Bastian pushed a stray hair from her jaw in his relief. "You were being stubborn about waking up. You know, I told you not to sleep."

Her gaze seemed distant, her tone thoughtful. "I tried not to." She eyed the horses, confused, before looking back at him.

No sarcastic retorts?

"You're back. Where's Jarrod?"

"Jarrod? Who's Jarrod?"

Opening her mouth, Rae blinked at him and then shook her head. "No one. Sorry, I... feel a little..." Her gaze trailed down to where he held her, and she furrowed her brows.

"We need to get moving back the way we came." Bastian changed the subject as he straightened his back. "You'll need to get up before I can..."

"Why?" Rae studied the material of his shirt, her eyes dreamy.

"I can't exactly stand while you're in my lap."

She smiled and stood, bracing herself on a tree. "I meant, why do we need to go back? I was planning to go to Drych."

Bastian rose, ignoring the pang of emptiness he felt. He busied himself with the bags on Zaili's saddle instead. "A Helgathian battalion is between us and there. They'll find those dead Reapers soon and will be on the lookout for anyone in these woods who might be responsible. Besides, we may or may not be carrying some stolen goods. I'll let you do the math."

"We? I took their coin. What did you steal?" Rae's eyes focused on him, but something about it seemed disconnected.

He flinched, but he'd need to get used to his new way of life. "Nothing quite as valuable, but I don't think it'll matter much if Helgath catches us." He abruptly changed the subject. "Isn't there a mountain pass that goes north? We could go that way instead, since I doubt we'd be welcome back in Jacoby." He finished retying their belongings and glanced at Rae, who stared at him with narrowed eyes.

"I think so, but..." She exhaled and touched her head. "It'll be cold, do you have anything warmer to wear? I have a couple blankets, and at least winter has passed..."

"The bag I snagged has some shirts in it, they should fit better than that tunic. Let's get going so we can stop at a stream down here in the valley to clean up. Any rivers through the pass will be ice cold."

"You remember that you work for *me*, right?" Rae muttered, stepping towards Syga. "You don't get to order me around, Colonel."

Bastian managed not to grimace at her nickname, thinking of Fenner. "You're right, but as the person you've hired to protect you, I strongly advise that you listen to me."

"I suppose I should be grateful you're doing your job *before* I'm bloody this time." Grabbing a fistful of her horse's mane, she mounted and closed her eyes. "You lead."

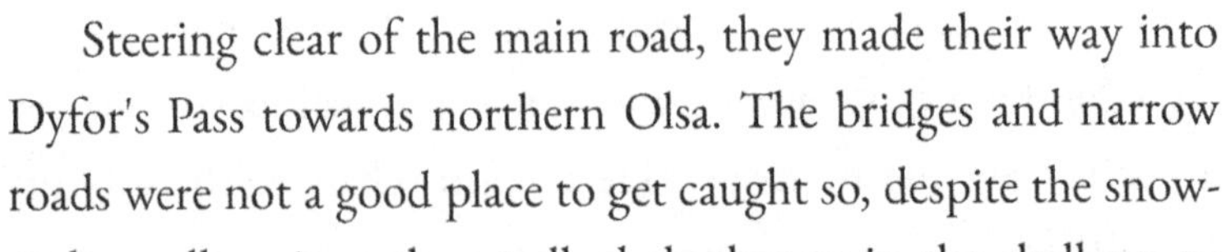

Steering clear of the main road, they made their way into Dyfor's Pass towards northern Olsa. The bridges and narrow roads were not a good place to get caught so, despite the snow-melt swollen river, they walked the horses in the shallows to disguise their tracks.

They camped near the shore at night and rode through the days. During the two nights after the fight with the Reapers, Bastian insistently woke Rae throughout, with shockingly little protest from her. Every time she closed her eyes, he feared they wouldn't open again.

"How did you do it?" Rae broke a prolonged, yet comfortable silence while they rode the next afternoon. "You said you knew a man who never woke, so how did you wake me?"

Took her long enough to ask, I suppose.

He tried to disguise his hesitation with a shrug. "I kept telling you to wake up." He wasn't sure how to explain what he didn't yet understand. "I guess you heard me somehow and listened."

"I heard you. Your voice echoed in my head, and it pulled on me."

"It did?" He slowed Zaili to saunter side by side with Syga and Rae. "You woke up. Isn't that the important part?"

Rae fell silent, and for a while, neither of them spoke. She'd added an extra layer of clothing to what she wore, a wool tunic beneath her cloak and gloves.

With the beginning of spring, frost only formed overnight while they had a fire to stay warm by.

"I'm surprised you didn't leave me there." She kept looking straight ahead for a moment before turning her gaze on him.

Bastian bit his lower lip. "I thought about leaving, but then I didn't. You were still alive, and I couldn't..."

Rae watched the sky. "Your hero complex will get you in trouble one day."

"I wasn't particularly heroic when I threw a knife at a fleeing man's back, Reaper or not. Besides... Why would I leave behind my only source of that headache oil?"

Rae smiled, but it looked half-hearted. Her demeanor had altered since the day with the Reapers, and he missed the witty side of her. "Not to mention income, right?" She smirked. "You wouldn't have been the first to rob a thief and feel justified..."

The thought tickled oddly in his mind. He wouldn't have even considered taking her things.

"I appreciate the wake-up, however you achieved it. I suppose I owe you."

"You don't owe me anything. I don't even know how I did it. Blank slate between us, all right?" Bastian looked at her with a smile.

"Ha. *Blank slate.* You're hoping I've forgotten that you kissed me."

A warm tingle passed through him with the memory. He fought back the smile by turning it into a disappointed frown. "Kissed *you*?" Wide-eyed, Bastian grinned his pleasure at seeing her wittiness returning. "I think you're remembering that a little inaccurately. Though I suppose you were suffering a severe head injury. *You* kissed *me*, Dice."

Rae chuckled. "Oh, so you do remember."

How could I possibly forget?

"You think I would've forgotten?" Bastian shook his head.

"It's fine. You were out of it. Probably didn't even realize what you were doing." The thought made his stomach feel hollow.

The way her gaze settled on him made him doubt his words, and she tilted her head. "Next time I'll be sure not to have a head wound then, that way you can't write off my actions."

Next time?

The river beside them rounded a bend and picked up speed, turning to frothing white-capped rapids. The game trail disappeared into a cliff side, rising out of the river's east bank.

The terrain jutted upward without leaving a path wide enough for the horses, forcing them to consider the alternative.

An old bridge spanned the twenty yards of rapids.

The rocky beach on the other side ran, unimpeded, farther into the pass which grew dense with pine trees. Their gnarled roots protruded from eroded crevices of soil, reached towards the water.

The rotted wood of the bridge looked anything but sturdy, riddled with gaps and planks hanging down into the flowing water.

Rae dismounted, leading her horse towards the dangerous structure. She glanced up and down the river, before arriving at the same unfortunate conclusion as him. "It might hold." A distinct lack of confidence tainted her tone.

"I'll go first." Bastian dismounted, taking up Zaili's reins.

The mare's ears twitched at the continuous roar of the

rapids, and she stepped back from the bridge.

"I'm lighter."

"Which is exactly why I'm going first. If it holds for me, it'll hold for you." Bastian eyed it suspiciously, planning the path he'd lead Zaili on.

The waters were too rough and deep to ride the horses through, leaving the bridge the only option.

"You any good with that bow you carry?" He eyed the tree line beyond.

Rae snorted. "You any good with that sword you carry?"

He smirked and shook his head. "Shoot a line across so I have something to hold on to in case the bridge fails. I'll tie it off when I get to the other side. Then we can push the packs over it, so they don't add the weight onto the bridge. Makes us and the horses as light as possible."

She considered him momentarily before retrieving her bow from her saddle, pulling a single arrow from the quiver. He handed her the rope from the stolen saddlebags, and she tied it to the arrow shaft.

"The rope'll change the way it flies, so aim high."

Her shoulders slouched, and she scowled at him. "Which way do I hold this again? Maybe you can show me." She lifted it upside down and gave him a dumb look.

Bastian frowned and crossed his arms.

"I got this." She handed him the loose end of the rope and stepped to the edge of the bridge. Lifting the bow, she nocked the arrow and drew it back in perfect form. Holding it taut, she angled the shot upward before letting it fly. The rope whipped past her, leaving plenty of extra length by the time it sunk deep into a tree on the other side.

Rae looked back at him. “Need me to show you how to tie that?”

It was Bastian’s turn to scowl as he walked up the hill behind them with the rope in his hand. He climbed the first tree he reached, tying it on a branch that gave the tether across the river an angle for their supplies to slide more easily across, but left enough slack for him to retie on the other side.

When he returned to Rae, she’d already removed all their packs from their saddles and reattached her bow.

Bastian slid his sword from his belt and attached it to one of his packs. “Just give me a moment to tie the rope before you send the bags across.”

Rae rolled her eyes. “Yessir, General Bastian, sir.” She gave him a faux salute.

Grumbling, Bastian approached the bridge, taking up the slack rope spanning the river. Holding his breath through the first steps, the lead hung loosely between him and Zaili. His feet tested each board before he shifted his weight.

Zaili took some convincing to move forward, but an apple did the trick. Coaxing the mare while minding his footing made the trip across the bridge feel far longer than it should have. The jagged rocks on the other shore bit through the thin soles of his boots, more of a relief than an irritation. He unbound the rope from the arrow, tying it around the wide trunk of the tree.

Before he could turn around, a bag thunked into his back, pinning him against the tree. He huffed, turning around to catch the second before it smacked him in the face. The slant of the rope didn't require much effort for Rae to assault him.

"Thanks!" Bastian yelled over the roaring river, but Rae only gave him a beaming smile and waved, pointing at her ears with a shake of her head.

She approached the bridge, testing her footing like he had, and Syga hesitantly followed. They made it halfway across before the horse balked.

A wild voice in Bastian's mind kept repeating itself, and he recognized Syga's fervent refusal. He tried to focus on it, calm the creature from where he was, but the effort felt silly.

Turning, Rae calmed Syga, stroking his nose. When she tried moving forward again, his eyes widened, and he briefly reared onto his hind legs. The wooden planks under his hooves wavered. As he landed and stomped the plank, Rae held fast to keep him from bolting but couldn't get him to keep walking as he tried to backpedal.

Unable to shout to Rae over the crash of the river, Bastian walked back onto the bridge. Leaning close to her, he shouted, "I'll get him." He took the reins from her hands, and she relinquished them. He gripped Syga's bridle just under his chin. Running a hand over the horse's cheek, he pulled the horse's head near his chest.

Familiar with the horses after the days traveling together and laying on his bedroll at night while playing with his newfound power, Bastian found Syga's voice. The techniques he'd learned on his family's horse ranch were far more effective when he could relay them directly.

A gentle thrum in his fingertips confirmed the connection, and Syga calmed. Guiding the creature from the base of his bridle, Bastian took a step backward, and Syga tentatively followed.

Even if he didn't understand his new abilities, Bastian felt grateful for them. When the voices began, he considered his mind had descended into madness. But when facing the Reapers, the Art had responded to his call, just as Syga did. Whatever was happening to him existed outside his mind, too.

Syga grew more confident, and Bastian slowed to let the animal walk ahead. His boot touched a soggy piece of wood, which buckled under the shift of his weight. He leaned forward, trying to regain his balance, and Syga sidestepped the bump with an irritated shake of his head.

The plank behind Syga snapped up, flicking icy droplets of river water across Bastian's face. A shudder passed through the wood, and the entire bridge groaned as it rocked sideways.

Bastian smacked Syga's rump, startling the horse into an instant gallop, sending splintering wood up around him.

Spinning, Bastian caught a quick look of Rae's wide green eyes.

She leapt towards him, grabbing onto the rope that still spanned the river with her left hand and reaching for him with her right. "Bastian!"

The bridge beneath him gave way.

His fingers touched hers for a moment of hope before they slipped apart.

Ice surrounded him. Rushing water froze him to his bones. At first, his body refused to move, to swim, only to be tossed back and forth within the current.

His feet couldn't gain traction on the slick riverbed, but he bobbed briefly above the surface, enough to get a cold lungful of air. Torn further downstream, he grasped for anything to stop him. His hands slipped off rock after rock until his fingertips found a rough enough boulder to grip.

Body seizing, he trembled despite how much he tried not to. His limbs burned, the cold tearing across his skin. His boots slipped on the stone, dunking him again into the water before he planted his feet against some unseen shape at the bottom.

The rapids tugged, but he fought to stay in place.

Gaining his bearings, he looked back up the river. The bridge had disintegrated into the white water, mossy boards floating past him.

He couldn't see Rae.

Chapter 9

RAE GRIPPED THE ROPE, SHIMMYING along it towards the shore. The bridge disappeared beneath her and she dropped to the ground once she reached safety. Scanning the water, she spotted Bastian as he resurfaced above the current.

"Shit."

He clutched a boulder, the river trying to rip him away.

Untying the rope from the tree, she used his sword to cut as much length as she could. Running downstream, she tossed one end of the rope into the water. The rope wasn't long enough, so she waded into the river, careful to keep her footing, before trying again.

"Bastian! Grab the rope!"

Glazed eyes met hers, and Bastian blinked hard at the rope as it floated near him. As if waking from a dream, he grasped it.

Wrapping her end around her forearm, Rae backed out of the water. Once her feet found dry ground, she pulled, piling the rope behind her as she reeled him in.

The abrupt loss of tension on the rope when he found his footing made Rae stumble backwards. She scrambled over the rocky beach, re-entering the water to help steady him.

His entire body shook, his skin a subtle shade of blue.

Removing her cloak, she draped it over his shoulders, pulling his arm over her neck. She grabbed his hand, his fingers stiff and freezing.

"I'll get you wet too," Bastian chattered in protest, trying to pull away, but his effort lacked strength.

"Shut up." She huffed, leading him to where Syga and Zaili had wandered into the tree line. Leaving him standing next to a tree, she retrieved a blanket but set it next to him on the ground. She tugged at the bottom of his shirt. "This needs to come off."

"Whoa, hey." Bastian's icy hands closing on hers. "I know you're excited and all, but this is hardly the time."

Rae growled and swatted his hands away. "This isn't the time to be bashful, you idiot. Help me take it off, or I'll cut it off."

Without further argument, Bastian untucked his shirt, the soaked fabric clinging to his body. He lifted the dripping bundle over his head, exposing the sun-kissed skin of his smooth chest. A ragged scar ran from his right side towards his belly button, the muscles beneath it solid and defined.

Why in Nymaera's name is he bashful?

He shivered and dropped his shirt as the cold air struck his bare torso. Wrapping his arms around his abdomen, he eyed Rae. "You gonna help me with the pants too? Or do I get the blanket yet?"

Rae reached for his belt buckle, unfastening it with impressive speed. "I'm more than happy to remove these if you need the help." She flicked the button at his waistband open with a quirked eyebrow.

"I was joking!" Bastian gasped, pushing her hands away again. "I got it. Can I have the blanket though, so I can at least pretend to maintain some of my modesty?"

Rae laughed and covered him with the dry blanket, wrapping it around him. "I'll get a fire going." She picked up her wet cloak. "Take the rest of your clothes off."

Gathering whatever wood she could find, she built a pit and retrieved her flint. She watched Bastian out of the corner of her eye as he held the blanket around his shoulders by pinning it between his purple lips. He shifted awkwardly under the blanket, leaning to untie the laces of his boots before stepping away from the entire soaked mess of leather.

His bare feet danced across the rocks towards the fire once it sparked to life, the blanket tight around him. It concealed his body, even as he bent to sit in front of the growing warmth.

Rae pulled both of her shirts over her head in one motion,

leaving her torso bare except the black cropped chemise he'd seen once before. The action exposed the tattoo of a fox chasing a sparrow, depicted in sketched lines of black ink. It ran over her ribs and extended below the wet leather breeches clinging to her legs.

"Um, what are you doing?" Bastian appeared to try, unsuccessfully, to focus on her face.

"You need body heat. Do you know anything?" She watched his eyes linger on her tattoo. Pushing her breeches down, she kicked off her boots, revealing the rest of the design and her meager cotton undergarments.

Bastian looked away, a bright flush rising in his cheeks.

Maybe this was all he needed to warm up.

Crouching in front of him, she poked his chest. "You going to make room for me under there? I promise not to peek."

Bastian's chest heaved with a breath that turned into a shiver. He opened his mouth but then abruptly closed it.

Rae sighed and pulled the blanket open, closing her eyes tightly to maintain her promise as she crawled onto his lap. Turning so her back rested on his chest, she pulled the blanket shut in front of her.

Finding his hands, she drew them around her midsection.

His body shook against her, his chilly skin making her shiver. But she held tighter to his arms, keeping the blanket around them. Stroking his arms, she massaged his muscles to warm them before moving to do the same to his legs.

His shaky inhales echoed in her ear, residual dampness on his chest absorbing into her chemise.

"I finally get your shirt off," she muttered, "and I can't even see you."

A breathy laugh tickled the side of her neck. "I'm sorry to disappoint." Bastian's cold hands traced up her sides, and he pulled her closer.

"You could've grabbed my hand, you know, instead of falling in the river. There are easier ways to get attention." Sensation prickled back into her toes as the fire grew.

He shuddered, resting his chin on her shoulder. "Are you sure it's not you who wants the attention?"

Rae frowned. "Would that be a bad thing?"

His arms tensed, body shifting slightly underneath her, and she settled further into his lap. "I suppose not."

"It's possible I enjoy your company. I'm not used to this."

"Used to what?"

Rae paused. "Being alone."

Bastian raised a hand and brushed her hair over her shoulder, encouraging her head back against his collar. "You're not alone. I'm here with you." His warming fingertips ran along the edge of her ribs, sending a tingle through her body.

"Saving me from loneliness. My *hero*." Rae turned her head to bury her nose in the side of his neck.

His chest vibrated with a laugh. "Well, not all of us can be thieves."

"Is one exclusive of the other?"

He gave a contemplative hum. "I suppose not. You've proven that to me twice now."

"Plus, you're the one with the hero complex *and* the stolen horse."

He shrugged, and she pulled her knees up to lean sideways against him while keeping the blanket tightly wrapped. Her hand rested on his chest, rubbing to generate warmth.

His hand closed firmly around her shoulder, an idle thumb tracing her skin. "Zaili likes me better than her last owner. I believe that qualifies as a rescue rather than stealing."

Rae resisted the temptation to tease him, trying to focus on warming him rather than the smoothness of his skin. "And you claim not to have a hero complex."

He tilted his head, nuzzling his face into her hair. He shivered with a soft sigh. "You smell good."

Her heart skipped a beat, having long noticed his clean, forest-like scent. She'd tried to ignore it. He may not be her typical type, being a law-abiding citizen, but he was plenty attractive.

What's the harm in enjoying his company, if it's mutual?

Bastian tensed in the silence, as if realizing what he'd said. He straightened his spine, pulling his head back from her.

Tilting her chin up enough to see his face, she paused in rubbing his chest.

His jaw, thick with a short, blond beard, looked tight, his gaze distant.

"Is everything all right?"

"Just..." Bastian hesitated, shaking his head. "A little fuzzy-headed from the cold, I think."

Rae slid her touch from his chest down his arm, where his skin still felt cool. "Can you feel that?" She heard a catch in his breath and a rogue thump of his heart echo near her ear.

"Hmmm." He hummed. "I'm not sure. Try again." His jaw flexed, and she smiled.

Running her hand back up his arm, she ventured up his neck to his hairline. "How about that?"

Bastian closed his eyes, his head tilting into her touch. "Why do I feel like you're teasing me again?"

"Teasing." She repeated the word. "I suppose it depends how you define the word."

"I suppose it does." His eyes fluttered open. He touched her cheek, his eyes on her lips as he traced his cold fingertips across her jaw. "What kind of teasing is this?"

Rae's pulse thundered in her ears, and she smiled. She lifted her chin and moved her lips against his neck. "The good kind, I hope?"

The unmistakable catch of his breath came again as she tasted his skin. A sharp inhale he didn't release.

She noted his hesitation and wondered if he had a reason to fight the intimacy he seemed to desire.

Did he suspect her potential to turn him in, somehow?

He could have recognized the second tattoo at the nape of her neck. A feather wrapped loosely around an arrow. A Helgathian soldier may be familiar with the stylized mark representing her position as a high-ranking ranger in the Ashen Hawks. She'd earned the right to have the spell-woven tattoo through her years of loyalty to the guild leader, and it provided a permanent beacon for her hawk to find her.

He let the breath out as his fingers touched her hip. The release of air coincided with a soft moan. "Rae." His voice dropped in pitch, sending chills down her spine. "I—" He abruptly stopped when she closed her lips against his neck, nipping at the skin.

"Should I stop?" She trailed up to kiss his jaw. Her hand slid to the side of his face.

His answer came in another raspy breath, daring to run his hand up her abdomen, between her breasts, to her chin. He encouraged her lips to meet his in a fiery rush, his tongue eagerly meeting hers.

I'll take that as a no.

Rae turned in his lap to face him, letting go of the blanket, though it was large enough to remain around them. She laced her arms around his neck, feeling his hand slide from her shoulder down her back. The kiss lingered, then renewed.

Letting a knee fall to either side of him, she pulled herself closer and his warming chest pressed against hers. Her hands explored the ridges of cold muscle on his upper back, eliciting new trails of goosebumps.

Rae leaned forward, applying pressure to encourage him to lay back without breaking the kisses.

He obeyed, lowering his body to the ground, the blanket protecting them both from the cold. As she came to hover over him, her hair fell to the side of her face. His hand drew down her side, caressing over her hip to the curve of her backside, tentatively exploring.

Her mouth left his, tasting his neck as she touched his abdomen, her hips settling on his.

Any doubt that he didn't want her disappeared as he let out a low groan.

Bastian's stomach flexed as her kisses lowered to his chest, and her fingers teased down the outside of his bare hip towards his thigh.

His hand grasped hers to draw it back up. Breath came into his chest with ragged heaves and his muscles tightened. Not an intimate tension, but one that radiated nervousness.

She lifted her mouth from him and looked up at his face. He looked unsure, and the pang of familiarity made her feel vulnerable.

Jarrod had looked at her the same way.

When his gaze flickered down to where she straddled him,

he abruptly closed his eyes and dropped his head back. "We should slow down."

Rae clenched her jaw at the undercurrent of regret in his tone. Rising from him, she swallowed back her embarrassment. "You have impeccable timing."

Bastian tried to take hold of her hand, but she dodged his touch. He quickly pulled the blanket over himself, wrapping it around his lower body. He pushed himself up. "Wait, I—"

"Don't. In case you're wondering, that's the *shit* kind of teasing." Grabbing her pants, she tugged them on, even though they were still wet.

His jaw tightened, and he scratched the back of his head. "I'm sorry. It's... It's complicated." He didn't continue when she threw one of his stolen shirts from the pack at him. He caught it and wrapped the blanket tighter, tucking it in at his waist to keep it in place.

Her anger flared, and she stepped back from him, pulling her shirts back on. "I swear to the gods, if you're married..."

He sucked in a breath but shook his head. "I need..." He shivered and pulled the tunic over his head, not finishing whatever thought had half-formed.

Rae shook her head. "I don't care." She walked away, leaving him by the fire.

So much for mutual attraction.

The cold air nipped around her, but it did wonders to jar her from the haze of being near him. She looked up at the open twilight sky, rimmed by the peaks of craggy snow-capped Belgast Mountains.

Din wouldn't be returning for another week or two, and she needed to keep Bastian around until she got word from the Hawks. Without the intimate connection, it would be easier to turn him in if she chose to.

Besides, he either belonged to another woman or felt a thief was unworthy of his affection. Neither option left her with the desire to want more from him.

Resigning to hide her damaged ego under the guise of maintaining a friendship, she took her time returning to their makeshift camp.

Bastian had dressed and sat by the fire with their cooking pot propped within it. The tension in his shoulders had diminished, and a collection of roots and foliage sat on the blanket at his side.

He stood, acknowledging her return with a glance before he took up the pot and walked towards the river to gather water.

While he went about meal preparations, she separated pieces of her hair and weaved a braid above her ear. Tight to her scalp, she continued it across the side of her head and behind her ear before braiding the rest of the length. After doing the same on the other side, the hair on the top of her head was still loose, so she gathered it and the braids into a high ponytail and bound it with a strap of leather.

When he returned and began to cook, the aroma of the tubers made her stomach grumble, and she debated retrieving the dried meat from her saddlebags.

"Should I hunt down a rabbit to add?" She kept her voice monotone.

Bastian wrinkled his nose. "Not necessary. I don't eat meat."

Her eyes narrowed. "You did the night we met."

He hesitated, looking at the pot as he stirred the liquid. "It's a new decision. And the stew won't need it. But if you need—"

"I don't." Rae clipped her words more than she intended. "I only thought you might."

Silence settled between them, the roar of the river nearby constantly reminding her of their nearly intimate time together.

"I'm not married." Bastian stirred the contents of the cooking pan he held over the fire. He avoided her eyes, remaining focused on his work.

"Forget about it." Rae shrugged. "I'm fine with keeping our relationship uncomplicated."

"Uncomplicated," Bastian repeated, his tone solemn. "Right. That's probably best."

She pursed her lips and stood, looking from his mouth to the fire.

"Why a fox and sparrow?"

She resisted the temptation to touch her tattoo through her clothing. She imagined the depiction of the two animals in play, scattering leaves and flowers around them. Shades of grey within the sketch gave it dimension, unlike the plain black ink tattoo on his shoulder.

C. 2603

★☆☆☆

A Helgathian military brand, marking his conscription year and rank. Lieutenant, she believed, maybe Sergeant. Either way, a surprising rank for a man so young. But she'd let him think she either hadn't noticed or didn't know what it meant.

She debated her answer as she pulled an apple from her saddlebag, wandering slowly back to him. "For my brother and sister." She sat down. "My father gave each of his children a type of *spirit* animal." The loss no longer felt raw, but she loved the permanent memorial on her skin.

"Isn't that an Aueric tradition?" Bastian glanced up but didn't hold her gaze.

Impressed by his cultural knowledge, Rae nodded. "It is."

"I was wondering, with how bright your eyes are. I've never seen human eyes so green. But I didn't want to assume you were half..."

"Quarter." Her heritage wasn't something she often spoke of, but she didn't have the penchant to lie to him.

Bastian offered her a steaming bowl of stew.

Setting her half-eaten apple aside, she accepted it. She

hadn't watched what he put in it, but it smelled of rosemary and thyme.

"What animal did your father give you?" He blew on a spoonful.

Rae paused, watching him. She'd never told anyone, but no one had ever asked. "A dragon."

Chapter 10

RIDING ALONG THE SHORE OF the river, the air bit through Bastian's clothing, and he fantasized about holding Rae against his bare chest again. His body craved the feeling of her skin against his. A stinging absence tingled where her hands had traced his chest. Where her lips left wet trails.

On more than one occasion, he had to shift in Zaili's saddle for a more comfortable position. Then, again, he'd recall the vision of her nearly naked form above him.

The desire for more threatened every fiber of his being, urging him to insist they stop riding and resume where they left off. He yearned to run his hands along her smooth, warm skin. Explore the curves of her feminine body, unlike anything he'd ever experienced.

She was gloriously perfect, everything he'd ever dreamt of. He'd had plenty of time to imagine while serving in the military. He'd partaken in plenty of lecherous conversations with his comrades, talked and heard about the glories of women. It should have better prepared him.

Despite the military's strict rules about fraternization among the ranks, human demand for physical touch often won out. Bastian abstained from the habits his fellows engaged in, determined to hold out for the right woman. He didn't judge those who sought comfort in the arms of other men, secretly envying the closeness, even if it wasn't for him. The more wicked heterosexual males lavished in raiding expeditions and their chance to reap what they wanted without reprise, but Bastian condemned their actions. When he took his own command, he ended it amid his troops through harsh discipline. He detested the greed of the Helgathian troops and their readiness to take what they wanted, regardless of who it harmed.

Rae proved a fierce reminder of his inexperience. And that remained the root of the entire problem.

Emotions overwhelmed him when she dared to venture too low with her hands, everything mounting into an impossible cyclone of panic. It surely left her more than a little embarrassed. He felt horrible for pulling away, but a lackluster performance would have been worse.

She'd be able to tell.

Being a man his age, yet never having been with a woman. Hells, he'd never even kissed one in his adult life until she'd surprised him five days prior on the other side of the pass.

The air of the forested valley blew in warm spring gusts, ushering in an early summer. Bastian took off his cloak, tucking it between the buckles on his saddle. He wore one of the stolen shirts from the Reaper camp, undyed tan linen tucked loosely into his breeches.

True to her word, she'd kept their relationship 'uncomplicated' after the river. Friendly, with her usual witty banter but lacking the previous teasing notes. Things had a certain thrill to them when the possibility of affection had been on the table. With it gone, he resigned to distance his emotions.

If only he could get the voices in his head to stop chattering.

As he rode behind Rae, he would have been distracted by watching her sway, but his headache peaked to a new intensity.

They'd worsened two days prior, but he hid it from Rae. The pain led to irrational irritability when he struggled to complete the most basic of tasks, like tying his boots, through the haze in his vision.

Rae was patient with him, helping when he asked and even when he didn't. He often woke to the scent of her medicinal oil already dabbed on his temples, but her care only made it more difficult to ignore his mounting attraction.

"Do you think we could stop at the next stream?"

Rae turned in her saddle to look back at him. "Again? We have plenty of water. We stopped yesterday."

"I know." Bastian frowned, closing his eyes to the invisible knife digging into his brow. "But can we stop again?" The icy mountain water didn't stop the voices, but it eased the rest of him.

When he opened his eyes, she'd slowed to ride next to him. "You're in pain. Even worse today? I was hoping they'd get better by now."

Her concern sounded genuine, but Bastian still wanted to snap at her. "I'm fine. The oil helps, but not enough anymore." He rubbed the sore spot over his right eyebrow, hoping it would relax the contracting muscles. "Water helps."

She sighed, and he imagined an eye roll accompanying it. "Is there one nearby?" She'd given up questioning how he always knew where one was.

He gave a quick nod, flinching at the motion, and steered Zaili to take the lead. They moved smoothly onto a game trail, towards a swollen stream nestled among the rampant flora springing from the warming ground.

Zaili's gait staggered as they neared the water, the pattern of sound in his head coming to a rumbling cascade of fear. Her exclamation of distrust overtook him and sparked a desire to flee.

Danger.

Zaili hopped, side-stepping and shaking her neck. Backing up, she snorted as Bastian laid a hand on her neck and pulled on her reins to quiet her.

He whispered to her with a flicker of his will, plowing through the cacophony of confused voices to utter a calming tone. The pain throbbed down his neck and into his shoulders, but Zaili calmed as a shrill neigh erupted from Syga.

Shaking his head, Syga stomped the ground.

"Easy, boy." Rae patted her horse's neck.

His nostrils flared, ears pinned back as he ignored her pleas. With a few backward steps, he abruptly reared up on his hind legs.

Rae adjusted in the saddle, clinging to the leather until his front hooves kicked higher in the air. With a yelp, she tumbled off and landed on her back in the dirt.

Swinging a leg over his saddle, Bastian slid to the ground. Even with the gentle dismount, the impact made his head throb, and he let the wave of agony settle before jogging over to Syga.

He snatched the horse's reins and pulled his head down with a firm grip. Through the haze, Bastian tried to focus on the jumble of agitation from the horse. The pain proved too much, and he resorted to calming the horse in traditional ways. Running his hand down his nose, he shushed away the nerves.

Syga resisted, but Bastian kept at it. The horse's ears swiveled, and he gave a dissatisfied huff, but his stomping ceased after a while.

Bastian turned his attention towards Rae, where she still lay exactly as she'd fallen. She stared up at the sky, catching her breath, but made no move to stand.

Tying Syga to Zaili's saddle horn, a wave of worry passed through Bastian with Rae's unmoving form. He stepped quickly beside her, turning his head to match hers. "You all right?"

Her gaze flickered to him, and she frowned. "My horse hates me."

"Maybe you should just ride with me." Bastian extended his hand out to her with an open palm.

She glared at it. "How chivalrous of you." Rising to her feet with his help, she squeezed his hand before releasing it and stretching her fingers.

His hand felt abruptly colder after she released it. He tried to hide his discomfort with a chuckle, but a flare in his head promptly stopped it.

The tension in the horses hadn't faded even though they stood still, their ears twitching.

"We shouldn't linger. Something spooked the horses..."

Rae stalked past him, ignoring him, and he wondered if he'd said something wrong.

"Dice?"

A tiny panicked voice sounded buried somewhere in the back of his mind.

She picked up her pace, jogging a short distance up the stream before falling to her knees with her back to him.

Curiosity propelled Bastian forward. Stepping around fragile new buds hidden just under the coating of the forest floor, he approached Rae from the side.

Her hands caressed a mound of black and grey fur in front of her. "Shhh... It's all right, little one." The care he'd recognized in her radiated through her comforting tone.

Who'd have thought a thief to be so kind-hearted?

Bastian's chest tightened.

Maternal.

His thoughts returned to Sindré and her threat.

I made the right choice.

The creature whimpered as she found a wound, and the buried voice cried out in Bastian's head. He squinted at two furry ears and tiny razor teeth chewing on Rae's offered hand.

"A wolf?" Bastian peered over Rae's shoulder. The creature couldn't be more than a few months old, his side matted with blood, yet he looked almost as big as one of his family's herding dogs.

Rae nodded. "He's hurt."

The fear in the little voice echoed, and Bastian frowned. "He's too injured to survive." He knelt beside her and the pup. He hoped she'd understand what he implied.

The poor thing is suffering.

"We should—"

"No." Her eyes flashed as they met his. "No. Don't."

"Rae." Bastian touched the back of her hand resting against the clean parts of the wolf's coat.

"No." Her voice was firmer, and she yanked her hand from his, grabbing his shoulder. "Help him."

"What?"

"I know you have a strange connection to some things and as much as you deny having the Art, we both know you have talent." She exhaled and steadied herself. "Can't you try?"

Bastian drew away, shock radiating through every limb. Panic at her blatant accusation made him cringe. He didn't know if he had the skill to heal, so how could she assume? Not all who had access could use the natural energies of the world in such a way.

The auer specialized in the life-giving powers associated with healing, but there were far more destructive styles.

There hadn't been enough time for Bastian to determine where his affinity lay. Sindré hadn't been forthcoming with any advice regarding what they'd done to him other than end any dreams of a family.

Bastian squinted at the whimpering creature. "It's just a wolf." Even though it felt far more complicated now, he'd been brought up to hunt the creatures that prowled his family's land. Saving one's life seemed a paradox.

The wolf whined, and Rae's jaw worked. "Please," she whispered, turning Bastian's face towards her. "Don't kill him until you've at least tried to save him." Her eyes bored into him and he wasn't sure he'd ever be able to deny her anything.

I can't keep hiding this. She's already seen it.

Bastian heaved a sigh, looking down to the ball of matted, bloody fur. "I'll take him to the stream. The water will help me focus."

Rae needed no more encouragement, letting go of his face to gather up the pup.

Bastian stepped away from her, taking a meandering path to the stream's edge. He stooped to take off his boots and roll up the bottoms of his breeches. Standing up, he met Rae, who held the furry form in her arms. She whispered down to the wolf pup, looking the part of a mother, and his heart unexpectedly swelled at the thought again.

He walked into the shallows of the stream, the cool water dancing between his toes. The voices calmed, some disappearing altogether, and he heaved a relieved breath. He turned back to Rae and held out his hands.

What's the harm in trying? Maybe something good can come of whatever is happening to me.

Rae gingerly passed the young wolf into Bastian's arms.

The creature let out a cry, snapping at the new grip before he sent a pulse of his energy to calm him. With a sigh, the wolf relaxed against him, and Bastian scratched beneath his chin.

Rae's steady breathing matched his slow steps as he strode deeper into the water.

All but the wolf's voice quieted, hidden behind the soothing song of the stream. His shoulders felt lighter, and he could breathe again when he stopped in the calf-deep water.

The voice in his arms sounded distraught, confused. But too weak to fight against the one who held him despite the desire to.

Delving into the energies around the wolf began tediously. It took earning trust first, a silent exchange occurring between him and the wolf that Rae wouldn't be privy to. He promised protection, comfort, relief.

The wolf took time to believe him, but gave way enough that Bastian convinced the wolf's soul to heal its body. He couldn't think of any other way to accomplish it. His energy merged with the animal's, feeling his pain, his fear, his instincts. He abruptly heard the sound the boar made when it charged the pup who'd ventured too far from his pack. And the patient licks given before his mother walked away with his four littermates. He'd clung to life for an entire day, and his stomach grumbled with hunger pains.

Bastian's energy sped the healing that the pup's body had struggled with. Already rife with infection, Bastian focused on those pieces first. His vision blurred, a brightness in the edges glowing pale blue and white. Wisps of power wove down his arm, encircling the pup, who whimpered. The process was painful, and he whispered reassurances that it would be temporary as he watched the torn skin knit together.

The process took longer than Bastian expected, but he'd had no clue what it would be like. When he saw the final piece of flesh pucker into a faint scar, then fade into the fur, his body weighed heavy. His eyelids drooped as he fought to keep them open.

The wolf's head popped up, his whimpers ceasing. He looked up at Bastian with bright, cognizant amber eyes. The instinct that might have encouraged him to bite Bastian before now ushered forth a pink tongue that licked Bastian's chin.

He squirmed, and Bastian quickly grasped tighter with both hands to keep hold of the creature as he stepped back towards the shore. He kept his eyes on the wolf in his arms, examining the flawless skin with wonder.

"He's hungry." Bastian frowned at how tired he sounded.

Without warning, Rae took his face in both of her hands and kissed him. It lasted only as long as a quick inhale, and he nearly dropped the wolf.

He barely had time to consider returning the unexpected affection.

As she parted from him, her brow twitched. She opened her mouth but closed it and pulled the young wolf from Bastian's arms with a grin.

He stepped onto the shore, his head ringing with the return of the forest's conversations. It helped wake him up, but his shoulders sagged.

"Hungry, huh?" She cooed at the pup, carrying him towards her horse. "Let's get you some—"

Syga stomped and snorted, causing Rae to pause.

"Syga will take some time." Attuned to the voices more than usual, Bastian deciphered the root of Syga's distrust. "Wolves chased him when he was a colt, so he's not fond of their smell. Zaili doesn't mind though."

Rae raised a brow, petting the wolf who climbed up her chest to drape his paws over her shoulder. "Then I suppose we're trading horses for now." She smirked. Stepping towards Zaili, Rae cautiously nestled the wolf pup into one of the horse's large saddlebags, removing the few objects still within before buckling it.

He barely fit, his big front paws hanging over the front.

Bastian recognized the glint in Rae's eyes that accompanied her teasing banter or surprising affection, challenging him to fight her proposed trade.

He touched his lips and frowned. "Why are you so damned difficult to say no to?" He sighed as he walked past Rae towards Syga, pushing more calm into the horse. It added to his fatigue, but he did it without doubting his ability for the first time.

Rae's playful expression faded as he passed her, and she averted her gaze to the pup.

Bastian's throat caught at the change in her demeanor, disappointingly recalling the time he'd said 'no'. When he'd been a damned fool. "Rae—"

"Don't." Her tone was gentle, but she didn't lift her eyes from the wolf who licked her wrist as she stroked his head. "I'm sorry. It won't happen again." Her tone sounded uncharacteristically soft, and he realized she referred to the joyful kiss she'd given him for healing the pup.

Gods, but I hope it will.

"I owe you an explanation." Bastian stepped towards her. "It's—"

"Stop, Bastian." She pressed two fingers to his lips.

He fought the instinct to kiss them.

"I understand."

Bastian sighed. "No, you don't."

Her eyes flickered to his mouth, and her fingers traced his upper lip before moving to his jaw, sending tingles down his spine.

"No?" Her fingers trailed back into the base of his hairline.

Her actions lit his body aflame, forgetting his fatigue.

"Rae, I've never—"

A sudden shift in the surrounding energies stilled his voice. He tensed, a thrum of power rippling through the trees. The chatter rose into one of excitement, anticipation. He lifted his chin, looking at the trees behind Rae. He tangled his fingers with hers, pulling her touch away from his neck.

The wolf yipped, squirming in the saddlebag.

Rae squeezed Bastian's hand but released it and stepped back, apparently also aware of it. Zaili and Syga were backing from the tree line towards the stream, and Bastian turned to scoop up his boots.

"Grygurr," he whispered. "We need to go. Now." He didn't hide the fear tainting his tone. He'd never encountered the intelligent humanoid creatures before but knew plenty of horror stories. He threw his boots into Syga's saddlebags, gesturing to the shore across the stream.

Rae stared into the trees behind him, not acknowledging his words. "Bastian."

Hurriedly walking to her side to grab her arm, he followed her gaze and found bright yellow cat-eyes watching them from the tree line.

The massive form, a full two feet taller than either of them, lumbered forward from the overgrowth. The short layer of fur on his face, smeared with mud, accentuated the feline features and upturned nose. Sharp fangs protruded over the edge of his lip, and his lynx-like ears twitched forward. Worn belts dangled across his concave chest, a bloodied axe at his side. Long, dexterous fingers tipped with claws reached towards the hilt.

Gripping Rae's shoulder, Bastian's pulse pounded in his throat.

Chapter 11

THE GRYGURR TOWERED ABOVE HER, more sinister-looking than Rae ever dreamt. His rear paws held him upright in a bipedal position, digging into the ground, claws extending and retracting.

Bastian squeezed hard on her shoulder, and she glanced behind them.

Another form emerged from the woods across the stream, tawny-furred with dark wildcat spots running down his sides.

They each wore a strip of cloth wrapped around their hips, their toned muscles flexing.

Rae stepped back, coming back into the urgency of the situation, and darted to her saddle to retrieve her bow from an antsy Syga. She yanked an arrow from the quiver and nocked it. Pulling back hard, she found the first grygurr in her sights.

Bastian hissed and grabbed her wrist. He tugged it down as she released the arrow, and it buried itself into the ground at her feet.

Rae gaped at him, opening her mouth to speak, but he cut her off.

"Stop."

Are you kidding me?

Another grygurr emerged from the tree line at their side, and she tried to face it. She twisted awkwardly in Bastian's grasp to take in the face of their new attacker, who sauntered forward. "Let me go."

Bastian focused on a fourth figure emerging from the trees, his grip holding steady.

The final grygurr appeared older than the others, leaning heavily on a crooked staff jangling with beads and bone tied to its top. Coarse tufts of white fur hung like a beard from his chin. The curtain of beads around his neck sounded like wind chimes with each of his movements. He looked steadily at Bastian, uninterested in her.

As the shaman entered the clearing, the other three grygurr shifted anxiously. None had drawn their weapons but stood with their fingers twitching.

The largest of them, the first who approached, chuffed and lowered his head. He parted his lips and a strange series of sounds came from his mouth. The guttural tones, linked with smooth vowels, reminded Rae of Aueric, though she didn't speak the language except for a few phrases her father taught her.

The shaman gave a stunted reply but didn't alter his focus from Bastian.

Rae's heart pounded as the enormous beast's fingers closed around his axe's hilt. She tried to pull from Bastian again, twisting her wrist free from his fingers.

He turned and wrapped his arms around her waist from behind, pulling her tightly into him. "Please, don't."

The grygurr tensed, one withdrawing his blade with a rasp.

The shaman glared at the one who'd drawn, and he lowered his head and slunk back with a grunt.

What in Nymaera's name is going on?

"Trust me," Bastian murmured in her ear. "Relax and don't look threatening."

Rae huffed. "That's a pretty big ask right now," she muttered but stopped fighting. She stepped behind him as his grip loosened, her back against his.

Bastian parted from her as he took a step towards the grygurr. His breath came in steady drops, but she could barely hear it over her heart. Adrenaline coursed through her veins, and she resisted the desire to attack.

Grygurr were vicious killers. Scavengers. They would kill them both and take all they had of value.

Bastian's desire to do nothing was pure insanity.

And I'm insane for trusting him.

She turned to watch as Bastian approached the shaman waiting near the tree line. He walked in the way she'd grown used to, uneven, silent steps.

The shaman's claws wrapped around the wooden staff, leaning with both hands to keep himself upright. A flick of his hand could have cut Bastian's throat open. His hunched back, typical of grygurr, was more exaggerated by his age.

Bastian slowed as he grew closer to the grygurr, their eyes glued to each other.

The big creature to her left shuffled in her peripheral vision.

The shaman dropped a hand from his staff, and Rae held her breath. She almost reached for her bow, but ground her jaw in determination.

Trust him.

The clawed hand didn't strike, but it extended towards Bastian.

The old grygurr muttered a word Rae strained to hear but didn't understand. "Rahn'ka." The shaman extended his hand further to encourage Bastian.

Bastian hesitated, his shoulders tense as he seemed to contemplate. He accepted the offered grip, and the grygurr's long fingers curled around his forearm. Bastian did the same, his fingers touching the tufts of fur on the underside of the grygurr's arm.

The shaman's steely blue eyes closed, his chin tilting down.

Bastian's shoulders relaxed and remained that way for longer than Rae cared for. She thought she saw the shimmer of Bastian's Art pass down his spine, a vague cloud of blue and white passing into a spiderweb over the ground.

"Rahn'ka." The grygurr opened his eyes and nodded his head. The great beast released Bastian and stepped back, leaning on his staff again. Stooping, the old creature gave a shallow bow.

Mirroring reactions followed from the other grygurr, their hands loosening from their weapons and their heads bowing.

Rae stepped back from the exchange between Bastian and the shaman, swallowing hard.

"I don't know what that means." Bastian bent to catch the shaman's gaze.

The grygurr smiled, his lips curling upward to show his yellowed, chipped teeth. He chuffed and shook his head. "Yeuh wull lurn."

"I will learn?"

The shaman only nodded with another toothy smile. He looked towards the grygurr to his right and said a single short word.

That grygurr turned, stepping back into the trees. The dense color of his coat vanished into the shadows quicker than Rae should have lost sight of him.

When she looked for the others, they'd retreated, too.

Bastian didn't move, watching the shaman as he turned his back and limped away.

Rae could still hear the jangle of his beads after he disappeared.

Bastian's back straightened, but he didn't turn to face her. The usual noise of the forest returned in time, and she spun to check the tree line around them again.

Huffing, Rae yanked her misfired arrow from the dirt and shoved it back into the quiver at her saddle, re-latching her bow. "Can we go now?"

"We should make camp." Bastian turned to her. "We're safe here and I don't think I'd be able to make it very far." His body sagged as he dragged his feet back towards her.

"Safe? How can you say that we're *safe* here? They'll kill us in our sleep."

Bastian found a rock near the stream's shore and plopped onto it, nestling his head in his hands. "They won't kill us." His tone made it sound like her statement was ridiculous. "They're heading back to their encampment to the south. If we leave their territory tomorrow, we'll be fine." He remained sitting, lifting one of his bare feet to pick pieces of rock from the bottom of his foot.

Rae gaped at him. How was she supposed to sleep knowing grygurr were nearby? Grinding her teeth, she resisted smacking some sense into him. How could he possibly know where their camp was?

She lifted the wolf from his saddlebag and retrieved a parchment wrap of dried venison to feed him. Unable to bring herself to speak to Bastian, she sat down with her back to him and offered some meat to the pup.

Her mind whirred. The potential to turn Bastian over to her guild hinged on her staying alive in the meantime. Not only alive but unattached to him, which also was proving to be a struggle. Even though he denied having the Art, she'd witnessed him use it more than once, but why had he refrained during his icy swim? Or to free himself in Jacoby?

None of this makes sense.

She let Bastian nap against the rock, dwelling in her thoughts.

When he woke, he stripped off his shirt and waded into the stream, the sun low on the horizon. After briefly submerging himself, he walked upstream a short distance, where an old tree had fallen across the water.

Sitting on it, his feet dangled into the water, and it ebbed around his ankles. His wet hair clung to his temples as he tilted his head back with his eyes closed.

The wolf pup played at her feet before running off to chase a leaf.

Rae stood and approached the base of the fallen tree, staying on the shore. "Are you done lying to me?" She spoke with more hostility than she meant.

Bastian's eyes shot open, and he turned his head towards her. "What?"

"Are you finished with the lies?"

He sighed, looking down, and kicked the water. "What lies?"

Fury built within her. "Are you serious? I asked if you had any ability in the Art, and you ignored me. You expect me to believe that you *reasoned* with the grygurr to leave us alone? I may be a thief, but you're the one who's dishonest." She'd stalked to the edge of the stream, unable to stop the rise of her voice.

He hesitated when she finished, chewing on the edge of his lip. "Not answering doesn't constitute a lie..."

"Don't patronize me. It's close enough!" She huffed and unlaced her boots, throwing them to the side one at a time.

"What do you want me to say?" Bastian looked up at her. He glanced at her bare feet but didn't move from where he sat. "You begged me to heal that wolf and I did it. I thought that was answer enough."

"We could have died."

He furrowed his brow. "When?"

Is he trying to piss me off?

Rae growled and stomped into the water, kicking it at his legs. "Blind trust isn't a quality I have, and you haven't earned it." She continued forward until she stood an arm's length from him, wanting him to look her in the eyes while he lied again.

"If you don't trust me." Bastian returned her glare, hopping down to stand in front of her. "Then why didn't you shoot those grygurr like you wanted to?"

Clenching her jaw, Rae huffed out a breath. "Hard to shoot while someone is redirecting my aim. It had nothing to do with trust. Give me a reason to trust you. Tell me the truth, for *once*, about *something*. Admit you have access to the Art."

"I have access to the Art." Bastian glowered, then sucked in a breath and averted his gaze. "I don't understand it. I don't know how it happened, but I have power. It started that day in those ruins. When the headaches started. I swear, I was inept before. If I'd have shown any talent in the Art when I was younger, the Helgathian Academies would've kidnapped me from my family and I'd still be there."

Rae let out a breath. "The headaches...?"

"They're related." He nodded slowly. "I've never had headaches like this before."

"What causes your headaches?" If he was in a truth-telling mood, she'd get all she could while it lasted.

He sighed. "I regret not being honest about my new access, but I promise it confuses me a hell of a lot more than it confuses you." His tone grew defensive as he turned from her, walking away.

Rae frowned and grabbed his arm, halting his steps. "Then tell me more about it. Tell me what you can do."

"You mean like saving your life?" Bastian's jaw tensed. "After hitting your head and refusing to wake up? I still don't know exactly how I did that either."

Rae let go of his arm, but neither of them moved. "I didn't ask what you've used it for. Can't you answer the question?" She ground her teeth. "What happened with the grygurr?"

"I just admitted I have the Art!"

"Congratulations! Is that where it ends, then?"

"It's complicated."

Rae scoffed. "Really inspiring trust. *Everything* is complicated with you."

He let out a low grunt and turned away, running his hands through his hair and down his face. It left the wet locks sticking up in places on his head. "It's just complicated. I can't explain things I don't understand. I don't know exactly what happened with the grygurr, but we talked. We communicated. I do it all the time with things around us. I hear the voices of everything. Syga. Zaili. That wolf. The trees. And sometimes I feel like I can talk back, and they listen—"

"Do you think I'm an idiot? You're insane." She gaped at him.

"I know! I know it's crazy. Why do you think I said nothing before?"

Rae fell silent, staring at him. Her chest heaved with her quickened breaths, and she shook her head.

I can't trust you.

She hurried from the stream.

"Dice." Bastian splashed after her, catching her wrist as she reached the shore. "I'm sorry that I haven't been honest. I didn't want to burden you with it too."

She jerked her wrist free from his grip. "Because that's it. There's you, and there's me. Two separate problems."

Bastian sucked in a breath and paused, recoiling from her. He stayed within the water, gazing at his toes. He swallowed, his chest heaving with the deep inhale.

"That's what I thought," she whispered, resigned, and turned away from him.

The water behind her splashed under his footsteps. His hand closed around her wrist and before she could twist free, he tugged her into him. Touching beneath her jaw, he brought his lips feverishly against hers. Cold from the dripping water, they tasted sweet as he encouraged her hips against his.

Rae sucked in a breath through her nose and closed her eyes. One of her hands ventured behind his head to grip his wet hair, while the other flattened on his bare chest. She tilted her head as he renewed the kiss, deepening it with a daring tongue playing against her lower lip. Her heart sped, and she moaned into his mouth, his grip around her waist tightening.

The looming fear of another rejection slowed her desire for more. Biting his lip, she tugged on it before letting go and looking at his face. His eyes shone when they met hers, his hand tracing her jaw before tucking a stray piece of her hair behind her ear.

"I want there to be an *us*."

"Is that so hard to admit?" She searched his eyes.

I can't turn you in.

Her thoughts raged a battle with her heart.

Bastian smiled. "I guess not." His fingers glided beneath her chin, lifting it so he could place a delicate kiss there before pulling back again. "I just want to kiss you. Nothing else for now. Is that all right?"

Nothing else?

She hardly understood his desire for restraint, but it appealed to her all the same. Somehow, the lack of haste felt intimidating. She'd sworn off serious relationships after the last one blew up in her face.

Her stomach fluttered. "I think that can be arranged." She already missed the taste of his mouth.

Bastian obliged her by returning to her lips, eyes shut tight as they succumbed to the rhythm of their mouths moving together. His hands ventured down her body, exploring her curves and eliciting goosebumps. He seemed cautious but kissed her fervently.

Grasping her thighs, he lifted her, and she wrapped her legs around his waist. Lowering her with him, he settled her onto his lap.

His lips strayed from hers, his stubble scraping against her skin as he kissed down her neck. Sighing quietly, she kissed his hair and ignored the rustle of the brush as the wolf pup charged towards them.

He yipped, pushing his body up against Rae's leg, paws digging in to wedge himself between her and Bastian.

Bastian groaned and hummed against her neck as his back arched to make space for the creature between them. He looked down at the ball of black and grey in his lap as Rae slid from him. "Really?" He gestured with both hands as the pup turned and chewed on his back leg.

Rae laughed, briefly admiring Bastian's bare torso with a cocked eyebrow before retracting her touch to pet the wolf. "He needs a name."

"I was thinking a leash." Bastian took her hand, entwining their fingers. "But a name only makes sense if we don't let him go back to the wild. Which would probably be best for all involved."

The pup's head swiveled back and forth between Rae and Bastian, one ear flopped over.

Rae tilted her head, and the wolf mimicked her motion, bringing a grin to her face. "I don't think so. He's coming with us. He won't make it all on his own. Besides, I think it's fair that I get to choose since it's my birthday tomorrow."

"Birthday?" Bastian tilted his head back. "Why didn't you say something sooner?"

Rae shrugged. "It's just a day."

"An important day." Bastian scooted beside her. "If you were home with me, Ma would bake a cake large enough for the entire ranch. And presents..." He nuzzled her neck with his nose, kissing her earlobe.

Sure sounds like a serious relationship.

Her cheeks heated.

He's joking, anyway.

A grin spread across her face, banishing her regret for mentioning it. "Home with you, huh? Seems a little risky to introduce a thief to your family."

He shrugged. "Maybe. There are worse crimes."

Rae tilted her head and caught his mouth with hers, kissing him in a move that felt too natural.

The pup yipped and threw his head against her chest, licking her chin.

She laughed, pulling away from Bastian.

Bastian sighed. "Fine." He scratched the wolf behind the ear as he leaned back. "Since it's your birthday. What's his name?"

Rae smiled as the licks ceased. She threw a stick, and the pup chased it. "Neco. It's Aueric for—"

"Death. That word I know. Seems appropriate with how close he got."

The pup ran back biting a large branch, not the one she'd thrown, and dragging it along the ground beside him.

Bastian pulled the wolf into his lap, forcing the pup to drop his discovery.

He yipped, squirming as Bastian lifted his chin to examine his face. Pink tongue flashed out and licked Bastian's chin.

"Do you like Neco?"

The little wolf howled.

"Neco it is." Rae threw another small stick, and Neco wriggled free of Bastian's hold to chase it. Before Bastian could respond, she slid into his lap and returned her mouth to his.

Chapter 12

LEAVING HIS BODY, BASTIAN STOOD from the shared bedroll and stepped over where he and Rae still slept. Her lips hovered near the exposed skin at his collar, his own buried among her hair.

Neco lay curled up at Rae's back, paws twitching as he dreamt.

Looking down at himself, he willed his hand to rise before his face. At first, he saw nothing where his hand should've been. A slight shimmer in the air, like thinned smoke, coalesced briefly into the shape of his hand as he imagined the way his fingers should be moving. He forced another breath and translucent strands between him and his physical body shuddered, his chest rising with a deep inhale.

Bastian sought to follow the bonds back to his sleeping form, trying to imagine pulling on them to grow closer to his body again, but it felt impossibly far away.

A dancing light in the tree line ahead caught his eye, interrupting the progress he'd made.

The campfire had dimmed to almost nothing, but the stars and moon fought to shine their light in the little clearing. The stream babbled as the tree's hazy outlines pulsed with energy. The auras of his surroundings radiated, yet produced no actual light of their own. They buzzed, their voices rising to an excited shrieking as a form lumbered through the trees.

Paws the size of a man's head padded silently onto the shore, the sand unmoved by the weight of the bear. Even on all fours, the creature was as tall as Bastian. The spirit's fur shimmered a pale blue-white, and they stared evenly at Bastian, the depths of their eyes glowing a deep azure.

The time has come.

The bass voice reverberated in Bastian's chest, and his heart stopped.

The bear strode forward, stepping across the water without disturbing the surface. They shook their ruff as they approached the sleeping human forms, their big navy nose prodding to investigate the blankets around Bastian and Rae.

With a sudden inhale, Bastian plummeted. He fell into himself with a jarring tightening of his muscles and opened his eyes. The embers of the fire glowed orange in front of him, and

Rae shifted within his embrace. He shuddered at the dream, lips forming a kiss on top of her head as he closed his eyes again. Neco's warm body swelled with breath against his fingertips.

Human child. The bear's voice reverberated over the others that returned with consciousness.

Bastian tensed again, pulling Rae closer. His last encounter with a spirit animal hadn't ended in the most ideal ways and instinctively, he sought to protect Rae.

I'll just ignore it, he thought.

Bastian shut his eyes, curling his body against Rae, shaking his head.

The bear huffed.

Bastian didn't feel a physical touch, but his body rocked as though the bear pushed against his hip. Slipping his hand from around Rae, he rolled to reach for his sword.

Stop.

Bastian froze, his hand halfway to the hilt of his sword when the command came. His head turned to meet the chilling gaze of the creature from his dream.

The bear towered over Bastian from where they sat on the ground. The dark flames of their eyes bore into his soul, pushing aside all thoughts of resistance as he abandoned his reach for the weapon. The bear leaned forward, bringing their nose directly to Bastian's face.

He held his breath as the bear opened their mouth, white teeth glittering in the moonlight.

A cloud of mist snaked from the spectral tongue towards Bastian, and he didn't have time to turn away before the white clouded his vision.

He blinked. Or tried to blink. But his eyes wouldn't obey the request. Everything within him tensed and then relaxed. He brought his hand back towards his body, only he didn't remember wanting to.

We don't have time for these games. The voice echoed through the strange silence in his mind.

The constant rumble of background voices disappeared from Bastian's consciousness, and he only heard the night sounds of the forest.

You will come.

The spirit bear turned, swinging their wide head towards the stream.

Bastian stood, slipping away from Rae, his body moving of its own accord. He fought, seeking all the power he'd begun to understand to get his legs to stop taking him towards the water.

It didn't work.

The bear waited at the stream's shore as Bastian walked beside them. His hand reached out to mingle with the fur on the bear's side, gripping it at the roots. It made everything in his arm tingle, like the air before a lightning storm. His bare feet stepped into the water.

"Bastian?" Rae's voice echoed behind him. "Where are you going?"

His steps faltered midway through the stream.

The bear huffed again, turning his hulking body to look at Rae.

"Nowhere you can follow." Bastian's mouth moved, and his voice spoke the words. It made his stomach rumble in agitation.

You can't possibly think I'll cooperate this way, Bastian thought towards whoever might hear.

"Come back." Rae's footsteps splashed into the stream behind him.

"Not now. This must be done."

Bastian growled in frustration, but his feet moved forward, anyway.

The bear shuffled beside him silently.

"Then I'm coming with you." Worry touched her tone.

"No!" The deep bass of the bear echoed within Bastian's voice. *"This is sacred knowledge, and you're unworthy."*

Bastian's feet reached the shore, sand squishing between his toes. Turning, he looked at Rae frozen in the middle of the stream.

Her ponytail was loose, the braids on the sides of her head a dark silver in the moonlight. Brows knitted together, she pursed her lips.

"You must stay away."

The bear paused between them, their monstrous body pressing against Bastian's, urging him towards the trees.

Bastian took a few steps backwards, trying desperately to memorize everything about the way Rae looked at that moment. He couldn't fight the suspicion in the pit of his stomach that it might be a while before he saw her again.

The forest remained oddly quiet as he stepped through the underbrush. The bear loped beside him, and Bastian ran, the power of the woods coursing through his veins.

The drunken sensation of power ebbed within all the muscles in his thighs and calves as he rushed through the forest. Each step brought more power, more surety to his strength.

He couldn't feel any pain on the soles of his bare feet, and no protruding branches struck his skin.

The trees grew denser and taller as they moved northwest towards the mountains.

Morning calls of birds echoed in Bastian's ears before they slowed.

As a soldier in the Helgathian army, he'd developed outstanding endurance, but even he couldn't have run at a sprint through the night before.

When they stopped, Bastian's chest barely heaved for breath. The morning air nipped his skin, slick with perspiration, but he hardly noticed as he stepped towards battered monoliths, ivy choked and stained by age.

The bear sauntered forward, stepping between the two sentry stones. As they did, runes beneath the layers of time crackled to life with a hum of blue energy. The vines recoiled, reweaving themselves to avoid marks on the ground.

Bastian paused as if he was being granted an opportunity to take in the sight before his steps took him forward again. His breeches, still rolled up from the day before, avoided the mud that covered his feet. He felt an unbearable itch on his neck, but his hand still refused to reach for it.

I'm here, he grumbled inwardly. *Can you let me go now?*

You've proven unwilling. The bear tilted their head back as they walked towards another set of monoliths sparking to life. *You don't understand the danger if you don't learn how to control this gift, Rahn'ka.*

The monoliths led to a fissure carved into the mountains. Greenery rimmed the stones beneath his feet, but the worn pathway was unmistakably man-made. The grey dawn hung in the air with a sprinkling of mist hovering on the tree line behind.

A rhythmic beat of hooves echoed through the damp air.

The bear stopped in the entrance to the crevice, swinging their head back. The creature rose onto their hind legs, twice as tall as Bastian. The hair on their neck bristled, lips curling to show their fangs.

Obstinate child.

Bastian spun around by the will of the spirit's power and witnessed Rae approaching from the tree line.

The horses stood behind her, roped loosely to a tree, with Neco in Zaili's saddlebag.

Rae had tied her hair back again, leaving the braids in place. Her eyes shone as she stared at him, mouth slightly agape, breath coming quickly. "Bastian. What's going on?" Her voice squeezed his heart. Her gaze locked on him, empty hands flexing at her sides.

Get rid of her, or I will, the bear snarled in his mind, dropping to all fours.

Bastian's entire body sagged. A steady thrumming pain spread through the muscles of his legs. The bear took a menacing step forward as he found his voice. "Dice. I'm so sorry, but you need to leave. You can't come with me. The answers I need to know more about my Art are here." He wanted to leave with her, but energies emanated from the sanctum behind him, and he needed to know their purpose.

Rae's presence somehow threatened his learning. The energy, which he guessed to be that of the Rahn'ka, vibrated in the bear behind him.

"I don't understand." Rae walked towards him, shaking her head. "Why can't I stay and help you? I thought..." Her words trailed off, leaving her unspoken meaning embedded in his mind.

Her kind is not welcome on these grounds. The bear spirit's massive claws grated on the ground.

"Stop!" Bastian held out his hands. His eyes darted to her feet, where they hovered on the edge of the stone path. "Don't come any closer. You can't help me. Take Zaili and go."

Rae narrowed her gaze but kept walking. "I won't just leave you."

The bear growled, the rumbling tone vibrating everything within Bastian.

"*Leave now, foolish girl!*" Bastian's voice shouted without his permission. His body reached for the energy around him, into the monoliths at his sides. His veins pulsed, the palpable power surging into him as his muscles tensed. It felt like lifting a great weight, even though nothing was in his arms.

Rae stepped onto the stone path but came to a stop. She stared at him, searching his face as she frowned. "What's wrong with you?"

No. Bastian begged helplessly as the bear lurched up behind him. The power came from them, too, the energies seeping deep into all of Bastian's muscles, coalescing into a tightly wound ball near his heaving chest.

Bastian's vision dropped, seeing Rae's approaching steps out of the top of his vision as he drew his fists up and crossed his forearms in front of his chest.

The explosion buzzed against his skin as the power his body gathered burst outward. The air rippled with heatwaves, a shimmering light radiating in a perfect sphere around him. The vines blew loose off the monoliths, their stone forms quaking as the shock wave struck them and then continued towards its target.

Rae gasped but had no time to seek cover before the blast threw her back. She hit the ground a few paces off the pathway.

Coughing, she staggered to her feet. Walking again, her chest heaved. "This isn't like you." She stepped towards him. "You won't hurt me."

The bear spirit didn't share Bastian's desires, and another growl echoed against the stone.

Please. Bastian's hands dropped to his sides.

The voices whispered in his head, offering words of acceptance as he took in their energy for himself. It pulsed into the veins at his wrists, his fingers twitching. One hand reached towards the monolith to his right, the runes flashing as he drew on the ancient power hidden deep in the stone. His other hand held out in front of him, the energy coursing in a thin white sheen towards his fingertips.

The power swirled like a tornado in his palm. It grew with each pulse of his arms, absorbing power. His vision flashed with blue-white brilliance that made it hard to see Rae.

"Bastian..." Her voice grew wary, tainted with doubt. "Please stop, you're scaring me."

Don't you dare hurt her! Bastian's demand fell on deaf ears as the power continued. It made his head swim in an odd sensation of euphoria mixed with his dread. He tried to force his hand down, stop it. Instead, the power twisted in his fingertips and with a flick, launched forward.

The swirl of energy raced through the air in a mote-filled cyclone. It picked up the dirt and leaves from the ruined walkway, leaving the carved stones untouched. It stretched as high as the monoliths, racing towards Rae like a tidal wave.

It ripped her off her feet, spinning her back through the air where she collided with a monolith and rolled to a stop near the horses.

For a terrible moment, she lay as still as stone. Mostly on her stomach, she moved, rising again to her feet to face him. As she did, the wind behind her picked up. Her ponytail whipped against her cheek, parallel to the ground.

The abrupt gust struck his chest, freezing his skin, causing him to brace his feet to remain standing.

The bear spirit dropped to all fours, eyes narrowing with a snarl.

Rae's eyes flashed as they met Bastian's, dazzling in the morning light. One remained its usual green, and the other altered to a new hue of vibrant yellow. Blood trickled down her forehead, across her brow.

The sun faded behind threatening rain clouds. A cruel mimicking of his emotions.

Without another word, Rae turned and jogged to the horses. With Syga still latched to Zaili, Rae mounted Bastian's horse and spun around in a hasty exit. A breath later, they were gone, and the sky cracked open with a downpour.

The rain soaked his hair, and his body shivered. It was the first instinctual response as he regained control.

Bastian whirled around. "How dare you..."

The bear's muzzle rippled with a show of teeth. The spirit shook their ruff, even though the rain passed right through their semi-corporeal form. Raising their head, they looked directly at Bastian.

You are Rahn'ka now. And you will learn. This is the only way. It's better you not be influenced by the falsehoods of an auer. Don't make me force you.

"Haven't you already done that enough?" Bastian took a step back. He ran his hand into his soaked hair, flecks of water spraying around his shoulders. "I don't see any other way to go about this. I won't step in there willingly after what you've done."

Very well. The bear shuffled away. *It'll be faster this way, anyway. Humans always were poor learners.*

Bastian's spine straightened and his body jerked forward. His steps were not his own as he crossed into the ruins beyond the crevice.

Chapter 13

RAIN PELTED RAE'S FACE LIKE tiny daggers as the horses tore through the trees.

Neco whimpered from his place in the saddlebag, but she didn't stop.

Bastian had attacked her, not once but twice. And she'd stood there like a daft fool and let him. She hadn't even retaliated.

Her heart pounded, and her hands shook, knuckles white as she gripped the reins.

As the rain subsided, Rae slowed the horses.

I'm an idiot. I should've stayed objective. He's a bounty.

Finding a large clearing of tall grass and a tiny trickling stream, Rae swung herself off Bastian's horse and retrieved

Neco. Mud splattered over the horses' legs and bellies, and she sighed. Cleaning them would be a job for the next day.

Putting the wolf pup on the ground, he huddled at her legs.

"I didn't see it coming, either," she muttered, answering the pleading look from the pup. "You think I should take his horse back to him?"

Neco barked, and Rae laughed. "Me neither."

As the horses grazed, Rae shared some dried venison with Neco and watched his antics. The wolf rolled around in the grass, chasing his tail and stumbling over invisible obstacles. It was enough to keep her mood light, but thoughts of Bastian lingered. Questions.

The attacks were out of character, but she couldn't deny what had happened. Her back ached, her ribs pinching with each twist of her torso. When she'd scratched an itch on her forehead, her fingers came away with smudges of blood.

Imagining Bastian's face, Rae's chest tightened. His eyes shone nothing like they had before. A flicker of glowing pale light tainted them like the raging cyclone she'd seen him wield. He'd been playing her the entire time, denying his knowledge of his powers. Using her for something, but what?

She'd outgrown her use, whatever it'd been, but it wasn't over. He'd see her again, whether or not he liked it, on his way back to Helgath.

Rae threw the stone she'd been pushing around on the ground, and Neco jumped up to chase it.

A screeching call drew her eyes upward to the tops of the trees, a dim familiar shape circling through the morning sky.

Smiling, Rae rose to her feet and held out her arm as she whistled.

Din swooped down from above, wings spread wide. His talons found her forearm, biting into her skin while his wings flapped to bring himself to a halt.

The metal cuff on his right leg donned a carving of the tattoo on her neck, bonding the two of them together.

"Good boy." She pulled the much-anticipated wrap of parchment from beneath the cuff. "Don't go far." Launching him back into the air, she breathed a deep inhale.

Approaching Syga, she unrolled the paper. The message inside was written in code, one uniquely used between her and Jarrod. The idea of an ally warmed her insides, and she wished he'd found her himself rather than return her hawk.

She considered what his reaction would be if he found out how Bastian had struck her. The soldier might not make it back to Helgath after all if Jarrod got his hands on him first.

The thought of returning to the Ashen Hawks, her family, brought an unwelcome mist to her eyes. Shaking her head, she tried to focus on her task. It didn't take long to find the rhythm of Jarrod's usual cadence, but the message wasn't all she hoped for.

Helgath is hunting a few deserters. Need more information to confirm identity. Are you still in Olsa? Theo wasn't your fault. You should have written sooner, I've been worried. Come home.

Guilt twisted her stomach. She'd never said goodbye to Jarrod beyond leaving him a note, and she regretted it.

Pulling her notebook and graphite from her saddlebag, she flipped to a blank page. She wrote her response in the same cypher without the hesitation she might have held the night before.

I'm sorry. I should have checked in. I'm just north of Bersali, in Aidensar. Planning on heading west soon. He has a military tattoo.
C. 2603
★☆☆☆
He says his name is Bastian. If he is worth it, come by boat and send Din with which port to meet at.

Rae signed off with the symbol of an arrow with an 'x' through the shaft and tore the piece of parchment from her notebook. She folded it and called Din back with a sharp whistle.

Jarrod would get the message within days, assuming he was still in Mirage and before she could change her mind, she sent Din off into the sky.

Resigning herself to solitude, Rae glanced around for Neco. It was difficult to see him with all the tall grass, and she saw no movement nearby.

Standing, she walked in the direction he'd gone in chase of the stone and tilted her head at a small area of trampled grass. In the center, the pup laid curled around the stone, fast asleep. Wind rustled the grass around him, Neco's ears twitching as he stirred.

Silence followed the breeze, hushing the chatter of the birds.

Syga snorted, and Zaili raised her head from the grass. Both horses perked their ears towards the east and for a moment, Rae wondered if Bastian had followed her.

Lifting Neco from the ground, she crept towards Zaili. Placing Neco in his seat, Rae circled the horse as Syga whinnied and pranced sideways. Still tied to Zaili, both horses backed up.

Rae grasped Zaili's bridle, shushing the horse, but her eyes remained locked on the tree line. At first, she'd hoped Bastian hadn't chased her. Now, she prayed it was him and not something worse.

When her eyes found yellow ones watching her, her heart leapt into her throat. "Shit, shit." She scrambled to mount Zaili as the largest grygurr from the day before emerged from the shadows of the forest.

Her bow, still latched to Syga's saddle, was out of her reach, but she didn't have time to retrieve it.

The grygurr hurled himself towards her with a cat-like yowl, and she yelped, kicking Zaili harder than she meant to.

With a high-pitched whinny, the horse rushed forward, galloping east with Syga keeping pace next to them. An aggravated growl grew distant under the pounding of hooves.

When they neared the opposing tree line, Rae dared a glance back.

The grygurr surged on all fours towards them, unrelenting in his charge. The curve of his back, striped with worn leather weapon straps, bobbed above the tall grass.

Rae kicked Zaili again, her breath coming in gasps as she debated how to reach her bow. She didn't need to look back to know the grygurr was gaining on them.

Steering Zaili closer to Syga, she took her eyes off the path ahead to focus on her objective.

When Rae lifted her feet from the stirrups, Zaili snorted and swerved to the side, dodging a tree and nearly unseating her.

Gripping a handful of mane, Rae growled and reached for Syga's saddle. With an ambitious breath, she released Zaili and yanked herself onto her own horse.

The snarl of a cat behind them made her hands fumble as she untied Zaili from Syga, letting the rope fall loose just as a tree parted the two racing horses.

Rae snatched her bow and drew an arrow from her quiver. Turning in the saddle, her heart stopped as she met the gaze of the grygurr again.

Close, much too close.

His giant paw lifted, and everything moved in slow motion as he drew three ragged claws over the side of Syga's rump.

Syga screamed, stumbling, but kept running.

Her aim temporarily faltered, but Rae found the grygurr in her sights a moment later. She stilled her breath and pulled the bowstring back.

As she loosed the arrow, the grygurr sidestepped, but it sank into the top of his shoulder. He howled, falling to the forest floor and vanishing from view.

Rae leaned to catch the loose rope to keep Zaili with her, but they didn't slow.

She thought the grygurr only grazed her horse, but when Syga's breath grew ragged, her heart squeezed.

Despite the desire to continue running, she brought the distressed horses to a stop in a thinner area of the woods. They panted, frothing at the mouth and nervously dancing as she secured them to a tree. Syga's movements were more sluggish than Zaili's, his breathing labored.

Rae sucked in a slow breath as she investigated his injury and cursed at the blood caked down the back of Syga's right rear leg. The three gashes bit deep into his flesh, the exposed muscle bubbling with fresh blood.

Rae swallowed. "Damn it, I'm sorry." She stroked Syga's back, and the horse nickered. "I should've killed that monster when I had the chance," she growled, retrieving medical supplies to clean the wound.

Syga tried to avoid each touch, sidestepping and pulling away from her care. It slowed the process and once she secured the wound so it wouldn't fester, Rae was exhausted.

Content to have a quiet evening, Rae made camp with Neco huddling close. Syga wouldn't cope well with more travel, and she didn't want to risk injuring him further. She had to hope she'd made it out of the grygurr territory and dissuaded the hunter from continuing his pursuit. But she kept her bow, an arrow half-nocked, at her side.

At least the rain stopped.

She lay on her back, staring up at the darkening sky. With one hand on her bow and one on the wolf, she drifted off into a troubled sleep.

The sound of a heavy body hitting the ground startled her awake, and she drew an arrow within a breath. But aside from the snorts and panicked huffs of horses, the night was quiet.

Her gaze darted to the side, adjusting to the darkness, and she dropped her bow.

Syga wheezed, laying on his side on the cool ground. Zaili nudged him with her nose, only receiving a weak nicker in response.

"Syga." Rae gasped and crawled over to her horse. Moonlight provided enough for her to see black veins spider-webbing out from the injury on his rump. Her stomach sank.

Some grygurr packs dipped their claws in poison before a fight. It'd been foolish of her to ignore the possibility. Even if she'd known, she carried no antidote for the obscure concoction coursing through Syga's veins.

His labored breath shook his body, flaring his nostrils. His mouth hung open, tainted with yellow froth.

Rae closed her eyes, willing strength into her soul. She couldn't let him suffer. Reluctantly, she rose from the forest floor and gathered her bow.

Neco whimpered as she stepped around to Syga's head.

"I'm sorry," she whispered, drawing the bowstring back until her arm shook. She tried not to look into his glazed, wild eyes as she readied her shot. Aiming directly at his forehead, she loosed the arrow with a sickening thunk.

Zaili cried out, and Syga stilled.

Unable to remain next to Syga's body, Rae packed up Neco and rode Zaili west.

Taking the life of an innocent creature never came easy, even when hunting. But something about putting Syga out of his misery took an extra toll on her.

If Bastian had been with her, he'd have been able to heal Syga. Hells, judging by their previous encounter, the grygurr hunter would never have attacked. The beast had been aiming for her leg and if he'd succeeded, she'd be the one frothing at the mouth with no one to give her a merciful death but herself.

Hot anger clouded her thoughts, and she instinctively looked beside Zaili for Syga. Her heart twisted at the absence.

This is Bastian's fault. He led me here. He must have known.

As she drew closer to the mountains, the trees thinned, and the sun beat down from its place high in the sky.

Her stomach rumbled, but she didn't want to risk stopping to cook a meal. A fire would draw too much attention if she was still in grygurr territory. Sustaining herself on whatever she could reach from her position in the saddle, she continued until they reached a shallow stream.

Zaili needed a break, so Rae dismounted but took her bow and quiver with her. The horse eagerly moved away, gulping water before munching on the grass near the shore.

The dried blood on Rae's forehead itched, and she rinsed her face. Drawing scoops of water, she cleaned her skin the best she could.

Neco peeked his head out over the rim of the pack he traveled in, sniffing at the air. He yipped, growled, and yipped again, drawing her attention.

Rae turned just before the cat snarl sounded behind her.

Dread overwhelmed her as the grygurr hunter tackled her across the stream, sending her arrows scattering from her quiver.

She shrieked, thrusting her legs up into the grygurr's concave abdomen, rolling backwards and away from the muscled form. Her fingers groped at the dirt behind her, searching for a weapon. As she found the shaft of an arrow, agony tore through her right side, and she screamed.

Nocking the arrow with shaking hands, she swiveled her aim back towards the vibrant yellow eyes. "Asshole." She shot her single arrow through his eye socket.

Chapter 14

THE POWER WHIRLING AROUND BASTIAN left him feeling drunk.

Minimal natural light penetrated the thick canopy of the outstretched trees. They sheltered the ancient ruins nestled in the canyon the bear had forced Bastian into.

Monoliths, like the ones at the entrance, encircled the clearing with a spiral of stones nestled among swaying grass. No wind blew, yet they danced with the energy humming against Bastian's very being.

Beyond stood an archway, rimmed with ivy that led to a darkened cave he couldn't see within. To the right of the stone circle were more crumbling ruins, but the shadows made it impossible to tell how deep they ran.

They walked side by side, Bastian's fingers tangled within the warm fur. The bear stopped at the edge of the spiral, shaking their ruff and urging his grip to loosen.

He wanted to look further into the ruins but couldn't turn his head. Instead, his eyes focused on a short rock altar stationed at the center of the spiral, a shallow bowl on it. Vines from the trees braided together, reaching towards the contents of the bowl. They didn't touch the surface, but basked in the dim glow as their tangle drew to a point.

Staring at the beauty, Bastian wished Rae could see it too.

The bear huffed, shaking their head again as if they could sense Bastian's thoughts.

You make this more difficult than it needs to be. Wouldn't you like to understand how to control your gift?

Bastian's body sagged as his control returned to his limbs. The cold grass under his feet soothed what pain he should have felt. "She wouldn't have interfered." He turned towards the spirit. "Your racism against auer doesn't make her guilty, as Sindré believed. Your acceptance of her would have ensured my cooperation. Isn't that what you want?"

You will cooperate, regardless. The more you struggle, the longer this will take. And you already know the necessity of it. The bear turned to face him, lifting its head to show its teeth inches from Bastian's face. *Auer are our enemy. Your enemy now, as a Rahn'ka. Their kind sought to eradicate ours because of fear and jealousy. She would show the same inclinations if she understood what you are.*

"What am I?" Bastian growled, stepping closer to the creature, despite all rational instinct telling him to run away. "What's this supposed gift they tricked me into taking?"

You're a Rahn'ka. The enlightened one. And you are the only one of us living. There can only be one now. The bear gazed, forlorn, towards the center of the circle. Before Bastian could question, the bear stepped forward. Their clawed feet trod on the stones, avoiding the grass as they made their way to the center altar.

The vines twisted and spun at their presence.

Bastian glanced behind him, the thought of running dominating his mind as he looked at the entrance to the ruins.

Rae had to be far away now. She had every right to run after what Bastian had been forced to do to her.

He cursed under his breath before he turned back to the bear, who touched their dark blue nose against the lip of the bowl on the altar.

Bastian considered the new information. "There's only one Rahn'ka? And it's me? What does that mean?"

Sindré didn't have the energy to explain beyond granting you the power you now hold, child. Nor is it their responsibility. It's my burden to carry through the millennia. Yondé must always be the teacher.

Voices surged in Bastian's head, and his hands shot to hold his temples. He'd been spared while the bear controlled him, but now they struck like a thousand stones pelting his body.

The pain drove Bastian from his feet, falling to the ground as he squeezed his eyes shut and tears welled. His voice joined the ones screaming in a chorus of demands and torments, urging him to listen. He caught pieces of languages he'd never heard, all begging him to do something he didn't understand.

A cold pressure touched his forehead, wedged between his hands. Coarse fur brushed his fingertips as everything departed. Lightheaded, nausea threatened Bastian's stomach as he forced himself from the ball he'd curled into. The spirit bear's nose pushed firmly to his skin.

Bastian breathed deep, savoring the barrier between him and the voices. "Yondé." He sought the strength of the creature's neck with his hands.

The bear pulled back, lifting Bastian to his feet. Their nose pulled away, but he refused to let go of the bear's fur. "You're Yondé, and you'll teach me?"

Yondé showed their teeth in what might have been a smile, but it was difficult to tell. The guardian spirit nodded once. *Yes. And the first lesson must be how to separate yourself from the well of spirits. Many Rahn'ka have failed to even reach me, driven mad by the exposure. But Sindré made a fitting choice. Your stubbornness may prove a benefit.*

Bastian grimaced at the lingering headache as it settled at the front of his head. But the voices didn't return as long as he kept a steady grip on Yondé. "Rae helped me through it."

Yondé growled.

"I have a lot of questions." If Bastian had to refrain from speaking of Rae to get answers, he'd have to resist the temptation.

Yondé huffed and guided him towards the center of the altar.

Bastian stepped only on the stones, cold under his feet.

I'd be disappointed if you didn't. You only have assumptions. But first, you must replicate my shield. Meditation will be necessary.

They rose onto their hind legs, clawed paws clumsily grasping the bowl on the altar and offering it up towards the vines.

They wriggled, parting to embrace the stone vessel, lifting it. Leaving the altar bare, Yondé thumped down to all fours and bumped Bastian towards it.

Sit.

Bastian eyed the narrow stone spot but lifted himself onto it.

The shrine will aid in channeling your power. It'll ease the process until you master the techniques.

Bastian pulled his feet underneath him, crossing his legs as he found his balance on the stone. "How am I supposed to master something I don't understand?"

The altar hummed with energy, tickling his senses.

Yondé stared. *With discipline and patience.*

Bastian rolled his eyes but closed them.

He imagined Yondé's shield surrounded him, even though their touch had ceased. It was thin, like a veil encasing him. It went beyond his body, engulfing any outreach of his power to protect it from forces trying to enter without invitation.

With the guidance of the buzzing stone beneath him, Bastian realized the voices never intentionally spoke to him. Everything, even his own essence, pulsed with a vibrant power that whispered of its own accord.

Bastian could only block it out, not make it cease.

He could even feel the surge of Yondé, its timbre like none of the others around. Different voices comprised their being, from many sources, each unique.

Instead of allowing himself to be distracted, Bastian focused on the thin sheet surrounding him. He couldn't explain how he sensed it, or how he touched it with his eyes closed, body unmoving. Yet, it happened as he breathed deeply, the shield contracting and expanding with each breath.

Precariously perched on top of the altar, Bastian did his best to focus. Sitting still for any length of time increased his restlessness. In the military, his desire to constantly train and practice had been a boon. It made him the soldier Helgath wanted him to be.

Bastian cracked his right eye open, realizing his mind had wandered.

Yondé snorted, rocking back to sit on their hindquarters. *Focus.*

"I can't." Bastian groaned, forcing his eyes shut again. He shifted on his hips, trying to find a new position. He could only focus on the way the rock poked his ass. So he shifted again.

Yondé made a sound like a sigh, and a tidal wave of pain followed. The barrier surrounding Bastian vanished, popped in the flood of voices that threw themselves at his consciousness. It was like being struck in the face, and his balance wavered.

The barrier returned in time for Bastian to realize the sensation of falling backwards off the altar. His back contacted the stone ground.

He could barely make out the azure afternoon sky through the trees acting as a roof to the sanctum.

Yondé's head swayed over him to block the view. The deep flaming eyes looked amused. *You can. You've already used the power in other ways. This is by far the simplest application. You're merely being uncooperative. Now get up.*

"I'll stay down here, thanks." Bastian forced himself to sit up, spinning to put his back against the altar. He bent his knees towards his chest, crossing them and putting his hands on his knees. "What exactly am I supposed to imagine?"

Your essence. Your ká. It's what you sense from everything else. But first, you must learn to use your own.

"And what am I supposed to do with it?"

It's a tool, like a blade or a bow. You must learn how to shape it.

"How?" Bastian sighed, irritated. He opened his eyes to find Yondé's snout only inches away. Instinct pulled his head back, where it hit the stone altar, making him wince.

Do you always ask so many questions?

"Don't you ever give a straight answer?"

Yondé made the sighing sound again, and a brush of wind blew through Bastian's hair with it.

Bastian brought his arms up to his chest, crossing them as his brow furrowed. "Why me? I've never had a lick of talent for the Art."

Precisely why Sindré chose you. We, too, were once without it. Until the gods granted us the power over ká, birthing the first Rahn'ka.

"Sindré." Bastian scowled. "Sindré didn't need to threaten Rae and force that choice on me. How is my inability to have children of use to you?"

Yondé tilted his head. *Sindré's methods are of no concern to me. They choose the Rahn'ka, and the tests vary.*

"But you said there is only one. And now that's me? Why now?"

Yondé circled a patch of grass as if contemplating before settling. *There were once many, but when the land broke into pieces, it disrupted our power. Our children became trapped, their power limited. But we, the guardians, pooled our energies to bless just one. There must always be one to maintain the balance. To battle the darkness.*

"Darkness?" A knot tightened in his stomach.

You're not ready for that knowledge yet. The time will come.

"Why?"

Yondé stared at him, the flames of their eyes boring into Bastian enough to make his spine straighten. *Not yet. Ask a different question, if you must continue this procrastination from your training.*

Bastian frowned. "What happened to the previous Rahn'ka? What led to Sindré choosing me?"

Yondé sat silently for a moment, but their gaze moved away from Bastian. Their head drooped, lips curling back into a slight snarl. *There have been several in recent years, all lost to madness before they could reach me. But Ailiena, the last I trained, was hunted and killed. Which is why—*

"Hold on." Bastian shifted away from the altar. "Hunted?"

Yes, hunted. Which is why you must learn to use your gifts. Ailiena had advanced well beyond my teachings, yet she still perished. You won't fare much better if you can't focus for longer than a bird's heartbeat.

Bastian heaved a sigh, running his hands through his hair. "Who hunted her?"

Your enemies.

"Auer?"

No, worse. They're servants of a being far older than the Rahn'ka. Humans tell tales of them. Shades.

"The children's stories?"

His father had told him numerous tales about creatures who left a trail of destruction behind them. Nothing lived where a Shade had traversed. When his mother's honeysuckle patch had abruptly died, his father suggested a Shade passed by. Bastian hadn't been able to sleep that night, imagining a black wraith creeping outside his bedroom window, plotting to murder his family while he slept.

All myth begins with some reality. Shades are real, and they'll hunt you should they discover your identity.

"Great." Bastian huffed. "Just what I need. Someone else hunting me down."

Yondé tilted their head to the side. *You're not afraid?*

"Oh, I'm afraid." Bastian wrung his hands together in front of him. "I had enough enemies before I became Rahn'ka, but now I can add auer and children's nightmares to the list." He looked up, and Yondé had settled their head down on their massive paws. "Tell me more about the auer and the Rahn'ka. What did they do?"

Too much to name. The auer are to blame for all our suffering as Rahn'ka. They don't trust what they don't know and stop at nothing to obliterate those they see as a blight on Pantracia.

"Are we talking about the same auer here? They hide on their island and don't seem to give a damn about anything else going on. Besides, Rae would never hurt me."

Do you believe you know her so well? The auer are masters at deception and manipulation. And they don't forget.

"In the name of the gods, she's only a quarter auer, Yondé. I doubt she's ever even met a full blood auer! They're not exactly common."

Yondé's lips curled back, and they gave a low warning growl, though didn't bother to lift their head.

Bastian threw his arms up in defeat. "Fine, fine. Auer are bad. Shades are bad. Everyone is hunting me. And all I must do is learn how to build an invisible wall, so my head doesn't explode."

It isn't—

"No, it's far more complicated. I understand that. You've made your point." Bastian pushed away from the stone, standing up. His feet tingled as he tentatively prodded at the barrier.

Then you're ready now? Yondé lifted their head to watch as Bastian climbed onto the altar again.

"As I'll ever be, I guess. Teach me."

Days bled together after Bastian figured out the trick to blocking out the voices. The constant glow in the sanctum made it difficult to determine the time of day unless he strained to see the sky through the trees. The cave beyond the altar held ancient texts, some crumbled beyond recognition, some in foreign languages and others newer and easier to read. He'd never been a studious learner, but under Yondé's guidance, Bastian learned to find some enjoyment in the old teachings.

Fortunately, it wasn't all about reading and meditating.

In the lumbering shadow of a monolith surrounding the altar, a sturdy root stretched across the gap between stones served as his bar for pull-ups.

Sweat ran down his face, muscles protesting as he drew himself up again. Navy tattoos of symbols and runes decorated the left side of his chest, shoulder, and down his left arm. Ink covered his old military brand, erasing the sour reminder. Helgath wouldn't be able to use the mark they'd forced on him to identify him anymore. Instead, he carried the marks of his new service to the Rahn'ka. They reacted to his sweat, glimmering like the motes of the sanctum when the moisture flowed over them.

With a huff, Bastian forced his shaking muscles into one more rise of his chin to the root, then dropped to the ground. His bare feet cooled on the stones, a buzz of power echoing up his aching body to follow the wrap of his new tattoos.

He ran his hand over his shoulder, feeling the charge as he rubbed his muscles. The flow of energy twisted around his fingertips, hand tense to contain the power as he brought it in front of him.

Yondé watched from the rounded archway framing the darkened ruins. Bastian suspected it led to a much larger complex, but the guardian hadn't allowed him anywhere near it yet.

The power flickered in Bastian's distraction, threatening to rush back into the place of origin amid his essence.

Bastian took a steady inhale, focusing on the constant hum of his ká to give the power substance. A white shimmer of motes and mist collected in his palm, his arm taut as if it weighed like stone.

Closing his hand abruptly on the mass, it thrust out both ends of his fist in a flash of brilliant light. The tints of white and blue formed a rod parallel to the ground. The tattoos illuminated, linking their power with the spear as Bastian thunked its base on the stone at his feet.

Turning to the monolith, he drew the weapon made from his power above his shoulder and took aim. With a heave, the spear propelled forward like a diving hawk in a great arc across the altar circle. The sharpened end collided with the ground in front of Yondé with a reverberating chime and puff of dust. The spear pulsed, motes coursing up its shaft as Yondé eyed it.

"Satisfied?" Bastian wiped the sweat from his eyes.

Yondé huffed, then rose from their resting place.

Yes. The bear turned, lumbering into the ruins behind him.

Bastian narrowed his eyes, watching Yondé fade into the shadows. As the old Rahn'ka spirit passed through the archway within, the motes of the sanctum followed like interested fireflies, weaving up to illuminate the runes carved within the stone hallway. Creeping ivy quivered, anxiously responding to the power Yondé brought.

Bastian sighed and followed. The spear buzzed as he closed his hand around the shaft. With a yank, he drew it from the stone.

Clenching his fist, the power loosened, dissolving into strands that trailed back into his palm. His back and shoulders burned as the tattoos darkened into the blue markings Yondé had helped him create.

"Am I supposed to follow you?" Bastian wasn't surprised when he received no answer. He couldn't assume Yondé would become less mysterious in only a few days. Bastian was thrilled he'd been able to accomplish what he had in such little time.

His tricks might be limited to the barrier that allowed him to remain sane and creating a weapon, but it seemed remarkable for someone with no previous experience in the Art.

If what Yondé had implied about Shades was true, Bastian didn't have time to take it slow.

Gritting his teeth, he crossed into the foyer of what might have once been a mighty building. The crumbled ceiling had fallen along the ground, dust and vines covering the debris. Tall trees above now protected it from the elements.

Pressure against the barrier Bastian now permanently kept in place increased, insistent to be heard. He opened the smallest of holes to allow the ká of the stone and foliage around him in. He didn't speak their language but understood what they expressed as he stepped through the second archway.

Fear.

Yondé was nowhere in sight within the domed atrium. It was as large as the training yards he'd been subjected to early in his enlistment. The carved stone floor led to steps, all dropping into an oval dirt arena at the center.

Bastian squinted to see the far end of the atrium, shrouded in darkness as the motes redirected back without journeying into it. His stomach twisted and his instincts as a soldier took hold. He froze to focus on the energy still stored within his muscles. His chest tensed, the runes rippling as a brush of power eked through them.

"Yondé?" Bastian kept his eyes on the shadows.

Something moved within them, slithering along the ground at the sound of his voice.

It's time. Yondé's voice echoed from somewhere Bastian couldn't see.

He couldn't look away as a shape formed within the shadows. Black rippled together into a mass, roiling like the waves of an upside-down whirlpool.

"Time?" Bastian tried to control the tone of his voice.

Your first test, Rahn'ka.

The swirl of tendrils fanned out, revealing a man. A cloak over his shoulders, a hood framing a grizzled, pale face. His greying red beard grew untamed, hair messily pulled back as he pushed the hood from his head. One stone-grey iris, the other a milky white. A ragged scar crossed the damaged eye, disfiguring his face down to his neck.

The Shade clenched his jaw, a hand emerging to unfasten the buttons holding his cloak in place. It dropped to the darkness with a ripple of power, flecks of something ash-like dancing into the air.

Somewhere within the voices, beyond Bastian's barrier, something wailed in agony.

Yondé's voice vibrated around Bastian. *Destroy him.*

Chapter 15

THE GRYGURR'S WEIGHT COLLAPSED ONTO Rae's legs, his blood pouring down the arrow shaft protruding from his skull and covering her leather breeches.

Her side scorched, her mind spinning as she wriggled out from under her attacker and away from the stream. Gasping for breath, fear clutched her chest.

Looking down the length of her body, she swallowed. Three gashes, like those on Syga's rump, stretched across the right side of her waist and lower ribs. Blood oozed from the open wounds. Burning accompanied the agony, extending around her middle and up to her shoulder.

"Shit." The hot taint in her veins spread into her limbs.

Neco bounded over and sniffed her wound. She shoved him away, but he returned to lick her face.

"This isn't good, little guy." She sat up. Whistling low, she prayed Zaili would obey. It felt far longer than the few painful breaths it took for the horse to approach.

Zaili's nostrils flared, and she stomped the ground, eyeing the still form of the grygurr.

Rae's body convulsed as she stretched for the stirrup to pull herself up. Her arm dropped helplessly to the side, muscles spasming. Breathing hard, she tried with the other hand but failed again.

Syga had collapsed half a day after contracting the poison, but she was much smaller. Returning and pleading with Bastian to heal her wasn't an option. She'd never find him in time.

Groaning, Rae rolled onto her good side and then her knees. Her heart pounded in her head as she defied the pain, grasping for the stirrup again. Crying out as she pulled her body up, she kept her right hand on her side to lessen the movement of her torn skin. She stood long enough to unlatch the bag containing medical supplies before collapsing.

Neco yipped and scurried away from beneath her, returning to lick her wrist, then face.

She steered him away from the specks of blood on the ground, relieved when he lost interest in favor of chasing a dragonfly that buzzed past. Eyeing her shredded clothing, she ground her teeth and ripped her shirt farther open.

The glimpse of exposed rib bone turned her stomach, and she rolled over, heaving.

Her hands shaking, she dumped the medical pack. She didn't have a fire to cauterize her wound, so stitching would have to do. Finding a nearby village with an apothecary to counteract the grygurr's concoction was her only hope for survival.

Threading the needle proved more difficult than she expected, unable to stop her trembling hands. By the time she had it ready, her entire body shivered. Even with the warm spring, she couldn't stop the cold growing within her.

Using a clean cloth, she wiped the wound as best as she could before her vision blurred.

"This won't be fun." Sucking in a breath through clenched teeth, Rae pierced her torn skin with the needle. She cried out with each stitch, fighting to keep conscious.

Neco nipped her wrist as she pushed the needle in. He growled, dancing around on the ground near her left hip. He resolved himself to curl into a ball, his amber eyes watching her, chin on his paws.

Tugging the gaping flesh closed, dizziness slowed her progress. As she finished the first and started the middle gash, her skin chilled and numbed.

After sewing each tear into a tight line, sweat coated her body.

Rae laid back on the warm ground and tried to control her shaking. The cloudless sky spun around her and as the adrenaline faded, so did her consciousness.

Rae stirred with a drunken sluggishness. She blinked, trying to clear her vision while Neco barked insistently. Two blue orbs had taken the sky's place. She blinked again, wincing as the pain of her side returned to the front of her mind, and moaned.

The orbs drifted farther away when she opened her eyes again. But they were not orbs at all. Eyes. Surrounded by tufts of white fur and pointed ears.

The grygurr shaman studied her from above, leaning heavily on the carved quarterstaff decorated with bone beads and feathers.

Rae's heart stopped before a sense of relief washed over her.

Put me out of my misery.

The curtain of beaded necklaces around his neck jangled as he righted himself from leaning over her, then dropped to a knee beside her.

Neco splashed in the stream, barking and growling at the shaman, but kept his distance.

What is he doing?

The shaman's throat rumbled, like a feline purr, and he pulled a vial filled with black liquid from his side satchel. He held it out to her, and she furrowed her brow.

"What is it?" Her voice shook. Propping herself up on her left elbow, she glanced at the dead grygurr and back to the shaman.

He stretched one of his long, gnarled fingers to her injured side and gently poked it, causing her to flinch more in surprise than pain.

She looked where he touched, grimacing at the black veins creeping over her midsection.

"Feh poi...zon." The shaman chuffed. "Curr."

Rae narrowed her eyes at him and then the vial.

Cure the poison? What do I have to lose?

The shaman plucked out the vial's cork before offering the potion.

She took it, lifting it to her lips, but he caught her wrist with a steel grip.

The grygurr guided her hand towards her wounds, pouring some liquid onto the stitches. The fire it caused within made her gasp and curl forward.

He urged the vial towards her mouth quickly after, and she drank it without hesitation. It tasted of cloves and bitterroot and stuck to her tongue, but she swallowed it all.

"Why are you helping me?"

"Go. No retern hare. Grygurr laand"

Rae saw her opportunity. "What is Rahn'ka?"

The shaman rocked back on his cat-like legs. Everything jangled with the movement. He quirked his head to the side and gestured a big hand in her direction. "Enmee. Enmee te auer. Damgger te auer."

His answer made sense, considering her last interaction with Bastian, but she'd hoped for new information.

Rae looked around, lifting a hand to shield her face from the sun.

Rocky crags and crevices provided ample hiding places, though not many large enough for a horse. All the same, Zaili was nowhere in sight, and she groaned again. Hopefully, the horse hadn't fled too far.

The shaman rose and, without warning, gripped her upper arms, hauling her to her feet.

Holding in a cry of pain, Rae kept her feet beneath her when he let go. The world spun as she glared at the ground.

Hold still, damn it.

In the corner of her vision, she watched the shaman.

He returned to his dead pack member, lifting the large body with little effort. Slinging the hunter over his shoulder, the shaman braced his steps with his staff. He waded through the stream, turning when he reached the other side to give Rae a final glance. Before she could ask another question, his dappled back disappeared in the forest's foliage.

Neco wasted no time in scurrying to her ankles, still barking.

"It's all right, Neco." She stooped to scratch his ears. The pain it sent through her side compelled her to abandon the effort, rising with a hiss.

Rae stared at the tree line where the grygurr had vanished, the burn of the poison subsiding. Looking down at her middle, she traced her finger where the black in her veins had been, and her throat tightened.

Swallowing, she whistled for Zaili. She waited for longer than the previous time, but the clomp of hooves echoed on the rocks as the horse tentatively returned.

Rae grabbed Zaili's saddle, thankful to have the support, and whispered comforting phrases to the horse.

Her side screamed as she mounted, and she had to adjust the angle multiple times before pulling herself into the saddle. Unable to lift Neco, she let the wolf follow on his own as they walked west towards Delkest.

Leaving the grygurr pack's territory was her priority, even if it meant giving up her chance to turn Bastian over to Helgathian authorities.

Chapter 16

WHAT ARE YOU WAITING FOR? Destroy him!

"You can't be serious." Bastian groaned. Staring at the Shade, his heart leapt into his throat.

All the horrible stories his father told him as a child resurfaced, eliciting an icy shiver down his spine. It didn't help his fear when everything around him also screamed in terror.

Black tendrils stretched from the Shade, snaking across the floor towards Bastian's ankles. The man hissed, his hand flexing at his side.

As the darkness advanced, the glimmering motes fled, taking Bastian's light source with them. The room fell to shadow, forcing him to strain to listen for movement.

Something wound up his right leg and yanked him to the ground with a huff. The force tightened, dragging him toward the deeper darkness where the Shade had stood.

Bastian threw himself to the side, clawing at the dirt, hoping his fingers would find something to grip. He willed his mind to focus on the ká around him, so he could envision the area by a different means. But nothing around him lived to produce the energy necessary.

His hand caught the sharp edge of a broken stone, and he tightened his hold to stop sliding along the floor. Fighting against the tendril's pull, he curled his body to build the tension in his muscles. His ká pulsed with building energy.

The power coursed from Bastian's legs to his arm. He slammed his palm to the dirt, focusing his will, and a ripple of light responded. It spread like waves in a pond, leaving a glow of pale light in its wake.

The light expanded, revealing the advancing Shade to his left. As he stepped, shadow plumed out from under his boots, collecting behind him in a mass of black. Both hands lifted from his sides, the dark mists following suit.

With a grunt, the Shade swung his arms forward, hands colliding together. As he did, a tidal wave of cold hit Bastian, the shadow momentarily enveloping him as it sent him flying back.

He collided with the distant wall, muscles aching as he struggled to get his feet beneath him.

As the shadow dissipated, remnants of the light he'd created shone again, creating a silhouette of the unmoving Shade. His tendrils lashed towards Bastian, giving him no time to gain his balance.

The Shade took another step, his onyx vines looping around Bastian's forearms. They pinned him to the rough wall, exposing his chest. Where the blackness touched, his skin scorched.

A cry escaped his mouth.

Bastian tried to clear his mind, but the looming approach of the Shade made everything in him numb. Forcing a deep breath, he closed his eyes to focus on the pain rather than what he saw. He struggled to free his right arm, but the tendrils held fast. He breathed hard as his muscles quaked, the pulse of his ká responding to the power.

Breath stopped with a vice grip around Bastian's throat.

He opened his eyes, finding one grey and one white eye piercing into his soul.

The Shade squeezed, nails biting into Bastian's skin as the tendrils snaked farther up his arms to his shoulders. More crept forward, wrapping around his ankles and lifting him from the ground.

Bastian's back scraped across the stone. He gathered the pain in his mind as he pooled all the power he could. Clenching his left fist, he rushed energy through his arm, focused into the inked symbols of his tattoo and the blood in his veins.

With a reverberation passing through his body, the shadow pinning his arm recoiled. A thin layer of shimmering white replaced it as Bastian expanded his ká. He collected all the physical strength he could into throwing a punch at the Shade, his fist catching the man square on his scarred jaw.

The Shade released Bastian's throat and sidestepped, hand rising to brush the blood from his lip.

Bastian took the moment to breathe and expand the rest of his soul. Expelling the shadows from where they held him, he fell to a knee and summoned what little he could borrow from the willing stone under his hands.

The Shade vanished into shadow, wafting to the floor in a billow of smoke. A rattling hiss resounded from the spot, and the heap of darkness unwound like a rope. Smooth black scales glinted with silver as a snake as thick as Bastian's neck rose before him.

"What in the hells."

Its mouth gaped, fangs reflecting the dim light of the room, and struck at him.

Bastian rolled to the side, finding his feet. Narrowly avoiding the lash of the serpent, his hand tensed to gather the energy stored in the marks on his arm.

In a flash of light, the spear erupted within his grip.

He stood, keeping the point of the spear aimed forward. The runes on its shaft radiated a new aura of light that allowed him to see the dead white eye, still scarred in serpent form.

"Good to know not all the stories are exaggerations. But you couldn't think of something more original?"

The snake coiled, shadow falling away from its head as the Shade returned to his humanoid form. A smirk graced his marred features, and he tilted his head. "More original? When you find yourself moments from death, you'll find my lack of originality the least of your worries." His voice sounded human enough but laced with the hint of a hiss.

"You know, like a crocodile or something. Or, oh! How about a badger?" Bastian stepped to the side, away from the wall and back down the steps towards the arena. He kept the spear pointed at the Shade, shaft braced against his forearm.

The Shade rolled his eyes. "You're stalling. Why not accept your fate like a good boy?" He advanced again. Tendrils whipped around Bastian's spear before he could react and turned it to the side.

Bastian didn't waste time trying to pull the spear back. He stepped into the charging Shade and brought his leg up to connect with his gut. Following the inertia of the spear, he thrust the tip into the dirt. Braced on the spear with both hands, he swung his full body weight around to kick the Shade.

An iron grip clamped on his ankle, interrupting his rotation and throwing him to the ground.

The Shade laughed as Bastian landed on his chest, sending shadowed tentacles over him once more. They whipped him around onto his back, and he attempted to roll towards his weapon.

The Shade tutted while standing over him, pressing a boot onto Bastian's reaching hand.

Bastian grunted as the tread of the Shade's boot bit into his hand. Fear rumbled through him, his mind concluding the only two ways this could end.

Either he had to kill the Shade, or the Shade would kill him.

He'd naively hoped Yondé was merely playing with him, and another solution existed.

The skin where the tendrils had touched felt as if it melted, deep grooves of torn flesh led to thick, hot trails of blood seeping down his arm.

He hadn't wanted to try again what he'd done to the Reaper to save Rae. He'd been afraid of it since his studies had revealed the depth of the damage he'd caused. He didn't understand what happened to the ká he removed from a physical body, which made him hesitate. But Yondé left him little choice.

Bastian pushed his head back into the dirt, looking up at the pleased smile of the Shade. He glared and found the one remaining voice within the arena besides his own and pulled.

The Shade's skin became ashen, and he choked on a breath as his footing faltered. The Shade's ká glimmered as it responded to Bastian's call, tearing it from the flesh it inhabited.

When the Shade didn't fall dead, Bastian hesitated. The shadows released him, and he sat up, reaching for the spear. His muscles strained as he pulled harder, grasping at the white-blue aura emerging from the man.

Bastian stood, leaning on the shaft of his spear as he looked, bewildered, at the stumbling Shade. The essence hovered between them, attempting to mingle with the energies gathered in front of his weapon, but it was trapped in a tug-of-war between Bastian and something he couldn't make out.

An anchor.

It trapped the Shade's ká in a horrible limbo between death and life. The bond prohibiting his death bubbled like a pustule, but its root reached into the fabric of the world itself.

Bastian shook his head, thudding the bottom of his spear as he released the energy. The ká snapped back into the Shade, throwing him onto the ground.

Bastian drew up his spear and stepped forward. His right eye stung, and he closed it to keep out the blood flowing from the wound on his head.

The Shade gasped for air, rolling onto his side as he coughed. He lifted a hand towards Bastian, palm out. "End it." He wheezed, grasping at his chest. "Don't put me back again. It's been enough years. Kill me or let me go. I'll abandon my master, I swear."

Years?

Bastian hesitated, narrowing his eyes. He lowered the spear, heaving a breath. "I won't kill you. Not if you surrender and do as you swear."

"You have my word." The Shade coughed again.

Kill him. Motes swirled from the ground to create Yondé's physical form beside Bastian. They turned their head towards him, lips parted in a snarl. *He deserves no mercy.*

"What?" Bastian turned towards the guardian spirit. "No. I won't. Not after he's surrendered. Honor—"

These creatures know nothing of honor. Justice must be dealt.

"It has. Mercy means more than vengeance." Bastian glanced at the Shade, who eyed him.

"Who are you..." The Shade's heels dug into the ground to move farther from Bastian.

Very well. If you lack the conviction... Yondé turned towards the Shade.

Before Bastian could reach out to touch the spirit, power pulsed through the ground. It coalesced beneath the Shade, gathering the minerals in the soil deep below. A spike of iron surrounded by white motes jolted from the ground, skewering the Shade's chest.

The Shade's eyes widened before his body fell limp against the blood-splattered stone.

"Nymaera's breath, Yondé!" Bastian gasped, shaking his head. Anger overtook him as he spun to the bear. He released his spear, and it disappeared with a flicker.

His death does little to pay for Ailiena's. Yondé spun and walked towards the doorway. *You should care for your injuries. You bleed.*

Bastian wiped his brow, drawing away his hand to see the blood. His right arm was a mangled mess, the skin torn with rotted, grey edges. The sight made his stomach clench, and he swallowed the rise of bile.

He needed to get out of the arena, away from all the death, to have any chance of healing himself with the power the Rahn'ka sanctum offered. Something told him it needed to happen soon, or the scarring would be worse.

Glaring at Yondé's haunches as they wove around a corner of the ruin, he growled a curse under his breath.

He chased after Yondé. Answers needed to come first. "He swore he'd abandon his master, which you also need to elaborate on... but you still killed him. His soul could've been redeemed."

Impossible. Yondé stepped to a welling fountain cut into the mountain's internal wall. The elegant three-tiered creation emptied into a shallow pool with a rim high enough to sit on. *Sit.*

Bastian obeyed.

Yondé crossed towards the water, sitting back to dip a paw in. As their claws touched the water's surface, energy passed up the bear's arm. The mist composing Yondé shifted, condensing into new shapes.

As their hand drew from the water, it changed to a human hand with thick fingers. The fur curled in on itself to form the flowing fabrics of a sleeveless robe, open at the chest to reveal a set of beads, like those the grygurr wore, against a dark bare chest. Yondé's deep blue skin matched the shade the bear's nose had been, their masculine arms uncovered.

They sat, a pair of white pants loose around their giant frame. Their eyes glowed the same as they always had, but now with a human face. A beard covered their wide jaw. Almost black hair, braided close to their skull, fell in long strands, beads and feathers nestled among the ends.

They still glowed with the energies of the ká that formed them.

"So you do have a human form."

Yondé, sitting, was taller than Bastian would have been standing. They smiled, their teeth still shaped like a bear's. *I do. And I understand your desire for answers, but you must heal first.* Their hand closed around Bastian's left arm, and he winced as the heat of the spirit's ká touched his injuries.

Bastian lifted his hand to push Yondé's away. His hand closed around their wrist. "Who was that Shade?"

Yondé tightened their hold to resist Bastian's push, causing him to gasp.

The pain turned into a strange tickling sensation, numbing his arm to his shoulder. He had to look to confirm Yondé's hand was still there.

Swirls of misty power sank into his torn flesh, tugging it back together in a sickening display that forced Bastian to close his eyes, glad he couldn't feel it happening.

When he looked again, Yondé sat before him, hands patiently in their lap.

Bastian eyed his arm, touching where the wounds had been carved into his skin. They were gone, leaving behind scars that wove around his right wrist, like vines around a tree.

"He was one of those I hold accountable for Ailiena's death." For the first time, their voice came through Bastian's ears rather than his mind.

"He killed the previous Rahn'ka?"

Yondé shrugged. "He is guilty in her death."

"So he deserved to die like that?" Bastian frowned.

Yondé returned the disapproving look. "You're unwise if you think it should have ended any other way. That creature would have killed you without a second thought. Yet you feel pity for him. Mercy."

"Yes. I do. There's always a chance for someone to change. People make mistakes, and that doesn't mean they won't learn to walk a different path. I refuse to believe that any human is beyond redemption."

"A noble thought. It'll likely get you killed."

"I'm just as likely to be killed if you keep pitting me against things I haven't learned about yet," Bastian grumbled. "I almost killed him. I think. That was his soul I was drawing out of him, wasn't it?"

"His ká, yes. Humans simplify it by calling it a soul, but if you'd rather consider it like that, you may."

"Even Shades have souls?"

"Yes, they are human. But everything has a ká. Even the stone at our feet has it if you know how to sense it. The ká of a living creature is more complex, it has more strands that make it up. Pathways for thought and the Art to flow."

"And Rahn'ka are what? Soul Artisans?"

Yondé grunted, shaking their head in a bear-like gesture that made the beads on their neck tremble. "An oversimplification, but yes. Rahn'ka may interact with all ká, whether it's a living creature or a blade of grass. You have the power to strip a thing of what makes it a part of the fabric of Pantracia. You may send it onto Nymaera's bosom, where she decides if and when it will return to life."

"That paints a bit of a different picture than what the temples preach." Bastian couldn't hide his skepticism. "Only sentient beings may journey to the Afterlife, and that's where they stay. Forever reliving either the good or the evil they've committed. That's not what happens?"

Yondé gave a wry smile, their deep blue eyes hardening. "Human falsities. But hardly your concern. You ask the wrong questions. It matters not what happens to the ká *you* send on."

"You mean something different happens to it if something else kills the vessel for the ká?"

"Open up your mind, Rahn'ka. Ask the proper questions."

Bastian sighed, rubbing his forehead. His fingers came away bloody, despite being healed, and it drew his attention towards his new scars. He eyed what the Shade's tendrils had done, considering the destruction of the natural life clinging to the walls in the arena. He hadn't been able to sense any pieces of their ká, though something should have remained behind for a time, even in death. A sliver of ká always lingered.

"Shades. Their Art drains ká, as well, doesn't it?" Yondé's mouth opened, but Bastian continued before the bear spirit could answer. "But it drains every drop of the ká surrounding them, leaving the practitioner's whole."

"And severs the tethers that guide a ká to Nymaera. Instead, they're drawn to a different hell, becoming twisted abominations previously unknown to Pantracia."

"Corrupted." Bastian found another name from his father's stories. "You're talking about Corrupted. The things summoners call to service."

Yondé looked surprised, narrowing their eyes. "I'm unfamiliar with the human's term for them, and nothing of these summoners..."

"It's a forbidden form of Art." Bastian's mind rushed to get the words out as he comprehended his discovery. "At least, it was. Rumor is that Helgath is dabbling in it. I guarded the training academies in Rylorn when I first joined Helgath's military. The sounds that came out of those towers at night made my skin crawl."

"Amalgamations made possible by the dark power Shades harness. The power comes from something beyond mortal man."

"I thought you said Shades are human."

"They are, but their master... is something else. It is your true threat, which is why you must never allow a Shade to live. If they discover what you are, they'll report back to the one they serve, and then you'll be hunted as Ailiena was. She showed mercy, like you, and it led to her death."

So even with all this power, the Rahn'ka can die.

A shiver ran up Bastian's spine. If the servants were as powerful as Yondé made them out to be, he never wanted to face their master. "So, what? I'm supposed to avoid them?"

"Isn't that what you planned to do regarding your human troubles as well? Avoid them?"

Bastian sighed, scratching the growth of his beard on his chin. "I was hoping they'd forget about me after a few years."

"Shades won't. Uriel, their master, is patient. It has existed for millennia. It was once the burden of our people to conceal its prison, but that time has long passed."

"Wait." Bastian's head shot up. "Prison? It can be contained? How?"

"That's not my knowledge to guard." Yondé shrugged. "It's far better to end an existence with death, is it not? I maintained that Shade here as a tool, and he served his purpose."

"So you killed him. Because his purpose was over, even though he swore he'd abandon his master."

"Shades can't forgo their service. It's etched into their souls. It binds them to their master, which is why you couldn't tear his ká from his body. The root leads back to Uriel, bound by their pledge to serve it. Even a Rahn'ka cannot sever the connection. It always remains like a rotting wound."

"If I can't kill a Shade with my Art, how do I do it?"

Yondé's lips spread into a fanged grin. "Why do you think I taught you how to summon a spear?"

Chapter 17

THE CLOAK DRAPED OVER RAE'S shoulders provided enough warmth during the day, but she shivered at night as she pressed west towards Delkest.

Neco trotted beside her and when dawn emerged, he joined her for a nap in the sun.

The young wolf woke her from her restless sleep with a wet nose, and her stomach grumbled.

"You need to learn to hunt." She pushed his muzzle away from her face while he licked her fingers.

Pulling out her map, she checked her location, and what western travel held for her. Her fingertip traced over the words *Eshlea Chasm*, and she smiled.

When she was a child, her father used to bring her there once a year to see the nearby lake's natural phenomenon. It happened near the start of every autumn, a brilliant show of light only known by her family.

Unbidden, her eyes trailed further west and looked at the name of her hometown.

Ashdale.

Rae swallowed, working her jaw. "We won't go that far west." She glanced at Neco, who yipped in agreement. "But spending the summer at a lake sounds pretty good, doesn't it? At least until I get Din back and can tell Jarrod I'm coming home."

She yearned to return to the Ashen Hawks, but the idea of riding back through grygurr territory tied her stomach in knots. If she wanted to return, she'd have to take the longer route through southern Olsa or take a ship.

But not from Ashdale.

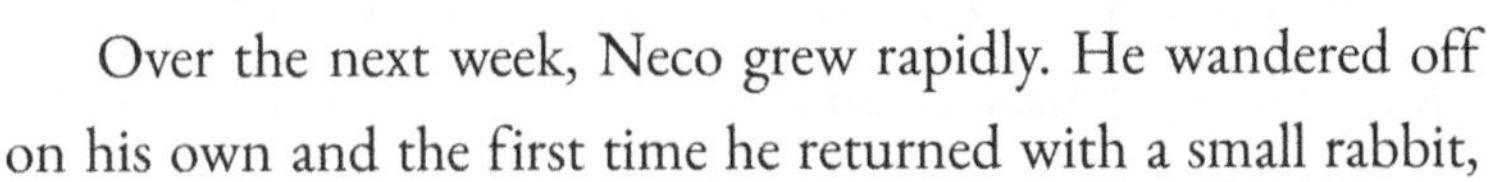

Over the next week, Neco grew rapidly. He wandered off on his own and the first time he returned with a small rabbit, she hugged him.

Her food stores dwindled dangerously low. Foraging with a side wound proved exhausting. She couldn't crouch easily, or climb trees, none of her usual methods for survival possible. Even her bow became obsolete in the treacherous mountain terrain. She couldn't risk using it with her balance compromised, so she stuck to root vegetables and ripe spring fruit.

Rae meticulously cared for her injury. The redness reduced only minimally, but the black in her veins had vanished and not returned. It'd heal, but jagged scars would undoubtedly remain. The injury hadn't marred her tribute to her siblings on her opposite side, giving her something to be grateful for.

The snow melted in the heat of summer, and they camped at the midpoint of the narrow mountain pass for several days while Rae harvested a plentiful patch of root vegetables, refreshing her depleted stores.

The subsequent venture down the other side of the mountain went quicker, with her side partially healed and the weather growing warmer.

Descending into the Delkest valley, game became plentiful and Neco doubled in size. He no longer looked like the half-starved pup he'd been when she found him. And judging by the size of his paws, he wasn't done growing.

As the second largest species of wolves, valley wolves were native to Olsa, and Rae suspected Neco to be one. The country's most vicious predator, beside grygurr, the creatures grew up to four feet tall at the shoulder. Locals told legends about how the valley wolves descended from a line of wild dire wolves, which grew twice as large and were famous for their role in Feyorian military tactics.

Rae couldn't take Zaili at anything but a walk, still healing, and Neco trotted next to them. He often veered off the uneven path to pursue squirrels and rabbits, vanishing for half the day. But he always found Rae when she stopped in the evenings, sneaking into camp to cuddle for the night.

When her eyes settled on the nostalgic lake, Rae breathed a sigh and brought Zaili to a stop. She picked a curve of oak trees facing the water to build a fire pit next to.

Satisfied the second batch of raven feathers she'd collected would be enough, Rae sat by the fire assembling arrows to fill her quiver from supplies she purchased in Eshlea's Chasm.

Neco laid on the opposite side, crunching on an antler he'd found.

The routine of attaching the iron arrowheads and trimming the fletching made her eyelids heavy. She slept only when necessary to keep her energy but even then, it was rarely peaceful.

Ever since the fire in Ashdale, she'd suffered from night terrors after traumatic events.

Bastian's attack, followed by the grygurr's, left her mind in a shattered state after having hardly recovered from the Reaper encounter. The cruel dreams often lasted for weeks, but even the foreknowledge of them didn't diminish their effect. Anxiety surged deep in her veins, and she dreaded each night for what awaited her after she closed her eyes.

Rae struggled through completing another dozen arrows before she admitted she'd have to sleep. Curling up on her bedroll, the dreams came fast.

Bright yellow eyes invaded her mind, and her side screamed in agony.

The huffed breath of a racing horse echoed around her, followed by a shrill whinny. Syga stood before her, an arrow jutting out of his forehead. His eyes were black, blood running from his wound and nostrils.

Her throat seized, and she grasped at an invisible force restricting her breath. Rising off her feet, her body rotated until she could see Bastian standing twenty paces away, his hands flexing. His eyes glimmered yellow, like the grygurr's.

It's a dream. It's only a dream.

Rae braced herself for the inevitable conclusion of the nightmares featuring Bastian.

His fingers twitched, and her neck snapped.

Gasping, Rae sat straight up, hands flying to her throat. Her heart pounded in her ears, the swelling darkness around her suffocating her sanity.

Neco whimpered and nosed her elbow.

She reached for him, pulling the wolf close and silently repeating the mantra.

Just a dream.

As she laid back down, Neco curled up and pressed his warm fur against her. He rested his head on her shoulder, and she stroked him until a feeling of calm reclaimed her.

Staring at the night sky, Rae wished for dawn. With no hope for more sleep, she tried to push the image of Bastian away, burying him with the yellow gaze of the grygurr. Her eyes burned as she shut them.

Three months later...

Autumn, 2609 R.T.

Rae threw a stone into the lake and watched the mirror surface break into ripples.

Summer came and went, and the green leaves brightened into oranges and reds of Valaran, the god of autumn.

The first time her father brought her to the lake, she'd been nine years old. The ride on horseback took two weeks, a daunting journey for a child. Her younger siblings stayed home with their mother, giving Rae time alone with her father. They spent weeks basking in the location's tranquility, waiting for the most glorious event her young eyes had ever seen.

"Should only be another night or two. But let's go look in the morning." Her father, Zeran, poked the fire with a stick. A log fell, dusting the smoke with embers. His topaz eyes shone in the firelight, with pupils smaller than a human's.

"How do you know when it will happen?" The warmth of the fire made Rae want to rub her cheeks. The autumn air came at night, balmy summer heat prevailing during the day.

"I don't want to spoil the surprise for you." He smiled.

"Do you know this place because you're auer? How come no one else is here if it's so amazing?" She hoped it didn't sound like a complaint. The hard dirt hadn't been the most comfortable place to sleep, and she missed her bed.

"We auer are more sensitive to the energies of the world, so yes, I suppose you could say I know because of our heritage." Zeran shrugged. "My father used to bring me here. Just like you will someday bring your children. This is our family's secret."

"I can't tell anyone but my children?" Rae tilted her head and eyed her father.

"Well, I told your mother, so perhaps you can tell your husband when you have one." Zeran gave her side a little pinch.

Rae made a face. "I don't want a husband. Someone telling me what to do. Sounds... tetous."

"*Tedious.*"

Rae stuck her tongue out at him, making him laugh. It was a rich, wonderful sound.

"The right man won't tell you what to do. He'll be your partner. One day you might change your mind."

"And if I don't?" Rae couldn't comprehend wanting to ask anyone's permission for anything.

Her mother constantly argued with her father, and he let her berate him usually without fighting back. Whenever Rae thought of marriage, all she could hear in her ears was yelling.

That life wasn't for her.

"There's no rule either way. But I rather cherish the idea of no man being good enough for my little girl." He pulled her shoulder in and kissed the top of her head.

She giggled and leaned into him, breathing in his earthy scent tinged with smoke.

Neco licked Rae's face, interrupting her reverie before the memory of smoke brought her mind some place darker.

Her fingers ruffled the dark fur near his ears, clenching the roots as he licked her again. She felt safer with him by her side as a formidable ally. Almost fully grown in height, his lanky form had some filling out to do. Though, as she laughed and pushed his wet nose away, he could've been mistaken for a harmless beast.

Desire to see the lake's event kept her there for months despite the possible danger of staying in one place. The display of color, undetectable to those unaware of its presence, would be worth it.

Rising from the ground, Rae looked up at the sky as a hawk called out overhead. It soared past, leaving her shoulders to slump as she thought of Din's prolonged absence.

She missed Jarrod and other members of the guild. The Hawks were her family. Brothers and sisters bonded by ink rather than blood. She remembered the steady poke of the needle as they tattooed her back. Some members had a sword instead of the arrow, sometimes an axe, a key, or daggers. A curved feather always surrounded a thief's chosen proficiency.

Some nights, as she snuggled her wolf, she could almost smell Bastian next to her. Each time his face surfaced in her mind, anger quickly followed. Sometimes fear. Her nightmares had reduced in frequency but still plagued her sleep, reminding her that Bastian wasn't her ally.

"Go get dinner, would you?" Rae playfully shoved Neco off, and he barked.

The black wolf loped past Zaili, disappearing into the trees surrounding the lake.

Rae sighed, admiring the surface of the lake reflecting the sky like glass. She threw another pebble.

A twig snapped behind her.

"That was fast—" Rae turned around. Her eyes met Bastian's, and she froze, momentarily wondering if she'd fallen asleep.

He stopped and stared.

Rae leapt to her feet, backing up and whistling for Zaili, who trotted over. Without looking away from Bastian, she unlatched her bow.

Bastian advanced from the tree line, his feet bare. He wore the same old breeches, but they were battered beyond repair. A loose, pale-blue shirt hung from his shoulders, tucked haphazardly into his breeches, the neckline open. A hint of new, dark blue ink poked out from under the fabric on his left collarbone. He carried nothing else. His unkempt hair grew long and wild, but his face was roughly shaven.

"Rae." Bastian breathed her name as she withdrew an arrow with shaking hands. He sounded exhausted and lifted his hands into the air. "Please, don't shoot. Even though—"

Lifting the bow, she nocked the arrow, drew it back, and set it free.

Bastian jumped to the side, lowering his arms to brace himself against the tree he slammed into. "Gods, Rae. Let me explain!"

"I'd like to hear you try." She nocked another arrow, side-stepping from Zaili as she put Bastian back in her sights.

He took a step away from the tree, holding his palms up and exposed. His lips drew together in a line. "It wasn't me. The power, the Rahn'ka Art took over and controlled me. Yondé attacked you, not me."

"Liar," Rae hissed and loosed her arrow again.

Bastian ducked, and it whizzed over him where his head had been.

She nocked another.

"Will you please stop shooting at me?" Bastian's voice rose. "Come on, you know I'd never hurt you. Not after what we've been through together."

Rae's hands shook, and her eyes burned. Most of his crimes against her had occurred in her dreams. Her mind showed her the image again of him ending her life, and her resolve hardened. Keeping her bow raised, she held the arrow ready. "Why are you here? How did you find me?"

"Rae..." His tone softened. "I've learned a lot in the last four months. I'm familiar with your ká, so I can track you fairly easily, it's just..." He stopped talking and shook his head. "It was necessary for me to stay, but Yondé shouldn't have attacked you. The guardians are bullheaded and not the biggest fan of auer."

Remembering her run from Bastian only brought her back to the moment the grygurr split her side open. "It's your fault!" The trembling in her hands grew too much, and she lowered her bow. The grygurr's growl vibrated in her head, and she shook it, grasping her scarred side. "I almost died because of you."

Bastian's hands tensed, twitching, as he lowered them to his sides.

Rae's heart thudded at the action, too much like how he killed her in her dreams. She whipped her bow back up and let her third arrow fly, but it sank into the ground at his feet. "Don't!"

A snarl followed her shout, and Neco barreled out of the trees behind her. The large wolf raced to stand in front of Rae, teeth bared and hackles raised.

Bastian's eyes widened, thrusting a hand out as if to ward Neco off with it. "Whoa, boy. You got big, didn't you? I won't hurt her."

She touched the wolf's back, crouching and grabbing a handful of his ruff as he kept growling. Closing her eyes, she gritted her teeth. Bastian's words didn't match the nightmares, and she struggled to find the truth.

After a few breaths, Neco fell silent and licked her face, prompting her eyes to open. The wolf whimpered, and she looked back at Bastian.

He still stood in the same spot, unmoving. He chewed on his bottom lip, scratching the back of his head. "Are you done shooting at me?" He dared a step forward. "What happened? I know it's my fault, but tell me."

Rae furrowed her brow and glared at him. Rising to her feet, she left her bow on the ground. "Syga's dead. And I nearly joined him."

"What?" Bastian gaped. "How..." His voice quieted as his shoulders sagged, and his persistent gaze lowered.

Still holding Neco's ruff, Rae swallowed. "The grygurr hunter found me." Her fear ebbed away, but her blood flowed hot.

Bastian remained silent, and she wondered if he'd heard her. He took another step forward before he spoke. "Gods, I shouldn't have been so naive to think you'd be able to walk out of their territory without me. Dice. I'm so sorry. You have every right to put an arrow in me."

"If I wanted to put an arrow in you, I would have." Rae eyed the arrow jutting out of the ground at Bastian's feet. She touched her side again. "You could've healed Syga, but all I could do was end his suffering. You could've healed *me*..." Her voice trailed off, and she cringed, looking at the lake.

I came here for peace, but where is it?

Bastian stepped loudly across the forest floor. He touched the top of her arm, his hand warmer than she expected, but she flinched away. "There aren't enough words to express how sorry I am. How much I wish I had been there. I'm sorry for all of it. For the grygurr. For Yondé's actions. For all the secrets."

Rae let go of Neco's ruff and encouraged the wolf away.

Neco licked her hand and trotted back to the tree line, content to return to his hunt.

Swallowing, she stepped back and looked at the man before her. Her eyes wandered over the exposed skin of Bastian's collar and narrowed at the dark blue ink on his skin. "And there are plenty of secrets, aren't there?" She lifted her gaze to his and tilted her head.

His hand rose, and she shirked further away. He quickly retracted his touch. "I don't want secrets between us anymore either. I finally understand what's been happening to me, and I want to tell you. Yondé be damned." He chewed his lip, his brow furrowed. "Are you afraid of me?"

"I'm..." Rae's voice trailed off, watching his hand for any sign of his power.

He turned his hands upward, offering his open palms toward her. "I'm still the same man."

"You killed me every night," she whispered. "Every nightmare ended the same. My death at your hands. Standing here, I don't want to fear you, but..."

"What can I do?" Bastian didn't reach for her again, taking a step back. "I swear by all the gods, I'll never hurt you."

"Tell me the truth." Rae eyed his newly tattooed skin. Without thinking, she reached out and touched it. "Was it you who attacked me?"

"No. It was—"

"Yondé. The one who doesn't like auer. And who is he?"

"It's complicated. But—"

"It's complicated?" Rae pulled her hand back, but Bastian caught it.

"Let me finish?" He squeezed her hand.

Rae frowned, glancing at her captured hand before nodding once.

Bastian brought up his other hand to nestle hers between his palms. "Yondé is an ancient spirit, in a way. But more complex. They're the collection of many Rahn'ka who preserved their spirits after death to become the teacher Yondé has served as for millennia. They're... a little impatient and prejudiced."

"And *they* believe I'm your enemy?"

"How do you know that?"

"The grygurr shaman told me."

Bastian searched her face as if trying to decipher more beyond her words. He held his breath as he drew her hand to his chest. "Is the shaman who I have to thank for you still being among the living?"

"He is. He gave me an antidote after I killed his pack member."

"I'm glad he found you when I couldn't be there. I'd never forgive myself if something happened to you."

"Something *did* happen. But instead of death, I have scars. What happened to you?" She nodded at the ink on his chest.

"Trust me, I have scars to show for it too. But the tattoo is a spell of sorts. It helps to keep a portion of my ká focused for a particular purpose. Yondé helped me create it with the Art I have now."

As much as his words made no sense, Rae couldn't help the hint of a smile at the corners of her mouth.

Bastian returned the smile, lifting her hand closer to his lips. "What's so funny?"

"Getting the truth from you." Her smile faded. "Why are you here?"

He narrowed his eyes but squeezed her hand. "I care about you. I never stopped thinking about you the entire time I was with Yondé."

"You care about me." Rae sighed. "Then tell me the truth."

He lowered their hands. "I am. This is the truth."

"All of it?" She stepped towards him.

He didn't back down. "There's more. It will take time to explain it all. I figured out what the voices I hear are, but it might not make any sense. The good news is I can block them out, so I don't get the headaches anymore. The only other truth that matters is how much I care for you. How much I want to be with you."

"So you want me today." Rae smirked. "What about tomorrow?"

"Of course. Always."

"You haven't exactly been consistent. You want me, you don't want me, over and over. What am I supposed to make of that?" Rae tilted her head.

"Well, it's more complicated than that."

"Everything about you is complicated, isn't it? Do you understand how confusing you are?" Her grip on him tightened, lowering their hands down.

"I don't mean to be confusing." Bastian took a step back, his eyes flickering down to their hands as she yanked hers free. "I'm bad at expressing..."

"Four months and you still haven't figured it out."

"I'm here, aren't I? I decided to come. I want you. I want this." Bastian gestured wildly between them. "I've never met a woman like you. I'm... confused, too."

"How about you come back in a few years when you've made up your mind?"

"I've made up my mind." Bastian's voice rose again. "Aren't you listening to me? I choose you. But there are extenuating circumstances."

Rae rolled her eyes. "Could you be *any* more vague?"

"It's not the easiest thing to admit out loud, all right?" Bastian paced a few steps in front of her. "Not for someone with my background."

Rae threw her hands up in the air and spun around. Snatching her bow from the ground, she stalked towards the camp she'd built. A simple ring of stones for a fire pit and a tent overhang under some trees.

"I've never been with a woman before!"

Rae halted in her tracks, slowly turning to face him. A thin braid fell beside her face.

Bastian averted his gaze, shuffling his feet in the fallen leaves.

Taking a few steps towards him, she tried to understand. "Never?"

Bastian huffed, not lifting his gaze. "Never. Hells, had never even really kissed a woman before you. Not... the way we have."

Gods, that explains so much.

Rae walked closer. "That's why? All this time, that's why you're so back and forth?"

"I kept trying to figure out how to tell you."

The other lies he kept from her paled with his admission, and she smiled despite herself. "You thought I'd care?"

A shade of pink crossed his handsome features as he continued to avoid her eyes. He looked at the lake instead. "Don't you? I mean, it's pretty embarrassing, all things considered."

Rae withheld her instinct to laugh since he'd likely take it the wrong way. She reached for his hand. "No." She smirked. "I find it rather..."

"Don't say sweet." Bastian took her hand.

Rae laughed. "I was going to say enticing."

He lifted his head. Their eyes met, and he touched her cheek, his fingers brushing down her jaw. "Will you forgive me?"

Her heart thudded in her ears with a mix of unexpected emotions. "I just might."

The smile he gave warmed his face. "That's all I could hope for. I didn't want to imagine I'd lost you."

Rae glanced at the lake, then back at him. "You had. I never thought I'd see you again. And if I did... I was certain it wouldn't be as friends." She cringed. "Sorry about the arrows."

"I deserved them." Bastian was quiet for a moment, looking at the lake as he took a step towards her. He chewed on his bottom lip, glancing behind at where she'd tied the corners of her tent to the trees. "How long have you been camped here?"

Rae paused, nerves rising in her stomach. "Three months, give or take."

Bastian sighed. "It feels like so much more time has passed, but so much less at the same time." He shook his head, strands of hair brushing his cheeks. He turned, drawing both her hands up between them. "There's so much I want to tell you. Everything that's happened."

Deciphering her thoughts on the matter would have to wait. Glancing towards the lake, Rae lifted her chin as the energy washed over her in a blanket of nostalgia.

Smiling, she shook her head at Bastian. "Can you tell me later? I came here to see this, and I'd rather not miss it."

Bastian's brows knitted together, but he turned to follow her gaze towards the lake. His breath stilled, then dropped in deeper than before. His hands warmed around hers, almost hot. "You feel that too? What is it?"

Rae gulped, her father's words reverberating in her memory. "I can't tell you. It's something that needs to be seen." Pulling away from him, she leaned forward and removed her boots. She'd done her hair in braids drawn back in a ponytail, perfect for swimming.

When she stood back up, Bastian no longer stood beside her. He walked towards the lake's shore, stopping with his toes touching the still water.

Rae grinned and ran around the shore of the lake towards an outcropping of rock that bordered it. She took familiar steps up the worn grey stone to reach the flat top curving over the water's surface. Diving off, the warm water erupted through her senses, dulling her awareness as she swam deeper.

Swimming down to the center of the lake, she entered the brilliantly lit narrow cave and her lungs burned. Her fingers brushed against the smooth stone, reflecting the glow from within. The colors grew more vibrant as she kicked and veered upwards through the submerged channel. Pushing off the cave's bottom with her bare feet, she burst into the familiar opening and sucked in a breath of humid air.

A flat sheet of rock the size of a large wagon composed the floor surrounding the open water she tread. The crystal ceiling curved upward, sparkling like gemstones. The air buzzed, a million wings beating against her soul. The water caustics reflected with life against the cavern walls, illuminated by a natural stream of the world's Art.

Rae's eyes stung, her throat tightening. It'd been too many years since she'd been here.

When the water rippled under her feet, she remembered she wasn't alone.

Bastian broke through the surface of the water, taking a quick inhale. He looked up, his eyes widening at the grandeur surrounding them. The pale light glowed on his bare, tanned skin. "I can see why you stuck around here so long." He swam around her. "Though I didn't think you'd be interested in something like this."

"Why not?" Her feet lazily moved beneath her. "Because I'm a cold, hard thief?"

He shrugged, the water sloshing against his shoulders as they briefly lifted from the water. The kaleidoscope of color accentuated his new tattoos. They ran further than she'd thought, curling from his chest up his collar to run down his left arm.

She wanted to touch them but refrained.

He swam closer to her. "Something like that. I'd expected to find a treasure stash of coins down here, rather than the Art." His foot brushed hers somewhere beneath the water.

Rae scoffed before reaching for him. She teased her hands up his neck and into his hair before shoving his head under the water. Swimming away, she reached the stone floor and pulled herself out of the water to sit on the edge.

He sputtered as his head resurfaced, but a grin lit his face.

"You have a wonderful opinion of me. You think I only value gold and jewels?"

Bastian crossed his arms on the rock edge, resting his chin on them, watching her.

Rae tried not to stare at him and his primed physical form, looking at the shimmering walls. Her soaked clothes clung to her, but the air in the cavern kept her warm.

"I do have a wonderful opinion of you. And it goes well

beyond merely what you value. There's so much more to you. And I want to learn all of it. Starting with how you know about this place?"

Rae focused on the colorful display. "Family secret. My father used to bring me here when it happens this time of year." She looked at Bastian again, feeling the weight of her father's words. "I'm breaking the rules having you here."

Bastian frowned, dropping his arms into the water. "I don't want to encroach on family traditions. I can leave if you'd rather?" He hesitated, running his fingers through his wet hair to plaster it back.

Rae smiled, goosebumps rising on her arms. "No." She shook her head. "I think he'd be relieved I'm here with anyone at all, even if you're not my—" Cringing, she cleared her throat. "Even if you're not my husband."

Bastian brought a thin wave of water with him as he lifted himself to the rock. His bare torso exposed, the tattoos weren't the only change. Thick flat scars ran down his right arm, starting at the elbow.

Water trickled through the creases of his abdominal muscles as he sat beside her, and she caught herself staring for a moment.

His eyes widened, but the smile on his face confirmed it was in teasing. "Husband? Was that the stipulation for bringing a man here with you?"

Rae smirked. "Yep. I hadn't planned on a visitor."

He laughed. A rich sound that echoed off the cavern walls, and the glow pulsed. "You'd like a husband then? To be married?"

Rae's cheeks burned, but she shook her head. "No. Marriage has never been a goal."

"Have you ever looked for it? I hear the right lover can sometimes be found in the most unusual place."

Rae shook her head again. "Haven't had the greatest luck with relationships."

He winced, glancing towards his feet. "I'm sorry about that."

"Who mentioned you?" Rae tilted her head. "Last I knew, we were never in a relationship."

"Not officially, I suppose. But I hoped you might be open to changing that?"

Rae shifted onto her hip to face him, debating things she never thought she would. "Way to cut to the chase, Soldier." A relationship with him? A man who probably hadn't even shared his real name.

He smirked. "Trying something new."

"Are you asking to court me? A cold, hard thief?"

Bastian's fingers entwined with hers. "Not so cold. And definitely not hard." He drew her hand up with his, the back of her hand brushing against his cheek before his lips formed a kiss on her knuckles. "I missed you and thought only of the moment I could do this again. It seems only natural to ask if I may continue to pursue your affection."

"So formal." Rae smiled. "Well, you came all this way, so I suppose I'd better give you a chance." She pulled him closer, letting her mouth hover near his. "Perhaps we should take it slow?"

He held his breath, and the release of it hummed across her lips. "Slow..." His warm hand traced her collarbone, slipping behind her neck. Tilting his chin towards her, his mouth brushed hers in a soft savoring of her lower lip.

Rae's heart thudded in her ears, her eyes slipping closed. "Mhmm." Leaning closer, she kissed his upper lip as her hand glided down his arm. "I can be patient." As much as she wanted his body, she needed to know his real name first.

Chapter 18

THE ART-LADEN CRYSTALS GLIMMERING AGAINST Rae's skin offered pure perfection. Her soft skin felt warm as Bastian ran his hands along the wet hems of her clothes. He could barely comprehend her words amid his pounding heart.

"Patient." The word seemed inappropriate. Her hot breath teased along his lip, yearning for more. "You may be far stronger than me," he whispered against her skin as he kissed her jaw. His tongue traced the lines of water that ran towards her neck.

Rae tilted her head to grant him better access, her breath coming with controlled speed.

The energies of the cavern vibrated against his skin, mingling with the sensation of Rae's soul tangled with his. He'd never been so aware of it before, but now he didn't know how he'd missed it. So close to her, it intoxicated his mind into forgetting all his previous hesitations. The embrace held so much more than mere physical touch.

As he returned to her lips, she ran a hand through his hair. He forced himself to reign in the desire to delve deeper, urging the kisses to soften. His lips tingled as he drew from her, his eyes opening to meet hers.

"I'd never have guessed how hard I'd fall for you when I gave you such a hard time on that rooftop in Jacoby."

Rae's brows twitched, and she tilted her head. "You mean you would've been gentler while you pinned me to the roof? You *were* gentlemanly enough to break my fall, though."

"I do what I can." He smiled. "But all things considered, I'm grateful. I wouldn't be alive if it wasn't for you. I hope you know that."

It wasn't only that he'd been arrested in Jacoby and would have been turned over to Helgath. He'd had plenty of time to think about how many Rahn'ka before him had gone crazy before learning to control the voices. He didn't want to consider the husk he might have turned into without her.

Rae studied him, considering his words. Her playful demeanor dimmed. "Neither would I." She ran her hand over his chin.

Leaning into her touch, he closed his eyes. It should have been black behind his eyelids, but his mind still processed the images formed by the surrounding energies. He didn't need to look at the crystals to see the majestic beauty they emanated.

Considering the significance of the cavern to her father's memory, Bastian desired to know more about her, but it felt unfair to question her. His chest tightened at the memory of his lies. He wanted to fix them, but his tongue refused to speak. It was easier this way, for both of them. Too much had happened between them for him to tell her the truth about Helgath.

She'll never forgive me if she learns who I was. I'm Bastian. Not Damien.

"I'm distracting you from the real reason you're here. I don't mean to."

"No. You're giving me a new reason."

Bastian's heart thudded, and he studied her eyes. "What does this place feel like to you?" As part auer, it was natural for her to have some ability. He'd witnessed it in the shift of weather while Yondé manipulated his body, though he hadn't heard of an Art capable of such control.

Rae's eyes narrowed, and she glanced at his mouth. "It feels like a buzz against my skin. Through my veins. Like heat in my soul or something. Why?"

"I can feel it, too." Bastian offered a smile as he took her hand.

He glanced at the crystals, studying the way the light glowed within them like a tiny lightning storm.

They grew in patches of color, mimicking stained glass.

"It's a new sensation I'm still getting used to, the Art. Did your father teach you how to use it?" Sitting beside Rae, he could not only feel the pulse of the cavern, but her own. It was buried deep, as if she shielded it the way Yondé had taught him to do.

Rae moved her face farther from his, shaking her head. "I don't have any ability. I can only feel this place because of my heritage."

Bastian frowned. "You don't know?" Something in her tone told him she believed it too. "I'm sure your heritage has something to do with it, but it's more than that. I can sense it, and what you did when Yondé attacked you only proves it."

"What are you talking about? I didn't do anything. Maybe your senses still need some tuning?" She ran her thumb over his lips.

Her touch made his mind wander, his stomach twisting in a pleasant knot.

As quickly as they'd come, his questions about her Art vanished. His mouth parted without his consent, closing to kiss the tips of her fingers. His body tightened as he gave in to the welcome distraction she offered with a soft sigh from her lips.

Leaning in, he claimed her mouth. He hadn't realized how much he needed it.

Needed her.

Her touch made goosebumps rise on his skin, a blissful numbness coalescing throughout his body.

Her lips responded to his, hungrily accepting the affection. Tangled pleasantly with his hair, her hand tugged him closer.

Bastian ignored her damp, cold clothing as it touched his chest. His fingers traced the hem of her shirt, following it down her side before he found the bottom. Wriggling within the wet material, he touched her abdomen, tracing her breeches before venturing up. His hand slowed as it slid over the subtle ridges of a wound he'd never felt before.

Sucking in a breath, Bastian broke from the fever of their kisses.

She watched him as his fingertips traced the unfamiliar lines.

"Shit, Dice," he murmured, his voice husky. "This is from the grygurr?" They curved all the way around her ribs towards her back. Imperfect edges confirmed she'd had to stitch it shut.

Rae pushed his hand away, backing up on the rock. Opening her mouth, he thought she might speak but instead, she closed it and fluidly slipped off the stone into the water. Without coming up for air, she disappeared into the depths.

Bastian cursed at himself as he shuffled to his knees. He looked after her, wanting to pursue. He always had to open his mouth. It was easier when it was preoccupied with other things. Taking a moment, he forced himself to breathe.

He eyed the crystals over his head, fascinated by their power. Reaching up, he slid a finger along the formation. Little jolts of energy sparked from the crystal into his skin, and focusing on the essence of the cavern came easily.

Its deep, thrumming presence answered him as he pushed his ká into it.

Bastian cupped his hand beneath the crystal as the weight of it shifted into his palm. Drawing away from the ceiling, he sat back on his heels and studied the thin shard against his skin.

The power within it swirled, trapped in the tiny vessel now apart from the whole. The light blue looked like when a ká manifested, and the tangle of yellow and green inside swelled and danced like fire.

Bastian tucked the crystal into his pocket before slipping into the water, whispering his appreciation to the cavern for the gift.

Familiar with the curve of the channel, the swim out went quickly. His lungs sucked in air when he reached the surface.

The sun neared the thick canopy of trees, and rows of clouds, like fields of blooming wildflowers, stretched towards the Belgast mountains to the east.

Bastian turned towards the shore, swimming in broad strokes to the shallows before walking from the lake. He ran his hands down over his pants, pushing the water out before roughly combing his hair back with his hands.

His skin chilled, but he banished the goosebumps with a simple thought that encouraged his ká to the surface of his flesh, drying the remaining droplets of water.

Rae stood at her camp, wearing dry breeches, but her boots still sat next to the shore. Her ponytail dripped as she put on a new chemise, facing away from him. She hung the wet one to dry next to her pants and shirt.

Neco laid several paces away at the tree line, enjoying the success of his hunt. His ears pricked at Bastian, but the wolf dismissed him and went back to his meal.

Reaching for a fresh shirt, Rae didn't turn to him, but he could see the three jagged lines over her ribs, curling slightly onto her back.

"Rae, wait. I might be able to... Uh..." Maybe she'd trust him, even if he didn't deserve it. "I can help."

"I don't need help." Rae didn't look at him, a hand on her side. "They don't hurt much anymore."

"Please." Bastian drew closer to her. "Let me see? I can make it so they don't hurt at all."

Rae met his gaze, and he recognized the feeling of mortality in her eyes. The scars reminded her how close she'd come to death, and he didn't blame her for not wanting to acknowledge them.

She swallowed and moved her hand, exposing the three lines running horizontally over her waist. The scars were raised and pink around the outside. Red in some areas stubborn to heal. She must have stitched them herself, but the threads had long since been removed. The skin puckered where the needle had pierced it.

Bastian stepped close, watching his right hand slide along the scars.

Rae flinched under his touch but stood her ground.

"It'll feel a little sharp at first... Then numb."

Taking a deep breath, the scent of her threatened to distract him from his purpose. But he clenched his jaw and dove into his access of the Art. He tentatively drew his hand away, setting it over the thin sheen of power her body held within its own ká. Touching it, his hand tensed as it hovered above her skin.

A heat passed from his chest and through his arm, the power of his ká working in tandem with hers. The power flared in a burst of pale flecks, misting from his fingers as he manipulated them against her aura.

She hissed, her body jerking as the pain he warned of came. Her body stilled as he wrapped his other arm around her smooth, tattooed waist. The heat in his healing hand altered to a distant burning, his awareness buried beneath invisible layers of power.

He pushed through the haze, tugging on the energies deep within her to urge them to his will.

The change came slowly, the scars paling as the swollen red edges faded. Starting at the end of the lacerations, the skin knitted tighter together, drawing smooth tanned skin over the marks until they were no wider than a blade of grass.

Lethargy eked into his muscles, his hand sore as if he'd been gripping a sword hilt for hours. He pulled it away, clenching his fist before he shook his hand to stretch the muscles. He loosened his hold on Rae, taking a step back as the heat of his ká flushed through him. Even touching her felt too warm, and he took in a grateful breath of the cool autumn air.

"There," he whispered, as if speaking louder would ruin his work.

Rae looked down at her side, pulling on the skin to see the scars. After a minute of silence, she lifted her gaze to him. With delicate movements, she stepped forward and touched his face before kissing him.

Bastian didn't know what he'd expected, but the kiss surprised him. His body tensed, her hand burning on his chin before he settled into the affection. Mouth moving against hers, he sighed happily against her lips.

When she pulled away, she smiled. "Thank you. I can't even feel them anymore."

"It shouldn't have happened in the first place, and I won't let something like it happen again."

Rae studied him. "I believe you."

A screech from the sky drew their attention upward.

She released him and jogged backwards, watching the sky.

Bastian felt the creature's energy before he saw the hawk.

Rae whistled two short, high-pitched blasts through her fingers, and lifted her arm.

The bird of prey dove, claws extended. He grasped onto her bare skin, the momentum forcing her arm down as she caught him.

Bastian took a step back to admire the view. Rae hadn't bothered to put on a shirt before the hawk's arrival, and the vision of her standing with such a majestic animal perched on her arm made his heart hammer.

Rae pulled a wrap of parchment from the bird's leg. Stroking his head, she scratched beneath his feathers. "Hey boy." She glanced at Bastian, unfazed by the hawk's talons puncturing her arm. "This is Din. My hawk."

Where was he when we met?

A brief wave of suspicion passed through him, but he buried it.

The hawk's head swiveled to look at Bastian, quirking to the side as if he understood the introduction.

"Nice to meet you?" He calmly greeted the hawk with his power, whose tentative, jumpy energy responded.

The hawk's feathers ruffled but then settled as Bastian's energy withdrew. Extending his hand, Bastian rubbed his knuckles against the hawk's chest, who cooed.

Rae raised an eyebrow. "He usually bites other people ..."

"Animals like me." Bastian shrugged. "But I have a bit of an advantage now. I can communicate with them, in a way. Din knows I'm not a threat, and I can ask permission before I pet him and know I won't get bit."

Staring at him, Rae hesitated. "Because of your power. Is that why you stopped eating meat?"

He looked up, meeting her eyes. The thought about his dietary change had barely registered over the past months, since foraging through the sanctum's gardens was routine. It surprised him at how quickly she made the connection. "I hadn't even thought about it that way, but I suppose so. It just stopped being appealing. But a plant's ká is distinctly simpler than an animal's."

Rae seemed to consider his logic and nodded, stroking her hawk. "Makes sense. You'll have a tough time convincing Neco to join you in your diet, but I'm happy to accommodate you with my cooking."

"You started cooking?" Bastian raised his brows.

Smirking, Rae shook her head. "No."

"So what you mean is, you'll eat my cooking that doesn't contain meat without complaining." He grinned.

"Yep."

Laughing, Bastian shook his head. He idly scratched Din's chest again while the hawk chittered at Rae.

"Stay close." Rae nuzzled the side of Din's head and clicked her tongue as she launched him back into the air.

Bastian eyed the minor scratches on her arm, taking it into both his hands before she could protest.

"It's fine. They heal quickly."

He squinted at the tiny white marks on her skin where they'd healed before. Rolling his eyes, he let go of her arm. "I'll save my energy then. Who's the message from?"

"I don't know yet." Rae unrolled the note and squinted at it.

Bastian curiously leaned to look at the scrap. It was a jumble of lines and symbols he couldn't make sense of. Not one of the languages in the books of the Rahn'ka. He narrowed his eyes, debating asking more.

Rae's brow furrowed as she read, and she turned from him to pace to the side without looking up.

He didn't follow her, trying to decipher each little change in her facial expression. The curious thought of why he hadn't seen the hawk before struck again. Din was an old companion and quite attached to Rae. He could sense that much. Bits of where the bird had traveled clung to the aura around his feathers. He'd come from the east along the Belgast mountains. The direction they'd originally traveled from.

"Dice?"

Her eyes lifted to him. "I need to go." She shoved the note into her pocket and retrieved a shirt from a nearby saddlebag. Pulling it over her head, she leaned back again to get a book. Crouching, she found a piece of graphite and began scrawling a message on a blank page.

"Go?" Bastian watched her write in the same coded lettering.

"Yes." She wrote several lines of symbols, then tore the parchment from the bound book. Looking up at Bastian, her face appeared grim. "To Ashdale."

"Ashdale? Isn't that where you're from?"

"Yes." Rae's tone sounded sour. She lifted her fingers to her mouth and whistled twice. Arm raised, she caught Din again with the same ease as before. She wrapped her response around his leg. As her fingers grazed the metal cuff, a subtle energy pulsed between her and the hawk. The odd connection radiated from a spot between Rae's shoulder blades to the cuff she secured her note beneath.

Bastian hesitated, watching as Rae gave Din another scratch, whispering something against his head, then pushed him off. His stomach knotted as he considered asking her about the connection with the hawk.

Now's not the time. It can wait.

"What's the hurry? From what you've said about Ashdale, I didn't think you'd want to go back."

"I don't. But I must. My... my father needs my help." Rae wandered the camp as if distracted, looking around her things. She glanced at Neco and over at Zaili, then back again. Anywhere but at Bastian. It made his stomach hurt.

She's lying.

"Dice." Bastian stepped towards her, holding out a hand. "Tell me what's going on."

She met his gaze, hesitating. "I don't know the details, but I need to go." Taking a step towards him, her eyes pleaded with him. "Come with me?"

He held his breath, looking down to meet her gaze. "Of course."

Why would I want to do anything else?

Yet, his gut roiled with uncertainty.

Rae's energies danced with agitation. Guilt clouded his new ability to sense the truth about her emotional state. It felt like he was prying into a private life he had no right to know about. He promptly blocked what turmoil her ká felt. It could have been for several reasons. She could be questioning her own decision to ask him to join her. He should feel grateful she wanted to be anywhere near him.

Distract her.

"After all, I'd be a pretty lousy future husband if I didn't come along. Especially after you shared this place with me." He steeled his insecurities into a teasing grin.

Rae's brow twitched, and then she smiled, but something else laced her expression. Perhaps he'd gone too far.

"That's true." Her words surprised him, and her free hand touched his face. "But are you sure? Do you have more... training, or anything? I don't want to screw up your priorities, especially considering I said I don't want a husband."

Bastian shook his head, ignoring the unexpected ball of disappointment in his gut. "*You* are my priority." He touched the back of her hand on his jaw. "No more training. At least not for now. I have nowhere better to be than by your side."

Taking a sharp inhale, Rae kissed him again, harder than before.

He'd missed the way she felt against him.

Drawing from the kiss, she buried her face against his neck, and he kissed the top of her head.

"I think I'll need some new clothes before we get to Ashdale, though." Bastian smiled.

Rae nodded against his skin.

Running his hands up her back, Bastian rested his cheek on her wet hair. She wasn't telling him the whole truth, but it didn't matter. Just being able to hold her was all he needed for now. She would tell him if it was important.

In the two weeks it took for them to journey to Ashdale, Bastian tried to contain the anxiety building within him. The only thing that helped was the new morning routine of their exercise together.

They shared cozy nights, and the only moments she truly looked at peace were while she slept in his arms. She'd told him of the night terrors she'd experienced over the previous months, but she never complained of more.

Neco vanished into the woods for extended periods of time, but Rae never seemed concerned, and he always came when she called him. At night, he'd curl up next to them and lick Bastian's fingers.

Bastian found what comfort he could in Rae's affection, as fleeting as it suddenly became. Despite her consistent assurances she wanted him at her side, he suspected it wasn't true.

His heart ached in thinking something had changed between them, but after what Yondé had done, how could he expect it to stay the same?

Ashdale met the jeweled sea with a slew of ship docks stretching towards the flat horizon. Seagulls squawked, circling the cobblestone streets leading to the piers filled with fishing vessels.

Dropping into the valley, Bastian eyed the burned-out husks of the village's north-eastern edge.

At least thirty structures, the length of several city blocks, were left in ruin. Nature had reclaimed the area, but autumn had stolen the leaves of the vines curling among the blackened foundations. Despite Rae's confession about Ashdale's scar, it still seemed vastly out of place on the landscape. The city spread south, curling around the charcoal ruins.

He wondered why they'd never torn them down to rebuild. Perhaps the tragedy she blamed herself for had been too great for the city to recover from. But it'd been an accident. A young child couldn't have prevented it.

He sat behind her on Zaili and squeezed her waist at the sight, feeling horrible for assuming the worst with her strange behavior. As he looked at the charred remains, he wondered if it all boiled down to her guilt for the destruction. It was a hideous reminder, and he couldn't blame her for not wanting to return.

His insides twisted with empathy, and he kissed her temple. "You all right?"

Rae shifted in the saddle before leaning back on his chest. She breathed a shaky exhale. "No." Turning her head to look at him, she rolled her lips together. "But I'm glad you're with me."

"Me too." He gazed at the lively part of the city. "Do you think anyone will recognize you?"

"I doubt it. Most of those who knew me well died in that fire. Besides, I was twelve. I hardly look the same."

"Makes sense." Bastian did a final silent inspection of the barrier between his mind and the oncoming wave of inevitable voices the city threatened.

The buildings, made primarily of stone, looked new and marked a change in the town's construction methods. The houses were identical near the center of town but grew more diverse as the city spread across the terrain. The outer structures boasted fertile fields and stables.

The bustling noise of the townsfolk muddled through the streets, people trading goods along the single major thoroughfare connecting to the docks.

Bastian steered Zaili through the archway of the town's south gate. "Should we get a room at the inn before we try to find your—"

"Yes. An inn would be best."

"I'd like to do some trading too, before everything shuts down for the evening." He still needed new clothing. Finding things that fit him properly had proven difficult in the tiny villages on the road to Ashdale, and they didn't have time to wait for a tailor's work.

"Why don't you do that while I try to locate where my parents live now?" Rae squeezed his hand resting on her stomach.

"Are you sure you don't want me with you for that?"

Rae's jaw flexed, and she nodded. "I won't approach them yet, I'll just find out where they are, if I can."

"All right." Bastian considered the mystery of her not knowing. He'd had plenty of time to consider why a message to visit her father would come from the opposite direction than Ashdale. He hadn't been able to determine Din's direction as he departed with Rae's response, but now in the city, he didn't recognize any of the energy patterns he'd felt on the hawk.

He'd avoided asking, but it felt foolish. They'd already both said they didn't want secrets between them anymore. "Rae. Can I ask something?"

She stiffened but nodded. "What is it?"

"Who asked you to come meet with your father? I only ask because Din came from the east when he brought the message."

Rae fell silent for a moment, still leaning on him. "A friend. I can't send Din directly to my father, it's why I don't know where he is."

"Instead, there's a friend acting as the middleman? Because Din can go to them? I wondered how your hawk could find you when you're always traveling." He'd already considered whatever connection he felt between them was the likely answer, but hoped Rae might confirm it willingly.

Rae nodded. "Din is bonded to me, so he can find me. With other people, it's more *complicated.*" She smirked.

He grinned, relief calming his tension. "Complicated? How so?"

Sighing, she shifted in her seat again. "It requires a charm. I have a limited number, but he can find those who hold them."

"I'd think you'd want to give one to your father, then. It sounded like you two were close."

"We were, but I haven't seen him since long before purchasing Din."

Bastian nodded, kissing her temple as they crossed into the city. Usually, whenever he asked questions, Rae would shut him out.

Time to stop while she's still being open.

They needed to stick together here.

Entering the city brought the usual anxiety, but he assured himself that this far from Helgath, no one would know to look for him.

The wide streets offered plenty of space for the pedestrian traffic, trade carts, Zaili and Neco to share. People gave the wolf a wide berth, suspicious glances flickering between him and his companions.

The shop signs swayed in the sea breeze and Bastian squinted to make out the names of the inns. The allure of a bed made him almost beg her to stop Zaili at the first one they saw, but something tugged him to encourage Rae towards an east-facing street. Between the gaps of the buildings, he could see a square with a fountain at the center. Beyond it, a black, burned archway loomed with wild growth attempting to reclaim the devastation.

"Falcon's Roost." Bastian pointed to a sign ahead of them. "Sounds appropriate."

"Din's a hawk."

He smirked. "Close enough."

Bastian didn't wait for Zaili to stop entirely before he slipped from the saddle, landing comfortably on the balls of his feet. He cleared his throat to gain the attention of the boy leaned against the entrance stairwell with a hat pulled over his eyes.

"Yessir!" The boy jumped to his feet. "Looking for room and board?" His thin black eyebrows came together as he looked at who'd woken him.

"We are. And some care for our horse too, if you don't mind."

The boy studied Bastian from head to foot, tilting his head when reaching his bare feet.

Bastian waved his hand beneath his waist, catching the boy's low, wandering eyes.

He jolted as if rocked from a dream. "Yessir. Sorry, sir. Yes." The boy pursed his lips together, as if struggling with a decision.

"You take the horses to the stables, right?" Bastian locked gazes with the boy to keep his attention upward.

"Yessir."

"Shouldn't you take the reins from the pretty lady?" Bastian gestured towards Rae as he took the saddlebag from her shoulder, lifting it over his instead.

The stable boy started again, hopping towards Rae with eager hands. Zaili snorted, and the boy let out a yip and jumped back. "Is that a wolf?" The boy squeaked as he backed up the stairs, and Neco yawned.

Rae patted her thigh, calling Neco to her side. "Dog." She scratched behind his ears. "Just a big dog."

The boy narrowed his eyes.

Bastian scooped up the reins the boy had dropped and held them out towards him.

"That's a really big *dog*." The boy eyed Neco before tentatively stepping forward and taking the reins from Bastian.

"He's harmless. Do we pay inside?"

"Yessir." The boy's eyes still lingered on the massive black valley wolf.

Bastian turned, leading the way up the stairs into the inn.

A distant ringing sound stopped him. He paused on the top step, the hairs on his neck standing straight up. He felt for the barrier he kept firmly in place. A pressure weighed on his chest, making his breath unsteady. It came from the northeast, beyond the line of buildings blocking the scorched ruins from view. It felt as if someone had knocked on a door but was gone by the time he opened it.

Shaking his head, Bastian blew out a breath and turned to see Rae staring at him.

"What is it?" Rae touched his arm.

"Nothing. Let's get inside so we can get to business before the sun sets."

"I'll get us a room, you go." Rae unclasped a small pouch from the inside of her belt. Holding it out, she gestured with her chin. "I forgot to give this back to you. I'll meet you back here for dinner."

He succumbed to giving back the saddle pack with her insistence and took the coin. "Where will you look?"

"I'll start with asking the innkeeper. Then some local taverns."

Bastian tilted his head, giving a teasing smile. "Purely for business? Or will you sneak some leisure in those visits too?"

Rae scowled but paused, thinking. She shrugged. "We'll see. Maybe someone will offer me a foot rub again."

He frowned. "Keep your boots on, Dice, and you can have all the foot rubs you want back at the inn tonight."

Rae smiled, but it didn't reach her eyes. "All right."

Bastian held the door open for her, watching her disappear into the dim interior. He descended the stairs as he considered Rae's response. He'd expected the usual teasing banter with his offer, but she hadn't reciprocated.

Maybe she isn't planning to meet me. Would she leave me here?

It could have been her intention all along. But it wouldn't make sense for her to wait until now and give him money to spend. Scratching his head, he turned towards the market, his back itching like spiderwebs tickled across it.

Chapter 19

AFTER ARRANGING A ROOM FOR her and Bastian, Rae hurried back outside with Neco. Grateful for the time alone, she tried to shake the weight on her shoulders after the message she'd received from Jarrod weeks ago.

The note instructed her to go to Ashdale. Jarrod, with a select team, would board a ship to meet her at a location not yet decided.

She'd vastly underestimated Bastian's value.

With the information she provided, Jarrod determined Bastian's real identity, and it seemed the Ashen Hawks had decided to acquire the infamous deserter, stepping into the role of bounty hunters despite it not being their norm.

In the back of her mind, she'd hoped to be wrong. Perhaps he hadn't lied about who he was, and she had no reason to turn him over.

But not only had he been a soldier, he'd been an officer.

A lieutenant.

The information Bastian knew about the functions of the Helgathian military would sell for thousands of silver florins. Helgath wouldn't tolerate an officer defecting. No one had done so before.

Rae had memorized the end of the note.

> *His name is Damien Lanoret. Get to Ashdale, we'll meet you. More instruction to come. Stay safe, he's dangerous.*

Her heart sank, and her lies to Bastian, *Damien*, came in half-hearted attempts.

Yet, he still followed her to her hometown. He trusted her, and her stomach twisted with guilt. Part of her hated that he'd lied to her and continued to do so, but how could she fault him? If he knew why she'd kept him around in the beginning...

A quick inquiry with the innkeeper when securing their room confirmed her parents no longer lived in Ashdale, which meant she didn't need to restrain her wandering. Yet, now she needed to explain to Bastian why her father wasn't even here.

More lies.

Rae sucked in a breath of cool ocean air, wandering through the streets of Ashdale.

Neco followed her, his ears pinned back against his head, nose whipping to identify smells he wasn't accustomed to. His discomfort pained her.

As the sun dipped beneath the ocean line, the skies blooming with twilight colors, Rae led Neco away from the streets. When they reached the border of the city, she knelt to scratch his ears. "You stay out here for now, boy."

He licked her face and whimpered.

"I know. But you'll be happier."

Neco shook his ruff before turning and loping into the trees, tail swishing behind him.

Turning back to the city, Rae stared down the cobblestone corridor leading to the sea. The docks grew dark, and she followed a trail of lanterns illuminating a sloping path towards the tavern district. The yellow glow of roaring fireplaces danced through the thick-paned windows, propped open to entice passersby with the scent of freshly baked pies and promise of ale.

Unable to bring herself to meet Bastian back at the inn yet, Rae sauntered to a stop outside the Hog and Sow Tavern, listening to the laughter booming within. Yearning for respite from her troubled mind, she pushed the door open and walked inside.

Warmth from the hearth engulfed her, and her shoulders relaxed. Several groups of people gathered, talking and gambling. Dice and cards scattered over tables, the noise deafening, but it offered a welcome, familiar environment. It drowned out her thoughts, but she needed an ale or two to squelch them completely.

A grizzled man with a dense white beard plucked at the strings of an instrument where he sat near the hearth, belting sea shanties the patrons occasionally joined in on. The sailor's lyrics told the tale of the foolish fisherman who fell in love with an alcan of the sea and drowned after she caught him kissing her sister. An alcan woman's jealousy was not to be tested, the moral of the song concluded.

Alcans, the water dwellers of Pantracia's people, rarely emerged from their ocean fortresses. But if shanties were to be trusted, it was always to meddle in the affairs of humans trying to make an honest living by the sea.

A barmaid walked past her, tilting her head in silent inquiry.

Rae nodded. "Ale, please." She passed the woman an iron mark.

Stepping farther into the room, she eyed a corner table, but a man's voice drew her attention.

"Blaine, stop starin', it's yer turn." The man shoved his shoulder into the young sailor next to him.

Rae raised an eyebrow at Blaine, who eyed her. His black hair cut short and a half-smile on his lips.

Without breaking eye contact, he responded to his friend. "Maybe she'd like to join us for a game, Tren."

Tren bellowed a laugh from his ale-rounded belly and pushed the dice into Blaine's open palm. "Lasses don't know how ta gamble, ye idiot. Roll 'em."

Blaine's muddy-brown eyes offered an apologetic glance as he closed his fist. They widened, along with his grin, as Rae walked towards the table surrounded by six men.

"Ye might be wrong, bud," Blaine muttered, standing and pulling out the empty chair next to him. "Want to join?"

"Only if you wanna lose your coin to a lass." She feigned a curtsey before taking the offered seat next to Blaine. She slid a few coins onto the table.

Tren's waspish eyes narrowed at her, and the rest of the men around the table laughed. They seemed to come from all walks of life, starting with Tren in his food-stained shirt with the sleeves pushed up his hairy arms, to a refined gentleman with his silver hair combed back, wearing a buttoned, embellished vest.

Blaine shook his head, curls falling over his forehead. "Six and three." He rolled the dice as the barmaid placed her ale down in front of her. Groaning at his roll, he passed the dice to her. "So, what ye wanna do, is decide—"

Rae interrupted. "Four, six." Rolling the six dice, she landed a mix of numbers, including two fours and a six. Setting them aside, the men chattered, and some tossed another iron mark towards the center of the table before she rolled again.

Two sixes and one four.

The men erupted in cheers, but Tren looked like he wanted to flip the table over.

Rae gathered the pot and took a long drink of her ale, already beginning to feel better.

An hour and four steins of ale later, the group roared louder than the rest of the tavern, upstaging the old man and his shanties. The crowd of tavern goers shifted their attention to the dice games, with Rae at the center of the excitement. Abandoning their chairs, the men stood around the table shouting in conversation and bets.

Rae scored another winning throw, and Blaine cheered along with the rest of the crowd. He crashed his stein into hers, and they both drank.

Tren slammed his mug down onto the table. Droplets of what remained at the bottom splattered out onto his shirt and beard.

She was one round away from beating Tren out of the rest of his coin.

Tren shook the dice in his palm, hushing the giggling onlookers around him. Silence built in the room as if it would somehow help him.

Blaine squeezed Rae's shoulder, and she stifled a tipsy laugh.

"Rae?" Bastian's voice broke the silence as he wriggled through the wall of observers.

Rae glanced behind her and grinned at the man who'd pledged to court her. To court a thief. "Bastian!" She clapped a hand over her mouth. "Hold on, he's focusing *really* hard," she whispered with mock seriousness.

Bastian looked different from the last time she'd seen him, so much so, that she almost didn't recognize him. His charming voice gave him away.

She didn't linger to look for changes beyond his cropped hair and trimmed beard before turning back towards Tren.

Blaine's hand slid to rest on her shoulder blade.

"Two and Five." Tren threw the dice and scored only one two, not qualifying him for a second roll. A collection of laughs and 'ooh's erupted from the crowd as Tren's face reddened.

His score wasn't enough to end the round, so they passed the dice to Rae. In the tradition of the last hour, Rae held them up for Blaine to blow on for good luck.

He obliged.

"One, six!" She threw them out onto the table. Among the numbers were two sixes.

Cheers rang as she leaned across the table to put the winners aside and gathered the remaining four dice.

Rae turned to Blaine but saw Bastian's fiery gaze in the corner of her eyes. She gave him a sheepish shrug as Blaine blew on her dice again before she rolled.

Three ones and a six.

Jumping up, Rae cheered, and the rest of the tavern joined in.

"Drinks on me!" She spun around with her arms up as Blaine scooped her winnings towards her.

The whole of the Hog and Sow roared in their appreciation as Tren swatted at his friend trying to give him a reassuring pat.

Rae finished her mug of ale and slammed it back onto the table, her senses dulled in her tipsy state.

Blaine grinned and wrapped an arm around her waist, pulling her towards him as she laughed.

Her hand went automatically to his chest, and she tried to stifle her giggles at his attempt to be smooth.

The liquor made Blaine's grip clumsy, and he stepped into her, but a man's hand stopped him. His eyes shifted down to the opposing force centered on his chest.

"Whoa there." Bastian pushed Blaine back from Rae, and he stumbled over his own heels.

She looked at Bastian without lifting her chin as he took a step into her, realizing Blaine's face, which she'd become accustomed to looking at, was only the same height as the top of Bastian's shoulder. She frowned at Bastian's collarbone.

The crowd had mingled together, and she leaned close so she could hear him over the ruckus.

"You missed dinner." He looked down at her.

"Don't worry." Blaine pushed Bastian's hand from his chest. "I took good care of her."

"Oh, I'm sure you did." Sarcasm tainted his tone, and he glanced at Blaine with narrowed eyes.

Rae hiccuped. "I ate pretzels!"

"Pretzels don't constitute a meal, Dice..." Bastian lowered his face to be level with hers.

She squinted and then shrugged. Eyes darting from Bastian to Blaine and then back again, she pursed her lips.

Bastian looked more handsome than she remembered.

When did his arms get so big?

She gripped his upper arm, feeling through the thin, grey material of his new shirt.

Bastian watched her with a raised eyebrow as she turned to do the same to Blaine's arm. She frowned and returned to Bastian's to compare.

"Can I get ye some dinner?" Blaine encouraged her hand away from Bastian's superior bicep.

Bastian wrapped his right arm around her as her eyes strayed to the table, studying the dice she'd been playing with. Her winning throw.

Rae chuckled. "I'm sure Bast will feed me." Reaching, she pocketed the pretty, colored dice.

Bastian's hand closed on hers, and she instinctively went to entwine her fingers with his, but he pulled away too fast. "She's spoken for." He dropped the dice she'd snagged back onto the table, and she scowled.

"Didn't look so spoken for when she came in alone." Blaine straightened, stepping challengingly toward Bastian.

Bastian's body tensed against hers, and he took a step forward too.

Rae snatched the dice back off the table, tucking them into her pocket as she wedged herself between the two men. "I apologize if you misunderstood, Blaine, but my affection belongs to this rather bulky man behind me. Thank you for the game." Turning, she pushed on Bastian's chest. "I want fresh air. Give up the pissing match." She did her best not to slur her words, but her tongue felt heavy.

Bastian narrowed his eyes but didn't speak. With another brief shove, he turned and started towards the door, taking her hand.

Blaine called after her. "You forgot your winnings."

Rae shrugged. "Buy another round."

Bastian guided her out of the packed tavern into the evening air. The roar of the people inside vanished as the door clicked shut.

Breathing a deep inhale, she chewed her lip and eyed Bastian, who observed her.

"I was worried when you didn't show up. I thought..."

Swaying closer to him, she lifted her chin and gave her most charming tipsy smile. "What did you think?"

He hesitated but didn't pull away. His hands closed around her waist as she slipped in against him. "I thought maybe you'd left town without me." His hazel eyes gleamed with uncharacteristic vulnerability.

"Now why would I do that?" Rae tilted her head and touched his face, running her thumb over his bottom lip.

His body tensed, muscles taut against her. He closed his eyes, bowing his head towards hers. Kissing her forehead, he sighed. "I don't know. But it felt like you were keeping something about coming here from me. Like you've been trying to pull away."

Rae pouted, desperately searching for a logical excuse. "It's hard being here." She walked a fine line between fiction and truth. "But I have no plans of leaving you behind, I promise."

He gave her a smile, nodding. "I suppose using dice games and cute gamblers as a distraction is a normal thing then?"

"Mmm..." She tilted her head back in mock thought. "Yep, apparently so. Reminds me of home. Is that a problem?"

"The dice game, no." Bastian kept smiling. "But the men... You might want to be careful or I may fall into a jealous rage." He playfully squeezed her waist.

Rae tugged on the front of his shirt. "Jealous? Over some sailors?" She scoffed. "The mighty Helgathian soldier?" She laughed at his frown and shook her head. "I only have eyes for you, *Bastian.*" His grip around her loosened, but she leaned into him and rose to her toes to kiss his chin. "Let's go for a walk? I missed you." She entwined her fingers with his, pulling him to follow as she stepped over the cobblestone street.

Bastian didn't follow, his grip tightening as their arms extended straight between them.

She turned back to him, and his head tilted down, eyes locked on the ground. "Rae, I... I need to tell you—"

"No, you don't." She pulled herself to him. "Don't tell me anything." She ran a hand through his newly cut hair.

He lifted his chin to meet her eyes.

"I don't need to know." Her hand trailed down his neck, and she leaned up, kissing him. His mouth responded, but she pulled away. "It's all right, *Damien.*"

Bastian's entire body stiffened, his hands dropping away from where they touched her hips. Tension filled the air between them as he took a step back. His eyes brightened, a flash of white light somewhere deep within them as they widened at her.

Shit. Should have kept my mouth shut.

Rae backed up from him, wondering through the haze of her tipsy mind if she'd made a grave mistake.

"What?" Bastian whispered, his mouth gaping.

No turning back now, you idiot.

She lifted her chin a notch. "Or is it more proper to call you Lieutenant?" The hairs on the back of her neck stood straight as she spoke the knowledge aloud.

He looked angry, and her heart thudded hard as he stepped into her. A hand closed around her bicep, the pressure enough to still her feet.

"Please." Bastian lowered his voice to a deep whisper. "Someone might hear you..."

The air thickened, becoming difficult to breathe.

"*Raeynna.*" A voice echoed eerily over the breeze, and she yanked her arm from Bastian's grasp.

Spinning around, she stared down the street. She couldn't see anyone. Her stomach knotted, mind dizzy enough to keep her eyes from focusing in the darkness. Few knew her full name. The inclination to walk towards the voice took hold before she could question it.

Boots scraped across the ground behind her, echoing in the night.

"You can't just say something like that and walk away." Bastian jogged ahead, stepping in front of her.

Rae focused on Bastian, but then she narrowed her gaze over his shoulder. "Would you like me to continue calling you Bastian?"

Something flickered in a distant alleyway behind him, and she tilted her head. A red and orange glimmer, as if candles lined the narrow side street. It vanished a breath later, wisping off into the air with another murmur of her name.

Definitely too much ale.

She shook her head and refocused on the man in front of her.

Bastian's shoulders tightened. "Yes..." He shook his head. "No." His hands came down on her shoulders, and he leaned to block her vision. "Will you look at me?"

Rae took a breath and met his gaze, but it made her stomach lurch.

Fire reflected in his eyes as if the entire town behind her blazed in an inferno.

Her breathing quickened, and she spun to search behind her. The sleepy streets sat unscathed. She stumbled back, and Bastian caught her, wrapping his arms around her.

"*Raeynna!*" The haunting voice shouted in her ears, and she gasped, wriggling free from Bastian's embrace.

"Leave me alone." Her voice shook as she stepped away from Bastian.

He raised his hands, exposing his palms to her. "Rae, you don't need to yell."

Rae didn't wait to hear what else he had to say, whirling to race through the streets back towards their inn. She needed to get away from that voice, the vague familiarity making her hands tremble.

Why did I come back here?

Bastian kept pace behind her, but he didn't touch her again.

As she neared the inn, her eyes were drawn down an alley to the fountain square.

"*Come here...*" The voice trailed off, slowing her steps. "*Come here...*"

She wanted to go inside, to hide from whatever was happening, but her feet took her towards the beckoning call. "What do you want?" Her eyes fixated on the rippling surface of the fountain. It shimmered with flames, and she shook her head.

Impossible.

"I want you to look at me." Bastian's vague shape reflected in the shallows of the fountain, haloed in crimson light. "We need to talk about this. About who Damien is, who I am..."

Rae hardly heard him.

Ripples spread towards her, their origin unclear in the darkened water. Each pulse made her skin feel hot. Invisible smoke stung her nose, making her eyes water.

"I need—"

A roaring in her ears blocked out whatever else Bastian might have said, and she winced, closing her eyes. Orange flames pierced through the blackness of her eyelids. Her eyes opened without her wanting them to, and the black, lopsided archway to old Ashdale glowed with living embers.

A figure, rimmed with a dancing red outline, held out its hand to her.

Rae backed up, bumping into Bastian again, but this time

his arms didn't encircle her. "No. This isn't real. It can't be." Tears trailed from her stinging eyes.

The apparition before her flashed, its pleasant face twisting in anger.

She blinked, and it became her little brother engulfed in flames. Innocent eyes staring at her. Lifting her arms, she covered her face. As she touched her cheeks, her body spun against her will. Something shook her, her entire body quaking.

"Dice?" Bastian's tone shifted to concern. "Rae, what's going on?"

When Rae opened her eyes, a face hovered directly in front of her, and she gasped.

A force clutched her ankles and whipped her to the ground in a single jerk. All the air expelled from her lungs in a huff.

The cobblestone blurred as a force dragged her backward. The blazing embers of the arch whipped past her before she even knew what was happening.

The dimly lit lanterns behind Bastian exploded in flames. Streaks of orange and yellow dropped from their housings to the ground, rushing in thick lines to charge after her.

Bastian's arm flew up to shield his eyes, his body disappearing behind the wall of fire blazing in her wake as something dragged her deeper into the charred area of the city.

She covered her face, kicking her legs to no avail, while her arms did little to block the images infesting her mind.

Her siblings, burning. And others beside them.

So many others.

Their screams and melting flesh. The smell terrorized her lungs, and she struggled to breathe.

Anger flooded her, but it wasn't her own.

Rae screamed, clawing at the ground beneath her.

The ground dropped out, and she fell. Landing hard on stone, her surroundings halted. The visions, unrelenting, engulfed her in flames. They licked up the walls, crackling and reaching into the sky.

The ghostly figure crouched over her, its mouth unnaturally wide with wailing.

Chapter 20

BASTIAN STOOD STARKLY STILL FOR too long, watching Rae vanish into the shadows of the burned-out streets after being torn from his grasp.

He didn't have time to process his regret, his fear of her knowing the truth about him. Of knowing he was Damien Lanoret. A failed lieutenant who refused orders and fled.

Traitor to Helgath.

Liar to the woman he cared for.

A rush of hot air struck his face, rustling the loose fabric of his shirt in the super-heated updraft. His arm protected his eyes, but he blinked at the two lines of fire racing after Rae's struggling body. They left a burning trail like oil on water.

He let his mental barrier drop in an effort to understand.

A mind-numbing wave of angered voices washed over him, the screams evoking his own as he grasped his temples. He fought to reconstruct the walls, building the bricks of his barrier to parse out what he needed to understand.

So much rage.

He ran as soon as his mind cleared enough, following the blazing trails as the voices shrieked in agony. Another scream sounded, but in his ears.

Rae.

The vibration of power against his ká made his knees weak, but he swallowed and steadied his gait. His emotions still catapulted around his mind, uncontrolled, as his stomach clenched imagining his true name on her lips. Thin lines streamed out of him, invisible threads connecting to the fabric of the Art without his permission. The pulse of his power rippled through the ground, buzzing like a hive of bees. The shift as he entered the charred streets seemed impossible.

How has no one else ever noticed?

He'd stirred something up, some lingering energy, he realized with a jolt.

This is my fault. My ká caused this.

He slowed, even though his mind yelled at him to catch up with Rae. The path of fire faltered, dropping to a short flame as he studied its source. It felt different from whatever spirits had risen within the ruins. Cleaner. He plunged his senses into tracing the origin.

All paths led in the same direction.

He ran, ignoring a rumbling fear in his stomach. It wasn't entirely natural fear. Places of death often resonated with a different frequency within the fabric, leading to feelings of uneasiness even among those not sensitive.

Human intuition and instinct can still be correct, even if they often ignore it, Yondé had lectured.

The fire crackled in Bastian's ears long before he saw it. He fell to his hip and slid to a stop at the edge of a gaping maw. The flames surrounded the boundary of a collapsed basement, a fog above glowing orange in the blaze.

Before Bastian could get to his feet, an invisible pressure on his shoulder threw him aside. Rolling onto his back, he reached for his ká. The force landed on his chest, pinning him.

The surrounding air erupted with pale blue light as he closed his fist in front of him, beams seeping from his tattoos down his arm. The spear manifested but struck nothing, ringing through empty air.

Sucking in a lungful of smoke, he focused on the faint outline hovering over him. The fog shifted as something moved through it beside him. He focused on the resonance of their energy and forced his ká to slow to match theirs.

Rae cried out below him, and the flames surged higher.

A force gripped his arm, tightening on the wrist holding his weapon.

Bastian flung his other arm in an arc, his knuckles tingling as they connected against an unseen shape, bucking it from atop him. He wrenched his wrist free, planting the spear's end on the ground to brace himself as he stood.

He reached for the flame, pushing his ká at it to draw energy from where it raged.

The power that controlled it fought him, but he coerced enough away to make the flames collapse briefly before blazing forth again. Using what he'd gained, he channeled it towards his left arm, preparing a shield within his ká.

Two distinct shapes paced, lumbering like a pair of men.

Bastian took a step back, his heel near the edge of the pit. "Rae!" He could sense more beings in the basement with her, at least two. One flitted around, never remaining in one place. His grip tightened on his spear as he channeled the power to shift its vibration.

He dared a glance behind him, catching Rae's wide eyes looking up at him. One green and one yellow, like they'd been when Yondé attacked.

She lay on her back, pinned by an aberration above her. Fire licked the flesh of her unmarred hands.

The fog in front of him shifted, and Bastian spun towards the open hole of the basement. He leapt over the shattered floor and took aim. Midair, he thrust the spear downward. He didn't aim for the spirits, but one swarmed up towards him with a cry. The spear thunked into the ground beside Rae's head.

He landed in a roll on the other side of the opening, huffing out a breath and struggling to get back on his feet. Lifting his left forearm, his shield materialized just in time to catch five glowing claws slashing across it.

A shriek reverberated from the basement, and he looked up just long enough to see Rae holding the spear. She'd thrust it through the apparition above her. The spirit disintegrated, and Rae rolled to the side, heaving the weapon to impale the second attacker.

Their energies dissipated, crumbling into the fabric still tingling with latent activity. The pulse of their rejoining caused the spirit attacking Bastian to hesitate, granting him an opportunity to slam his shield under its chin. The thing fell back and before it could scramble free. He slammed the razor bottom down into its chest. It screamed and vanished as its companions had.

The chaos ceased.

The fog stilled, the buzz in his ears silenced.

He rose, heaving for breath. Stepping to the edge of the pit, he peered down at Rae.

She stood in the center of the basement, feet touching the still-flickering flames. Her gaze lifted to meet his, and the fire calmed before the clouds above released a downpour.

Rain washed away the fog, hissing as it squelched what remained of the inferno. Wisps of steam attempted to rise, only to be pulled down by the steady stream of water falling from the sky.

Rae slowly sank to her knees, water cascading over her face and soaking her clothes before Bastian could consider helping her up.

He breathed in the power forming his shield, and it slid back into his skin. His tattoos darkened as he dropped into the basement, motioning towards the spear embedded in the far wall. It drifted through the air, unaffected by the rain, before it collapsed into pale trails of energy disappearing into his skin.

"Are you all right?" He knelt and touched her cheek, brushing away trails of rain only to watch them reform.

Rae shut her eyes and leaned forward, slumping into him.

He wrapped his arms around her, drawing her against his chest and burying his face against her soaking hair.

Her body shook, but she held him tightly. Breaths came in ragged gasps without words.

Bastian closed his eyes, running his hand over her hair and hugging her close with the other. Rocking to his knee, he accommodated their gradual slide as mud thickened.

Something solid shifted under his weight.

Looking down without releasing Rae, he eyed a rectangular outline sticking out from beneath his knee. The pouring rain left clean patches, washing away the dirt and ash. Stretched across the undamaged leather-bound cover were the wings of a dragon, mouth wide as it curled around a distinctly Aueric symbol Bastian didn't recognize.

He tore his eyes from the curiosity to focus back on Rae. He kissed her head. Letting his barrier weaken, he relaxed when nothing of the spirits remained. "They aren't coming back."

Rae lifted her head from his chest and looked at him. Tears rimmed her red eyes, irises green again. "No. They're not."

The rain eased, turning to a light mist in the air.

He touched her chin. "I'm sorry this happened."

If I'd been more in control of my emotions...

"It's my fault." Her tone sounded hollow as the rain cleared. "I shouldn't have come back here... The fire that killed everyone was because of me, not the lantern."

"No." Bastian shook his head. "Your Art might have escalated the fire, but you didn't do it on purpose. It was because you were being bullied. You can't blame yourself. Emotions and the Art are delicately entwined."

Rae pushed away from him and rose to her feet. Looking around the burned cellar, she rolled her lips together. "This was my home."

Bastian didn't rise immediately, glancing at the ground and the book. He leaned forward, as if to brace himself as he stood, and his fingers slipped around the cover. If this had been her house, the coincidence of an Aueric text with a dragon was too much to overlook.

He drew the book behind him, slipping it into the back of his breeches under his shirt as he stood. "Do you want to leave?" He took her hand in his, hoping she wouldn't pull away.

Rae nodded, running her free hand over her hair.

"But we still need to talk. About a lot of things."

She eyed him, her expression impossible to read, and his stomach fluttered with apprehension. "I suppose we do." She looked away.

Leading her to a crumbling wall, he braced a foot against it and laced his fingers together to create a step for her. Once her boot settled in his hands, he lifted her up, and she pulled herself out of the cellar.

Rae reached down for him, and the hovering tension within him faded.

Bastian didn't prompt her to speak as they walked back to the inn in silence, and he resisted taking her hand. Instead, he watched the streets for signs of activity from the residents. Someone must have seen something, yet no one had emerged from their homes.

Perhaps activity like this is common here. And no one cares to investigate anymore.

The dilemma of the ghosts accounted for in his mind, it wandered to more selfish topics.

How long has she known I've been lying to her?

Fear of losing her rivaled the thought of her turning him over to Helgath. Worse, she might hate him. But it hadn't all been lies, and she needed to know that. It'd been naive to think he'd escaped so cleanly.

No one ever has, and I'm not that lucky.

In the safety of the room Rae had arranged for them, Bastian secured the lock. He debated jumping straight into asking her the questions burning in his mind, but her appearance softened him, and he offered his hand. "May I?"

As Rae turned to him, he warmed his ká, drying his body and clothes the same way he'd done at the lake.

She looked at his hand, and he swallowed. It was possible she no longer trusted him, depending on how recent her knowledge of Damien was. Granting him a modicum of relief, she accepted his hand. A moment passed as he spread his focus into her.

Once her clothes were dry and her hair no longer dripped, Rae found her voice. "Thank you, Lieutenant."

Bastian cringed. "How long have you known?"

"Does it matter?"

"Yes. To me, it does."

Rae held his gaze. "Since you failed miserably at selling your armor. I've been chased by enough of your comrades to recognize it. Just took me a bit to match your face to the posters I'd seen."

She'd stayed, despite the lies he told her. It made his throat clench. "And you never said anything." Steadying his breath, he forced himself to remain in control of his ká as he looked away in shame.

"Really? Calling you Soldier and Helgathian doesn't count as saying anything? Besides, you didn't want me to know."

"Can you blame me? And then this whole Rahn'ka thing made it so much more complicated..." He groaned as he lowered his head, lacing his hands behind it.

"No, I don't blame you. Perhaps you can understand why I didn't say anything either. Would you have stuck around? With a thief? Being the most valuable man to a rich country?"

Bastian contemplated all she said. "You're from Helgath too, aren't you? Not originally, I know you're not lying about what happened here."

"How did this become about me? I never lied about where I was from. You just never asked where I went after leaving here."

Bastian sighed and shook his head. "That's not what I meant. But I'm sorry. You didn't lie. I did. But so much of what I told you is true too."

"Is it?" She walked to the bed they were meant to share and sat on the edge. "Tell me what's true, Damien, if not your name, heritage, or history."

Hearing her say his name sent a shiver through his body. It felt odd. He'd grown so used to being called Bastian that it almost didn't seem right to be called Damien again. But somehow, it sounded right in her voice.

"I didn't lie about who I am now. Maybe it's better that you call me Bastian because Damien died, in a way. He died when he said no to orders and walked away." He laughed dryly. "I never imagined I'd make it this far. I'd resigned to facing death, but it felt foolish not to fight. And when the Rahn'ka..." He trailed off, taking a step towards her.

Crossing his arms tightly against his chest, he watched her for a reaction. "Why didn't you turn me in if you knew all along? I'm sure the reward is handsome at this point. No one's lasted this long."

"Oh, it is. But you were kind to me and rather handsome yourself." She tilted her head to the side. "I'm a thief, but I'm not greedy. I had enough coin at the time to risk getting to know you before making a rash decision."

Bastian chuckled. "You're a generous thief then, letting a soldier get the best of you." He paused, forcing his hands to drop to his sides as he walked to her. Stopping directly in front of her, he looked down to meet her eyes. "I didn't lie about how I feel about you. Thief or not, I've fallen hard for you."

Rae blinked slowly as he knelt before her.

He brought a hand up and placed it on her knee, watching it as it caressed over her breeches. "What decision have you come to? What happens now?"

Rae's shoulders tensed, and her jaw flexed. "Have your desires changed?"

"No. Nothing would have meaning without you."

Smiling, Rae touched his jaw, encouraging his chin up. "Neither have mine. I want to call you Damien. I will keep your secrets. I swear, I pose no threat to you."

His stomach fluttered. "Damien." He repeated his own name. "I suppose it still fits. Lieutenant, not so much."

"Can I ask you something?" Rae's shoulders relaxed.

"Of course." He touched the back of her hand.

"Why didn't you tell me? I understand that you didn't trust me when we met, but... why did it take you so long?"

"Shame... Regret. I couldn't fathom why you'd stay. Not with who I was and then how I lied to you. With everything else going on, I couldn't stand the thought of losing you. You're the only reason I'm still alive."

Rae leaned forward and ran her hand through his hair. "Sometimes lies are necessary," she whispered. "But they can be fixed, right?"

"I hope so. I don't want there to be anymore between us."

"Me neither." She sounded half-hearted.

"Let's start here." Damien reached behind him with one hand. He withdrew the book he'd found from his waistband, holding it up to her.

Rae's brows knitted together, and she let go of him to take the book, brushing dried mud off the spine. "What's this?" Running her palm over the cover, her eyes widened. "Where did you get this?"

"In the basement. I spotted it when it in the rain. It seems amazing that it didn't burn in the first, or this second fire. There's an odd energy around it, but I can't place it. I thought you'd want it since it's from your old house. You had other things on your mind when I found it."

Rae traced her fingertips over the dragon before flipping the cover open.

Inside, the pages were in perfect condition. Scrawled on the first page was a single word.

Raeynna.

"Is that your full name?" Damien peered at her across the book.

Rae's mouth fell slightly agape as she stared at the page and nodded. She turned the page, but the next was entirely blank. Yet, she didn't tear her eyes away.

He frowned, looking at the white pages. "Is it a journal?" He tried to sort out the sensation prickling the surface. "I'd hoped for more than blank pages."

Rae's gaze darted to him. "You can't see the writing?" Turning another page, she pointed at it. "You can't read that?" Her finger pointed at nothing.

"No." Damien's brow furrowed. "You can?"

She nodded, returning her attention to the book. "It's from my grandfather." Rising from the bed, she paced towards the back wall as she read.

Damien stood but stayed out of her way, watching. "It's important then. Good. I did something right." He offered a joking smile, even though she was absorbed by the book.

Breaking her focus, Rae looked at him again, and her shoulders drooped. A haunted look glazed over her face, and she gently closed the book, placing it on a table. "Did they show you anything?"

"They?" Damien controlled his instant reaction to comfort the look in her eyes. "They who?"

Rae turned from him and walked to the west-facing window.

The black sea reflected the half-moon, shining silver on the rolling waves.

"The spirits. Did they show you the fire? The people burning?"

"I saw the fire, but that was you, not the spirits." Damien stepped behind her. "I could sense the line that tied you to it. But that was all I saw, other than the spirits themselves."

Rae fell silent, staring out the window.

His stomach clenched. "What did they show you?"

Lifting her hands, Rae began unbraiding her hair. "All the people I killed years ago. I heard them screaming. I felt their anger, their pain, the smell..."

Damien took her hand from her hair, drawing it towards him. "Let me?" He gestured towards the bed, tugging on her hand.

She followed, sitting again as he crawled behind her.

Rising on his knees, Damien pulled gently at the intricate braids to loosen them as he gathered his thoughts. With the unraveling of each braid, the soft scent of her drifted into his senses. "They don't feel anger, or pain, anymore. Those are merely echoes belonging to things that aren't those people anymore. It might be made of what's left of their energies, but it's not them. They've passed well beyond by now and are at rest with Nymaera."

Rae sighed, letting silence fall between them for a few moments before she responded. "Do you know that, or are you just trying to make me feel better?"

"I know it." Damien kissed the top of her head as he finished pulling out the braids. Still touching her hair, he found comfort in twisting her brown locks around his fingers. "I did learn a lot from Yondé. It's kind of my thing to know all about how ká behave... Souls."

Rae nodded. "Thank you." Turning and tucking her legs beneath her, she looked at him with a subtle smirk, hand delving into her pocket. "So no more dice games?" Lifting her hand, palm up, she displayed the three lapis lazuli dice she'd stolen from the table.

Damien gave an exaggerated sigh, tracing his hand down her arm. He plucked a die out of her palm. "I put these back."

Rae shrugged. "I left plenty of coin to pay for them."

He returned it to her hand and leaned back, running his fingers through her loose hair. "I see my decision to call you Dice is still perfectly appropriate." He twisted a lock around his finger.

Chuckling, she shook her head. "I've never had a pet name before. Maybe I stole these to live up to the expectations of it."

"All those men and I'm the first?"

Rae laughed. "*All those men*? Is that how you think of me? I've only been in one serious relationship before you."

He quirked an eyebrow. "So this is a serious relationship?" He gave a slow smile. "You forgive me for all the lies?"

Her posture straightened as a hint of color touched her cheeks. "I do. And... I don't know if it's *serious*, I just meant... Well, I'm not—"

He touched her jaw gently. "You don't have to explain. I jumped to conclusions, what with Seth and now Blaine..."

"I'm just comfortable around men, they're predictable. I wanted the distraction, not the rest of it." Rae smiled and pulled her loose hair into a ponytail. "His arms were half the size of yours." She nodded, as if it was the most interesting part of the interaction. "I checked."

Damien laughed, and his entire body lightened with it. He leaned back on his elbows, stretching his legs out over the side of the bed. "Is that what's important to you?"

Rae wrinkled her nose. "Not the only thing." She kicked off her boots and crawled over him. "There are many other factors to consider when choosing a lover."

She settled pleasantly on his hips, and his blood warmed.

"Am I still in the running?" He shifted his balance to support himself with one elbow, the other free to touch her thigh, caressing upward.

Rae lowered her face to his and ran the tip of her nose up his neck before kissing below his ear. "You're the only one in the running, Lieutenant."

His body tightened beneath her, and he wasn't sure what emotion caused it. But they were alone, and no one would hear. He brought his hand up her side, tangling his fingers within her hair to guide her mouth to his. The feeling of her lips sent jolts through him, excited to hear her say his real name and rank. It made it even more real, as if the rest had all been a dream.

Rae's mouth moved against his before she parted from him enough to speak. "Damien..." She kissed his upper lip.

He quivered and rose to take her mouth again, but she pushed his chest down. Letting himself fall back to the bed, he looked up to meet her eyes as she hovered over him. "I enjoy hearing you say that name more than I expected."

"Does that mean I don't have to go back to calling you Bastian, Mister Lanoret?" Rae lowered her body to rest against his.

"In private, please, no. Though it might take some getting used to again. You don't regret losing Bastian?" He grazed his fingernails along her neck, watching the slow line of goosebumps they created.

Rae rocked her hips, evoking a short groan from him, and smirked. "Last I checked, I get both of you." Her expression grew serious. "And as much as I want you, I still think we should take this slow. So if you'd rather, I can stop now."

"I'd rather not." Damien watched the trail his hand caressed down from her neck, passing bravely over her breast. "But I'm happy just kissing you."

She kissed his mouth again. "Who said anything about just kissing?" Her lips moved to his neck, kissing down to his collarbone. Looking up at him, she quirked an eyebrow. "Unless you're not up for it, I'd like to show you this thing I can do with my tongue."

Damien's eyes widened, his heart missing a beat before thudding at a far faster rate. "Dear gods, Rae. Do you really have to ask?"

Chapter 21

UNDER NORMAL CIRCUMSTANCES, RAE WOULD'VE felt on top of the world. The night together left her deeply satisfied, but when the sun rose, her heart sank.

Plagued by the reality of the situation, she escaped their room while Damien slept, in search of fresh air and a clearer mind. He fogged it up, making logical thought difficult. Rolling around in the sheets together, not sleeping, didn't help.

He'd proved to have a natural knack for physical romance, despite his lack of experience. And she had plenty of fun providing him with a night he wouldn't soon forget.

While not exactly as slow as it could have been between them, they left things yet to be discovered. It left her excited, imagining what it would be like. She craved closeness with him more than she expected, but wondered if she should let it happen.

He'd come clean with the truth, but she hadn't. Not really. Deception had never stopped her from enjoying men before, but with Damien, it was different. When he held her, he held more than her body.

Guilt wrestled through her. She couldn't tell him her true motives, or at least, what they had been. When they'd talked that night, and she'd told him she would keep his secrets, she meant it. From here on out. The first step would be to get the Hawks to back off, and that was no easy feat.

Will he forgive me?

Rae walked from the city, up the shoreline to the north. Sand squished beneath her boots, damp from the recently receded tide.

Jarrod would know what to do. He had a way with things like this.

Rae had no doubt that if Jarrod knew how she felt about Damien, he'd turn around and go right back to Mirage and leave them be.

But it wasn't so simple.

A team was on their way, with the goal of capturing Damien. They didn't know about his ability in the Art, but they knew enough. She didn't want to imagine what Damien could do to her guildmates if it came to a fight.

The idea of continuing to lie to Damien made her nauseous, but if she broke protocol now and didn't meet them, her allies would assume she'd been compromised. They wouldn't hesitate in killing Damien in his sleep if that happened.

Rubbing her temples, she sat on a low boulder and watched the sea waves roll in and out. As they did, she re-braided her hair along both sides of her head, leaving the hair on top, before pulling it all back into a ponytail. Imagining Damien's hands undoing them again, she wondered if he'd woken yet.

A screech echoed above her and drew her gaze. Sighing with relief, she whistled and held her arm up.

Din soared down and landed with a tight grip on her forearm, claws biting into her skin.

"Good boy."

The bird chittered as she scratched behind his head.

Pulling the parchment from his leg, she unrolled the message.

Din hopped off her arm, stretching his wings as he waited on a piece of driftwood caught on the rocky shore. He eyed her before he buried his head beneath his wings to preen.

Board the Herald. It departs on the half-moon.
The captain is already paid and expecting you.
Meet you in Porthew at Birch Bay Inn.

Rae swallowed her nerves, realizing she didn't have her notebook with her to write back. She'd have to use the same parchment and turn it over. Without her graphite, she found a piece of charcoal debris to write her reply. Luckily, it was abundant in Ashdale.

> *Change of plans. Stand down. Will explain in person in Porthew.*

Wrapping it around Din's leg, she said a silent prayer that Jarrod would listen.

"Go to Jarrod." The hawk hopped onto her arm, and she launched him back into the sky, watching his form disappear into the distance.

Redirecting her gaze, she searched the sky for the moon. Finding its faint shape near the horizon, she groaned. She had to hope she hadn't missed the departing ship she was supposed to be on.

Rae jumped when a yip rang out behind her. Spinning around, her shoulders relaxed when she saw Neco. "Hey, you." She stroked between his ears. "I don't think you'll like the next leg of our journey."

The wolf cocked his head, and she sighed.

"Come on, maybe it won't be so bad." She started back towards the inn.

Taking the beach as far as she could for Neco's sake, she approached the inn from the sea, seeking the back door. She climbed the stairs to the second floor with Neco padding noisily beside her, his nails clicking on the wooden steps.

Rae opened the door to their room and looked towards the bed.

Damien laid on his stomach, arm propping up his pillow with the entirety of his back exposed.

She admired the stretch of tattoo, which she was still getting used to. The runes were nothing she could understand, dominating his left arm and shoulder. Waking him with soft kisses along his spine came to mind, but her mischievous side won out.

Keeping her voice low, she closed the door behind her. "Get 'im."

Neco bounded onto the bed with a gleeful bark, slamming into Damien with a wet nose and slobbery kisses.

Damien woke, shouting, and then shoved Neco's chest before the wolf stubbornly wiggled his head back through his hands to give more kisses. "Damn it, Neco!"

Rae grinned, but a storm cloud lingered in the back of her mind.

Neco nipped at his wrists, jumping towards the bottom of the bed, lowering his chest towards the mattress. In the tussle, the sheet slipped lower on Damien's waist, granting Rae a peek of his naked body.

Damien looked over Neco's head, spotting her leaning against the door. Tugging up the sheet, his cheeks flushed.

"Shy?" Rae tilted her head.

Neco thumped to the floor, tongue lolling out of his mouth.

"Modest." Damien frowned.

"You weren't so *modest* last night." She approached the bed. Touching the edge of the sheet, she raised an eyebrow at him.

He watched her hand, then glanced up with a daring look in his eyes. Both hands still gripped tightly to the sheet, held against his abdomen.

Rae let her gaze trail down his bare chest, lingering at where his hands held the sheet, and then returned to his face. She shook her head. "You're a fine-looking man, you know that?"

"Oh? Enjoying the view?"

She crawled over the bed, unable to resist the draw of his earthy scent. "I am." She gave him a long, drawn-out kiss. "Is that a problem?"

"Not at all." His breath tickled against her lips. He must have abandoned his hold on the sheets because his hands caressed her waist and drew her into him again. He savored her lower lip, and she hummed her response before pulling away.

"I hate to cut this short, but we have to go. I got word that my father is in Porthew, and there's a ship leaving today. We should try to get on it."

He pulled gently away, giving a little whimper, not unlike one of Neco's. "Already? I suppose I should get dressed then."

It was Rae's turn to groan. "Such a shame." Rising from the bed, she stepped to the floor. She turned her back to him but peeked over her shoulder. "Want privacy?"

Damien slipped to the edge of the bed behind her, standing despite her playful glance. He stepped against her, his bare body touching her back as he wrapped his arms around her waist and kissed the side of her head. "No. I want you."

Rae closed her eyes, wondering if the Herald would leave without them. She had half a mind to let it. Turning in his embrace, she claimed his mouth again. Letting heated kisses reignite between them took only a matter of breaths before she pulled away. "Stop seducing me. You know I can't resist."

He laughed, rich and warm, making her want to melt into him. "I apologize. I don't know my own power." He glanced away from her towards where she'd thrown his clothes the night before.

Neco laid next to his tunic, head on the floor, peering up at them.

Damien's eyes narrowed at the wolf, and he released her waist, stepping away. His movement seemed less bashful, but he kept his back to her as he tugged on his breeches.

Regardless, she shamelessly admired the view.

"What about Neco?" Damien laced his belt. "I can't imagine a ship will take a wolf. Nor that a wolf would much enjoy a ship."

Rae sighed. "I was hoping you could use your weird mammal connection to explain that to him. It might be time to let him go be a wild wolf."

Damien's face quirked with an amused smile. He glanced at Neco and knelt. "You hear that?" He looked at the wolf, scooping his tunic up in the same movement. "*Weird mammal connection*, she says. Little does she know it isn't just mammals, but that might be too complicated, huh?" He ruffled the fur on Neco's head, standing as he pulled on his shirt and looked back at Rae.

She rolled her eyes. "I'm sorry, your *everything that lives* connection. Or can you speak to the dead too?"

"Haven't tried yet." Damien shrugged. His face grew more serious. "What do you want me to tell Neco? I don't think you know how attached he's gotten to you. He won't be happy in the wild."

Rae's shoulders drooped, and she settled down onto the floor, patting the space in front of her. She didn't want to disappoint the wolf. He'd been a loyal companion for nearly half a year.

Neco rose, trotting over to her and draping his large body over her lap. It knocked her back, but she braced herself with an arm.

Stroking his ears, she sighed. "I don't know. I'm attached to him, too, but the sea is no place for a wolf. Especially a valley wolf. I'd like to think we'd see each other again. Maybe he can venture south, since we're going to Porthew."

Damien sighed as he positioned leather bracers at his wrists. He crouched beside her and Neco. "You're right." He kissed Rae's temple. "Let's see what Neco wants then?" He shifted his attention to the wolf, hand brushing down his neck to scratch under the wolf's chin. Damien's eyes locked with Neco's, and the wolf tensed in Rae's arms, responding to something she couldn't hear. His ears went back, and a whimper sounded from his chest. He leaned against Rae, pushing his shoulder against her chest.

"He's trying to express that he promises he won't bite anyone if we let him come." Damien sat as if accepting this would take longer than he thought. "At least I think that's it. Either that or something about not chewing up any more... something."

Rae hung her head. "He ate my other pair of boots."

Neco whined, and she hugged him.

"Oh, you sensitive furball. I forgave you for the boots. Maybe he can meet us in Porthew?"

"I'll try to express that. It's not exactly like talking, but I'll make sure he knows you aren't mad about the boots too." Damien moved closer, knees touching Rae's thigh as he reached for Neco, who avoided his gaze now.

"Come on, boy. Work with me here." Damien bounced Neco's chin a little in his hand before they both grew still in an intense exchange of looks.

The wolf whined, but then he stopped, and his body relaxed. He dropped his head against his paws, looking up at Damien. Neco licked Rae's fingers but then shifted his weight to crawl off her lap. He shook, like after climbing out of a pool of water, and then pushed his nose under Damien's hand.

Damien sighed, and the room filled with their breathing again, as if they'd all held it during the process. "He understands."

Neco looked at Rae and bowed his head as he sat in front of her. His tail wagged back and forth as he licked her chin.

"Good." Rae wrinkled her nose at the wolf's breath. "He's an accomplished hunter, and he'll do fine on his own for now."

"I could help guide him." Damien turned towards her. "Since we're familiar with each other's essence. I'll do what I can to help him get to Porthew. He's rather insistent that he'll meet *you* there. He doesn't care about me."

Rae laughed. "Those boots must have tasted good." A pang resonated in her heart.

Damien stood and leaned against the wall as he tugged on his new boots. "You said there's a ship leaving today?" He frowned as he looked down at his feet, grabbing the top of the boot at his calf and trying to wriggle it around before doing the laces.

Rae leapt to her feet. "Yep." She snagged her pack and slung it over her shoulder. "I'll be back, I'm not sure when it departs."

"Well, I'm almost ready if you want to wait? We could go together."

I need to get to the ship alone first.

Rae cringed inwardly but nodded. "All right. I need my bow from the stables, and we should probably sell Zaili..."

"Probably best. Zaili doesn't like the ocean much, so she'll be happier staying off a ship too. You think I'll need anything else?" He gestured up and down to the loose grey tunic, secured at his wrists. It fit snuggly at his chest and shoulders. "This is all the clothing I own."

"Uhhh..." Rae tried to focus on what he was asking instead of how flattering it looked on him. "Maybe. I should check to make sure the ship won't depart without us, though. Do you want to deal with Zaili while I do that?"

Damien frowned. "Am I going too slow?"

"Yep."

"Go." Damien sighed, rolling his eyes. "I'll catch up."

She stepped over to him and pulled him to her for a quick, hard kiss.

Neco followed her out the door as she left, and she didn't deter him from keeping at her side as she hurried to the docks. The last thing she needed was for the Herald to leave without them. Jarrod would have her head.

The haze of the morning still hung in the air, a light mist curling its way up the Delkest coastline. The docks already buzzed with the excitement of trade as fishermen brought their catches ashore to sell to the locals before the rest were loaded onto trade ships. Cries of seagulls mingled with shouts of men, emerging from the mist like phantom voices until she grew close enough to make out the massive vessels moored on the piers.

She inquired with the dockmaster to the ship she sought and controlled the sigh of relief when the matronly woman pointed her towards the Herald's berth.

Rae saw the figurehead at the front of the ship first, an ethereal carving of a woman swimming among strips of fabric that curled like waves around her. Her long, delicate fingers held a horn shaped of coral and seashells to her lips. Painted in swirling gold lettering against the bow behind the alcan figurehead was *The Herald*.

The masts rose into the mists until she couldn't see them anymore, spiderwebs of rope rippling in the sea breeze as it blew over the saltwater waves. Little port holes rimmed the front of the ship, turning into wider latched shutters.

The ship stretched along the docks the length of a city block. The gangplank had to switch back before it reached the top, running parallel to the ship instead of straight up to it like all the fishing dinghies across from it. It seemed out of place in the Ashdale harbor.

Rae stepped up to the bottom of the gangplank, Neco at her side, and a shadow beside her shifted within the mist.

A slender person stood from where they sat on a pile of barrels pushed against the bottom ramp, a long coat billowing around their boots. They brushed back their hood, exposing a head of stone-grey hair cropped short to their head. The stunning deep burgundy of their eyes with pin-point pupils confirmed one thing. Auer. Which explained how a man could look so pretty.

"You took your time." He eyed Rae from her feet up as if confirming her identity. "Ashen Hawks are usually punctual."

Rae tried not to scowl. "I only received my instructions to seek your ship this morning. I apologize. I hope I haven't delayed you."

He shrugged. "The storm that sped our journey probably slowed your hawk. I'm glad you're here, though. The captain is growing impatient and desires to make way. She'll be pleased to hear you're ready to depart." He glanced behind her with a curious smirk. "However, I don't see your cargo."

Rae sighed. "He's coming, and he isn't to know any of this." Her tone became serious.

The Ashen Hawks had a sterling reputation, and she expected to receive the same respect she would give. Even at her young age, Rae was no apprentice within the Hawks.

The man lifted his hand and acted like he was sewing his lips shut. "Not a word." He lifted three of his fingers to his forehead before bringing the swooping gesture down. He offered his hand. "Lygen. I'll be your liaison while aboard the Herald."

"Rae." She accepted his hand.

He shook it with a firm grip, eyeing the wolf at her side.

"What's the relationship I am to understand between you and your charge? So we don't disrupt your business..." Lygen's hands settled behind his back.

Rae swallowed. "As far as your crew is concerned, we are merely traveling together. But he is *mine* and I will not tolerate any of your crew getting any ideas. His safety is paramount."

The auer's eyes sparkled. "Interesting. But the Ashen Hawks' priorities are no concern of mine, nor my shipmates. The crew will be told you are merely travelers. It is easier that way."

Rae nodded once. "Perfect. His name is Bastian. Unless you need anything from me at this moment, I'll go fetch him."

"A name is more than Jarrod gave us. The coin was good enough to stop the questions. The Herald and her crew are discreet. We don't need to know more. But there will be limitations to where you, or Bastian, may go on the ship. I ask that you respect them, regardless of our separate business deal. I'll await your return to show you to your quarters. But I must ask about your shadow." Lygen gestured down to Rae's side. "Our captain isn't the most welcoming to... dogs?" He gave her a teasing smile.

Rae looked down at Neco and shook her head. "Not to worry, he isn't joining us aboard."

"Shame. I would've liked to see the look on the captain's face."

Rae smirked. "You're welcome to borrow him for your cause until I return."

Lygen shook his head. "She'd like to speak with you once we're at sea. In private."

"Of course." Rae dipped her chin before turning to take her leave. Her boots were silent on the docks as she made her way back to solid ground.

Neco's nails clicked behind her through the cobblestone streets until she reached the southern edge of the town.

Sighing, she eyed the wolf. "This is where we part, Neco." She knelt and scratched his ruff. "I'll see you soon, all right?"

Neco huffed, pushing his forehead against her chest and licking her chin. As she pushed him back, he nudged her hand with a small whimper. After another wet kiss on her chin, he hopped away, loping into the woods.

Rae watched him go, and when he looked back, she smiled.

His big black body vanished into the morning shadows of the trees and Rae sighed, feeling distinctly alone.

"He'll find his way." Damien's voice came from behind her.

Rae jumped and spun around, narrowing her eyes at him. "How did you find me?"

Damien smiled. "I told you before. I can always find you." His hand rested near a new pouch secured to his belt, buckled shut. "Do you want me to explain how?" Her bow was over his shoulder with her quiver.

Rae tilted her head and raised an eyebrow. "I suppose it doesn't matter. Though it does rather interfere with my ability to be sneaky. Do you always know where I am, or do you need to... look?" She walked to him, lacing her arms over his shoulders.

"Little of both. I have to focus when you're not close by." He wrapped his hands around her waist. "*Is that a problem*?"

Rae rolled her eyes at his re-appropriation of her catchphrase. "No. It's actually strangely comforting."

"Oh, good. I wasn't sure if I could stop."

"Are you ready to go?"

"As ready as I can be. Considering we're headed back towards Helgath." He frowned a little.

"We're going south, it's hardly closer to Helgath. Are you having second thoughts about coming with me?" Her eyes searched his.

"No." He reached up and touched her jaw. "I said I want to be with you, and that's true. And I trust you."

Her stomach knotted. "You'll be safe."

They walked hand in hand back to the docks.

Lygen met them as promised and introduced himself to 'Bastian,' casting a discreet glance at their entwined hands.

They climbed the gangplank and emerged on the deck as the sun broke through the mist.

The mist surrounded the sides of the ship, as if they sailed on a cloud, the blue sky above them. The back of the ship rose to two different levels of deck, open wooden staircases on both sides.

Rae's boots stuck ever so slightly to the freshly tarred wood.

They followed Lygen to the front of the ship, descending a short ramp leading to a double doorway centered in another level of deck. He swung a door open and held it for them.

The suffocating hallway had a single unlit lantern hanging at the center, natural light squeezing through the musty windows above the doors.

"Your cabin is the one on the right." Lygen pointed ahead.

Damien got to the door first, twisting the iron knob.

Spacious for a ship, the room boasted a double bed, pushed into a corner, under a row of portholes. At the right stood a desk with an angled cover latched shut like all the cabinets and drawers built into the bulkhead.

"How long to Porthew?" Damien faced Lygen, who offered a courtly smile.

"Week. Maybe a little longer if we hit rough waters. It's likely this time of year, so I hope you don't get seasick. I'll be back shortly after we've launched. I know the process can be fascinating for those without experience, but it's safer if you stay within your cabin until I come back to give you a tour of the ship and to take you to meet the captain. She's eager to meet you both."

"She?" Damien's brow tightened. "A female captain?"

Rae scowled at Damien. "Are you kidding?"

"It's not that." Damien took a step to the side. "It's great! I just wasn't expecting it on this side of Pantracia."

Lygen grinned, amused by their exchange. "Our home berth is Ziona... If that helps explain at least a little. And there's no finer captain than ours."

Rae supposed she couldn't blame Damien's surprise, but it still made her roll her eyes. "I look forward to meeting her." She eyed Damien, walking farther into their room. "Next, you'll tell me only men can be thieves."

"The good ones, yeah," Damien mumbled under his breath, but a smile played on his lips.

Rae laughed and held up his newly acquired pouch, turning to face him. "You sure about that?"

Damien's hand flew to his side, grabbing at the belt where the pouch should have been. He frowned as Lygen let out a melodic laugh.

"I'll let you two settle in, then." Lygen closed the door behind him, leaving Damien and Rae alone in their quarters.

Damien narrowed his eyes on his pouch. "What do I need to do to convince such a mighty thief to return my property?"

He took the bow from his shoulder, propping it in the corner with her quiver.

Rae smirked, tossing the pouch in the air and catching it. "Your property?" She tilted her head. "Where did you get this coin? A horse isn't worth that much."

"I earned it. Fairly through trade."

Rae scoffed. "And what did you trade?"

"Open it. But look in the little grey pouch inside first."

She turned sideways and did as instructed, nerves rising in her stomach. Unlatching the buckle at the front, she peered inside. There were several smaller bags, and she recognized his coin purse she'd returned to him. She eyed a velvety green pouch suspiciously as she plucked out the grey one. It was heavy, bulging with the sharp edges of whatever it contained.

Damien walked up in front of her and took his larger pouch from her hands, holding it in front of him so she still had access while she undid the ties on the grey linen bag.

She peeked inside, and her eyes widened. Glancing at Damien, she poured a handful of perfectly cut precious gemstones into her other palm. Her heart sped. "Where did you get these?"

Dread washed over her.

"I found them," Damien said as if it was the simplest thing. "Well, made them, sort of. A benefit of being able to manipulate the ká of a stone. I can help it become this."

Rae gaped at him and shook her head.

Why is he showing me?

His hand touched her wrist, tightening around it. "I don't want you to worry about me. You won't have to be the one supporting us all the time. I just have to be smart about how often I trade them."

Us.

Rae rubbed her forehead and tipped her hand to return the stones into their pouch. "All right... I won't worry then..."

Damien chose the little green bag from the pouch next and held it out towards her. "Now open this one."

Rae didn't reach for it. "What's in it? Gold?" Her gaze remained on him, looking for any sign he might suspect she'd originally planned to turn him over.

Is he trying to make himself more valuable than his bounty?

"It won't bite, Dice." Damien bobbed the little drawstring bag in his hand. "It's a gift. For you."

Her stomach flipped, but she swallowed and took the small bag. Without hiding her hesitation, she pulled the opening while tipping the contents into her free hand.

A cold necklace tumbled into her palm. Within the pale blue crystal, swirls of color sparked to life when it touched her skin. Silver curled around the shard, like vines growing on a pillar, ending with a spiraled loop hanging from a chain.

Rae stared at the piece of jewelry. Her surroundings blurred as she focused on it.

This is from my father's cave.

Damien broke the silence that hovered. "The cavern gave the shard with the knowledge it was for you."

Men had given her gifts before, often jewelry but nothing close to this.

Taking a shaky inhale, she looked at Damien. "I..." She shook her head. "It's beautiful." She looked back at the necklace.

The inch-long pendant hung on the most delicate silver craftsmanship she'd ever seen.

Lifting the chain by the clasp, she offered it to Damien. "Would you?" She held her ponytail to the side after he took it and turned around.

He draped the chain around her neck, the crystal resting right above her sternum. He did the clasp, fingers tickling her skin. When he finished, his hands traced down her arms, encircling her from behind. "I'm glad you like it." He kissed her earlobe.

Rae closed her eyes, a hand on the pendant. "I do. I love it." Turning in his embrace, she sought a distraction from her guilt. Her mouth met his, drowning her fear of him learning the truth. But she had no intention of letting him be taken to Helgath.

Pulling away, she made a hasty decision. "I have something for you too, though it's not nearly as pretty." The words spilled from her mouth before she could second guess.

"For me?" He sounded surprised and touched her jaw. "I hardly deserve a gift, considering everything."

"Then it's a good thing I wouldn't call it a gift. More of a..." Rae shook her head and stepped around him, leaving his embrace to open the pack resting on the bed. "You don't have to take it if you don't want to."

Digging in her bag, she found a small leather case at the bottom. Pulling it open, she withdrew one of the two remaining bone whistles charmed for Din to find.

Rae turned to Damien and held it out in her palm. "We can train him to link your name with it later, but I thought maybe..."

Damien studied the little white cylinder, etched with black ink runes. Pursing his lips, he reached and took it slowly. "Should I be suspicious that you're planning on abandoning me, requiring long-distance messages?" A small smile accompanied his teasing, which made the words sting less. He tucked the whistle away into the pocket of his breeches, bringing his hand back to enclose it around hers. "You don't have many of those things, do you?"

"Three." Rae touched his chin. "I'm not planning on leaving your side, but I wanted you to have it, just in case, even if I can't foresee—"

"Dice." Damien squeezed her hand, lifting a finger to her lips. "You don't have to explain. Thank you." He traced her lower lip with his thumb as he stepped into her.

Her fingers slipped to tangle briefly with the collar of his shirt, touching the warmth of his skin beneath it as he leaned over and kissed her forehead. Another kiss followed, caressing her temple.

Burying her hands in his hair, she urged his lips to hers. The heat rose quickly between them, but she pulled away before it consumed her.

He breathed a sigh against her lips, gasping for air as he leaned his head against hers. “What is it?” His voice dropped to a deeper tone.

“I could tell this was real,” Rae whispered. “Between us, this. I could always tell.” She met his gaze, wishing to burn the message into his memory. “Do you understand? This is real.”

Damien touched her cheek, his fingers hot against her skin as he brushed back the escaped hairs from her secured braids. “I know.”

Chapter 22

LYGEN INTERRUPTED THEM, MUCH TO Damien's disappointment.

The heat Rae caused in his blood made him crave every part of her. From the feel of her fingers on his skin, to the little gasps from her lips.

An addiction to her formed, and nothing could convince him to stop it.

The Herald looked big from the outside, but wandering up and down the steps and ladders during their tour only made it feel larger. The fortune of such a ship being in Ashdale at all was incredible. And Rae had booked passage in a luxurious room for sea travel.

"Are passengers like us normal for your ship?" Damien trailed slightly behind as Lygen led them out of the crew quarters, a narrow space with several heights of hammocks hung in rows.

"Not terribly unusual." Lygen glanced back. "We trade in whatever kind of transport we can. We have the space to provide for guests, so when the opportunity presents itself, we'd be foolish to turn down the coin." He gestured towards a doorway with a sliding panel blocking it. "The aft cargo hold, but you aren't permitted beyond this point." Lygen stepped onto the set of steep stairs, climbing back towards the galley and armory. The former being encouraged for guests to visit, the latter strictly off-limits.

"What about the starboard bow? You didn't show us that."

As he walked onto the main deck, Lygen stepped aside for Damien and Rae to join him. "Empty space. We lost that section of the ship in an accident a few months back, and it's full of water from the patch." He narrowed his gaze at Damien. "You seem familiar with ships. Spent time on them?"

"My uncle. He used to captain one. I played on it as a kid."

Lygen made an accepting sound as he continued.

Rae looked at Damien with a raised eyebrow but didn't voice whatever thoughts she had.

"Shall I take you to the captain now?" Lygen's stiff demeanor and polite attitude made Damien uncomfortable. He hadn't spent much time around auer but had studied plenty during his military academy days. Of course,

Helgathians didn't have the best opinions about their eastern neighbors.

"Sure." Damien shrugged. "Does she often bother with meeting those you transport?"

"It's her policy to meet all who board her ship. Regardless of the nature of their arrival, as guests or cargo for the brig."

Damien frowned, wondering why a trade vessel like the Herald would market in transporting prisoners. He'd watched the crew they'd walked past, trying to get a feel for who they were.

Human ká were more complicated than animals. It felt like trying to study a single raindrop in a monsoon when he sought to piece together thoughts or emotions of people.

The energies at sea differed from those Damien had grown used to in the forest. The water pulsing on the hull of the ship brought a rhythm to the power it offered, but it left him uneasy. Too many people he didn't know, or trust.

This is for Rae. She needs to get to Porthew.

He wasn't about to leave her when something far deeper was going on. She'd been acting strangely, but he couldn't put a finger on what it was that convinced him of it.

They walked up the aft stairs to the level below the helm. A carved decorative pair of doors sat propped open, their scene done in a relief like the figurehead. An alcan woman leaned against a rock jutting from the sea, her horn summoning a storm of waves and alcans on the backs of orcas.

Stained glass windows framed the doors, though some patches were filled with a block of wood rather than glass.

Damien examined the captain's quarters beyond, light streaming through wedged-open windows at the back. A breeze caught the swaying fabric hanging from a full four-poster bed set to the side, the wall behind it full from floor to ceiling with books. Opposite was a set of well-worn, overstuffed chairs beside a table with a collection of bottles and a tea set.

The captain stood near the front of the room, hunched over a larger circular table rimmed on one side with chairs. The rest of the chairs occupied the space in front of another row of bookshelves.

Her elbows against the table, she peered down at maps. She held a piece of graphite and a compass in one hand, tapping it against her alabaster cheek. Her hair was pulled back in a single, long deep brown braid, which reached all the way to her mid-back.

She stood straight, tossing her tools down on the table as she heard the three of them approach. Her black boots came to her knee, cinching in cream-colored linen pants. Despite being on her own ship and in her own quarters, a sword hung at her side.

"You must be our passengers." The captain held a hand to Rae first. She offered a smile, showing vague age lines near her mouth.

Damien guessed her to be in her thirties but did a double-take when he looked at her stormy blue eyes. Something about them wasn't right. It took a moment for him to realize that her pupils were oddly shaped. Like a partial crescent.

"Rae." She introduced herself with an air of formality Damien hadn't expected, taking the captain's hand. "It's good to finally meet you, Captain."

Damien glanced at Rae.

Finally?

"You, too. Jarrod speaks very fondly of you." The captain shifted her grip to offer it to Damien.

He took it, his mind whirling at the mention of a name he'd heard before. "Bastian."

Who in the hells is Jarrod? She's said that name before.

The captain gripped his hand hard, requiring him to release his hold first. "Wish I had better news, but it looks like we might hit rough water over the next couple of days." Her wrist rested against the hilt of her sword like an ingrained habit. "Best if you stay in your cabin when that happens. Ship's deck is no place for land walkers during a storm, and I don't fancy fishing you out of the water."

"And we don't fancy going for a swim." Rae nodded. "We have no problem abiding your rules, and Lygen has already made it clear which areas are off-limits. Rest assured, we respect your boundaries."

Damien resisted all temptation to raise an eyebrow at Rae.

She had to be lying. There was no way she'd so willingly accept such restrictions. She'd be casing the cargo holds as soon as a storm hit while everyone else was distracted.

"Good." Looking at Damien, the captain lifted her chin. "If you'll excuse us now, I need a word alone with Rae. Lygen will show you back to your cabin."

Damien frowned and glanced at Rae. His stomach curdled with anxiety, twisting like seasickness.

Rae glanced sideways at him, nodding once without the vaguest hint of surprise. "Of course."

"Well..." Damien swallowed. "It was nice to meet you." He turned to Rae. "I guess I'll see you in the cabin in a little while?" He put his back to the captain, which made his skin crawl. Something about her felt wrong, leaving him uneasy. He tried to tell Rae with his eyes.

Rae locked her gaze on his, and with the most serious expression he'd ever seen, she motioned with her eyes for him to leave. "I won't be long."

Lygen stepped into Damien's vision, gesturing towards the doors.

Releasing his hold on Rae, Damien followed the auer out of the cabin. Before he could turn back around to exchange a final glance with Rae, the doors clicked shut.

Arriving back in the room, Damien promptly sat on the bed and unlaced his boots. When the first twisted free of his foot, he groaned in relief and threw the torture device to the ground. The other came off easier.

Briefly rubbing the sole of his foot, he crisscrossed his legs and straightened his back. His barrier had thinned from the pressure of all the crew around. He'd caught them watching him as he returned to his cabin. It made him more uneasy, still unable to determine the ship's true purpose.

The Herald's crew was one of the most diverse he'd ever seen, albeit most of his prior experience had been in Helgath. At least half the crew were women, which seemed appropriate with its home port. Damien only knew what the Helgath military academies had taught about the matriarchal country, and none of it was kind considering their centuries-old rivalry.

The anxiety of what the captain and Rae could discuss kept him from being able to relax. The name Jarrod came back to his memory, and he wondered if he was the friend Rae had been communicating with her parents through.

A sickening feeling coalesced as his mind forced him to consider that perhaps Jarrod had been the one other relationship she had admitted to.

But why are they still friends, if it's over?

Pushing the thoughts of politics and Rae aside, he fought to clear his mind.

Rebuild your barrier. Stay objective.

Damien sucked in a deep breath. His body numbed as his ká warmed. With each flickering change, the next action became easier. Soon, all he could sense was the slow swell of his lungs with breath and the ebb of his ká as it solidified the boundaries of his aura.

The door slammed, jolting Damien from his trance. His shoulders jerked and eyes snapped open to see Rae bolting the door behind her.

Fury sparked through her eyes as she stalked into the room, kicking off her boots. She didn't acknowledge his presence, unlacing her vest.

"Your conversation went well, I take it?" Damien untucked his legs to touch the cabin's wooden floor.

Rae pulled off her shirt, tossing it onto the bed. "Yep." She dropped to the floor to begin pushups.

Damien twisted on the bed, rolling to prop himself up with one arm while he watched her work out her frustration. "And now you're exercising?"

"Mmm." Rae lowered herself into a second set. "Helps with more than hangovers."

His eyes traced the defined muscles on her back before he could control the desire. "What'd the captain want?"

"Oh, the usual. Berate and demean."

He frowned. "About what?"

"Apparently my methods as a thief need a drastic amount of work." Rae lowered herself to the floor and rolled over. Staring at the ceiling, she caught her breath before rising into a sit up.

"Who's she to judge?" Damien scowled. He slid off the bed, taking his accustomed position of holding her ankles.

"It doesn't matter." She met his gaze for the first time.

He leaned forward against her knees and caught her mouth for a quick kiss as she rose into another sit up. "Should I go give her a piece of my mind?" He grinned, teasing.

Rae growled. "You'll do no such thing." She sat up once more and touched his face. "She doesn't know what she's talking about, anyway."

"Please don't stop on my account. I was enjoying the view, though this one isn't bad either." He smiled. "I could suggest alternative physical activities to burn off some steam." He doubted it would distract him from the burning questions in his mind.

Starting with who Jarrod is.

Rae gave him a devilish smile. "You know, with all the women on this ship gossiping about you, I'm sure you could have your pick." Standing, she rummaged through her pack, putting her book on the desk before giving up her search for whatever she'd been looking for.

Damien stood, creeping up behind her. He wrapped his arms around her bare waist, humming in her ear. "Oh my... Is it your turn to be jealous?"

"Apparently," she grumbled, jaw flexing. Turning in his embrace, her eyes bore into his, brimming with unreadable emotion. "You're mine."

"You have nothing to worry about. I am, most ardently, *yours.*"

Rae's brows turned upwards in the middle, and he wondered what else she felt under her obvious distaste for other women's wandering eyes. "Promise?"

He paused, smoothing her brow with his thumb, then cupped her cheek. "What's wrong? Something's bothering you."

Rae looked away, stepping from his touch.

He frowned, catching her wrist to guide her towards the bed. "Of course I promise."

A smile twitched the corner of her mouth, and she climbed onto his lap after he sat. "This is going to be a long week." She brought her mouth to his in a delicate kiss. "At least we have a bed."

"Better than what I was expecting." Damien traced the line of her spine. "It's amazing how lucky you were to find a ship to Porthew with a captain who knew of you beforehand. What are the chances?" Despite Rae's apparent frustration, he refused to let her distract him from his questions. As he spoke out loud, an unfamiliar nervous energy returned to his stomach. "I'm not sure I trust the captain."

"I'm not sure I do, either." Rae slid next to him while a hand pressed on his chest to encourage him to lie with her.

The bed felt comfortable beneath him, and he couldn't help the satisfied moan as Rae nuzzled against his side.

She played with the bottom hem of his shirt.

He thought for a moment she would elaborate, but when she didn't, his nerves only grew.

Perhaps a different subject, then?

Turning to his side, he chewed on his lip while he studied her face, touching her temple. "Will you tell me who Jarrod is?"

Her gaze darted to his face, and she remained silent for another breath. "A friend."

The hesitation suggested far more.

"Just a friend?"

Rae tilted her head. "Now, yes..." She sighed. "But no, he wasn't always *just* a friend."

A flash of jealousy flitted through him, adding to his nerves. "How long ago?"

"How long ago did it start? Or since it ended?"

"Both? How long were you together?"

"Almost two years, but we've been friends since I was thirteen. It ended a year ago or so, maybe a little more."

In most societies, two years was enough time to court, wed, and have a child. The line of questioning didn't help Damien's nerves, but he needed to know. It felt important, even though he didn't understand why.

"You said his name before." Damien heaved a breath. "You asked where he was when I woke you after that fight with the Reapers."

Rae nodded. "I know. I was confused."

"You thought he was with you?"

Running her hand through his hair, Rae shook her head. "Maybe. Even after we split up, he was always there for me."

"Why didn't it work out between you?"

Rae met his gaze evenly. "I wasn't the kind of person he wanted to be with."

Damien stared at the thin embroidery lines on the blanket between them, picking at the threads. Not only had she been with Jarrod for years, but he'd broken it off with her. He couldn't help the next burning question. "Did you love him?"

Rae sighed. "Damien..." She touched his face. When he didn't look at her, she took a deeper breath. "Yes, I did... and I still do, just... in a different way."

The coiled jealousy sparked, tightening his throat. Damien cleared it as he reached to take her hand, hoping the physical contact with her might help assuage the bitterness. "What about me?"

Rae smiled. "What *about* you? I'm here with you. Because I want to be. Jarrod is my closest friend, but you're the man I want to *be* with. It never would have worked out with him, and nothing will change that."

He met her eyes, her hand running back through his hair again, making his entire body ache. The green of her irises seemed bright in the dim room, assuring. All he wanted was to wrap himself in her warmth.

He took her hand, bringing her palm to his lips. He kissed her skin. "I'm sorry. I'm still new to all this."

"Believe it or not, it's rather new to me, too." Rae pulled herself towards him to kiss his lower lip. "Just as adamantly as you claim to be mine, I feel the same. Don't worry about Jarrod, or anyone else."

"Anyone else?" Damien couldn't help the brief smile. "How many have there been? I'm starting to seriously question my decision to become a soldier rather than a thief."

Rae laughed. "I told you. Only two relationships."

Damien traced her bottom lip with his thumb. "When you say two... who's the other beside Jarrod that I need to kill?"

"You, you idiot. And you don't need to kill Jarrod. I think you'd like him." She gently bit his thumb, sending a pleasant tingle down his spine. Almost enough to distract him.

"I doubt that." He frowned. "What about un-serious relationships?"

"You ask a lot of questions." Rae smirked. "What about them?"

"I'm curious." Damien shrugged. "But I suppose I could stop asking if you'd give me the proper motivation."

Rae rolled her eyes. "I've been with a few men, but most of those encounters didn't last longer than a night. I've kissed more than a few, and I couldn't possibly count how many I've flirted with. Does it matter? My profession lends to rather unique necessities and sometimes the need to thoroughly distract a man. Or a woman."

"Again, I picked the wrong profession."

Rae shook her head and her brows knit together. "I disagree. You're too honorable a man. I don't think you'd be satisfied with my line of work. Besides, it's all empty. The physical is shallow and those single-night affairs never granted me whatever I was searching for."

Damien smiled, touching her chin. "What about this?" He leaned in to kiss her lower lip. The kiss slowed, but as it renewed, he felt as if he could melt into her.

She inhaled through her nose, returning the passion for a moment before pulling away. Meeting his gaze, her brows twitched. "What I have with you is deeper, and I wouldn't trade it for all the men in Pantracia."

Holding her so close, everything in Damien felt immensely right. Peaceful. Even the power of the Rahn'ka grew satiated by Rae and her words. He realized in the moment of clarity how much he'd always need her.

"How did I get so lucky?" Damien kissed her jaw.

Rae closed her eyes, using her hand to redirect his mouth to hers. Apparently unwilling to answer his last question, she rolled him onto his back again. The weight of her body rested on his. After several heated kisses, she pulled back enough to speak.

"Make love to me," she whispered, lips brushing over his.

His heart thundered, his entire body responding. How desperately he wanted to.

Touching her side, Damien urged her to the bed and followed readily. He lifted his body above hers and nestled between her legs as they wrapped them around him, mouth hungrily taking hers. His hands explored down her body, savoring her curves through the thin chemise. Breaking the heated kisses, he trailed his lips along her jaw, nibbling beneath her ear.

Rae's back arched, and she held her body tight against his. Without pause, her hands ventured back into his hair before tugging at his shirt.

A bell somewhere above them tolled.

Damien's shirt flew to the floor, and the bell rang again.

Distant shouts of the crew penetrated their cabin. The rising nervous energy of the crew pulsed against his senses, forcing him to acknowledge the brutal interruption.

Inhaling sharply, he broke the kiss but refused to move away from her.

"For fuck's sake." Rae groaned as the bell kept reverberating through the walls.

"That's not a storm." Damien kissed her neck regardless.

The ship listed to one side, turning.

Rae gripped his sides, and the touch left his skin buzzing like a lightning storm. "How am I supposed to be useful when all I can think about is you? Besides, we were told to stay in our room."

"A good point." Damien trailed his lips lower on her body. The pressure on his ká from outside sources demanded his attention, but he focused on Rae. He noticed the elevated ecstatic energy of her ká as it danced against his. He could feel her frustration, her desire. It mounted against his, making his muscles tremble.

With their energies tangling together, the rest of the ship vanished from his mind despite the persistent ring of the bell. It faded to a distant thrum, buried beneath the sound of Rae's sharp breaths as he lifted her chemise over her head, his lips caressing her breasts.

Grabbing her thighs, he pulled her to the edge of the bed and stood. She sat up, unbuckling his belt and whipping it off to the floor. He reached to help, but she swatted his hands away, unfastening the buttons of his pants with a flick of her deft fingers.

Meeting his gaze, she tugged his remaining clothing down, teasing him with an admiring glance and graze of her fingertips over his skin.

"How could I ever even look at anyone else?" Kissing beneath her ear, Damien urged her back, lowering to the floor in front of her. "I only want you." Hands trailed down her abdomen to make quick work of the fastenings of her pants.

"I will only ever be yours." Rae watched him slide her leathers from her legs.

His hand traced up the inside of her thigh, teasing as he stood to return to her lips. She inhaled deeply, the sound enticing him closer as she scooted further onto the bed, and he followed.

The pit of his stomach hummed, every part of him aching in anticipation for what would come. He could imagine no better way to explore such undiscovered territory.

The taste of her skin while his lips trailed down her body encouraged Damien's energies to focus on nothing else. He felt only her and the tantalizing reaction to each subtle touch. The heat of her tormented every fiber of his being, and he couldn't resist anymore.

Rae pulled him closer, her heels encouraging him forward as he slid into her. The sudden rising fire threatened his control, and he stilled. He met her gaze, and she ran her hand through his hair. He touched her jaw, lifting her lips to his in a tender kiss.

After a breath, Rae rocked her hips, and he gasped. They moved in tandem, rising with passion once more. Urgency mingled with euphoria, the vibration of her moans against his lips once again testing his resolve.

When Damien slowed to steady himself, she kissed him harder and pulled him deeper with her legs. His body shook, and she cried out into his mouth, sending him plummeting over the edge with her. His breath came in ragged gasps, arms no longer able to hold him above her. He sank against her chest, and she held him there.

Rae's lips formed a kiss on his neck, legs still tight around him. "I think I might be as lucky as you." His skin muffled her voice, and she gently bit him.

He groaned, unable to form words. Lifting himself just enough to see her face, he traced the line of her collar. The small crystal had fallen beside her neck, glittering among her hair and the bedcover. Unable to resist the temptation of her reddened lips, he claimed her mouth to kiss her hard.

Rae's hand buried into his hair, tugging on the roots. Pressing her forehead to his, she broke the kiss. She opened her mouth but hesitated, her breath still coming quickly.

Touching her lower lip with his thumb, he tried to steady his heart. "What is it?"

Swallowing, she shook her head, but her eyes were glassy. "Just happy."

He smiled and nodded as he nuzzled against the side of her head. "Me too." The smell of her hair lulled him into a state of relaxation, rivaling any he could accomplish under Yondé's teaching. The strands of his ká lay in a similar state among hers, utterly satiated.

Against his will, the state of calm allowed the exterior voices to return. Accompanied by the insistent toll of the bell on deck, it cruelly rocked him from the lingering ecstasy. "Should we check what's happening?"

"Probably." She breathed deeply. "But I can't move until you do." Smiling against his skin, she nipped him again.

He groaned, trying to regain control of the rest of his body. It came slowly, and they both gasped as he pulled away. He slid to the ground, plucking up their clothes and trying to remember how to fasten his pants.

Rae dressed and then laughed at him, still fumbling with his buttons. "You all right, Lieutenant?" She crossed to him and completed the task for him.

He grinned at her. "Just recovering. What can I say? You've got me a little dazed." Watching her, he abandoned dressing himself.

Rae smirked, pulling his shirt over his head for him. "And I'm happy to repeat the process at our next opportunity."

"Promise?" The rocking of the ship had displaced the quiver and bow, and he quickly collected the arrows to replace them.

"Promise." She took the weapons at his offering and slung them over her shoulder. "Shall we?"

The bell tolled constantly now, and the ship listed to the starboard side.

With a nod, Damien unlatched the lock and yanked the door open. He didn't bother with shoes.

When they emerged from the short hallway, chaos roared

across the main deck. By the way the sailors moved, weaving in and out of each other, with others climbing up the rigging, it looked well-orchestrated. While they shouted to each other, no one stood idle.

Looking at the aft deck, a dark-skinned woman stood shouting orders that were echoed back. Damien had enough knowledge to recognize her as the first mate.

Lygen wove through men making their way below deck, approaching Damien and Rae as if he'd been waiting to see them emerge.

Damien ignored him, taking a step towards the port banister, staring at the vessel approaching the Herald, preparing to broadside her. The burgundy sails made her country of origin unmistakable, and his heart clenched.

Rae came up next to him. "Helgathian Armada. You need to get back inside."

"You both should." Lygen's voice interrupted before Damien could respond. "We're no strangers to fighting Helgathians."

"Then you should know what's about to happen," Damien growled. "She never should have gotten this close."

Lygen frowned. "Let us worry about it. This isn't your concern."

"Like hells it isn't."

The Helgathian ship creaked and groaned as her helmsman threw her into a sharp turn.

Rae's hand closed on his forearm. "*Bastian*," she said between gritted teeth. "Go back to our room. Please."

Damien's head spun as adrenaline coursed into his system. "Not if I can be of help here. I can't sit inside while everyone else puts their lives at risk." The guilt of him potentially causing the ship's attack wouldn't allow it.

Fear flashed through Rae's eyes, and she let go of Damien's arm, averting her gaze.

"Get back to your cabin. This isn't a request." Lygen's face darkened. "I don't have time to argue. You won't be any help without a weapon."

"Then give me a weapon." Damien glowered.

Rae walked away, pulling herself up the side rigging. She climbed toward the Herald's sails and swung a leg over a high horizontal beam.

The guilt in him doubled as he realized Rae's likely anger.

But how could she ask me to sit this out?

Lygen sighed, then thrust a rapier from his belt into Damien's hand. "Stay out of the way."

Something thunked beside Damien, and he turned to see an arrow, its tip aflame, jutting out of the banister.

Lygen cursed in Aueric. With a gesture of his hand, power surged through the auer. A misty cloud of water vapor passed from his palm to quench the fire, and the embers sizzled.

Damien dared a look after Rae, just as she loosed an arrow to take out an archer on the Helgathian ship. A breath later, the sail directly behind her tore, the punctured hole catching flame.

The first mate shouted, and crew raced to secure the sails, a flurry of activity surrounding Rae.

Another flaming arrow struck, nearly piercing Rae's thigh, and she glowered. She grabbed the fiery shaft with her bare hand and nocked the blazing arrow herself. She sent it back to the archer it came from. Her eyes scanned the Helgathian ship, and Damien followed her gaze to the captain.

Before she could take a shot, the Herald lurched, a boom splintering through the deck as the Helgathian ship collided with them.

Rae's beam shook, and she slid sideways. Grabbing onto the rigging before she fell, she hung from one arm. Gracefully, she lifted herself and wrapped her legs around the beam.

Damien gaped in wonder. He wouldn't have been able to accomplish the task. Despite the rising adrenaline, he still felt distant from their passion.

Hanging upside down, she locked her ankles together and drew the bowstring back.

"You can't be serious..." Damien muttered as she took aim.

Loosing her arrow, Damien watched it fly toward the opposing captain. It exploded midair as it struck an invisible force. The shield pulsed outward, rippling like fabric in the wind. The radiating energy made Damien's ká hum, and a faint amber light shimmered in a domed barrier surrounding the Helgathian ship.

More projectiles struck it, sending an array of shudders across the surface from each shot the Herald's archers took. The ranged attacks from Helgath ceased.

The barrier swelled to cover where the two ships' banisters met, secured with ropes. The Helgathians didn't even bother guarding the entrance to their ship.

Damien looked up, searching for Rae, but couldn't find her before deflecting an oncoming attack. He'd seen plenty of fights before, but none in such a claustrophobic environment.

I need to warn her about the barrier.

Men shouted from aboard the Helgathian ship, and uniformed naval soldiers threw themselves across the gap between the ships. They clashed with the Herald's crew, a thunderous battle erupting as Helgath charged beyond the barrier line.

Most of the Herald's crew avoided nearing the barrier, but a young crewman lunged forward, axe in hand to sever the bonds between ships. His body struck the shield with a rattling pop, and he screamed. His skin blackened, charred beyond recognition. His body seized and collapsed onto the deck.

The Helgathians passing through the barrier didn't suffer the same fate. The charms they carried allowed them an unfair reprieve from the battle. When injured or exhausted, they retreated to trade places with a fresh soldier.

The deck grew slick with blood, and several souls departed Damien's awareness, vanishing beneath the waves to join Nymaera. Too few were Helgathian.

Damien hastily made a decision and spun, searching the deck for one of the fallen Helgathians.

A body lay halfway between the barrier, legs sticking out on the Herald's side.

Damien rushed forward, grabbing the man's ankles and pulling the body back. He rolled the corpse, snapping the arrow sticking out of his neck, and tore at the buckles of his armor.

The squelch of sticky steps behind him demanded Damien's attention, and he abandoned the search in time to bring his borrowed rapier up to catch a sword from striking his shoulder. The soldier withdrew his attack, remounting a new one to take advantage of Damien's crouched position.

Damien rolled over the corpse he'd searched, his left hand closing around the charm at the dead soldier's chest, tearing the thin leather necklace.

The attacking soldier's eyes locked on Damien's fist, and his face turned serious. Glaring suspiciously, he rotated the hilt of his blade, body tense.

Damien circled with the soldier before he lunged without warning. Instinct and muscle memory took hold, and Damien's blade caught the other above his head. With his palm against the flat of the blade, he braced a foot behind him and pushed the man off.

The soldier's body went rigid as an arrow sank into his head. He dropped limply to the deck.

Following the trajectory, Damien found Rae standing on a different beam than she'd originally occupied. She drew her bowstring back again, but it looked like she aimed straight for him.

Don't move.

He flinched and held his breath when her arrow flew. A breeze rustled his hair, the feathers on the arrow's fletching tickling his ear as it whipped past his head, and a grunt echoed behind him.

Spinning around, Damien faced his would-be attacker before the man collided with him. He must have been running when Rae shot him, because the full force of his body threw Damien to the deck.

Pain washed through his chest and arm. Shoving the man's limp body away, Damien eyed the knife buried in his left shoulder. The hilt stuck out from his tattooed flesh, his shirt staining bright red. It was high, close to the joint. If the man had stabbed him from behind before Rae shot, it would have been his heart.

Somewhere, he heard Rae shout something, and then she was at his side.

"I'm fine." He grimaced, trying to sit up. Each time he made progress, his hand would slip. He let go of the sword hilt and looked down at the knife.

"Stop moving. Leave it until we have something to stop the bleeding."

Easier said than done.

He understood the logic of keeping the blade in place, but looking down at the piece of steel, wholly wrong in his shoulder, he wanted to tear it out. His shirt clung to him, soaked with blood. He hoped not all of it was his.

"Help me up." Damien reached for Rae. He sucked in a breath, trying to compartmentalize the pain. He urged his ká to focus on the area, numbing as much of it as he could.

Rae pulled his good arm over her shoulder and hauled him to his feet.

Before she could chide him for it, Damien tore the knife from his shoulder with a hiss.

Rae scowled at him. The shade of her right eye shifted as clouds gathered to block the sun. "Why do I bother? Fight battles, get stabbed, risk being—"

"Behind you." His tone, dulled by pain, sounded far less dire than he meant it to.

A Helgathian soldier plowed towards Rae, a boarding axe raised in one hand.

She whirled around and lifted her arm to block the swing. The handle crashed down on her forearm, just under the weapon's head.

The sound of bone snapping echoed with her yell as she fell back into Damien, the break bulging against her skin. Her bow clattered to the deck.

With the tumble, Damien skirted to the side, and the axe dug into the wood of the mast just over his right shoulder. His arm encircled Rae, holding her to him as he kicked his foot at the soldier's gut. He wheeled backward, sputtering and leaving his weapon behind.

The clouds broke, rain pouring down and slicking the deck as it purged the blood from the planks.

Rae twisted from Damien's grip, using her uninjured arm to tear the axe from the mast in time to block an attack coming from behind them.

Damien lifted the knife he'd torn from his shoulder, channeling power into it. The effort made his head feel light, and the blade glowed orange as if fresh from the forge. Before he lost the nerve, he tore open his shirt and pressed the flat side of the blade to his shoulder wound. He cried out as it sizzled against his flesh.

He fought to keep his knuckles clenched and, instead of dropping the blade, he threw it. It sunk into the chest of the attacking soldier, propelling him back with the impact. He hit the ground at the feet of another, who stared at Damien in rage.

His angry, battle-hardened face was one Damien recognized as the Sergeant he'd surpassed.

"Lieutenant Lanoret." Rynalds used a voice too calm for the battlefield. "Didn't expect to see you here."

A rush of thoughts coursed through Damien as he dove to the deck, searching for the items he'd dropped. He clutched the barrier charm and struggled to rise.

"Stay down!" Wildly swinging the axe with one hand over Damien's head, Rae gutted another nearby Helgathian. The weapon flew from her grip, skittering across the deck. Yelping, she tucked her broken arm to her side and grasped Damien with the other.

He yanked her around the mast, putting it between them and Rynalds as quickly as he could. In the moment of pause, he tied the necklace's leather strap around her neck. He pulled open the collar of her shirt and dropped the iron pendant against her skin.

Chapter 23

"LIEUTENANT!" A VOICE CALLED FROM behind the mast.

Rae's heart jumped into her throat before she could ask Damien what he'd just tied around her neck.

Damien flinched, turning to face the soldier who said it. "Sergeant Rynalds." He bobbed his grip on the wet rapier in his hand. Rain flowed down the blade, dripping off the tip.

"You're coming with me, Lanoret. To face punishment for your crimes." Rynalds glowered. "You're going to make me a rich man."

Rae stepped around Damien. "Like hells he is." She yanked a stray arrow from the mainmast to use as a weapon and lunged for the hulking man's torso.

Rynalds grabbed the arrow's shaft, forcing it down as he struck her across the face with his other hand.

Rae stumbled back, shaking her head to clear her vision as Damien wove past her.

A metallic taste tainted her mouth.

When her vision cleared, Damien's left arm was twisted behind his back and a new gash marred his jaw.

Thunder rolled through the sky, rain dripping off her chin.

A pair of brass knuckles shone in Rynalds's left hand as he jerked back on Damien's injured shoulder. "Still just as bad at grappling, I see." He smirked and swept Damien's feet out from under him with a hook of his ankle, using the momentum to push them towards the barrier.

Rae held her breath as Damien's body met the barrier, but passed through it as if nothing were there at all.

Damien's skin glimmered beneath the fabric of his shirt. The pale-blue light of his power shone, and Rae watched as the wisps trickled down his arm. The marks of his tattoo glowed beneath his shirt, following the paths of the runes Rae loved to trace.

The Art flared in a blinding flash of light, extending into the shaft of his spear. The razor point erupted towards Rynalds, who shouted and threw Damien ahead of him.

Someone shoved Rae to the side, and she lost sight of Damien. She maneuvered through fighters to gain a new vantage from farther down the ship, in time to see Damien rip a charm, identical to the one he'd given her, from a soldier's neck.

Rae touched the necklace he'd given her.

It makes them immune to the shield.

Damien faced the barrier, leaving his back exposed to Rynalds's advance.

"Behind you!"

But it was too late.

Rynalds threw a muscled forearm at the back of Damien's head. The blow struck his shoulder in his late attempt to dodge, forcing Damien against the banister. He dropped to his hip on the ground, dodging another blow. Pushing off, he slid along the slick deck towards the barrier.

The Sergeant caught him before he made it all the way through.

Brass knuckles crashed down, slamming into Damien's right wrist, below his clenched hand holding the charm. Rynalds yanked on the leather necklace, wrestling it from Damien's hand while the Rahn'ka's arm remained within the barrier.

Rae raced towards him, but she couldn't reach him before the barrier reacted, a horrible crackling sound with a flash of amber followed by Damien's scream. Her hand closed on his wrist, silencing the barrier's assault before it could do worse damage.

Damien fell back onto the Herald's deck, and Rae landed on her knees next to him. His arm shone with red and black blistered skin. He tried to pull it into his body but cried out when he touched his destroyed flesh.

Rae moved behind him and grabbed him under his arms, lifting his weight in the crook of her elbows. She dragged him away from the barrier and raging battle, her forearm howling at the effort.

Herald crew swarmed between them, forming ranks and pushing Helgath back.

"Shit." She came to a stop on the safer side of the ship. Rain sizzled on his arm, and she wondered if it made the pain worse or helped numb it. "This is why I told you to get below deck."

Damien's eyes glazed over, but his good hand closed on her bicep. "The necklace will get you through the barrier. It has to touch your skin." He grimaced, drawing a shaky breath. "Destroy their ship from the inside. Use the Art to do it."

Rae pushed his hand away. "I can't. I don't know how. I haven't read enough, and I've never—"

"None of that matters." He pointed up to the stormy sky. "This is you, not nature. Just let go of that thing you've been holding onto inside you. All the fear, the pain, whatever's been on your mind. The Art will answer."

Rae shook her head, rain falling from her face. "What if I can't?"

He squeezed her arm, his grip firm. "You can. Just stop overthinking it. Besides, if you don't... we'll all die."

Rae tilted her head with a scowl. "Way to leave me no choice. At least my last hour was memorable." She frowned. "If I die, I'm coming back to haunt you." She gave him a hard kiss, and he returned it. When she pulled away to look at him, she tried to burn his face into her memory in case she didn't get a chance to see it again.

He touched her cheek. "Come back to me. I need to tell you how much I love you."

Rae's heart lurched, and she closed her eyes as she let out a half-hearted laugh. "Bold declarations mean more when they aren't given at the brink of disaster. Try again when we aren't about to die." Something about his face made her want to make bold declarations too, but she held her tongue.

Damien smiled, but it was weak. "Go, Dice."

"Don't bleed out while I'm gone." Rae's arm throbbed, but she fought to stay focused. The thought of boarding the Helgathian ship alone made her knees weak.

The roar of battle crashed around her while she waged her own internal war.

He's crazy, I don't know how to use the Art.

Gritting her teeth, she scaled the rigging as fast as she could with only one viable arm. She hooked the ropes with her left, reaching a wide horizontal beam. Its tip nearly touched the barrier, and she gasped, balancing on the slick round wood.

"This isn't how I die," she whispered. "Shit... This is the stupidest thing I've ever done. And I've done a lot of stupid things."

She needed to make it over the gap to a similar beam on the Helgathian ship, and that would require sure feet. With the rocking of the ships in the growing storm, the landing would be impossible.

Pushing away the desire to delay longer, Rae tensed before sprinting ahead.

One boot landed in line with the other as she ran over the narrow beam.

Reaching the end, she held her breath as she launched herself off. She soared through the amber barrier while imagining the wind gathering beneath her. Her skin tingled as she passed through the shield, but the sensation passed without pain.

A gust of wind burst up beneath her, propelling her farther than she expected. One boot connected with the Helgathian beam on the other side of the barrier, but her tread slipped on the wood, and she fell forward. Her good arm grabbed hold of the only rigging it could.

The rope she grasped fell loose, swinging her down to the main deck below. Letting go at the last moment, she rolled to a stop and pushed to her feet. Her chest heaved, and the looks of shock on the soldiers' faces mirrored her own.

Among them, the scowling face of Sergeant Rynalds emerged. He stepped from the crowd, moving towards her, his brass knuckles gleaming.

Rae lifted her right hand, forcing herself to stand still. Surrounded by enemies, she wondered if Damien's faith in her had been misplaced. Her mind numbed as she struggled to do as he instructed. Seeking the shackles locking away her power, she focused on the sky.

"Hey, Rynalds." She tried to buy herself some time as a rumbling inside her heated her veins. "Can't we talk about this?" Her Art swelled, answering her call in a rush. Relief accompanied the flood of energy, and hope prickled at her mind.

Rynalds gave a wolfish grin. "Not a lot to talk about. But I should thank you. I have a feeling having you will make Lanoret more cooperative. What with the way I saw him looking at you and all..."

"Having me?" Rae stepped back. "I'm just here for a visit, real short, I promise." A dam somewhere inside her will strained in excitement as storm clouds swirled above her, waiting for a demand.

Rynalds jerked his head to the soldiers beside him. "Restrain her."

The men answered, plowing forward, and their hands clamped down on her.

Rae cried out, her arm screaming. Her connection, nearly bursting, needed something from her, but she struggled to comprehend what. She focused on Damien's face.

Let go. Let go.

Rae exhaled, blocking out the sensation of being pulled across the slippery planks. With her breath, she found the walls she'd built without realizing it. She let go of her fear of what lurked behind and welcomed what nature was ready to provide.

In a flash of light, thunder cracked. Lightning ripped from the sky, exploding the planks around her. Electricity vibrated through her bones, the bolts striking her in a deafening crash.

Her body arched, ablaze with heat and energy. Awareness left her senses, consumed by blinding light and noise. The air buzzed, the surrounding rain evaporating in a wave of steam. Every hair on her body stood straight up.

The shouts of soldiers around her disappeared when the wood shattered beneath her feet, glowing cracks forking across the deck, thunder booming in a flurry of destruction.

Rae screamed, the ground under her boots giving way. All hands vanished from her skin, and she fell.

Cold water engulfed her, but her limbs wouldn't move. Opening her eyes, the salt burned. She looked up at the surface of the ocean.

Flashes of lightning echoed across the waves, fading to a dim light trickling through the dissipating clouds. The shadows of debris floated all around her, the water churning as the mass of the ship's hull sank.

Her body felt heavy, and the last of her air bubbled from her lips. She drifted down, the light at the surface dimming the deeper she got.

An unfamiliar energy pulsed around her, urging her to breathe. Giving in to the instinct, she sucked water into her lungs. It stung at first, but then dulled. Like breathing thin air at the top of a mountain. Despite allowing her to live, it failed to strengthen her muscles enough to swim.

Her eyelids slid closed, leaving her alone in silent darkness.

The water swelled, a hollow sound in her ears.

Something grabbed her around the waist.

Bubbles trailed up her body, tickling beneath her clothes. Breaking through the surface came with a rush of sound, screams and cracking wood.

Somehow, she couldn't breathe. Air touched her face, but she choked, unable to draw it in.

Forcing her eyes to open, Rae squinted at the bright sun. Struggling to maintain consciousness, the next thing she knew she was flat on her back on cold wooden planks.

A force struck her chest, and she coughed. Her body curled to the side, and she sputtered the water from her lungs, spitting it onto the deck. Gasping in the freezing air, Rae shivered. She blinked, trying to focus on the person leaning over her, dripping saltwater on her face.

"Good. You're alive." The captain flipped the soaked tail of her braid over her shoulder as she took in a breath. She stood, her silhouette blocking the sun from Rae's eyes. "Now, I'd like you to explain why you brought a Lanoret on my ship."

Rae winced, grabbing her injured arm. "Who?" Dread spiked through her.

"Don't play coy with me. I heard his name when his comrade said it."

Rae closed her eyes, shaking her head. "Where is he?" She tried to look around from where she lay. "Is he all right?"

"Depends on the definition." The captain wrung the water out of her sleeves as if they hadn't all just nearly died. "You're lucky I don't kill him myself considering the family blood in his veins. But he's where he should have been this entire voyage. And you've got some explaining to do before you can see him."

Rae let her head fall back to the deck with a thunk. "He has no loyalty to Helgath." Her eyes steeled on the captain. "And if you kill him, I *will* sink your ship."

The captain chuckled and shook her head. "I suppose you would. But I'm hoping we can be more civil than that. Shall we at least agree to chat before you go about summoning any more storms?"

Rae frowned. "Works for me. I'm pretty tired now."

"I sure hope so." The captain crossed her arms over her chest. "It is curious how protective you are of the deserter, considering the reward for his return to Helgath doesn't require him to be alive. It'd be a lot easier to collect if he wasn't."

Rae sat up and coughed, shaking her head again. "I don't give a shit about the reward. I told you before. You don't know what you're talking about. The last thing I want is to turn him over."

The captain quirked a thin eyebrow at Rae, the side of her mouth following it in a half-smile.

A small crowd gathered around them, all eager to watch.

Lygen stood behind his captain, his face difficult to read.

"What I wouldn't give to see Jarrod's face when you tell him you fell for a Helgathian soldier. If I hadn't witnessed you save my ship with my own eyes, I wouldn't have bothered jumping in after you." The captain heaved a sigh and snatched her sword from a crew member who'd been holding it. She laced the belt and re-buckled it. "Lanoret will remain in the brig until we reach Porthew. I'd suggest you not persuade me to throw you in with him."

Rae glowered, rising to her feet, her broken arm close to her waist. "I appreciate you taking a swim on my behalf, but if you hurt him, you'll wish you let me die."

The captain adjusted the sword at her side, stepping towards Rae. She didn't hesitate in getting in close, her face an inch away. "Before you threaten me, you best remember you're on *my* ship, girl."

"It's only a ship while it floats," Rae hissed through her teeth. She turned away, but the captain caught her broken forearm, and Rae yelped, yanking it away.

The captain didn't reach for it again. "Lygen." She spoke without looking away from Rae. "See to her broken arm, then escort her to visit her lover. We'll talk later."

"Yes, Captain."

The captain glared at Rae for a moment, then turned, and Lygen stepped in to take her place. Starting up the stairs towards her cabin, she shouted at the crew as she passed them. They responded by dispersing, plucking up shattered pieces of ship from the deck as they went.

Lygen's ruby eyes narrowed at Rae's arm and he ran his fingers over the fracture bulging under her skin. "We should go to your cabin before I begin the healing process." His face looked gentle, caring, as opposed to the captain's stern one. "It'll be more comfortable."

"Did you heal Damien?"

"As much as I could. He was distraught when the Helgathian ship sank with you still on it. I had to knock him out to keep him from jumping into the water after you."

Rae cringed. "Thank you."

Lygen gave a wry smile and gestured towards the guest quarters. "Injury inflicted by the Art is beyond my ability to heal. Damien is still in rough shape and will need ongoing care for the burns on his arm."

She swallowed but let Lygen lead her. Crossing through the doorway, her eyes flitted to her book, which had tumbled to the ground, open. She picked it up, placing it back on the desk, and hoped the auer wouldn't ask about it.

Lygen gestured to the tousled bed as he stripped off his long coat, tossing it over the back of the desk chair. Beneath, he wore a simple white shirt, the sleeves rolled up and stained at the edges with blood. It clung, soaked by the rain, to his tanned skin, and Rae looked at the floor instead.

"I'll have to set the bone first."

Rae sat, picking up a stray arrow from the floor. Her mind wandered to Damien and their recent use of the room. The pain of holding her arm out for Lygen stopped the thoughts, and she put the arrow shaft in her mouth, biting down with a nod.

Lygen gave her no warning. He grabbed her arm and yanked, sending a fresh wave of pain and nausea through her. The arrow helped quiet her scream, but only marginally. With his other hand, Lygen pushed on the fracture, popping the bone into alignment.

Another shriek escaped her mouth, and the room spun. Closing her eyes, she gasped a breath and dropped the arrow from her teeth.

Lygen closed his hand around her forearm, never letting up on the pressure as his palm warmed. He stared intently where he worked, as if breaking eye contact would ruin whatever spell he wove beneath her skin.

Rae breathed hard, biting back a whimper, bracing with her good arm to stay upright.

Lygen's grip loosened, and the heat faded. "I can't heal the break completely right away. I need to maintain some energy to continue to work on the crew, and breaks like this are better for me to heal in stages. My power is limited."

Rae nodded, catching her breath. Pain remained, but not as severe as before. Purple bruising discolored her arm, but at least the bulge had been fixed.

"Hold it, and I'll tie a splint."

"Thank you." She held her arm steady.

Lygen snapped the head off an arrow after retrieving it from the floor. He used it to brace her arm and wrapped it with strips of cloth he tore from a towel tucked beneath the bed.

Rae stared at the arrow shaft. "A little too fitting, if you ask me."

Lygen gave the faintest hint of a smile. "We auer are resourceful, after all." He looked up, meeting her gaze. "I'd suspected you shared some of our blood before, and your shifting eye color confirms it."

Rae furrowed her brow. "My what?" She stood, sidestepping Lygen to cross toward the small oval mirror mounted to the wall.

One green and one yellow iris looked back at her. She looked closer. "Shit." She sighed. "Have they been like this the entire time?" Blinking, she willed the green to return to both, but nothing changed.

Lygen's voice sounded like it was coming from a different part of the room. "They've been like that since the captain fished you out of the water."

Rae turned around and frowned at him standing by the desk.

His hands cradled the book as he turned a page, his brows knitted together.

Clearing her throat, she raised an eyebrow. "Can I help you?"

Lygen glanced up, unfazed. "This is Aueric." He traced a finger down the page. "I can sense the energy that makes it more than a blank journal. It's a loq'nali phén, isn't it?"

Rae stalked over to him and pulled the book from his hands. "I don't know, but it's mine."

Lygen shrugged and leaned against the wall near the desk. He made the movement seem graceful. "Well, we aren't related, or I might have been able to read it. Those of us with mixed blood aren't the most common on the mainland."

Rae snapped the book shut and put it down on the other side of the desk. "No, I suppose not. I haven't met many. I assumed you were full-blooded."

"No, my mother was a rejanai. With her banishment from the homeland came mine by default when I was born. Her decision to marry a human male didn't help the matter, of course. But you're not the first to mistake me for pure. I take after my mother."

Studying him, the softness of his jaw would have been from his father. Along with his slightly wider pupils.

"Auer blood aside, I've never seen the Art used the way you did today. It was remarkable. Much like whatever Damien did to summon that weapon. Two Helgathians with a unique style of the Art would be the last thing I'd suspect to find sailing towards Porthew. It could've been the pair of you who brought the Helgathian Armada down on us rather than our ship's sorted past."

Rae gave him an unimpressed look. "It wasn't. One of their men admitted seeing Damien was a surprise. And professional courtesy dictates you keep this information to yourselves."

"Merely making conversation." Lygen frowned. "We are no lovers of Helgathians, and that alone will keep your secrets safe."

Rae sighed. "I apologize. Your captain has a way of putting me on edge."

"She speaks her mind, and it can be off-putting." Lygen shrugged. "She's grateful for the risks you both took today, even if she doesn't show it well. But it's best to let her process the events in her own way. Damien will be safe, and you'll still be able to care for him. Keeping him in the brig helps her... *mourn*, in a way." He heaved a sigh and leaned away from the wall. "Did you want to go see him now?"

"I do." Rae tilted her head. "What do you mean, mourn?"

Lygen hesitated in front of the door, turning to her. "Are you familiar with Helgath's persecution of privateer vessels used during the third Dul'Idur War?" The question seemed out of place and made Rae quirked a brow.

"That was twenty years ago, but yes." Rae's knowledge of the matter stemmed from her time with the Ashen Hawks, or else she'd never have learned of such events. "Helgath still holds a vendetta towards any privateers hailing from Ziona."

"The Herald was one of those ships, and Andi captained her back then too. She might not yet look middle-aged, but she's been sailing since before your human parent was born, I suspect." Lygen held the door open for her before following her onto the deck. "The Helgathian admiral tasked with hunting down the privateers caught up to us about a year ago. Captain Andi made a bargain with the admiral and exchanged herself to keep the crew safe. They crippled the ship and left us stranded, which the first mate at the time wasn't too happy about. He and Andi were... close, and he rallied the crew to make the repairs and chase after them. The admiral tortured the captain for days before we caught up."

"What does the admiral have to do with Damien?" Rae wondered if they'd known each other. The pieces of various conversations clicked into place. She cringed. "It was Damien's uncle, wasn't it?"

Lygen glanced at her and nodded. "Admiral Gyrin Lanoret. And he did a lot worse than torture the captain. He murdered our first mate right in front of her. Andi killed him and sank his ship for that."

Rae stopped at the top of the stairs leading down into the ship's interior, gaping. "Shit." Her stomach sank.

"Now you understand." Lygen turned to face her. "You couldn't have known. Hells, Damien might not even know. Word about death at sea can take months and depending on when he deserted..."

"He might not know his uncle is dead." Taking a deep breath, Rae debated her options. "Could I speak with the captain before seeing Damien? I won't bother her for long, I promise."

Lygen gave her a confused look but nodded. "She'll be in her quarters. She may be willing to speak with you. No harm in trying, I suppose." He gestured towards the aft of the ship where stairs on either side led to upper decks.

Rae tried to sort her thoughts as they made the short trip to the captain's quarters, wondering how she'd feel if someone killed Damien in front of her. The thought brought bile to her throat.

When they reached the double doors, Rae rapped on one and waited for an answer.

"Enter."

Trying the handle, the unlocked door swung open.

Andi sat in one of the overstuffed chairs near the back of her cabin, legs crossed. In her hand, she swirled a glass of amber liquor, the other holding an open book.

When her eyes caught Rae, she frowned, clapping the book shut. "I won't be changing my mind about the boy. There's no point in trying." She glowered, setting the glass down and tucking the book between her thigh and the armrest. She took up a bottle and poured more of the drink, filling the glass.

Rae held up her hands and shook her head as Lygen shut the door behind her, staying outside the room.

Smart man.

"He can stay in the brig. That's not why I'm here." Rae lowered her hands.

Andi narrowed her eyes but didn't look back at Rae. She picked the glass up and brought it to her lips for a long gulp, wincing. "Then why are you here?"

"I wanted to apologize." Rae stood in place. "I understand now who, what, Damien represents to you. Who his *uncle* was. I didn't know, and I didn't mean to cause you unnecessary pain, as I'm certain I have. Sounds like the admiral got what he deserved, at least."

"Lygen can never keep his mouth shut." Andi pursed her lips before letting out a sigh. Leaning back to the table beside her, she drew up another cup. It chimed as she flipped it right side up on the table, and she poured an inch of amber alcohol into the fresh glass. With a subtle gesture of her head, she summoned Rae towards her.

Rae eyed the glass and hesitated, but joined the captain. "An auer trait, perhaps. I occasionally suffer from the same affliction."

That got a smile from the captain, and she offered the drink towards Rae. "I never would've guessed." The half-curl at the edge of her lips confirmed the sarcasm. "Though alcan's are known to be a little hot-headed, so I suppose we're both victims of our lineage."

Rae accepted the glass, raising an eyebrow as Andi motioned for her to sit. Taking the seat, she smirked. "Explains how you could swim so deep to save me."

The captain shrugged, lifting her glass for a slow gulp. "Things to thank my harlot father for. Came to shore just long enough to plow my mother. His blood helps with life at sea. But it's not for everyone."

"Still salty that Jarrod stayed with the Hawks instead of joining you?" Rae smiled as she drank.

Andi gave a wicked grin. "He told you about that, did he?"

"He tells me everything. If it makes you feel better, he was tempted, but the Hawks are his family."

"You are a close-knit bunch. Loyal almost to the point of blindness. I hope you understand why I said what I did in our previous conversation. Though now I see why it angered you so."

Rae sighed. "I do and believe me, I damned my feelings from the start. But it's not shallow like you think, and it's not a play. He's also nothing like his uncle."

"The boy proved his attachment when he nearly launched himself off our deck. It took four men to restrain him before Lygen could put him down. You've got him hooked, and he's a hell of a catch. Perhaps too good for you to let go, family ties notwithstanding. Gyrin Lanoret wouldn't have risked his own skin to help someone blow up a Helgathian warship. Your Damien is either very brave, or a complete moron for making the choices he has."

Lowering her glass, Rae shook her head. "I'm not letting him go. I told you before, and I meant it. This isn't about the bounty. I... I care about him, more than anyone else."

Andi picked up the bottle, refilling Rae's glass. "More than Jarrod? He speaks highly of you and always has. I don't think he's over whatever was between you. What if he wanted you back?"

Rae couldn't help but smile, chuckling. "I love Jarrod like a brother. He's been my closest friend and ally for years. But he doesn't and won't want me back in that way. I guess it's difficult to compare the two, but what I feel for Damien surpasses anything I do for Jarrod." Taking a gulp, she added,

"Jarrod will make someone very happy one day, but only when he's ready."

Andi gulped the rest of her glass down before she refilled it. "Beware the jealousy of men, Rae."

"Jarrod won't be jealous."

"I wasn't talking about Jarrod."

Rae laughed. "Once they get to know each other, Damien will like Jarrod. Just watch, Captain, one day they'll be friends."

Andi winced with a drink. "While we're in private, call me Andi. No need for formalities here. I've been allies with the Hawks long enough to allow you the familiarity."

"Maybe with the Hawks, but not with me. Does this mean we're *friends*?" Rae teased, a buzz hitting the back of her head.

Andi gave a short laugh. "Not yet. But give it enough bottles and perhaps."

"If any of the Hawks can keep up with bottles, it's me." Rae smirked. "As long as I sober up before Porthew, we're good."

"About that." Andi took a drink, then leaned forward, cradling the glass in both hands. "Does Damien know the reason you're taking him to Porthew? His face this morning made it clear he has no idea who Jarrod is."

Rae cringed. "No. He thinks I'm meeting my father."

Andi hissed. "You're playing a dangerous game."

"I know. But I'm going to meet with Jarrod in Porthew. I've already told him to stand down. I'd like to avoid Damien learning that I'm a Hawk."

Andi chuckled. "I don't know which is more amusing. The idea of Jarrod standing down, or you thinking you can keep that secret." She held up a hand before Rae could protest. "I'm sorry, but you have to admit it's foolish."

Rae sighed. "I'll tell him, eventually. Once I clear things up with Jarrod." She swirled the liquid in her glass.

"Beware the jealousy of men." Andi lifted her eyebrows to emphasize her repetition. "*They'll be friends.*" She laughed. "You'll be lucky if the two don't kill each other."

Groaning, Rae leaned back in her seat. "It'll be fine." She downed her liquor. "I'll make it work somehow." Placing her glass on the table, she studied Andi's face. "Will you tell me about your previous first mate? From what Lygen said, he sounds like an honorable man."

Andi gave a baleful smile, her eyes focusing somewhere behind Rae. "His name was Finn."

Chapter 24

DAMIEN GLARED AT THE IRON bars blocking him from finding Rae.

After she vanished into the ocean, he'd feared the worst, despite never losing the feeling of her ká. Beneath the worry hung a deep sense of pride. She'd done what he'd known she could and destroyed the warship in a glorious onslaught of lightning.

The loss of life hovered in the fabric around him for a time, but the Herald had lowered her sails and resumed the journey before he could sort out if any survived.

Selfishly, he hoped they hadn't. Guilt wracked through his chest at considering the number of soldiers dead, but there was no choice. They'd have killed him and Rae, along with the crew of the Herald.

He rubbed the lump on the back of his head and winced. The prick of pain couldn't compare to the way the rest of his body felt. His left arm burned as if a thousand bees still stung it, and he battled the instinct to swat at them. Lygen had wrapped it in some pungent gauze restricting his movement.

As if there's anywhere to go in this stupid cell.

Yelling did little but give him a headache, so he'd resigned to sit on the narrow cot shoved against the ship's hull. There wasn't even a guardsman for him to express his displeasure to. They left him alone as their sole prisoner.

Across from his cell, the heavy metal doors swung open with the sway of the ship, clanging shut with each wave. He couldn't even sleep to pass the time with the constant noise.

With his eyes closed, he leaned his bare back against the wall. What remained of his shirt had been stripped away to work at his plethora of wounds. Sighing, he thudded his head back against the wood in time with the swaying cell doors, using the vibration to distract from the constant ache of his burned arm.

Repeating his new-formed ritual, he sought Rae's location by sensing her energy. He took a steady breath to focus his power through the haze of his ongoing discomfort. The process dragged on like he was back with Yondé in the first days of training. The currents of his ká slipped through his fingers.

Damien finally found her, but the answer didn't make sense. He frowned, thrumming his head against the wall again. "Come on..."

"Something wrong?"

Damien's eyes snapped open, and he pushed off the wall to sit up.

Rae sat cross-legged on the other side of the bars, watching him.

"You're here." Damien furrowed his brow. "I thought my senses were lying to me."

"I would have said something sooner, but I thought you were asleep." She rose from the floor.

He couldn't help the dry laugh. "Sleep. I don't think the captain meant for me to sleep." His back straightened when Rae withdrew a key from her pocket and unlocked his cell door.

Instead of opening it for him, she stepped inside.

He gathered the strength to stand, eager to take the freedom he didn't think to question. But before he could move, the iron door clanged shut behind her. The lock clicked back into place.

She crossed the small space and sat on the cot beside him, her left arm wrapped and in a sling.

"What are you doing?"

"Joining you." Rae looked him over. "Lygen healed the knife wound?" She touched the grisly pink scar interrupting the flow of his tattoo.

"I guess that's what happened. I don't think I was conscious."

Rae tilted her head. "He had to knock you out, to keep you from diving into the water."

"*Had to* is an interesting way of phrasing it." Damien frowned. "I wasn't going to let you drown."

"I don't think I would have. Besides, Andi swam after me and pulled me out."

"Andi?"

"The captain."

Damien's brow furrowed, but his body relaxed at her touch as she ran a hand up his abdomen. He turned to her, touching her chin. "I'm glad you're all right." He kissed her forehead.

She leaned into him, and he wrapped his good left arm around her waist. Burying his face in her hair, he sought the comfort of her scent and caught a whiff of something else. "Have you been drinking?" He pulled back in confusion.

Rae laughed. "Maybe. Helped numb the pain after Lygen set my arm."

Damien frowned, considering the locations on the ship he'd sensed her. One had been the captain's quarters. He'd expected she'd be in there receiving an interrogation, not indulging in a round. He grumbled. "It's cute that you're playing into the romantic idea of locking yourself in here with me, but it's unnecessary if you want to get back to whatever you were doing before."

Rae's shoulders slumped, and she leaned away from him, looking at her hands. "Would you rather I go?"

An immense wave of guilt washed away his frustration. He sighed. "No. I'd rather you stay." He entwined his hand with hers, lifting the back of it to his lips. "I'm sorry."

Looking at their hands as he lowered them to his lap, she took a slow breath. Her green and yellow irises returned to him. "I have to tell you something." The vibrant color of her eyes somehow suited her. Other subtle changes within her energy confirmed the acceptance he'd urged her towards.

He focused on the glimmering yellow of her iris, the topaz hue echoing the Art inside her. "The captain probably overheard Rynalds and realized who I am. And that's why I'm down here instead of up in our cabin... I'd hoped our efforts to save the ship might have persuaded her to overlook my bounty. But no such luck?"

Rae blinked slowly. "You're still disembarking with me in Porthew."

Damien quirked his head and frowned. "What? How did you manage that?" He'd assumed the captain to be opportunistic, not foolish enough to let go of a prize.

Rae pursed her lips. "A little whiskey goes a long way to help understand someone. I'm sure the threat of me sinking her ship would have kept her to her word too, but some things work better than threats."

Guilt festered inside him again, realizing his anger towards Rae had been misplaced. She'd been working to secure his freedom, not frivolously socializing. He looked down at their entwined hands, resting on his thigh. "Then I owe you an apology. I shouldn't have doubted."

Rae shook her head. "No need. Andi is more reasonable than she seems."

"Since you're on a first-name basis now, does that mean I can get out of this hole?"

"No."

"No?" Damien didn't know what he'd been expecting, but nothing so finite. "I thought you said she'll let me go?"

"In Porthew. It didn't matter what I said, she can't trust you. And Damien, I can't blame her."

"Because I'm a Helgathian deserter?" If Rae supported the idea of him being locked up, it had to be something else. His grip on her hand tightened.

"It's a lot more than that. It's about your family. There's history there."

Damien frowned. "History?" His mind raced. "My father's been discharged for decades. Even then, he and my brothers only served inland. We would never have had any interaction with a pirate ship like this one. I've already realized that there's no way this is a trading vessel, not with—" He cut himself off when Rae tilted her head.

"That's what I need to tell you."

"Right." Damien leaned forward. He winced when his right arm flexed, pulling on the damaged skin. "What is it?"

"Gyrin, your uncle. He's dead. The captain sank his ship."

"What?" Damien's eyes widened. "How?" His father's brother had been a novelty when Damien was young, visiting Rylorn with his father. He'd met the proud, rigid man several times, though hadn't seen him in at least eight years. "When?"

"A year ago." Rae slipped off the bed to kneel in front of him. "News travels slowly from sea. You must have left before..."

Damien sucked in a breath, steadying the wave of regret. It was foolish to feel it. He'd lost his family when he deserted.

He closed his eyes, saying a silent prayer to Nymaera for his uncle, anyway. "Gyrin was obsessed with hunting a pirate captain named Andirindia Trace." With a sigh, he slid off the edge of the cot. He ignored the jarring protest of his body, wanting Rae close. He smiled despite himself, brushing a strand of her hair back from her cheek. "What possessed you to book voyage on a pirate ship?"

Rae stared at him as if he'd asked her the color of the sky. "I'm a thief. You expected me to collect references and choose the most legitimate ship? And she's not a pirate. She's a privateer."

He laughed. "Semantics. And I suppose I should get used to doing things the less-legal way. I understand why Andi might end up confronting my uncle, but why kill him and still hate me?"

Rae fell silent, and her gaze drifted away.

"Tell me."

Swallowing, Rae sighed. "He captured Andi, tortured her for days, and then killed her lover in front of her."

"Gods... I'd heard stories about how brutal Gyrin could be, but I never wanted to believe them. I thought I knew a different man. Service to House Iedrus and the throne can warp a person into something unrecognizable. I don't want to know if I could have become like my uncle..."

Rae's eyes darted up, and she touched his face. "You're nothing like him. There isn't a trace of cruelty in you." Leaning forward, she tilted her head and kissed him.

The taste of her helped dissuade any argument he might have given. He eagerly returned the affection, despite the dryness of his lips. He pulled away, twisting a strand of her hair around his finger.

"You were pretty amazing with all that lightning. I'll consider myself lucky you didn't do that to me when Yondé attacked you. And I'll get used to the eyes."

Rae released him and kissed his neck before moving back to study his face, color touching her cheeks. "I'll figure out how to make them green again, hopefully by the time we get to Porthew."

"I don't know, I kind of like them like this." Damien smiled, touching her cheek.

She tilted her head into his touch. "Perhaps, but until I get a better grasp on my ability, I'd rather not openly display that I'm a freak. Lygen said he's never seen the Art used like that before, and he's auer."

"But he's still an auer away from Eralas. They might know more there. Or that book?" He shifted back from her to straighten his legs to one side, lifting his damaged arm onto the edge of the cot.

"Lygen said it's called a loq'nali phén. Something tied to my family's blood. And something tells me I'll have plenty of time to read it over the next week."

"I suppose I won't be able to serve as a pesky distraction." Damien frowned, glancing back at the cell. "I was rather hoping to further explore our earlier affections. I guess we could hang blankets up over the bars." He teasingly nipped at her neck, nuzzling near her ear. "I'm shy, remember?"

Rae grinned. "I'd call you many things, but I don't know about shy anymore."

"Not with the right audience. Now I know what I'm missing."

Rolling her eyes, Rae shook her head. "It's only a week, and then you'll miss nothing."

He gave a soft moan, and her body tensed in his hands. "I can be impatient, you know."

"Just think." Rae tilted her chin to kiss his jaw. "We could have been doing this since the bridge incident."

He laughed, kissing her neck. "One of my few regrets." Lifting his head, he touched her jaw. "You will consider staying in here with me, right? But I guess it'd be forward of me to ask you to sleep here too."

"I can be here as much as you want. Nights included."

"You'll have to excuse the rather dismal amenities. But perhaps you wouldn't need to be here *all* the time..."

Rae laughed. "Sounds fair. But I want to be near you, even if it's in here. Someone needs to care for that arm of yours and make sure you get fed properly."

"What about your arm?" Damien looked down at the sling. "I can't do anything about my own outside a sanctum, but I could help with yours. Even with my injury, I have access to plenty of power."

"Why do you need a sanctum for yours but not mine?"

Damien hesitated. "It has to do with how power cycles during healing. When I heal you, your ká is focused on that but still requires mine to guide it. I can't do that for myself. My ká can't heal and *be healed* at the same time. A sanctum allows me to use the guardian's ká to guide mine."

Blinking slowly, Rae averted her gaze to her wrapped forearm before pulling the sling over her head. "You could break out of this cell easily, couldn't you?"

Damien shrugged as he ran his hand over the bandage on Rae's forearm, unwrapping it one-handed. "I could. But there's hardly a reason to. They'd just put me back in here. If I wanted to stay free, I'd have to do some damage to make the crew afraid to try. Which doesn't seem right, even knowing that they're pira... privateers." He slipped his hand beneath her arm, supporting the break. Letting the bandage drop to the floor, he studied the clouds of bruises on Rae's skin.

"And you were worried you'd end up like your uncle." Rae scoffed, watching his face.

"I guess you're right. After I'm done with your arm, could you please tell the captain I'd be willing to help with any of the injured crew? To give Lygen a break." He didn't see the harm since most had likely seen him use the Art already.

He didn't wait for her answer before he focused on the tug of the surrounding energies. Even at sea, plenty of life existed to help fuel the transformation of Rae's ká, encouraging her body to heal. Lygen had done the difficult part of setting the bone, which Damien couldn't have done in his condition.

The pulse of the waves against the hull thrummed against his power, and he found the correct paths to elicit the soft blue haze over her arm.

The bruises faded first, progressing through all the stages of healing before her skin ran smooth and flawless again. The bone was more difficult, but the power dove into her flesh to hurry the process.

Rae remained mostly silent through the endeavor, but her eyes squeezed shut once he started repairing the bone. A hiss escaped her lips, but she didn't retract her arm. Her muscles twitched under his fingertips.

When he released the energy back to where it'd come, lightheadedness overcame him, and he closed his eyes to let it pass. He squeezed her arm while he welcomed the temporary darkness, sequestering the voices in his mind once more. The expulsion of power diminished the mental barrier he'd constructed between himself and the pain in his arm, but he gritted his jaw to hide it from Rae. The burn throbbed, and he swallowed the threatening nausea.

"Better?" He sought the distraction of her voice. "Should be like it never happened."

Rae circled her wrist around and smiled. "Like it never happened. Thanks. And I'll let the captain know." She touched his forehead. "Do you need anything? Food? Water? A bucket?"

"Maybe a pillow?" Damien laughed. "But some food would be good too, especially if I end up needing to heal more. Working the Art makes me hungry. We'll worry about a bucket later." He shook his head. "For when you're *not* around."

Nodding with a smile, Rae stood. "Then I'll be back with food and comfort." When he opened his mouth, she continued. "No meat. I know. Don't go anywhere."

He laughed again and shook his head. "I'll resist the temptation. But I do have one more favor to ask."

Rae tilted her head, waiting.

"Could you lock those other cell doors shut?"

"Might be more fun to attach bells to them."

Damien sighed, pulling himself to his feet. He touched her chin and kissed her forehead. "That's exactly the kind of torture I knew you'd be capable of."

Chapter 25

One week later...

"HOW ABOUT ANOTHER DRINK?" ANDI grinned, eyeing Rae up and down.

A cloudburst had struck while Rae maneuvered the rigging after enjoying the sunset from the crow's nest. She dripped from every limb, even though the rain had stopped. An unwelcome shiver passed through her bones.

"It would warm you right up. You look like a drowned rat." The captain put a hand on her hip. "Or do you need to get back to that boy of yours?"

Nodding, Rae looked down at herself. "I told that boy of mine he'd see me soon, but after I tuck him into bed, I think I'll come back and join you for that drink."

Andi gave a short laugh. "You know where I'll be." She glanced up at the sails, swelling as the northern breeze filled them. "If this wind keeps up, we could be in Porthew by tomorrow evening."

Smiling, Rae descended to the brig. Her boots whispered on the wood as she approached Damien's cell. A faint glow emanated from it, and she peered in through the bars.

He sat cross-legged on the cot, hands resting on his knees with his eyes closed. A pair of orbs fluttered like fireflies above him, their pale-blue light illuminating his features. His face looked peaceful, and he smiled as she approached, even though he wasn't looking at her.

"Were you just sitting there keeping track of my location?"

The cell looked far more comfortable than it had before, filled with pillows and blankets she'd pilfered from various parts of the ship.

"Among other things." One of his eyes opened to just a small slit. He closed it again and rolled his shoulders back. He was slow with his right, a twinge of pain passing over his face as the skin stretched beneath the loosely wrapped bandage. "I heard the rain, but you look more like you took a dunk in the ocean."

Rae laced her arms through the bars, resting her elbows on a horizontal crossbeam. "Andi called me a drowned rat. I was hoping you'd help?"

Damien snorted and shook his head. "Is that all I am to you now? A convenience so you don't have to change?"

Rae grinned. "*Among other things.* Is that a no? I suppose I can go back to *my* cabin and get undressed all alone instead."

Damien stood, stepping barefoot across the cell towards the bars she leaned on. "Maybe I'd like to help undress you instead?"

"Hmm..." Rae tilted her head. "And I bet you'd graciously offer your body heat to warm me up, too."

"*Very* graciously."

"Unfortunately for your grand plans, I have a date with the captain and her bottle of whiskey. Plus..." She looked up and down the open corridor. "You're a little shy for public affairs, remember?" Quirking an eyebrow, Rae drew back.

Damien reached through the bars, catching her. "It's the only thing dissuading me." He tugged her towards him and touched her temple, fingers brushing up over her braids.

Rae's blood warmed, the familiar rise of desire invading her senses. "Captain thinks we might reach Porthew tomorrow." Nerves danced in her stomach.

She'd received no word from Din, and the silence left her more than a little uneasy. It wasn't like Jarrod not to reply to such an important message, but she prayed the stormy weather delayed her hawk yet again.

"Now you're just teasing me." Damien traced his fingers down her neck, eliciting a tingle of energy through her. Heat, different from what he could ignite with his touch, made her take in a quick breath. Steam rose from her clothes as the water evaporated and left her dry.

Damien withdrew from her, leaning his forehead on the bars. "Should I wait up?"

Rae lifted his hand to her lips and kissed his knuckles. "Probably not. If this is our last night aboard, the cap and I might get a little rowdy."

"Could you at least pretend to miss me while you're there? I'm starting to feel like I should be more jealous of Andi than Jarrod."

Rae grinned and kissed him through the bars. "I don't have to pretend. And in a day, I can show you how much I mean that."

"And I look forward to it," he whispered, returning the kiss. "Have fun."

I love you.

The thought made her swallow, but she didn't dare say the words out loud.

"I'll be back later." She tore herself from the cell to return to the main deck. Passing by the first mate, she tipped her head in acknowledgement. "Keryn."

"Rae." The dark-skinned woman replied with a similar nod. "Evening plans with the captain again?" She gave a knowing grin, white teeth flashing in the lamplight.

"Am I so predictable?" Rae laughed and crossed to the stairs leading to Andi's door, where she knocked before pushing it open.

Andi sat in her usual spot, a full glass already sitting on the table beside the overstuffed chair. One leg crossed over the other, it bounced lightly while she read a book in her lap. She glanced up at Rae's entrance, but then returned to the book as she blindly reached for the bottle and poured another glass without needing to look.

"Keryn's going to think we're having an affair," Rae mumbled, taking her usual seat.

Andi snorted, and Rae might have thought it uncharacteristic before getting to know her. "Keryn's just jealous. It's not good practice for the captain and first mate to get drunk at the same time, so our usual escapades are reserved for when the Herald is docked."

Rae picked up her glass of whiskey. "I'll enjoy the lack of my importance, then."

Andi quirked an eyebrow over the spine of her book. "Even if it leads to rumors?" She snapped the book shut and tucked it between the cushion and her thigh.

Shrugging, Rae sipped her drink. "Rumors hardly bother me. Of all the things people could accuse me of, having an affair with their captain is the least offensive."

Andi chuckled again as she lifted her glass to her lips. She narrowed her eyes as she drank. "How are you dry already?"

"Perks of that boy of mine." Rae smiled through the anxiety in her gut.

"He seems rather handy to have around. Perhaps it would be in my interest to seduce you into staying aboard, gain him by proxy."

Rae grinned. "Might be able to get Jarrod by proxy too, then." She crossed her legs, leaning back in the chair.

Andi hummed, bobbing her leg up and down. "A tempting proposition. Though, I can already tell a life at sea isn't for you. It'd feel like caging a bird if I asked you to stay."

"Perhaps that's why I became a Hawk. You're right. As much as I look forward to *working* with you in the future, I'm craving dry land, among other things."

Andi gave a knowing grin. "*Among other things.*" She gave a comfortable sigh as she settled back into her chair, resting her glass on the arm. "I can hardly imagine a life off this ship anymore. Jarrod tried to convince me to speak with Sarth about joining the Hawks when the Herald was crippled after that battle with Gyrin. But I couldn't let the old girl go." She glanced around the room. Shrugging after a moment, she looked back at Rae. "What about you? Staying a Hawk despite all this unpleasant business?"

"Probably until I die." Rae understood Andi's attachment to her ship. "The unpleasant business will pass, but they'll always be my family."

Andi smiled and lifted her glass towards Rae. "To the family that we choose. Gods damn the ones we don't."

Mirroring the movement, Rae clinked her glass with Andi's and took a gulp. "Couldn't agree more."

They grew silent for a moment while Andi lifted the bottle to top off both their glasses. "Jarrod was always so damn secretive about why *he* joined the Hawks, but I know family problems when I see them. Seems to be a common theme, I'm guessing?" She eyed Rae.

"I can't speak for everyone, but that rings true for me at least. I was close with my father, but my mother..." She shuddered. "I can only hope I never see her again."

"How long has it been?"

"Nine years."

Andi let out a low whistle. "You can't be older than twenty-five, so you must have been young. Fifteen, sixteen?"

"Twelve. I'm twenty-one."

"Too damn young. And the Hawks found you?"

Rae nodded. "I started stealing to get by and I tried to lift Sarth's coin purse."

The captain's eyes widened, a laugh trying to escape mid-gulp. She swallowed, wincing, and coughed, leaning forward. "I suspect that went as well as I imagine."

Laughing, Rae shrugged. "The leader of the Ashen Hawks is more patient than you would think. My induction and training started immediately, which is why I outrank most of the guild members much older than me. It was a difficult rise, though. You'd be surprised how many men don't enjoy taking orders from a teenage girl." Quirking a brow, Rae took a drink.

"There's nothing quite like a man with a damaged ego."

"I think it's why I got close to Jarrod so quickly when he joined. He never once questioned my authority, as minimal as it was at that point."

"Jarrod always seemed to be good with orders, but do you think he'll listen to your stand down?"

Rae paused. "I don't know. My hawk hasn't returned with a message from him confirming. He's probably confused, especially since I haven't seen him in so long."

Brows knitting together, Andi leaned back. "Why's that? From what Jarrod always said, it sounded like you two were inseparable, romantic relationship or not."

Mouth slightly agape, Rae huffed sheepishly. "We were. We are. I just... I left this past spring. It's the longest I've ever gone without seeing him. I'm still a Hawk, but I needed a break."

"A break? I didn't know Hawks got breaks. Sarth just let you leave?"

"No. I didn't tell anyone. I left Jarrod a note, but that's it. I couldn't stay and be much use, so I decided I needed some distance. Now, I can't wait to go back."

"What happened?" The captain lifted the bottle, offering it wordlessly towards Rae, who nodded. Pouring liberally, Andi filled their glasses again.

"A reconnaissance job went sideways, and one of our young recruits got captured."

"That happens though, part of the risk you sign on for, isn't it?"

"Yes, and he knew that protocol dictates not to say a word to authorities and wait for rescue. But he didn't wait. He confessed to crimes of espionage against House Iedrus, and they executed him before I could try to get him back. I led the job. He was my responsibility, and the brave little idiot claimed he was from Feyor to keep the Hawks out of it. A kid protecting me didn't feel right, and I didn't cope well."

"I could argue that you're not much more than a kid yourself, Rae." Andi frowned. "Sometimes you can't save everyone. It's a hard lesson, but one you'll have to bounce back from, or the guilt will destroy you. Kid made his own choice."

Rae nodded. "I understand that better now, but I needed the distance all the same to sort my thoughts. Didn't think I'd meet Damien, let alone... you know."

Andi chuckled. "Fate has a funny way of working sometimes. What's next? You can't be thinking you can take Damien home to meet Sarth."

Cringing, Rae shook her head. "I don't know. I want to go back, but I don't want to leave Damien. He might just have to join the Hawks." Even as she said it, she recognized the impossibility.

"That boy needs to stay as far from Helgath as he can. They won't stop looking for him until they know he's dead."

Rae's shoulders slumped. "I'm open to suggestions."

Andi took a long gulp, swishing the whiskey around in her mouth. She winced as she swallowed. "Find a nice, quiet spot in Isalica. Marry the idiot, have lots of babies. Forget the Hawks and live a life full of... you know."

Looking at her glass, she swirled the amber liquor. "I don't want marriage... I don't even think I want children. Maybe. I guess I should ask Damien what he wants."

Andi laughed, shaking her head. "Gods, you've got it bad." She lifted her glass in a mock salute before downing the rest of it. "Going from *I don't want marriage* to, *maybe we should talk about it*?"

Rae laughed. "I meant children. I'm not sure about that. I'm positive on the marriage thing, though."

"Why no marriage?"

"My mother and father fought constantly. Berating, demeaning, blaming... I don't want that." Rae finished her glass, setting it on the table, her mind blurry.

Nodding, Andi emptied the rest of the bottle into Rae's glass. "I think we need another bottle."

When Rae woke up the next day, the brig spun. The bars wobbled in her vision, and she closed her eyes with a groan.

How many bottles did we drink?

Rae couldn't remember, but the memory of the captain walking into her own desk made her laugh. A wince quickly followed as her head pounded.

"Well, good morning." Damien's voice stabbed in her ears. "Or should I say afternoon?"

"Don't yell at me," Rae whispered, covering her face with her arm.

His laugh didn't feel much more merciful than his voice.

Peeking at him, Rae scowled. "Laughing at my misery." Her eyes focused, and she raised an eyebrow as he rose back into her vision.

With his feet wedged under the edge of the cot, he did sit-ups towards her. Gloriously shirtless.

Suddenly, her headache felt less paralyzing. "Exercising while your woman sleeps off a hangover... you're too good for me."

He gave another small laugh with the exhale as he sat back up. Leaning forward, he placed a gentle kiss on her forehead then descended with his back to the deck. "You're too cute to wake up. Drool and all."

Rae groaned and rolled onto her back, staring at the ceiling. It had been a long time since she'd drank too much, but her nerves compelled her desire to forget her situation.

After dragging herself to her feet, Rae acquired food for herself and Damien, and the supplies she'd need to redress his arm. During a quick word with Keryn, Rae learned they'd arrive in Porthew before sunset. Her stomach churned.

Where are you, Din?

The rest of their last day at sea passed with no word from Jarrod, and Rae tried not to show her anxiousness. Finding any excuse to stay away from the brig, she packed their belongings but failed in her attempts to read her book. Unable to focus, she resorted to climbing up and down the rigging to keep her body busy.

Damien emerged from below deck as the Herald neared shore, and Rae dropped from her position on the ropes to land next to him. Setting foot under the sky for the first time in days, his apparent relief almost helped her relax. He stood at the banister facing the hazy silhouettes of Porthew's stone buildings, haloed by billows of smoke from their chimneys.

Rae admired how the twilight sky reflected in his gaze. "Feel good to be free again?" Her eyes darted to a large bird in the sky, only to see a seagull instead of her hawk.

"It does." Damien heaved a gentle sigh. "I'm grateful the captain is still willing to overlook the bounty. I don't think I could handle another cell."

"Then you best keep that girl of yours safe." They both turned towards the captain's voice. Andi smiled at Rae. "I've grown rather fond of her."

Damien stiffened as he eyed the captain. "You won't have to worry about that. I'm rather fond of her myself."

Rae's cheeks heated, but she smiled, raising a hand. "I'm also pretty capable of keeping myself safe... On dry land, at least."

Andi shrugged. "Your capability isn't in question. But you can't protect yourself from everything. There are some things only *he* can." Her eyes locked on Damien, and he shifted closer to Rae.

"I am sorry, Captain. For the actions of my uncle. I understand your apprehension towards me and don't hold any ill will for your decisions."

"Good." Andi pursed her lips. "But forgive me for hoping we don't encounter each other again. However... I suppose I may tolerate your presence if Rae is with you."

Rae grinned and stepped forward, meeting Andi midway for a hug. "I hope we meet again."

"Let's make sure it's under better circumstances next time." Andi released Rae from her embrace.

Nodding, Rae acknowledged Andi's secondary meaning. "Next time, I'll bring the whiskey."

Chapter 26

DAMIEN'S ARM THROBBED WITH EACH movement, but he gritted his teeth to hide it. The darkness of the brig had been a blessing for the healing burn, but that didn't diminish his joy at glimpsing the sun above Porthew before sunset.

Long shadows of twilight draped across the wide roads fanning out from the docks. Business slowed in the approaching chill of the night, the townsfolk returning home to their families and hearths.

Damien welcomed the comfort of solitude, the barrier of his mind relaxing in the void of commotion. It enabled him to focus on blocking the pain in his body instead.

Stubbornly, he insisted on carrying the pack he and Rae shared, even though it prohibited him from being able to hold her hand. It left her with nothing to carry since her bow vanished during the battle with the Helgathian vessel.

She asked for directions from the dockmaster on how to find the Birch Bay Inn.

"Is that the inn your father is at?" Damien tried to catch her gaze as they turned down the roadway headed south.

Rae stuffed her hands in her pockets, licking her bottom lip before biting it. "I don't know." She peered down side roads as they passed them.

Something felt horribly wrong with her. Damien could sense it even without her suspicious glances. He forced himself to stifle the nervous sensation in his chest, threatening to make him question everything again. "Why the specific inn then? Do you know it?"

Rae focused on him with matching green eyes. The topaz in her right eye had faded to return to the green over the week.

Damien missed it.

She nodded. "Mhmm, I've been there before. Long time ago, though, and I don't remember exactly where it is..." Her voice trailed off as she looked down another alley.

Damien stopped, shifting the pack on his shoulder as he turned to her. "Rae, what's going on?"

She frowned. "Your shoulder hurts. Will you please let me take the pack? Nothing is going on. I just want to get somewhere so you can rest."

"I'm fine. I can handle carrying a bag. That's not what's causing you to glance down every alleyway we walk past."

Sighing, Rae shook her head. "I'm sorry, I guess I'm just nervous. I feel like ghosts are hiding everywhere, waiting for me to let my guard down." Looking at the ground, she twisted the toe of her boot on the cobblestone.

Damien stepped to her, gingerly touching her waist with his injured arm. "Nothing is hiding in the shadows. We're out of danger for now." He kissed her temple, inhaling her calming scent. "Let's get to the inn. I don't know about you, but I'm dying for a bath."

Rae leaned into him before nodding. "A bath sounds wonderful."

They kept walking, and Rae's sideways glances lessened. Guilt flooded through him for questioning her. He couldn't blame her after what happened in Ashdale.

In the distance, the inn's sign swayed in the breeze. The tavern on the ground floor, beneath the rented rooms, appeared dimly lit by a candle or two. The people of Porthew must have retired early for the evening, since no music or chatter echoed from within. Either that or the bustling tavern down the road was just more popular.

Rae opened the door, and tiny bells jingled at its corner.

He followed in behind her, scanning the empty bar, tables, and chairs. Not even the innkeeper stood at the traditional post behind the long wooden bar.

The door shut behind them, an eerie silence prevailing as Rae led the way farther into the vacant space.

"Is it usually this unpopular?" Damien's voice reverberated around the barren room even at a whisper.

Light flickered from the dying hearth, its crackle one of the few sounds other than Damien's footsteps.

Rae turned to face him, pushing his chest. "Go back outside."

Damien's brows furrowed, his stance unmoved. "What?"

Movement flickered in the amber light of the fire behind Rae, and Damien's breath caught.

A man lunged from hiding behind her, his dark complexion barely visible beneath his hood. Simultaneously, someone wrenched Damien's arms behind his back, the pack falling to the floor. The burns on his arm flared, and he couldn't stop his cry of pain.

Boots thundered, and Damien counted four men, including the one restraining him.

The man behind Rae grabbed her around the waist, and she gasped. He whirled her to the side, letting go as she rolled over a tabletop to land on her feet on the other side.

Damien shoved back against his attacker. Bracing himself, he threw his head back, and it connected solidly with the face of the man attempting to hold him. He followed by stomping his foot down and spinning in the man's grip to twist his arms free.

The large man, dressed heavily in black with a hood over his head, stumbled backwards, reaching up to his bleeding nose.

In a rush, Damien breathed into his power, drawing up his ká through the tensing of his left arm. The two other men clambered over the bar, knocking the stools towards him as Damien swelled the energy of his ká into a bubble around him.

Gripping his hand into a fist, a ripple of pale light erupted at the edge of the barrier, smacking the stools back into the base of the bar and striking the men.

They flew back in unison, both crashing into the back wall as bottles and wood exploded at their impact.

With the use of his power, the agony in his arm tripled, and he grimaced as he hugged it against his torso. He glanced in the direction Rae had been thrown, watching her leap over the table back towards the fight.

The man who'd thrown her gaped at Damien. He drew a wicked-looking dagger from his black cloak before he charged.

"No!" Rae yelled, but Damien planted his foot behind him, bracing for the thrust of his energy.

His ká pulsed at his fingertips as he outstretched his hand towards the attacking man, streams of his power reaching through the air towards him.

The man skidded to a halt an arm's length away, dark eyes wide, and Damien moved to plunge the glowing mist of his own essence against the man's aura.

As he did, Rae dove between them, her back to Damien's attacker. One hand held out towards Damien, her other grabbed the man's wrist and stilled his weapon.

She was too close for him to stop the flow of his Art in time, and Damien's ká tangled with hers.

Gasping, Rae staggered in place, wide-eyed, and the man wrapped his arms around her waist again, pulling her away from Damien.

His instinct to pull and tear the soul he held vanished, and Damien released the intention of his power as fast as he could. Shock struck his stomach like a punch, causing him to recoil. He cried out with the dissolution of his power, arm throbbing. He hunched forward, only to be torn upright when an arm wrapped around his throat, arching his back.

"Stop!" Rae shouted from the arms of her captor, sucking in a breath as the two men in black cloaks charged again.

Thunder cracked, vibrating the floor.

Feet slowed in surprise as eyes turned towards Rae.

"Stop. Break off." Authority echoed within her tone.

The arm around Damien's throat tensed, but not enough to cut off his air.

Damien wasn't sure who she spoke to, but decided it had to include him. He froze, the man behind him doing the same. They both stopped their struggle against each other and remained static.

The two advancing men halted as well, looking from Rae to the man holding her from behind.

"Dice?" Damien watched her.

Her right eye showed the faintest tones of yellow, but quickly faded as her breathing calmed.

The man behind Rae let her go and spun her around by the wrist. "Are you insane?"

She backed until her back touched Damien's chest. Whirling around, she glared past Damien's face. "Braka, let him go."

The big man didn't listen, giving a grunt instead.

Damien's hand closed on Braka's wrist, keeping his energy ready.

Rae met Damien's gaze, and her jaw flexed. "Please don't hurt them."

He narrowed his eyes, but something in hers begged him. With a slow exhale, he released his hold on his power, letting his body sag in Braka's grip. He tried to hide the wince as his left arm twisted.

The men exchanged looks, and Rae turned around to face the one who'd grabbed her and seemed in charge. "Stand down."

"Give me one good reason." The leader pushed his hood back and rubbed his short black hair. "You're standing in front of the biggest payday we've seen in a long while."

Damien's heart sank.

Rae didn't move. "Because I love him... and I outrank you."

Damien's stomach fluttered at the word 'love' in a way inappropriate to the situation. His grip on Braka tightened without him meaning to. He wanted to respond, tell her how much it meant for him to hear and that he loved her too, but her second phrase gave him pause.

The leader's shoulders slowly relaxed, but his expression hardened as he examined Damien. His brows furrowed, but he said nothing as he mulled over her words.

A strained silence settled in the room before the leader gave a curt nod. "Break off."

Braka let go of Damien so abruptly he nearly fell. He stepped back, and the other two relaxed their stances, whispering to each other.

Rae glared at them. "Give it a rest. Sky is still blue."

Damien rubbed his throat as he turned and looked at Braka's displeased grimace, his face smeared with blood.

The big man sniffed, rubbing his nose with his sleeve. "That fucking hurt."

Taking a step to Rae, Damien touched the small of her back. "What's going on?" He wrestled with the only conclusions his mind could reach, and he didn't like the implications.

The leader glared at Damien, but his gaze softened as it moved to Rae. "You *did* write the last note." He shook his head. “It was a break from your usual routine. I assumed the worst.”

Rae gulped and glanced at Damien before walking to the man who’d apparently been concerned for her safety.

Damien grimaced.

The friend she was sending Din to.

Rae touched the leader’s forearm. “I’m sorry.”

The man’s arms engulfed her in an embrace that made Damien’s jaw flex. Rae whispered something, and he kissed her hair.

A growl threatened his chest as Damien realized who Rae had been communicating with the entire time. “All right, I think I’m owed a bit of an explanation here,” he snapped, his face heating.

Releasing her hold, Rae turned to the Rahn’ka. “Damien, this is Jarrod.”

Kind of figured that out.

The jealous blaze escalated as he glowered at Jarrod, the man he’d imagined holding Rae, and now he saw it. How dare he have the audacity to greet her in such a way after breaking her heart? His stomach roiled.

“Jarrod.” The name tasted acidic. “Wish I could say it’s a pleasure. But it’s not. And that doesn’t explain what’s going on, Rae. Why is Jarrod here?”

Rae crossed back to Damien, her eyes locked on his. “Can we talk in private, please?”

Jarrod motioned to the back staircase. “Rooms are empty, plenty to choose from.” His tone suggested he'd protest if they wanted to leave the inn.

Damien watched him, trying to pick apart the stoic look on his face. All black clothes.

I should have guessed Jarrod would be a thief too.

Damien forced his gaze away from Jarrod, turning to Rae. “After you.” He grunted as he lifted his injured arm, gesturing to the staircase.

She stepped across the room again, ignoring Braka and the other two men who mumbled among themselves. As she walked past Jarrod, he caught her upper arm.

Damien resisted the urge to tear Jarrod's hand away from her.

“If the hawk flies...”

Rae nodded. “I know. When's sunset?”

“Midday, tomorrow.” Jarrod let go of her, and she weaved her way around fallen chairs and tipped over tables to reach the stairs.

Damien followed, plucking their pack from the ground as he did. Cautiously turning, he kept an eye on Jarrod as he walked past him. He didn't like leaving them downstairs while he and Rae spoke. Or being anywhere near. His mind whirled wildly with assumptions and questions.

Picking a room far down the hall, seemingly at random, Rae entered and locked the door behind Damien. "I know you must—"

"What in Nymaera's name is going on?" Damien interrupted before he even put the pack down on the bed. "Jarrod? He's the *friend* you've been communicating with this entire time?"

Rae stared at him. "Yes."

He groaned, running his hand roughly through his hair as he crossed to the open window. He pulled the shutters closed, latching them. With an absent flick of his hand, two wall sconces fluttered to life with the glow of his ká rather than fire. "Why?"

She paused. "To decipher your identity and coordinate your capture."

The pit of Damien's stomach dropped out. He felt nauseous, collapsing on the bed as he stared at the floor, trying to breathe. "Everything, every moment, was leading to you getting me here to Jarrod? It had nothing to do with your father."

But she said she loves me downstairs.

Even if it'd been in a moment of desperation, he clung to the hope it brought. He closed his eyes, focusing on his breathing while he waited for her answer.

"That was the plan, at first. But before we boarded the Herald, I wrote and told him to stand down. I didn't have my things with me, so when my reply method changed, he assumed I'd been... compromised by you."

"Compromised." Damien mused at the word and shook his head. He looked at her, trying to understand. "Is it true then? Did I compromise you? I'd hate to get in the way of your *biggest payday in a long while...*"

Rae held his gaze. "Not in the way Jarrod thought. I struggled with the plan from the beginning. I didn't know who you'd become to me, but if I broke protocol and didn't show up... They'd have thought the worst, found us, and killed you in your sleep. I came here to tell Jarrod face to face that we aren't turning you in."

Damien had avoided putting the pieces together.

Helgath. Protocols. Coded messages. Ranks.

He'd questioned why she didn't belong to a guild when they first met, and she'd even challenged the notion. The one thing about her that didn't fit the usual operation of the most infamous criminal guild in Helgath was Rae's presence in Olsa. Ashen Hawks never strayed far from their nest for long periods of time.

Chewing his bottom lip, he retraced the lines of logic he'd previously ignored. "What's at midday tomorrow?"

Rae crossed the room to him but stopped a couple of feet away. "The inn is a safe zone until midday tomorrow. Means they've secured the building. It's just code language we use sometimes."

"And *we* is—"

She interrupted before he could say it. "The Ashen Hawks."

Hearing it confirmed made his breath catch as he lowered his gaze to the floor.

The whole guild probably knows about me.

He winced with the thought. The hope he'd amassed crumbled.

"I can't believe how stupid I've been." Damien sighed, rubbing his face. "It's a miracle I made it out of Helgath at all, considering how dense I am." He looked up at her again. "If the whole thing is called off, why didn't you tell me the truth?"

Rae grimaced. "Would you have come with me to Porthew if you knew the Hawks waited here? I needed to explain to Jarrod in person or else he never would've stopped hunting you."

"What I would've done doesn't matter. You never gave me the choice."

"I was afraid of losing you." She closed her eyes.

Damien hesitated but stood to face her. "How can I make this any clearer to you? You'll never lose me, Dice." He touched her chin, guiding her eyes to meet his. As much as he wished he could stay angry, he understood. He'd done the same thing with his own secrets.

Damien stepped towards her and kissed her head, letting out a sigh as he did.

Rae relaxed against him, and her arms slid around his waist, avoiding his hurt arm. "Is it trite to tell you I'm sorry?" His chest muffled her words. "A part of me is, but a bigger part isn't. If I hadn't pegged you as a target, I wouldn't have broken you out while I was drunk." She looked up at him. "And I'd have lost my chance to fall in love with you."

Touching her cheek, Damien smiled. "I guess I'm grateful too, then. Through all this mess, we still know *this* is real. I love you, too." He drew her into him, bringing their lips together in a tender kiss that made everything in him numb. He broke away slowly.

"Are you sure Jarrod has enough say to call off the guild entirely?" Damien resisted pulling too far from her mouth. "Or you? Seeing as you *outrank* him?"

Rae kept her face close to his and raised an eyebrow. "I've called them off, so it's finished."

He smirked, his hand encouraging her hips closer to his. "You have the influence then… I'll have to be careful not to let all this power go to your head."

Rae smiled, her eyes glittering. "You're really not going to leave me? You forgive me?"

"I'd be incredibly hypocritical if I didn't. I meant it when I said I'd never leave you again. I'm staying here, regardless of how foolish it might be considering there are four Ashen

Hawks downstairs and one in the room with me. I don't want a life without you in it."

Rae's smile widened. "They'll stay downstairs, but think of it more as protection than confinement."

"Well, the privacy is much better than my last cell." Damien smirked.

Rae pulled his mouth to hers, tilting her head and kissing him so abruptly that Damien lost his balance. He fell back onto the bed, taking her with him as the pack thunked to the ground.

Chapter 27

JARROD SCRUNCHED HIS NOSE OVER the rim of the ale Braka poured for him. He hardly believed what he'd heard. Rae being in love... seemed unfathomable with the life she lived.

Of course, she loved me once.

Luckily, he hadn't told Sarth or the rest of the Hawks about Damien and swore the three accompanying him to Porthew to silence.

Loyalty ran thicker than blood between the Hawks. They'd never cross each other, not even for a bounty like the one offered for Damien. If Rae truly cared for the man, then the deserter was as good as one of them.

Unfortunately, based on the way Damien had glared at him, Jarrod wondered how he'd take the information Rae hadn't told him yet.

Maybe we'll get to see the money after all.

Content to dine on the food in the kitchen and help themselves to the kegs behind the bar, Jarrod ensured his crew didn't grow too rowdy by putting a hard limit on their indulgences.

"We came all this way…" Braka downed a stein of ale. The two pieces of cloth stuffed up his nose caused his voice to sound nasally. "And she loves the guy? This is *Sika* we're talking about. Are you sure she hasn't been drugged? With all the stories you told me, I figured we'd find her eager to be rid of Lanoret."

Braka's unfamiliarity with Rae led him to only ever refer to her by her guild name. The tradition named the thieves after animals, and Rae's came from the stealthy black cats bred by Feyor to act as infiltrators and spies. Smaller than a panther but bigger than a bobcat, the predators were rarely caught, or even seen, which fit Rae perfectly in Jarrod's opinion.

"Love concoctions are a load o' horseshit." Melner picked at the food on his plate.

Jarrod laughed dryly. "I think she's serious, and you better listen to her. You know how she gets when you don't take her for her word."

Melner snorted. "I ain't worried bout her no more. Did ya see the Art that Helgathian used? Bounty didn't say nothin' bout him bein' a practitioner."

Jarrod's gaze narrowed at the restored flame of the tavern's hearth. "No, and Rae never mentioned that either. I'll ask her tomorrow."

"You thinkin' she'll tell you?" Veck raised an eyebrow.

"Course she will."

Veck shrugged. "I dun' know. She's holding a lot back since she left the Hawks. Does she even have the right to break us off anymore?"

Bile rose in Jarrod's throat, and he stood to face Veck. "You're still a free man 'cause of her. I think we owe her a little more loyalty than that. Besides, even if you doubt her authority, don't you dare doubt mine."

As Veck pushed to his feet, his chair scraped across the tavern floor. His stormy blue eyes darkened beneath his thick blond eyebrows. "I paid my debts according to guild law. I don't owe her nothin'. And you're just a big lump of mush 'round her, so she rides you however she wants, like a beaten mule."

Jarrod growled, swinging a fist at Veck's jaw.

The impact jerked the thief's head up in time for Jarrod to land a second blow to his gut before kicking him back with a booted foot.

Veck collided with a set of chairs, toppling over them into a heap on the ground while he cursed and heaved for breath.

Braka rose to his feet next to Jarrod, pushing up his sleeves.

Melner stood, still holding his mug in his hands, taking a long drink while he eyed back and forth between Veck and Jarrod.

Veck coughed and spat blood onto the floor.

"Mules kick hard, ay Veck?" Braka chuckled.

"How about you watch your mouth." Jarrod glowered at the downed thief. "Or we can keep this going, if you'd prefer."

Veck wiped his mouth with the back of his hand and shook his head of long blond hair.

"Either of you got somethin' to say about Rae's status in the Hawks?" Jarrod looked at Melner and Braka.

Melner settled back into his chair and popped a foot up on the table in front of him.

Braka sat down with a thud. "Not over here, boss."

Lowering himself to his seat, Jarrod looked at the blazing hearth. A lot of effort had gone into their journey to Porthew, but he'd never cross Rae. Past lover or not, she was his closest friend and confidante. She knew things about him that no one else did and had never once judged him.

Veck picked himself up off the ground, dabbing at the break in his lip, then collapsed into one of the chairs he'd tumbled through. He faced away from Jarrod, likely hiding his glower.

"What's the plan?" Melner gulped his ale.

Taking a deep breath, Jarrod sighed it out slowly. "We'll figure it out in the morning. But for now, Damien Lanoret is off-limits."

"Lucky bastard." Melner rocked back on the legs of his chair, and Jarrod smiled. "Course, you're the one who'd know how lucky, wouldn't ya, boss?"

Jarrod scoffed. "I think *lucky bastard* covers it quite well."

Braka gave a deep laugh, leaning towards Jarrod with a smirk. "It's true then. You and Sika had a thing?"

Jarrod gave the newer hawk a sideways look. "Been listening to rumors, have you? Aye, we had a *thing*."

Melner gave a knowing smile behind Braka's interested expression.

"So what happened between ya? I get a girl looking like that one, I ain't lettin' go."

Jarrod ground his jaw. "Mutual agreement that it wouldn't work." He still loved Rae, but not how Damien might.

"Didn't look like it wasn't workin' the way you kissed her back there," Veck muttered darkly over his shoulder.

"We're *friends*," Jarrod growled. "Am I not allowed to be relieved to see she ain't dead?"

Braka opened his mouth to ask more, but Melner interrupted.

"Give it a rest, ya big sod. Can't ya tell he don't want to be talkin' about it." Melner kicked the bottom of Braka's chair. "Nymaera's name, ya sure are thick."

Jarrod stood. "I'm getting more ale. Then I'm gonna check what else is in the kitchen. When I get back, there'll be no more talk of me and Sika."

Jarrod woke in his chair by the hearth, hood still over his head. While he scrounged up breakfast, Rae came down the stairs with freshly braided hair.

Jarrod glanced behind her but didn't see Damien. Smiling, he crossed the room and hugged her. "I was worried about you." The rest of the men had wandered from the inn in search of a hot meal, giving him the opportunity to be himself with her.

"I know. I'm sorry." She returned the embrace.

"Where's your man?"

"Sleeping." Rae gave him a sheepish smile. "I need to get some fresh bandages for his arm. Food would be good too."

Draping an arm over her shoulder, Jarrod guided her to the door. "Let's go then, and you can tell me how Andi is doing on the way." He gave her a knowing grin. "Did you two get along?"

Rae laughed. "Not at first."

While she filled him in on their journey, Jarrod led her to the edge of the city. They fell into comfortable conversation while walking side by side.

A dense stone wall surrounded Porthew, an old remnant of days of war. In the years of peace, businesses and farms had sprung up beyond the open archways, including an apothecary shop.

She found bandages and salve but then suggested they return to town to find a bowyer.

They followed a simple dirt path, the wall on one side, an open field of tall Olsa grass on the other.

"I never thought I'd see the day you *lost* your bow."

Rae rolled her eyes, shrugging. "It's likely floating in the ocean somewhere. Lost for a good cause, though."

Jarrod paused, walking beside her in silence as he studied her profile. He sighed. "You're sure about losing the bounty on your Helgathian?"

Rae nodded without pause. "I am. I know what it took to come here with the others, but I can't turn him over. He's—"

"It's all right, Rae. I get it." Jarrod squeezed her shoulder. "I just wanted to make sure. I already told the guys he's off-limits."

Rae sighed, and her face brightened with a smile. She opened her mouth to speak, but paused. She narrowed her eyes at the open gate ahead, leading back into the city.

A figure appeared beneath the stone arch, a dark hood drawn over his face.

Something about the way he stood facing Rae made all the little hairs on the back of Jarrod's neck stand straight up. They stopped walking, and the air stilled.

Jarrod's hand instinctively found the hilt of his dagger.

The man quirked his chin up, revealing the sharp line of his jaw. The edge of it was disfigured, boiled and burned with juts of angry red blossoming across his cheek and neck like branches of a tree or the fork of lightning. One of his eyes, deep in the damage, donned a leather eyepatch.

"Gods..." Rae backed up a step.

"Rae?" Jarrod drew his weapon.

"Rynalds," Rae whispered. "He should be dead."

Footfalls thumped behind them, and Jarrod whirled around to find two men clad in thick leather armor, their weapons drawn. One leapt for Rae, while the other wielded a heavy blade at Jarrod.

Chaos rose amid the din of noise echoing off the wall, more men emerging from the towering grass.

Diving to the side, Jarrod's back collided with the stone wall. He turned to see Rae pinned to the ground, two soldiers with their knees against her legs and back. They wrestled shackles onto her, locking her wrists behind her back.

Jarrod lashed out at a soldier who brought a sword down towards his head. He spun around him, burying his blade in the weak point of his armor at his waist. The man fell, grappling Jarrod's shoulder to stay upright.

Shrugging the man off, Jarrod lashed out with his fists, landing a few hard blows before two more soldiers joined against him. Striking the wall with his face and chest, they twisted his hands up behind him.

Jarrod braced to push off with his feet and flung the mob of soldiers back with him. They tackled him to the ground, fists slamming into his head. The world spun as strike after strike knocked the air from him, and he choked on his own blood.

"Where is he?" Someone shouted, and Rae exhaled, crying out.

Jarrod cringed.

They're looking for Damien.

He tried to look at Rae, his vision tainted red with blood. He could only make out her body, her face turned away from him.

She spat at a soldier. "Go fuck Nymaera."

Another blow hit her.

Boot steps scuffled across the ground towards Rae as the figure from the gate grabbed her hair, forcing her head up. His hood had fallen back, revealing that the damage extended into his cropped salt and pepper hair.

Someone wrenched Jarrod's chin, straightening it before punching him so hard his teeth rattled.

"Answer me, girl, or your friend over here is gonna pay for your stubbornness."

"Don't tell them." Jarrod's vision flashed white with the crashing wave of pain as a boot collided with his ribs.

Rae cried out. “Stop it!” She growled and dirt shuffled beneath her boots before a man thumped to the ground. “I swear I’ll kill you all.”

Opening his eyes, Jarrod watched Rae twist her legs around one of their attacker’s necks, nearly snapping it before someone intervened. A boot connected with her jaw, jerking her head up. She groaned, rolling onto her side, hands secured behind her back.

“Kill him.” Rynalds turned his good eye towards Jarrod. “Unless *you* feel inclined to tell us where Lanoret is.”

Jarrod gritted his jaw. Hawks never snitched. “If you’re going to try to kill me, make sure you do it right. Otherwise, I’ll slit your throat while you sleep.”

Rynalds narrowed his eye, then shook his head as if disappointed. “Make it slow.” He patted one of the men holding Jarrod on the shoulder.

A flicker of light danced across a steel blade plunging towards him. A searing hot pain stabbed under his ribs.

Rae screamed, sobbing as his breath faltered.

Jarrod closed his eyes, trying to block out the sensation of warm blood pooling beneath him.

A second stab next to the first made him gasp, forcing his eyes open towards the bright sky.

Everything numbed as the blue darkened to black.

The story continues in...

PURSUIT OF THE HAWK

www. Pantracia.com

THEY WANTED HIM... UNTIL THEY SAW HER POWER.

Now Rae's trapped without her magic, locked in a cell bound for Helgath. With no sign of rescue, hope dwindles the farther they take her from Damien.

Discovering Jarrod on the brink of death, Damien travels between worlds to find out what happened to Rae. Betrayal jars him off course, putting his life in the hands of the thief he'd sworn to despise. Damien must confront his fears, returning to Helgath with unexpected allies.

Weaving bonds thicker than blood, Damien and Jarrod must overcome prejudice to face what awaits them. If they don't face it together, they'll lose Rae forever to a fate neither of them could have ever predicted.

Pursuit of the Hawk is Part 2 of *A Rebel's Crucible* and Book 5 in the *Pantracia Chronicles.*

Made in the USA
Monee, IL
12 March 2024

54373272R00260